PRIVATEER

STEVE DAHILL

Jumpmaster Press
Birmingham, AL

Copyright

Edited by: Ghia Truesdale
Artwork Generated by Midjourney
Cartography: Jude Dahill

Library Cataloging Data
Names: Dahill, Steve, (Steve Dahill)
Title: *Privateer* / Steve Dahill
5.5 in. × 8.5 in. (13.97 cm × 21.59 cm)
Description: Jumpmaster Press™ digital eBook & paperback edition |
Alabama: Jumpmaster Press™, 2018 - 2024. Alabaster, AL 35007
info@jumpmasterpress.com

Summary: A feisty American shipping heiress must assume control of her father's smuggling operation. She attempts to outmaneuver creditors, her crude, salty crew, and daring captains with a death wish, while the fledgling United States and powerful Britain battle off the Atlantic coast during the War of 1812.

ISBN 978-1-964526-13-3 (eBook) | 978-1-964526-03-4 (print edition)

1. Historical Fiction 2. Sailing 3. Boston History 4. Pirates 5. Revenge 6. Privateer 7. Age of Sail

Printed in the United States of America

PRIVATEER

STEVE DAHILL

Dedication

I would like to acknowledge, with all my love, my wife, Cathy, and our children, Katie, Maura, and Jude who all grew up with wind in their hair and ocean spray in their hearts.

Table of Contents

1. Flying Jib   2. Jib   3. Main Course   4. Spanker

In 1814 the British Empire blockaded the transport of American goods from many ports on the Atlantic coast. Armed American privateers—converted merchant ships—were instrumental in the war effort as the United States Navy only boasted a handful of Naval warships to Britain's eight hundred. Privateers helped even the score; they were light, fast, and were granted legal protection by the U.S. government if they sailed carrying a "letter of marque" allowing them to attack, capture, or sink enemy ships. During "Mr. Madison's War" of 1812, many Americans, including leading powerbrokers in the East became disillusioned about American 'independence' and were financially motivated to a return to British rule whereby trade was more profitable. The British, meanwhile, had their sights on the vast continent west of the Mississippi, and therefore encouraged American conspirators who might become their allies.

The War of 1812 lasted two years and eight months. In 1813, after a year of hostilities between America and Britain, Napoleon's massed armies continued to threaten Britain and her allies. While England fought for her life, the United States opportunistically declared war on

Britain under the pretense of protecting fair and free trade at sea when the real objective was to commandeer lightly garrisoned Canada. With the miniscule U.S. Navy up against Britain's massive Royal Navy, the United States was not only outgunned, but her mid-Atlantic coasts were blockaded tight, commerce stifled. Once Wellington dispatched French armies, America could do little to prevent his tens of thousands of hardened troops from landing on the Maryland shores. To disrupt Britain's sea trade the island nation so desperately needed to survive, thousands of private American sailing ships therefore were transformed into privateers armed with canon and decks overflowing with men anxious for the spoils of war. A successful outcome for either combatant was anything but assured.

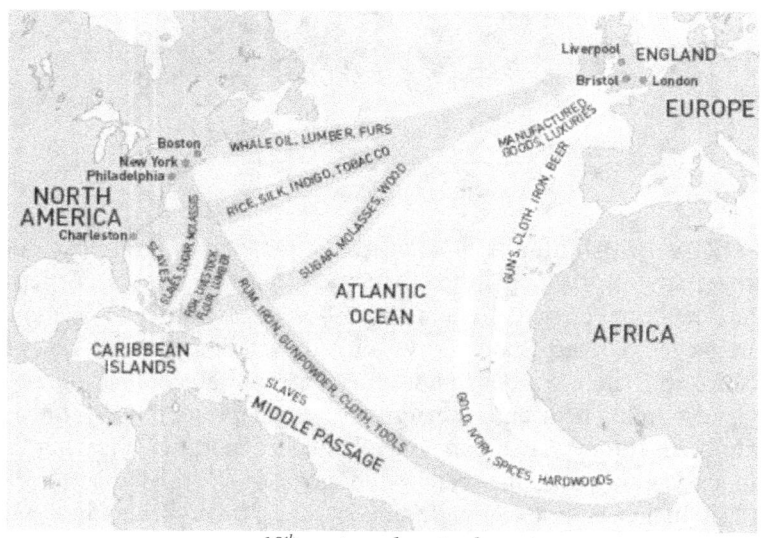

19th-century slave trade routes

Book One

A Gamester's Hope

Chapter One

Newport, Rhode Island and Providence Plantation, 1813

Thomas Hammond perched on the edge of his polished maple chair and described the most exciting day in his twelve years. "Every citizen of Newport would agree it was a momentous event, Father!"

"Our ship was mauled, Thom," declared his father, Colonel Samuel Hammond, having surveyed the damage to his valuable brig.

"But our captain never flinched, sir!" Seated between his father and his sister in their grand dining room at Great Hill manor, the lad retold the action: when the twelve-gun privateer *Rattlesnake* attacked the more powerful British ship, *Scepter,* armed with twenty-four cannon. Even more astounding, Thomas had returned home safely to Great Hill, alive and able to recount his tale, despite a splinter wound to his cheek that three inches lower would have taken off the boy's head. "When the enemy appeared, he went right at them!"

"Bow-down?" Colonel Hammond asked.

"Yes, Father. He *dared* them to hit us, which they did with no effect."

"'No effect', indeed," Colonel Hammond ruminated. "The damage to *Rattlesnake's* broken spars and split rigging will consume the better part of a fortnight to repair." And the payments Hammond and Company owed to the men from Providence were far past due. The Colonel had counted on this latest cruise to fulfill his solemn obligations. Time was running short, and neither his captain nor his ship was ready for another cruise. "Tell me about injuries, son. I have just now read my absent captain's cursory account of nine crewmen *'out of Action'* and *'five men buried over the side'.*"

"Father, yes, a few. One lad from Middletown lost a hand, but the cook saved his arm with a tight tourniquet—"

"Thomas dear, please tell us about our Captain Jordan?" his sister interrupted. "Did he conduct himself with valor?" Emma Hammond, a charming young woman of nineteen years, had waited patiently to inquire about the Captain Jordan's wellbeing. "Surely his daring action shall embellish his reputation as the most audacious privateering captain on the coast."

"Captain Jordan was marvelous, Em! He stared the enemy straight in the eye! He took us in close, despite their best attempt to stop us…" Thomas took another mouthful of steamed cod and boiled potatoes. "Our captain did not for a moment hesitate…" *Despite a heated argument with the mate*, Thomas mused to himself, having promised his captain to keep secret certain events on board *Rattlesnake*. "…and when the smoke from the enemy's guns suddenly cleared, the captain cried out *'No merchantman can reload in under five minutes, lads—and* 'Snake *can do it in three! Bring us closer!'* he cried to the mate. Our sprit boom, Father, nearly snagged the enemy's mizzen shrouds—but we had them dead to rights!"

Together, the Hammond family relished a meal of fresh fish, venison, and early summer vegetables from nearby fields of the Great Hill estate. Despite the plentiful food and his relief that Thom had escaped serious injury, the Colonel's mood ran foul. His head was racked with ongoing pain due to his many concerns. War, his errant wife, their children, and a growing debt due to an insubordinate captain were stressors that had reached an unsustainable level. His privateer, *Rattlesnake*, had returned to Newport with only the proceeds of a badly damaged prize-ship. The colonel poured himself another glass of sherry from one of his wife's many travel mementos, an exquisite crystal decanter she had shipped back from Venice accompanied by a brief note mentioning she was staying on.

Colonel Samuel Hammond, *Rattlesnake's* owner and one of the wealthiest ship owners on the North American coast, had many questions for his son—even more for his mysteriously absent captain. With *Rattlesnake's* supporting shrouds severely ripped apart due to the enemy's initial, unanswered broadside, his captain had risked crashing

Rattlesnake's entire rig of masts, spars, and sails to the deck when he ordered a reckless tack onto a new course. Without the web of secure stays, her masts risked collapse, the ship might have been lost altogether. The captain, one Captain Cornelius Jordan, had threatened the brig and the lives of fifty men on an unnecessary flashy maneuver that a more sanguine captain would have avoided. *Why,* Colonel Hammond would demand of Captain Jordan, *did you place mayhem ahead of profit? And jeopardize my son's life!*

Colonel Hammond continued to listen carefully to his son's enthused telling. He struggled to see a picture of a true account of the battle. Alongside other lads near his son's age, youngsters like Thom Hammond helped the fighting sailors in battle by retrieving powder and shot from the ship's magazine below deck. The zeal of youth, however, did not provide them with a protective shield from the pandemonium of flying hot iron and maelstrom of splinters. Imagining his son crouched as ordered behind the protection of the gun deck's heavy bulwarks, the colonel tried to hide his apprehension. He had surprised even himself when he allowed Thom to ship with Captain Jordan on the Hammond brig the boy had named *Rattlesnake*. The fact that Thom had survived to tell his tale said more about good fortune than it did about Captain Jordan's acumen or attention to the lad's well-being.

The colonel looked across the table at his dear daughter Emma, named Mary Celeste at birth, after his mother. When Emma was a very young girl, she insisted that her own eponym, Mary Celeste, be abbreviated "M" for Mary; and as she grew, "M" morphed into "Em" that became a term of affection. These days, she answered only to "Emma"—an unvarnished name well-matched to her sprightly spirit. Colonel Hammond noted with dismay, however, how his daughter listened with particular interest to her brother's adventure. He was not sure which concerned him more—young Thom's questionable account or his intelligent daughter's keen attention to what surely had been—by the mauling the ship had suffered—a murderous sea-action. Colonel Hammond tried to enjoy the dinner celebrating his boy's safe return, yet his thoughts kept turning as well to his wife's vacant seat at the dining table. Caroline Hammond was presently engaged in an extended European tour—purportedly to take in the ancient monuments—though the colonel knew otherwise. Her abrupt departure stung like a hammer blow, given the reasons she had left. His wife did not understand the many pressures he faced nor the distasteful choices he had made to keep the family's fortunes afloat.

The colonel wiped his chin and regarded their two children. His wife would have objected vociferously to Thom's sea-going adventures. She had insisted the boy's place was ashore with tutors learning a useful trade. *And our blooming daughter*, Caroline Hammond had chided him with a sigh as she had packed her many trunks, *is overdue for a suitable husband. A pretty maid*, his cross wife had told him, *must not tag along with her father each morning, not to his office, nor near the pier where young sailors with tar under their nails and lust in their hearts watch our angel's every swaying step.*

As Thom's account wore on and the venison dwindled, Colonel Hammond's troubled mind churned. His thoughts turned to his most successful, young captain, the insubordinate Cornelius Jordan. Hammond's instructions had been to capture enemy merchant ships without undue damage or injuries. Instead, Captain Jordan had towed a mast-less wreck into port under a jury rig, a hollow victory in this war of economic survival. And Colonel Hammond's letters to five Newport families conveying their sons or husbands would not return, had to go out in the post before he might find the relief of his pillow that night.

"And Captain Jordan?" Colonel Hammond asked Thom. "Tell me of his tactics under fire." Emma sat straighter, eager to hear of her captain's valor.

Thomas, attuned to his father's suspicions about the captain's violent tendencies, held back. The boy sidestepped, focusing instead on the excitement of his first encounter with the hated British enemy. That splendid day weeks ago rang clear in the boy's memory. He wished he were still clinging to a backstay, shouting with glee as brave crewmen reloaded their massive cannon. The more he recalled the fraught drama of that day, however, the more the open animosity between the first officer and their steadfast captain rang in his head. He decided not to burden his father with that part of the story; Thomas felt that he alone understood his captain's stout heart, but the mate's obvious terror in the face of battle had been an emotion he did not understand.

"I've never seen such courage, Father! Emma, our captain defied the enemy! All our men cheered!"

Men still standing, that is.

North Atlantic Ocean. Two Weeks Prior

Though *Rattlesnake's* first mate Ebenezer Briggs was lured to the privateer's life with promises of riches unavailable to men ashore, privateering's brutal reality mostly offered only privation, lonely cruises over empty oceans, and pain. At an early age, Ben Briggs had learned to navigate through dangerous New England shoals earning him an officer's commission on a merchant ship. With war declared, his ventures as a merchant seaman abruptly ended when suffocating British patrols and blockades closed many American ports. New England harbors remained open in the early months of the war, but once Royal Navy line-of-battle ships and speedy frigates were freed from European duties, they arrived, choking harbors from Eastport to Charleston. Armed American vessels only slipped out of east coast ports under the cover of gales and strong offshore winds, the risks high, penalties severe. Nevertheless, like many ambitious seamen, Ben Briggs gratefully accepted a commission on Hammond and Company's newest privateer—*Rattlesnake*—a heavily armed converted coastal brig with a *letter of marque* license to capture British-flagged merchant vessels.

Though not a seasoned fighting man, young Ben Briggs knew enough about sea battles to recognize that the captain's plan as they approached a menacing prize was reckless, or worse, a deadly mistake. Lured by the captain's promises of gold, Ben Briggs was nonetheless overly protective of his own well-being, an anomaly among *Rattlesnake's* fifty men who stood bare-chested against an ocean of harm; men ready to kill for a taste of fortune.

Ben Briggs' sandy sun-streaked hair shone against his ruddy skin. His eyes squinted uncomfortably in the morning sun as he stared across the two hundred yards of gentle ocean swells that separated *Rattlesnake* and the massive English vessel they had chanced upon minutes before through the lifting mist. From the quarterdeck where the captain stood alongside the owner's son and the helmsman to the crowded gun-deck,

Ben Briggs looked into the faces of *Rattlesnake's* sweating crewmen. Each man hunched over his cannon thirsted for a quick action and the rewards to follow. Even so, each man appeared apprehensive about Captain Cornelius Jordan's course of action. For the captain's most recent order—attack head-on—the crew showed scant enthusiasm. Ben Briggs shared their trepidation. The crew hovered over their loaded cannon with slow-lit matches and waited impatiently for the captain's order to steer away so *Rattlesnake's* cannon would come to bear and fire a deadly first volley. Instead, Jordan ordered *Rattlesnake* to sail directly toward the larger enemy ship, exposing the Yankee brig's unarmed bow.

"Prepare your larboard watch to board with axes, pikes, and pistols," Captain Jordan calmly ordered, his eyes never looking at the field of battle nor at his men. Instead, he closed his eyes and basked in the sun's increasing warmth. He opened them briefly to pat young Thom Hammond on the shoulder.

"Watch this, son," Jordan said to the lad who smiled broadly.

After an awkward silence, the captain peeked out from under his broad-rim hat and gave his new first mate his full attention. "She's a packet, Mr. Briggs. An *unarmed* packet of the Dempsey Line from Liverpool, if I've not mistaken her pennant. We shall take her with ease if she does not protest."

"But she's not yet backed her sails, Captain," Ben noted, the nearest men nodding.

"We *shall* take her," Jordan insisted.

Briggs reluctantly looked along the deck. The men saw what he saw: their target was not lying hove-to, prepared to surrender to American privateersmen crawling up her side. Instead, she appeared ready to turn upwind and fight. Briggs noted the crew's attention was fixed on their officers—loyal eyes now questioning the captain's high-risk plan to charge an enemy whose cannon might be hidden behind disguised gun ports. If Captain Jordan had guessed wrong, if their prey turned hunter and unleashed heavy cannon, the packet could blow the smaller, slightly-built *Rattlesnake* out of the water.

From under his hat, Captain Jordan peeked and saw Briggs turn toward the crew. Yet he remained at the taffrail standing tall in a fine blue naval jacket nattily matched with white pants, silk stockings, and shoes polished as bright as the brass bell that hung by the wheel. His hair, long, clean, and lightly perfumed was pulled tight behind his lace neck-cloth. With his back to the men on deck he spoke to his first mate in a voice the entire crew could hear.

"Mr. Briggs, note her sides! Do you see gun ports? She is unarmed as clear as she is poorly sailed, lollygagging over the waves instead of making her escape. She has not enough men to both sail proper and fight at the same time. My Newport lads will take her, eh boys?" Jordan turned to the men, though their response to his rallying was as tepid as a pot of hours-old tea.

Briggs felt burning shame at this public rebuke; he prided himself that the men took him seriously, that he would protect them. He shook his head in silent protest and gripped the larboard rail so hard he thought he might crack the oak with his heavily calloused fingers. Ben Briggs had proven himself these past months by leading armed sorties against small merchant vessels and isolated, unprotected villages on England's West Coast. The young officer—nigh twenty-two with ten hard years at sea—had demonstrated he could fill *Rattlesnake's* hold with captured cargo while still protecting his men from unnecessary bloodshed. He knew from sad experience far out at sea, wounds from sharp swords and lead balls often led to gangrene, amputation, and too often, a feverous death. Captain Jordan, however, did not share his first mate's consideration for the survival, never mind the good health, of his crew. The captain, bent on spoils, led his men straight into a potential slaughterhouse.

"Briggs, we must not show temerity before the enemy!" Jordan's words rankled in Ben's head.

Ben had no ready answer to thwart his captain's accusation that effectively turned his measured caution into "temerity before the enemy". *Hell,* he thought, *we need a plan, not just boldness!* At a crossroads, Briggs focused instead on escape. If the day turned against them, they must either trim the brig's spanker and rake the enemy's stern firing their six larboard eighteen-pound cannons into the enemy's unprotected, gilded cabin, or ease all sails, fall off to larboard, and fire a concentrated broadside before the other ship could rake the privateer's gun-deck packed tight with bare-back men and combustible charges. Either course was preferable to charging head-on, turning at the last moment in order to bring the ships alongside each other, and board fifty men with orders to kill.

First Mate Briggs had to admit Cornelius Jordan cut a dashing image of a bold privateer captain during the recent spring *soirees* in Boston and New York. And here on the glassy Atlantic waters under a humid May sky, that image matched reality. The problem as Briggs saw it, however, was that the image presupposed a successful outcome; yet here today, their dashing captain had placed *Rattlesnake* in unnecessary danger. If Ben Briggs could have found another path to the wealth he desired—accumulating enough capital to build ships of his own design—he would have gladly pursued it, leaving the fighting to men with stronger stomachs. Out here on open waters—with two heavily-armed ships ready to throw tons of hot metal at the other with the intent to tear sails, spars, and lines while ripping men apart—was not the life Ben sought. Before he could build ships, however, he had to survive the morning.

Rattlesnake slowly approached the ship from Liverpool.

The light wind wafted from SSE with occasional puffs that lifted both ships on the Atlantic's gentle swells. *Rattlesnake's* main course and topsails flapped, struggling for shape as the crewmen adjusted braces to find whatever pressure existed forty feet above deck. Briggs studied the other ship's rigging. He watched her men controlling the braces on deck. Suddenly he heard a muffled sailing command from across the water. British sailors scurried to their larboard side facing *Rattlesnake's* undefended bow. The enemy's spars rotated to catch the wind, her flying jibs and staysails were trimmed in tight, and the ship beat closer to the wind. The enemy turned into attack position.

"Captain, she's gained the speed to cross us! We must fall off and bring our guns to bear!" Briggs shouted with an urgency no one could construe as a strategic alternative: it was a counter-command to the captain's orders. It belied an ominous threat nearly as dangerous to *Rattlesnake* as the enemy; her officers disagreed, their vehemence no longer disguised.

The captain glared at his first mate. Speaking slowly in a voice as steely as his unsheathed sword, he said, "Mr. Briggs, on only your *second* privateering voyage, how is it you know more about our business than your captain?"

Briggs' rejoinder was cut off by an urgent cry from forward. "Captain, they're opening gun ports! She's running out cannon! Ten, sir!"

Deta:hed, Jordan ignored the warning. His cold eyes stared down Ben Briggs. He looked over his shoulder, up at the sails, and casually toward the enemy ship. He turned to the bow and spoke loud so the entire deck could hear.

"We shall continue on this course, Mr. Briggs!"

"Captain, she's backwinded her mains'l," cried a crewman on the foredeck

To s ow the larger ship and steady her rocking motion so her fire would er.pt straight and true, her captain had allowed her sails to catch the wind from forward, squaring her so her guns bore directly down on *Rattlesnake.*

"We shall have a more stable target then!" Jordan replied.

Briggs felt the weight of fifty men staring at him. He swallowed hard, his fist to his forehead. "Aye, sir. Boarding party's ready. Our starboard broadside is aimed at her rig—"

"Nay! Lower the guns," Jordan commanded. "Spray their gun deck with grapeshot. We shall kill these people."

Briggs obeyed, aware the enemy might be planning the same murderous tactic. *If an exploding canister of small metal balls and broken glass can tear through a ship's solid oak topsides, what'll it do to a man's bare chest? Does he die painlessly unaware or stagger stupidly in searing agony, his hands unable to stanch an unrelenting flow of blood?* Ben's stomach loosened and he tasted his breakfast. He considered the rail but realized the stars in his eyes might cause him to fall overboard. His deep-set fear of drowning faded with the even greater terror of the impending enemy broadside. Ben Briggs regained his feet and his wits.

Although *Rattlesnake's* mission was to capture prizes while avoiding damage in material or injury to her crew, Cornelius Jordan was a man who not only welcomed, but thirsted for the smoke and thunder of cannon fire. The instant the enemy cannon appeared like a pack of wolves from a forest's edge, the captain's original plan to board would no longer do. By trimming her sails and increasing her speed the British ship had cut off *Rattlesnake's* overtaking course or any possible flight. Her massive hull loomed like a fortress. *Rattlesnake* had nowhere to go but straight in.

Sucking deep breaths, Briggs wiped hair from his dripping brow. *Rattlesnake* must counter the enemy's latest move—now! The crew's eyes—a mix of fear and urgency—pleaded for such a counter. *Rattlesnake* could sail nimbler than the behemoth across the swells. If she could maintain the weather-side wind advantage—which dictated each ship's position—she would gain considerable advantage. Yet the command to bear off waited for the captain, while he fitted his smooth leather gloves. Like the sun unmasked from a fast-moving cloud, Captain Jordan finally turned and looked at Briggs, his eyes glazed with a killer's lust. *Good men will die this morning,* Briggs told himself, *because of this man.*

"Captain," Ben Briggs tried one last time, "her cannons are aimed at our gun deck! We must bear away and fire!"

Even if the captain had agreed, shouting "Turn and fire!" in a voice as loud as a thousand rushing beasts, his words would have been lost by the deafening crash of the British volley. Enemy cannon shot whistled close overhead, tearing *Rattlesnake's* sails and splitting her lower rigging. A shroud, tightened as hard as iron, snapped like a broken cello string. More curious than angry, the captain looked up at the swaying mast. His eyes lit up like a prize fighter who had absorbed his opponent's best punch. Jordan raised his sword.

"Lads, they missed high!"

High indeed, Briggs thought. *Their next volley will not.*

"Thom, go below or take cover!" he cried to the owner's son, standing in awe, oblivious to the dangling damage high above his head.

Broken spars, loose lines, and flapping sails caused *Rattlesnake* to slow, losing maneuverability and her previous tactical edge. Briggs squinted through the smoke wafting from the expired enemy guns: Only a few had fired in unison, navy-fashion. *Might Captain Jordan be correct? Has the enemy an insufficient complement of sailors to trim sails, fire weapons, and reload, all the while fending off a boarding from a determined hoard of privateersmen?*

Another chest-pounding blast erupted. Briggs' hopeful illusion and the captain's ill-founded premise quickly dissipated in the suffocating cloud. A hot wind scorched inches above Briggs' head as he crouched. British cannon balls, now aimed lower to kill exposed privateersmen, slashed through *Rattlesnake's* forward deck rails and bulwarks propelling splintered shards of Newburyport pine into the soft skin of unfortunate crewmen who had ill-timed their duck. On cannon number two, three men dropped with fearsome lower injuries: one poor man's leg ripped off at his thigh, another's scream showed a kneecap turned into a pulp of shattered red bones and mangled tissue. The deck near the injured ran slippery with blood despite sawdust strewn for traction. Dying and stricken men screamed in pain, pleading for *help* or *God* or *Mother*. As the wounded were carried below, *Rattlesnake* silently sliced through the water. Bow-down, she closed. Her cannon ready, her captain tough, not.

"Their rudder, sir?" Briggs yelled out above the din, trying to sound like a reasoned, loyal officer, unclear of his captain's intention, offering sober alternates in the fast-changing chaos. *We could sail past her stern, cripple her steering, and regroup,* Ben thought. *Boarding her now is impossible!* Briggs blocked the stench of burnt powder wafting from the enemy's guns, and coughed violently. Spitting downwind, he locked eyes with the captain.

"No, Mr. Briggs," his captain countered. "Aim your starboard guns at her deck. Prepare the elevation of your larboard guns and be ready to fire at her mizzen mast. After our first broadside, we shall wear ship and you may fire once the smoke clears."

Briggs looked for a man to help him guide the captain down a safer path. Staring back at Briggs was fellow crewman, Quartus Gant, the ship's gunner, a tall, burly local Newport lad of few words about Briggs' age albeit with fifty pounds more muscle and a somber expression.

"Quartus!" shouted Briggs.

Gant's rich blue eyes resonated with a language Briggs understood; *steady,* the gunner's expression said, *this is not the time.* Encouraged, Briggs tore his sight away from the gunner who returned to aiming his weapons. Suddenly a third loud explosion ripped the lull—a single shot passed so close to Briggs' head he felt the concussion of displaced air. *They're aiming at the captain and me—the murderous buggers!* Ears ringing, he grabbed the rail, his arms numb from wrist to elbow, his sight blurred. After a long moment of confusion, his vision cleared. He recalled his foolish promise to mind Colonel Hammond's twelve-year-old son who sailed on this voyage, Thom's first. Briggs looked around the crowded deck of injured men and debris. *Was the owner's son crouched safe as instructed? No, damn it!* The boy was standing, mirroring the captain's defiance, head unprotected by bulwarks, flouting all logic! Thomas Hammond, an intelligent, imaginative lad, stood grinning, soaked in the glory of his first sea battle.

"Thomas Hammond, *down*, I said!" Briggs screamed as another shot missed his head by inches sending the boy's mop of brown hair flying. The iron ball smashed a longboat stowed on deck through and through and split a main shroud before it crashed into a gun crew of five men and boys whose bodies flung to the deck and bulwarks in an unrecognizable mass of broken, ripped parts. Thomas, dazed but still standing, touched a three-inch splinter embedded in his cheek—*higher by two inches and he'd be dead,* Briggs reprimanded himself. The boy acted on instinct and yanked out the bloody trophy and held it with a weak smile. *There is no honor Thomas,* Briggs thought, *in merely surviving.* "*Down*, Thomas!" he ordered once more. Thomas retreated hesitantly to beneath the chest-high bulwarks and crept aft, away from the gun deck. Briggs returned to his duty directing the cannon. The one-sided battle would soon be over if *Rattlesnake* did not return fire. Only sixteen yards from the enemy, they had time and sea room for only one final move. "Starboard guns are ready, sir! Shall we steer down and fire?" He waited. "Captain?"

Rattlesnake's bowsprit was seconds from snagging the enemy's spars and rigging. If they rammed the other ship's massive hull, the smaller, lighter *Rattlesnake* would sink. Captain Jordan turned to Briggs with a toothy smile.

"Aye, Mr. Briggs."

"Hard over, Mr. Wickham!" Ben roared the command for which every man on deck was praying. "Let loose our windward sheets and braces!"

The brig turned like a wild horse trapped in a paddock. She came abeam of the British ship, her six starboard guns in level firing position. *At last!* thought every privateersman as one.

"Mr. Briggs, sir, look—the gunner!" screamed Thomas Hammond.

He grabbed Ben's arm and pointed: the ship's gunner, Quartus Gant, carried packed bags of black gunpowder, stepping over injured men and debris. He appeared oblivious to the mayhem. Thom had noticed that the enemy's last volley had severed the recoil line on cannon number two. Without its heavy restraining line, the massive cannon, once fired, would fly backwards on its carriage wheels unhindered, and crush anyone in its path. Briggs reacted instantly. He mounted the first cannon and launched off its oak carriage the instant before it fired. He crashed into the gunner chest-high and the two sprawled to the deck in a knot of arms and legs doused with spilled black gunpowder.

The captain dropped his sword and screamed, "Fire!"

Rattlesnake's six starboard cannon exploded in tight, well-aimed crescendo while the untethered cannon shot backwards past the two men's feet and rammed into the mast. Flying splinters forced Briggs and Gant face-down onto the seams of the blood-slicked deck. The gunner, first to rise, inspected his uninjured body and looked down at the sprawled first mate. *Had this human projectile saved him accidentally or was this an act of unselfish valor?* Briggs rose slowly. The two men nodded in disbelief—amazed they still enjoyed use of their limbs. The blood streaked on them belonged solely to injured men lying nearby. The gunner and first mate locked arms in recognition of a primal bond formed in the thick air of smoke and confusion. Their day, however, had just begun.

"...and after that broadside, Father," the boy continued, unconsciously fingering his raw, splinter battle scar, "Captain Jordan ordered the lads to wear ship—a smart move! It brought our loaded larboard guns to bear as well. He went right at'em!" Thomas looked for reinforcement from his father, though only Emma nodded appreciation. His squeaky voice raced on, breathless with excitement. "Captain Jordan positioned *Rattlesnake* close alongside the Indiaman, waving his cutlass and threatening to sink them if they did not strike—"

"Are you saying, Thom, Captain Jordan positioned *Rattlesnake* aside a larger ship that had not yet surrendered?" asked Colonel Hammond. *What if they changed their mind and shot the damned fool's head off,* thought the colonel. He would speak to the captain... once he located the scoundrel. *Rattlesnake,* Hammond's most valuable ship and the key to restoring his dwindling fortune, had returned to Newport harbor battered yet again. The full force of the Hammond shipyard must work, day and night, to ready her for sea before November gales shut down the English shipping lanes. She required new sails, starboard-side shrouds, stays, and ratlines. His ship's paltry return—suffering expensive damage with only a single damaged prize sent to auction—improved neither his financial situation nor peace of mind.

Only days before had he received disturbing news from his banker and longtime partner, Matthew Westerly: the Colonel's promised payments were overdue—to multiple obligations. For a merchant such as Colonel Samuel Hammond, rumors of peace between the United States and Britain (his former primary trading partner), should have been welcomed news. But Hammond and Company ran blockades with war material; food and supplies for American cities along the coast sold at extraordinarily high prices. And he also smuggled guns, powder, and contraband to whomever paid the most. The problem was, as the colonel saw it, for every three ships he sent to sea, only two returned. When long-brewing hostilities were formalized one year earlier in 1812, he had outfitted the largest and fastest of his schooners and brigs with heavy cannon and armed crews. Their charter, under government-issued *letters of marque*, authorized the designated ship—formerly a merchant vessel, now a 'privateer'—to chase and capture British merchant ships. Ships laden with valuable cargo, most sailing from the British West Indies *en route* to London, taken under a privateer *marque* propelled owners like Colonel Hammond to extraordinary heights—*if* his privateers were lucky not to meet escorting British men-of-war and *if* they returned home. War was good for privileged privateer owners like Hammond; a long war potentially better. Peace would quickly restore normal trade, especially with Britain which, for Hammond, would be a mixed blessing, if not a curse, as it would abruptly end his privateering windfall. Until he settled burdensome debts to which he had regretfully over-committed during the heady days of the war's first months of unmatched captures, he remained stuck in the mud. Privateering was one of only two remaining trades that could replenish his coffers fast enough to meet all his obligations; of the two, a ship with a *letter of marque* was the only way to avoid dishonor. Upholding his family's sterling reputation was as important to Samuel Hammond as his children's well-being. Unfortunately, he was running out of time. The colonel needed an accurate tally from *Rattlesnake's* latest cruise, yet by the time he had arrived at the pier to greet his ship, Captain Jordan had already left the ship.

"No, Father, *Scepter*—" Thomas turned to his sister. "That was the prize's name, Em, from Liverpool—It lay in tatters. They could neither clear the debris nor fire back. *Rattlesnake*'s six larboard guns were aimed down their throat! You should have seen our captain waving his cutlass, Father. He was magnificent!"

"'Ta_ters...'" the colonel muttered. This latest prize was therefore worth far less at auction. *Damn that captain!* Unlike Emma who tallied the ledgers and understood how a rate of return on investment relied heavily on the condition of the taken property, Thom looked up sharply as if to convey, *We are at war.* Hammond tacked. "And, Thomas, what's this about the gunner and Mr. Briggs?"

The colonel needed men who understood the business principles underlying privateering's legal thievery. He was considering first mate Ebenezer Briggs for a command, a promotion requiring prudence coupled with intelligence; traits he regretted Captain Jordan woefully lacked.

"Mr Briggs recognized cannon number two had ripped loose. Well, I pointed it out, Father. But with no regard for his own skin, Mr. Briggs shoved the gunner to the deck just as the cannon fired and recoiled with great violence. It was Briggs who saved Quartus Gant's life!"

"Yes, yes, Thom, but tell us more about Captain *Jordan*," Emma badgered her brother. "Did he conduct the battle with discretion?"

The colonel looked at his daughter. The damage to *Rattlesnake* proved beyond doubt the captain had fought with great violence. But with *discretion*?

Thomas gulped another mouthful of chowder. "Aye, Em. Captain Jordan was about to lead the boarding party, each man armed with pikes and swords. He would have been the first over the side—"

"I thought you told us the captain did *not* board *Scepter*?" The colonel pried, beginning to see the picture.

"No, Father... but he was *ready* to board! And cut off their heads!"

Thomas' smile as wide as the polished table was long, his bright face shone in gleaming candlelight reflected off crystal goblets. The colonel pondered his son's enthusiasm although he did not share the boy's admiration for the captain's tactics. He had instructed Jordan to operate with cunning not brutality; a privateer's cannon were for *warning* shots and defense, not ship-to-ship action against a superior force! The *Rattlesnake,* a converted coastal packet, could sail extraordinarily fast, especially upwind in a moderate breeze, though she had been built extremely light—her hull, not double-planked like a warship, could not withstand even a six-pound shot. Any British warship—even a single-mast cutter with a handful of light cannon—could sink her. The colonel had instructed his captain to use the brig's speed in a surprise approach, board an unarmed prize with overwhelming numbers then fly away—under full sail if an enemy man-of-war appeared hull-down on the horizon. Instead, this captain thought he was Captain Isaac Hull aboard one of '98's heavy American frigates.

To Emma's thinking, however, a fighting sea commander leaping from his ship in a mad rush to overpower a larger force was as heroic as anything Lord Nelson had done in his fabled career. And this most recent action! Two of the enemy's three masts had been toppled by only six shots! No other ship-to-ship action in this war had been so deadly accurate, not even *Constitution* or *Constellation*, each of which carried fifty-two heavy guns into battle.

"Did our captain escape injury?" the young woman asked her brother.

"His eyes were awful red, Em. And his energy lagged terrible after the battle. He collapsed in his cabin for two days. The ship needed repairs. So, we sailed home." Thomas turned and implored his father with renewed energy, "Father, the captain never backed down! No ship escaped us without a great chase. He commanded we set a full press of sails at all times—even in a gale—"

"Did we lose any men, Thom, during these 'great chases'?"

Thomas stared at his plate. *Rattlesnake* had gained a sordid reputation under Jordan: a ship sometimes as dangerous to her crew as to her enemies. Colonel Hammond recalled Jordan's uneven scrawl in his captain's log: The captain had not distinguished between crewmen who died in the thick of smoke or men who fell from aloft in a storm. He listed each man's death the same: *"Died PerForming His DuTy."* The boy had been encouraged by the fellowship aboard to keep mum about the reality of a privateersman's life at sea. Yes, men died from disease without a surgeon on board. And yes, men washed over the rails in the night when a rogue wave broke, or lost their footing climbing to a yardarm to shorten sail in an icy gale. Thomas remembered Captain Jordan once made a courageous effort to locate a lad who had fallen over the sides during a chase off Newfoundland. With a furious scan of his brass spyglass across endless whitecaps, the captain had refused to abandon hope—although he never slowed the chase. *The captain had had no choice*, Thomas reminded himself; no coming about was possible in seas the height of a gabled roof. The lad, George his name, from near the Taunton River, was never seen again by any but fishes.

"One. A boy from Tiverton. He was careless aloft, Father." Thomas would say no more; even this admission felt too close to betrayal of his captain.

Emma had stopped listening. Her concern focused on her brother's description of Captain Jordan's well-being. *The stress of command in battle must tire a man's soul*, she worried. The daring captain had only his own wits to make decisions upon which many lives and much bounty rested. Over countless voyages this past year he had delivered the prize-ships her father and their Company sorely needed, providing her with imported fashions from England and France and a comfortable life at the magnificent Great Hill manor brimming with crystal, golden drapes, and oil paintings from Boston, New York, and the European continent. Captain Cornelius Jordan brought glory and victory in a dreary war desperate for heroes. She must congratulate him soon... *in person*. She smiled thinking of the occasion and what she would wear.

After the taking of *Scepter*, ashore and resting for two days, Ben Briggs sat at the *Scarecrow Tavern* on a well-worn maple bench and nursed a robust local ale. The drink filled him though he fretted about the voyage he had, by God's intercession, survived. That, he vowed, would be his last privateering cruise under Captain Cornelius Jordan. Though it was late in the season to find another officer's berth, his dream of fortune could only happen with privateering cruises. But sailing under Cornelius Jordan would likely end his life before the Lord intended. His dream the previous night lingered and he had trouble filing it away: standing next to Jordan, the air filled with spindrift, then smoke masking waves of blood before the ship and everyone on it disappeared into a black cauldron of boiling oil. Call it a warning, perhaps, or recognition of his near-miss. Either way, Ben needed a way out.

A rugged young man with a trim build that belied his strength, Ben Briggs struck strangers as taller than his six feet. A sailing master who could climb masts with the most agile top men, Ben was known to share the burden of fighting an icy gale alongside his able-body crew. In his most recent two month-long cruise aboard *Rattlesnake,* he had displayed special skills handling the ship's wheel despite the North Atlantic's changing conditions. In that voyage, he had earned the respect of the ships' crew—a mishmash of former Navy men and port-side thugs—all hoping, like Ben—to score a bounty that might set them square for life once ashore. Ben Briggs kept his dreams to himself; he trusted few with his ambition to build the fastest sailing ships seen on any ocean.

Ben Briggs looked at other men as a utility: a trusted crewman or a necessary supplier; a friend or an enemy; an enabler or an impediment. And though a night ashore in a distant port after a cold, lonely voyage might find him in the company of a comely girl whom his coins attracted, he avoided most social engagements when home in Newport. Nor did he pursue with long-term intent or any particular enthusiasm the young women he met in town or at county fairs. His spirit was too much taken by salt air to be captured by a girl's enticing smile and a confining dalliance sure to follow. His few attempts at casual courtships had ended awkwardly—one, a local minister's daughter who presumed his benign interest was of a more permanent nature. Shunned by her family when he backed away, he avoided Sunday services for the next year.

Scarecrow Tavern's battered door suddenly swung wide. A burley young man strode in. His bulky shadow immediately darkened the small room as if he had brought a cloud inside with him. Briggs smiled for the first time in days.

"Q!" Briggs waved over his new friend, *Rattlesnake's* gunner, Quartus Gant.

This was a fellow with whom he could enjoy thick ale and re-live that calamitous morning when against the odds, they had taken *Scepter.*

Quartus Gant felt genuinely indebted to the first mate who had saved his life and, unusual for a loner, enjoyed Ben Brigg's salty company. Together the gunner and first mate could make plans. And although neither realized their hopes were as varied as mountain and wave, they both correctly sensed their destinies were intrinsically tied. Taller and more muscular than Ben Briggs, Quartus Gant wore a face darkened by the sun, rough even by seaman's standards though shaved clean of whiskers. The gunner seldom smiled, but when he did it might follow with a sharp witticism or incisive observation. If he had other friends or family, he never said; Brigg never asked. Perhaps today by the open tavern window with flowers scenting the approaching path, and given their shared memories of a recent escape from death, Quartus Gant might reveal his inner thoughts. Briggs pushed a full tankard across the table. Gant took it gratefully and gulped half. The two kept their voices low. Though prize money weighted their pockets, they wanted no notice from port-side whores or former shipmates. For the first time since they had disembarked from *Rattlesnake*, the two men had the opportunity to converse in private.

"Did Jordan share his plan with you?" Gant asked right off, then took another deep draught, dragged his sleeve across his lips, and hailed the waiter for more.

Briggs glanced up, recalling the carnage on *Rattlesnake's* deck. He shook his head.

"No, I had no notion—"

"Cause he *had* no plan," said Gant. "He acts on the first thought that enters his perfumed little head."

Briggs nodded. "We'd be dead if we weren't lucky."

"Aye," Gant answered. "Jordan assumed the Indiaman was unarmed. Then he assumed they'd miss." After a few quiet moments Gant added, "They never miss when you expect'em to."

The gunner stared absently at the dark earthy foam in the mug that looked to him like whipped whitecaps where below the deep ocean surface lies still waters, a calm, eerie place where sometimes answers are revealed.

"Did you see him stow two of *Scepter's* chests in his cabin? For 'inspection' he said. What do you make of it?" asked Briggs, although he had a fair notion.

"He can inspect the devil for all I care. What if he tickles a few bracelets for his women?"

Briggs let it lie, then added, "A shot nearly took the boy's head off. That would've cost me my commission. I promised the colonel I'd watch the lad. Either way, it's probably my last cruise on *Rattlesnake*. The captain—"

"—is a damned *fool!* Oldest trick for a square rigger in light air sailing with only a mains'l... Backwind it and even an ugly lugger like *Scepter* would lose her headway. Jordan made no provision for her move. He left us exposed."

Briggs realized Gant understood the finer points of ship-action: Perhaps he had once fought aboard a man-of-war? Quartus Gant, more warrior than merchant, seemed immune to guilt as he overpowered an enemy with his fist or knife. Once during a fight on a rolling deck, Briggs had witnessed him take a life without remorse while sparing another in the same minute. Gant objected to firing the ship's cannon into the hull of a defenseless prize where blood would spill without purpose or glory. Yet Gant had no patience for strategy when his blood was up and a boarding loomed. Briggs, by contrast, enjoyed a more deliberate outlook when action threatened. Ben carefully weighed crew commands for their intended or causal effect. His plans for battle factored not only wind and swells, but the atmosphere he sensed aboard a ship and the energy or fear he saw in his men's faces. He prepared for every violent confrontation like a politician, ready always for the unexpected. Over the course of many weeks fighting alongside each other or during quiet legs returning to port, the two young men had earned each other's confidence. They agreed they might advance their careers faster as a team and so formed a pact. For Gant the loner, dependency was a new and uncomfortable condition. For Briggs the dreamer, his ambition for the first time was tied to another man.

One night at sea, the two had stood on deck in the early evening dog watch, Gant taking his turn at the ship's wheel, while Briggs shared his innermost musings. He spoke slowly and with passion about how a few more privateering voyages would make him rich enough to buy a schooner to trade along the coast. Eventually he might build ships of his own design. Gant had listened patiently as he looked to the trim of his sails. Lighting a pipe with his hands, his knees guided the spokes on the wheel in the gentle breeze.

"Aye," Gant had said. "And you'll need sturdy men."

Quartus Gant, without any apparent joy in his heart, understood Ben Briggs' dream. Yet years before, when Briggs spoke of his ambition with his parents and sister, they had looked at him with blank eyes, his father warning of unknown offshore dangers, his mother of mysterious foreign diseases. His sister, however, had nodded her support, smiling at him as she knitted. As miles turned to leagues, leagues to cruises, and cruises to campaigns, Ebenezer Briggs had warmed to the possibility his dreams might come true—to sail a ship of his own build to distant harbors, the fastest, most beautiful sailing vessel the world had ever seen. Investors would queue at his door to secure cargo space for their precious spices and teas. He would replace slow and uncomfortable packets with sailing chariots of speed and luxury fit for the most discerning passengers. To awake with his dream a reality, he needed first to make his fortune like men from Boston were doing in the exploding China trade. To accomplish that, he must overcome the deathly downside of privateering: either learn to survive the violence or escape from ruthless sailing masters like Captain Cornelius Jordan. Perhaps his new friend Q could show him how.

"Jordan only needs direction." Gant leaned across the table. "The *'Snake'* a smart ship. Jordan attracts the right sort... the best top men and able-bodies. They go privateering with Cornelius Jordan because he takes more prizes than any privateersman—even the Newburyport sloops. Think on it." Gant took another long swig. His eyes never left Briggs.

Ben *had* thought on it. Truth was, he felt terrified to sail under Jordan again. Gant must not see his fear or learn he had lost many nights' rest with visions of loose cannon atop dead men strewn along a red slick. He answered his friend honestly, "A smart ship will get us nothing if she's lying on the bottom, Q."

Gart ignored Briggs reticence, having sailed on too many smugglers and slavers to let this rich opportunity pass. He could brave the *'Snake* without Briggs, though a growl down low in his gut hinted that his drinking mate was important to his future.

"Then we'll keep her atop the waves." A belch resembling a chuckle escaped Gant's throat. "When I'm leadin' the fightin' and you callin' the shots in his ear, we can focus his attention... in a more purposeful manner."

"Tell him how to fight? I don't see it, Q," Briggs objected.

Gant sensed Briggs was losing heart. But he also saw a sober strength necessary to steer the easily distracted captain. Gant's breathing slowed. He took a long slug that emptied his tankard. Where other men might pound a fist, raise a voice, guffaw, or roll an eye to sell their point, Gant sat patiently. After the empty space had set the table, he spoke at a deliberate pace.

"Most men got no influence on him, Briggs. But *you* do. He knows you're smart. You sometimes back off when he barks, but you're usually right and he knows it. Me, he sees my skill at the wheel or with a bloody knife in my hand. If we work together, we can save him from his worst impulses. We can drive him to our advantage. Good for him, he don't die. Good for the owner, we bring his ship home full of bounty. Good for us, we'll get rich." This was the longest speech Ben Briggs had ever heard from Quartus Gant. Each word sagged under great weight. The gunner wiped his chin after his long, final swig and leaned in. "I don't see me sailing under him again without you, Briggs. And I don't see you bending his will by yourself. But I'm telling you… he's only one man." Despite his premonition of violent death standing near Captain Cornelius Jordan, Ben Briggs heard a calm confidence in Gant's voice that steeled his own resolve. "Jordan will lead us to our fortune," Gant promised, his hand extended. "Or we'll take his ship."

Chapter Two

A pot of steaming black tea wafted fragrant notes cf the Far East. In silence, Emma Hammond added sugar to one of the porcelain teacups on her father's office desk. Arranging the saucers artfully beneath the remaining cups, she slipped away without a sound. Distracted, Colonel Samuel Hammond gazed out the window watching the *Rattlesnake's* first mate Ebenezer Briggs walk briskly toward the pier and the Hammond and Company offices. He suspected that behind the standard, orderly list of captured goods and an unemotional recap of damaged spars and crippled men, the mate could paint a more accurate portrait of the recent cruise than his own son's wild depiction. Confident footsteps climbed the office stairs.

"Good morning, Colonel." Ben Briggs smiled earnestly, his eyes steady.

"Where's Captain Jordan?"

"He begs your forgiveness, sir—he hailed a schooner to pick him up off Brenton Reef. A Bristol packet we spoke off Point Judith relayed his mother had taken ill. He feared the worst this time. He expects to be down the bay by the end of the week. Our tally, Colonel."

"This is the second time this season that poor woman has faced eternity," countered Colonel Hammond, his tone ironic, "She has remarkable recuperative abilities."

"Sir?"

Glowering, Colonel Hammond did not ask what else Jordan had disembarked *with*. After a brief review of the captured cargo manifest, Hammond looked up.

"Master Briggs, our situation in this war has turned…" He affected a deliberate pause. "…delicate." Briggs did not respond to the non-question. *Good,* thought the colonel, *a young man who listens.* "I require my ships return in good order. I expect a certain profit."

He swiveled his chair and reached for the teapot. Pouring, Hammond tilted his head toward *Rattlesnake's* second in command indicating he might help himself to hot tea.

"Aye, Capt—!" Briggs stopped, smiled, and corrected himself, "Thank you, Colonel Hammond. After being at sea, I find it hard to drop sea-talk, sir." Ebenezer Briggs was determined to present himself as man of business not a deck hand.

"Thomas spoke well of you, Mr. Briggs. Told us you were gallant… instrumental in directing the ship in battle. You saved a man—Quartus Gant, our new gunner? Tell me."

"I was fortunate, sir." Briggs scratched his cheek. The latest voyage was a confluence of lies. If his privateering career were to continue, he needed support from both his captain and the owner. Truth only slows down the day. "And your son helped us reposition a gun—he set the altitude and range."

"So he told me. I was asking about the gunner."

"Thomas noted the recoil lines on cannon number two were severed by the enemy's first broadside. He alerted me to the danger just as the gunner crossed behind it."

"You shoved the man out of the cannon's path?" Colonel Hammond asked casually; he sought insights from Briggs about his attention to details, any evidence of a quick wit and competent decision-making process, not a retelling of a story he already knew.

Briggs realized his brush with gallantry was not the impetus behind the owner's questions, and expounded, "I had no time to warn him, nor could I disrupt the gun crew—their cannon was aimed. When it fired, the gunner would have been crushed. A leap was the best among the bad choices I faced."

Hammond heard what he wanted. The mate's priorities were ship, crew, self—in that order. *Good man.*

"And Thomas stood his ground?"

"Yes, sir. Everything happened in a flash. I believe it is important for men to overcome their fears and attend their duty despite the mayhem and the injured mates around them. Your son understands this.

He learns fast. We often talk during our watches. He has a keen eye for tactics and action."

"As I feared," the colonel responded. "The boy has a 'keen eye' for the bloodlust of fighting. And he has a stomach like mine—girded for war. But he must develop a keen eye for profit as well, or our enterprise will suffer." Imagining his young son standing on a deck amidst the bloody engagement, Hammond grew uncomfortable. And the mate sitting here, angling for a command—*Does he think I am oblivious to the obsequiousness of his agreeable tone?* Nevertheless, he relaxed, recognizing the first mate appeared to have genuine affection for Thomas. *Briggs will keep my lad safe.* Hammond decided to trust this young officer, despite having once trusted Cornelius Jordan.

"Keep a sharp eye on Thomas. Send him below deck during any future attacks."

"Yes, sir." Briggs nodded.

"As I said, our business is at risk," said Hammond regarding the able young man. *Fond of my son. Brave in action. Intelligent enough to remain silent when a rejoinder does not improve the conversation.* Yet an ambitious man like Ebenezer Briggs must not slide from one of life's unplanned events to another while depending on serendipity to make his fortune. Hammond decided to open a door. The Providence syndicate needed new blood. "We have a duty, Mr. Briggs, to our investors. We return them profits only a privateering enterprise can deliver during war. I need crews, fighting ships… and loyal officers." Hammond stood and paced to the open window. Shutting it, he turned to Briggs, and spoke softly, "Mr. Briggs, I need captains who display not just cunning but discretion as well."

Is he offering me a ship? Ben wondered, barely concealing his joy. *Befriending Thomas was a smarter move than I anticipated! Strange—to be genuinely fond of the entitled son of a rich man.* It was obvious to Briggs that Thomas had told his father about their recent voyage. Briggs wondered if the boy's telling truly reflected a morning when terror and crippling fear had nearly overcome him. The colonel leaned in and stared. Ben waited, disappointed when Hammond offered nothing further. *You must wait*, the colonel's silence advised him. *Watch and remain loyal. You will be my eyes.*

Briggs answered the colonel simply, "Yes, sir." The meeting appeared over and he remembered an earlier promise. "Ah, sir, forgive me, the gunner, Mr. Gant, has proved a valuable seaman. I ask that you give him an officer's commission. He's a good man, sir."

"Is he a sailing master?"

"He can navigate around any shoal in New England."

"Would you trust him with your life during a storm hard against a lee shore? Would you trust him with your ship if she were everything you owned in this world?"

"I would stand beside him in battle or in a hurricane," Briggs answered straight.

"I hear he is unfriendly."

"He has not had an easy life. But he knows the ship. He's a skilled navigator, particularly through the narrows. He leads our fighting lads over the rail."

Colonel Hammond was surprised Ben Briggs had not seized upon the opportunity to advance his own career. Instead of blowing his own trumpet or offering a critique of Captain Jordan's shifty behavior, Briggs' oblique answers reflected deep intelligence rather than an unwillingness to be forthcoming. And the only thing he asked for benefited another man. Another honorable young officer to complement Briggs on a ship under the aggressive Captain Jordan might bring needed balance. And despite some barely concealed patronizing, Briggs had answered his owner's questions forthrightly. He spoke the truth yet said nothing unnecessary—a special skill for an even more dangerous commission Colonel Hammond had in mind.

"I shall inform the captain I've rated Mr. Gant second mate. But he'll retain his gunner duties, as well."

"He'll be grateful, thank you, Colonel."

Colonel Hammond had many dire needs: capital and profits most of all; finding honest men for a dishonest business; securing larger ships swift enough to run into blockaded ports. Yesterday he had got word that not one but two of his older coastal ships, a small brig and a topsail schooner—despite careful routing he himself had prepared—had been captured by British patrols, and were to be sold at auction. Since neither was an armed privateer, his men should find their way home eventually. But the ships and their cargoes were lost. For every three merchant ships sent out, two foundered in storms or were captured. A Hammond privateer must, therefore, return with a cargo of stolen enemy riches every six weeks in order to keep the enterprise solvent. The key was to regularly send ships to sea with sober captains and hearty seamen hunting in places where Samuel Hammond had been informed that enemy naval patrols did not venture. By what means Hammond learned about these unprotected zones, however, had a cost sure to harm him if discovered. The colonel sighed as his weary body begged for rest.

Hammond looked to Ben Briggs. "Here." He took a risk. Colonel Hammond handed a small canvas envelope with a wax seal imprinted "*H*". It was not addressed. "As you're second-in-command, Mr. Briggs, I'm giving you instructions in the event *Rattlesnake* is captured by the Royal Navy. Contained herein is..." Unconsciously, he hesitated, searching for a more precise word. "...*information* meant for our friends as well as for our purported enemies. This war cannot and must not continue. Trade is at a stand-still, imports down by nearly 80%, our feeble government's coffers are near-empty without trading customs duties. Our great state of Rhode Island cannot even procure sufficient grain or corn for our mills. I rely on profits from trade with England yet today their fleet blockades most major harbors. My associates and I disapprove of Mr. Madison's folly—" He cut himself short. *Our profits are drying like salt on tarpaulin.* "However, to secure an honorable peace with people who arm Indians in our western territories and encourage them to slaughter our farmers is... well, a challenging balance." He paused to look directly at Ben, in rapt attention. "Our New England states have continued close ties with our former mother-country. Some, not I, would consider seceding from these United States in order to rejoin Britain. This possibility keeps the British administration more favorable to our needs than to the vile Federalists who have been at our throats for a dozen or more years!"

"We have indeed encountered fewer patrols off Boston, Colonel," Ben added to demonstrate awareness of the precarious conditions upon which trade must navigate.

"All due to our New England sympathies for a great empire fighting that tyrant from France. Without the Royal Navy, Bona's thirst might drive his fleets west, suffocating our coasts. Madison's latest embargo may push us to bankruptcy, or worse, dissolvent of this brittle Union. Some call our country a group of united states, rather than the singular United States. Madison had not considered *that* in his ploy to favor western voters."

"I see," Briggs answered feebly, wondering about the purpose of the colonel's harangue.

Hammond cleared his throat. "Back to you, however. If *Rattlesnake* is captured, I need the ship returned to a neutral port. Once there, I need her officers offered parole and my crews treated humanely. This letter entreats any commander of an enemy ship you might encounter to show my men justice under British law and the rules of war. In return, this letter... offers certain arrangements that our enemies will value. It may save your life, Mr. Briggs. Guard it well." Colonel Hammond paused considering how much more he could safely share with the young first mate. "Your responsibilities, however, end when you deliver this. You are only an emissary. Do not assume a more active role." Colonel Hammond saw Ben Briggs not only understood the game but signaled with knowing eyes that he agreed to its rules. The colonel added one last instruction. "And Mr. Briggs," The colonel reached to reopen the window. "There is no reason for Captain Jordan to know anything about this."

Not long after Briggs left with a noted bounce in his step, the colonel's daughter slid into the office.

"Father, you appear washed-out today." Emma observed his sagging posture as she took her desk beside his. "Your partners should meet the sailors they sponsor, no?" Colonel Hammond's look of surprise did not deter her, and she pressed on. "Rather than confine yourself with your associates this month in your smoky library, why don't we invite *Rattlesnake's* captain and officers and a few other Newport friends to join them in an afternoon *soiree* on our lawn? I shall undertake the invitations and arrangements—peaches, your favorite, are readily in supply as are the season's first strawberries. The alewives are running and we shall have fresh bass. What do you say, mix pleasure with business?"

"Emma, a splendid idea," replied the colonel but then added in a by-the-way voice, "We shall present my partners with an opportunity to grill my privateersmen directly. Perhaps they can explain how to steal a fortune," he said, and then murmured under his breath, "…without getting killed."

"What was that you said, Father, at the end? Your voice escaped me—"

"Nothing my dear."

"Father, what has you so agitated these past weeks? You do not enjoy the company of your so-called friends, and despite the war, we have the most successful *letter of marque* ships in Newport. Is it… Mother's absence?

"No." The thought of Caroline drew his brows tightener. "It is our political situation. I need not bother you with its machinations."

"Bother me? Father, it will help you to confer with someone who loves you dearly."

Colonel Hammond looked at his handsome daughter; she had grown quickly from a sprite into a woman of striking style, with a keen intelligence. Though she hid her sharp thinking behind a *façade* of delicate smiles and sly sighs, he knew she inherited his intellect that paired well with her charm and beauty inherited from her mother.

"Look at the ship, Emma," he said, pointing out the window. "I've got a score of men repairing damage with hammers, timber, and rope from the lofts. Here—read the tally of the costs! We cannot afford Captain Jordan." Emma's smile disappeared as she studied the invoice he gave her. "I'm not of a habit to wait for my captains once they've tied-up," the colonel ranted as Emma placed it in her pile of bills. "Our captain apparently disembarked off Point Judith and returned home. His expenses are high, yet his returns are far less than I expected."

"Father, he brings the war to our enemy's shore, does he not? Not since Paul Jones in the War of our Independence has an American ship dared attack the British home islands. And I hear the British insurance rates have increased substantially due to the loss of so many of their merchant ships. Surely this will help us negotiate a peace?"

"Either that or they may send Arthur Wellesley to the Virginia coast with forty thousand war-hardened soldiers once he and his allies dispatch Bonaparte."

"Yes, but Father, did not *Constitution* maul *Guerriere* and *Java* last year? Those actions infuriated the English public, or so says my cousin Ceci."

"Daughter, our heavy frigates enjoyed far more firepower than their so-called British counterparts. Those were mere pin-pricks to the enemy. They have over eight hundred warships, many of them two and three decker first-rates. America can float not more than a dozen frigates."

"But we have our privateers. They are making their mark."

"Indeed. However, privateers are not enough and cannot confront British men-of-war. Once Napoleon is defeated, Britain will turn their full armed forces against us. My friends and I feel that must be prevented at all costs, now, before Madison forgoes free trade in return for his dreams of unhampered western expansion. This would be to our great disadvantage. I fear we would find ourselves worse off than before the war."

"You do not admire our President's policies, then, Father?"

"President Madison started a foolish war, Emma. He used the pretense of British impressment of our sailors. The truth, I and my friends suspect, is quite different. With the British Empire exhausted and financially strapped from twenty years' fighting Napoleon, we struck when we thought they were weak and unable to counter our quick foray to take Canada. That, as you know, failed miserably."

"So what is it you fear the British shall do, Father? They have protected their North American dominions and we are no threat to their sovereignty—" Emma paused at her father's pained expression.

"Britain lost a continent, Emma. They want it back."

"Britain would never be able to conquer our United States! They tried before. They failed."

"Their naval activities—armed sorties of lethal squadrons of frigates and cutters bolstered by indiscriminate blockades—has turned this into a war of economic survival for the States along the coast, while the inland frontier faces Indians armed with British weapons and military guidance. I fear they want to squeeze us, leaving us with only our coastline, while they rape the west for their own harvest."

"I see."

Emma had neither a rejoinder nor a solution for her father's predicament, though she sensed walls closing in. She studied her father, older now than even the month before; where his neck had been firm, it now drooped extra flesh like a drying sail. Where his eyes had pierced, they now darted from side to side. What bothered her the most, however was a slight shake to his left arm. Before, when they played cards as a family beside a fierce hearth, he had dealt the cards with a steady hand, and a grip as firm as it was in trade.

"Please take some tea, Father. And return to the manor early today for a rest in the afternoon perhaps? I will make plans to host your friends."

Friends. A curious word, Hammond thought to himself. The word failed to accurately describe the syndicate of ruthless merchants, bankers, and power-brokers he had helped assemble with the objective to find an alternative escape from the Administration's bumbling war effort. What had started out as a forum to discuss methods and counter-strategies to Madison's had, however, recently devolved into heated arguments between two belligerents that leaned toward direct intervention in the affairs of state. Hammond was unsettled with this. It was one thing to float proposals through back channels in the capital; it was quite another to attempt to outflank one's own elected leaders. Some manner of negotiated peace with Britain was preferable to watching profitable trade dry up like an empty clam shell on a rock. Samuel Hammond, therefore, had at the outset of the war offered to contribute the returns of one out of every three privateer cruises to a common fund for the syndicate's use to secure peace favorable to like men-of-trade. Now however, his commitments had fallen short. *Damn that Jordan!* And the antipathy in the group against him had reached a crescendo. Hammond recognized the short slide into treachery for men whose vision seemed increasingly more about their future elevated roles than for any merchantman's economic advantage. In particular, the colonel hoped his trust in his banker, Matthew Westerly, had not been misplaced. For two decades, with only bumps on the path to mutual prosperity, they had worked well together as accommodating banker and grateful trader. Then war erupted.

Westerly had recently introduced to the syndicate a new member from Providence: Geoffrey Lancaster Morris, a wealthy businessman and a rumored player behind the curtains of power in Washington, D.C. Morris, from the beginning, however, had cast an unsettling and overbearing influence within the group. When Morris pressed his urgent views across the table at their monthly syndicate meetings—often held at Great Hill—he half-rose while pointing a long, scraggy finger at whomever his scorn was directed as if his digit could spew hot lead and fire. On one occasion, Hammond felt Morris' accusatory digit in his face; though he did not rise to the insult, he did notice Westerly had seconded the provocation. Increasingly, Morris and Westerly spoke with a single voice, demanding that higher returns from syndicate-financed privateer voyages be delivered for a vague "Purpose" (meant to alleviate restrictions on trade by some unspecified means) on a schedule set by Morris. Since the colonel owned the most tonnage, his was the highest contribution. The money gathered, Morris claimed, was necessary to set in motion the path to peace. On that the group had agreed. Geoffrey Morris' tactics and plans for the funds, however, were laced with secrecy backed by a forceful manner and an ego without bounds. Hammond might have tried to dilute his influence with the group but Westerly made it clear that his own relationship with Morris was rock-steady, and if Hammond expected the same easy flow of capital for his future ventures—legitimate or otherwise—he would need Westerly's continued largess. Hammond ruefully accepted these conditions. War has its price, he consoled himself. He held his tongue even as Morris and Westerly displayed scant sympathy if a Hammond privateer returned empty to Newport, and ever less when captured by a British patrol, or sank with all hands.

Colonel Hammond slouched in his office chair. He felt suddenly lightheaded, his breathing constrained by a tightness in his chest—evidently, he suffered with more angst about the upcoming syndicate meeting than he dared admit. Captain Jordan's strange absences added to his unease. To top things off, young Thomas Hammond, his son at home, had packed a sea chest, soon to return to war. The colonel hoped he had not erred. His wife would have fought him bitterly on this, but she remained overseas. He prayed that on the ocean his boy would grow fast. At least Emma remained close by, a dear comfort.

Brandy and cigar in hand, Colonel Hammond sat in his library at Great Hill. It had been a long day, the ship a mass of repair activity. He waited for Emma; her questions about business—and affairs of state—had, in recent weeks, become more insightful. The colonel had been tempted to bring her further into his private world, but when he saw her cheery smile and gay spirit he thought not: a shame it would be to mix his sordid undertakings with such promising innocence. Though behind the knowing eyes that managed the company's ledgers, he sensed she would not remain uninformed for long. The first Hammond and Company voyage to Whydah would soon return, and he had no ready explanation for its ample profits when Emma pointed out on her ledger that the ship had departed only three months earlier with a cargo of rum, bound for Livorno.

"Did Captain Jordan appear at last at your office this afternoon, Father," asked Emma, serving him from a tray of assorted cheeses and sliced fresh apples.

"He did not. Only the mate. A fine young man."

"Oh. I was so looking forward to running into Captain Jordan today. I will send a boy to him with a personal invitation to our *soiree*, Father. I am sure he will attend, and you two can conduct your business here at Great Hill." Emma smiled thinking erroneously that she had settled things. "He is a wonderfully successful privateersman, is he not, Father? A brave man, he must be, and so skilled! Our Captain Jordan has captured more tonnage of British shipping than any ship's master on the coast. Cousin Ceci said they wonder along the Connecticut shore how Hammond privateers are so successful at avoiding the British patrols! Are we more skilled or just lucky, Father? Ceci insists we must have magic up our sleeve."

"How do you respond to such foolish conjecture?"

"I tell her privateering is a successful trade *only* if one avoids the Royal Navy. That is how we conduct our cruises. And I tell her that our captains are more courageous than other privateersmen."

"Indeed, courage…" Hammond trailed off forcing himself to study the ledger in his daughter's tight script, its subtle flourish indicating her sex. The colonel had kept from her the syndicate's most recent plans as well as other risks he took to protect the family fortune. No one else must ever learn how his captains, alone among scores of privateers, were able to find British merchant ships unescorted. Hammond suspected Jordan knew his secret, however. In order to mute his renegade captain's curiosity, he did not police the captain's strange comings and goings with the diligence required. Now, however,

Jordan's absences had become steady, the returns from *Rattlesnake's* successful voyages painfully insufficient. The solution had become clear: he must find a replacement for *Rattlesnake's* current master. The upcoming voyage and planned assault on English Channel shipping would be Captain Cornelius Jordan's last cruise under the Hammond and Company pennant. Colonel Hammond thought to share this with Emma, then held off. Instead, he said, "Captain Jordan is a clever man, I grant you, my dear. Though I fear his success will cripple us if he continues his violent assaults."

"And yet you allow my dear Thomas to accompany him? Father, he is but a tender boy!"

"He will learn fast from the lads. Plus, First Mate Briggs is a sober man and will send Thomas below when cannon are run-out. I met with him earlier. I shall introduce you at our gathering—"

"I shall be quite busy with our guests," Emma interjected as she straightened and looked at the colonel directly. "Father, I sense I do not enjoy your complete confidence. I've examined the latest ledgers. There is something amiss—"

"That is enough for today, Emma. You are right, I am weary. A man must sometimes follow a path that keeps his enterprise afloat." The colonel waved her attention away. "Regarding Mr. Briggs. Your mother and I think it is high time—"

"For me to find a husband? Yes, I know her mind. Or at least I *did* before she left us."

"She'll return home when the time is right. Then you must choose a husband."

Emma Hammond felt her mother's absence sharply, yet Caroline Hammond's return would mean the end of Emma's freedom. "I am far from the thinking you and Mother share—" Before Emma could continue, a knock sounded on the front entrance.

A maid appeared. "Captain Cornelius Jordan, sir."

Emma lit up like a star shooting over a moonless sky.

Chapter Three

Alone in her bedroom the next morning, Emma Hammond slid behind a small walnut desk beneath a bay window splashed with sunshine, and she admired the east lawn. Beyond, the meadow grasses fell to a rocky shore that bounded her family's Great Hill estate and eased the viewer into a seascape of marsh and tidal flats. When summer heat peaked, she rested in this quiet alcove each afternoon. At her desk she wrote orders for goods her father had requested and arranged for deliveries of ship provisions: salted cod and beef, fresh vegetables in season, lime juice, of course, to thwart a sailor's misery of scurvy. In her delicate, particular hand, she inked notices to their captains to appear in Newport ready to slip heavily laden Hammond ships into New York, Boston, or Chesapeake ports. After completing a day's paperwork at home, she filled a leather pouch with instructions carefully ordered by topic and priority. She called for a boy to deliver her accounts to Colonel Hammond in his office overlooking the pier, a short trip around the cove into the bustling port town. Often, after a midday meal, she would join her father in his office for a few hours where she enjoyed sitting near him at her own tidy desk. Afterwards she was free for pleasure—to write of her life and dreams, most often in the form of letters to her cousin Cecelia Appleton in New London. With Ceci, she shared her plans for lavish parties to be held on Great Hill's sloping lawns and vine-covered porticos. She described small fishing schooners sailing past the point and imagined enemy British ships hovering nearby offshore. Often, she told her cousin how she longed to visit what lay beyond a half day's sail (the furthest she had ever ventured).

One year younger than Emma Hammond, Cecelia had been Emma's favorite cousin since they had spent every family holiday together while growing up. Their rambunctious letters to each other often revealed sprawling tales of fantasy and illusion about life's possibilities if the stars aligned and if they wished ardently enough. Emma enjoyed writing these fluid letters, one of her few escapes from the drudgery of Newport during this choking offshore war. Having completed organizing the stack of invoices to be paid—for merchants whose mills were stocked only because Hammond vessels had avoided British patrols—Emma wrote a letter to her cousin. Musing, she glanced out the window and waved at her dear brother Thomas on the lawn. He waved back, thrusting into the air a long stick he had sharpened. For the hundredth time this week, Thom dispatched an imaginary throng of armed combatants who had breached his redoubt of lawn chairs. While her brother had been out to sea for weeks, Emma had missed his cheerful company. Without Thom, life at Great Hill became unbearably tense, elevated largely because their mother had sent a letter stating her intention to remain in England with Emma's aunt. Caroline Hammond's London-born sister provided a haven for the Newport denizen, even in wartime. In Emma's estimation, this created a situation whereby her father's sad eyes at reading the missive revealed he had not previously considered possible. Her father's kindling stress enflamed due to a constant line of well-dressed visitors who arrived in stately carriages and four from Providence and Boston. These men—smoking outsized cigars and sporting polished, bejeweled walking sticks—required elaborate meals, imported brandy and claret, tobacco, and sometimes a guestroom for the night. These evening dinners fell to Emma to arrange, often with little notice. If talk ran late and tempers simmered, she could feel a sort of malevolent pressure descend on Great Hill like an early morning miasma blocking the view of Rhode Island Sound. Her father met with his visitors—"associates" he sometimes called "friends"—without obvious amity. Some evenings the meal and clamor lasted until the wind died away entirely and the leaves stopped their rustle, which by day camouflaged the men's raised voices. At night, the silent air carried angry threats to Emma's room above. The heated tones piqued her curiosity, and if she so desired, she listened fervently to their talk and often scribbled notes so she might press her father on what manner of business or government affairs were taking place at Great Hill.

Sharing particulars with her cousin Ceci, Emma wrote on expensive parchment—unlike the rough, canvas worksheets she used at the shipyard office. She hoped her uncle Josiah would let Ceci visit this summer to escape the windless heat of Long Island Sound. Her Connecticut cousin complained the breezes along the Sound were so feeble they could not even ruffle the edges of a lady's skirt.

...my dear Ceci, I remain conflicted trying to understand the truth about Rattlesnake's *most recent voyage. Thomas appears quite impressed with her Captain's success and says not a bad word about his talents, bravery, or skill. My father, however, views him differently. I fear the truth lies in between. The Captain says he is one of the Roth's, the wealthy whaling clan from Mystic. Do you know them? I cannot describe my feelings, but when I hear the Captain's name, my chest compresses with a great weight. And after recent voyages, he has paid us his respects here at Great Hill, during which times I dared not even speak to him, or engage his gaze. Am I suffering from the guilt of forbidden love? Am I a silly girl pining after a man who is at sea most months and will not likely survive this war?*

I also heard the Captain and my father argue last evening.

"Why?" my father asked the Captain, "Why did you not fire first? Instead, you meekly accepted their broadside and then a second without any response... a volley that killed good lads, severely damaged my ship, and almost sank her?"

Captain Jordan's answer was cryptic but enthusiastic (he might be wrong, Ceci, but he <u>never</u> has the slightest doubts!): "Indiamen usually do not shoot straight, Colonel. This ship was an exception," he said. "Their broadsides hit their mark, I grant you. But I thought they should empty their cannon first before firing our own. We would then board the broken vessel and take an easy prize."

My father spoke of the five lost lives and to this, curiously, Captain Jordan had no retort. They turned to a discussion about the next voyage—to the Azores and the British Isles. Shoosh, I should not share this with you! Rattlesnake *will be refitted and re-crewed with dispatch and Captain Jordan will have Mr. Briggs as his mate once again along with our new gunner, a Mr. Quartus Gant.*

The Captain speaks enthusiastically about each man to the Colonel. Young Mr. Briggs, only a few years my senior, is fair-haired, pleasing to look at, and lively in conversation. The new mate, Mr. Gant, however, is an enigma—I suspect he hides his true feelings behind his severe countenance. Though despite his angry looks, Mr. Gant has a silky, mysterious way about him. I venture he is a man of deep passions and vitality if he was freed from the bridle that chokes him. I have invited our three officers to a grand reception on Great Hill's south lawn later this week before they sail.

I must rush away now, my dear. I own every detail of the preparation. I very much look forward to it.

Captain James Breton of *HMS Fortitude,* a thirty-two-gun British Royal Navy frigate built during the Peace of Amiens, reread his orders. Never had he seen such duplicity on the part of the Admiralty, nor could he fathom its reasons. If the Crown were ever going to undertake the initiative in this war, their fleets must do more than chase smugglers and blockade. If he were in government, an army led by Arthur Wellesley with cannon, cavalry, and the best and most experienced troops from the Iberia campaigns, would be deployed to America forthwith. *The Empire must go at them with everything we can bring to bear,* he thought. *A Nelsonian approach. Instead, this...*

"Send for Mr. Clarke, if you please," Captain Breton ordered the steward outside his cabin. Seconds later, the summoned first lieutenant appeared hat in hand. "Lieutenant, in this conflict with the United States, our orders instruct us to attack their shipping and frigates with utmost energy. It seems, however, that we are to allow certain American vessels from a particular trading house to pass through our blockades. You see the logic in this, do you not?"

The captain steamed. He wanted to sink *all* American ships no matter their cargo. *Incomprehensible!* England had outlawed slavery in the year seven and was bound to enforce oceans free of the slave trade. Yet had this policy been partially suspended? *Like a man partially hanged*, the captain fumed. He looked up at his stoic second—a trusted young man smart enough not to answer. The service did not ask a lieutenant to find logic or ill in Admiralty orders. Even to comment risked censure. *Follow and die*, was ingrained. Nevertheless, Lieutenant Harry Clarke looked at his captain with aligned concern.

Captain Breton was not usually long-winded, or so candid.

"Certain American slavers and merchantmen from the Hammond line are free to transit. We shan't stop them. But Yankee men-of-war… especially *privateers…*" He said the last with careful, slow emphasis. "…we are ordered to sink them."

"Yes, sir."

"I have sympathies for Admiral Warren, however, that I dare not express, even to him. The Admiralty has asked that his North American fleet accomplish the impossible! Hunt and sink the heavy American frigates. Patrol the sea lanes of hundreds of ports along the entire Yankee east coast, even to New Orleans! While his fleet is doing that, he is expected to provide protection for our convoys sailing from the West Indies. And in our hours of leisure, we are to chase and sink the enemy's privateers!"

"Sir, their privateers number over six hundred ships. As reported in the London dailies."

"I damn well know that! Six hundred! They swarm like pests on the Southern Ocean." Captain Breton examined the charts on his desk. His lieutenant leaned over. "You've heard of Jordan, of *Rattlesnake*?"

"Aye, sir."

The entire British Navy had heard of Cornelius Jordan and *Rattlesnake*. All England, Scotland, Ireland, and Wales had heard of Jordan and *Rattlesnake*. For nearly ten months the murderous privateer had attacked English ships in port and while in transit to the islands' west coasts, stealing and setting fire to countless millions of pounds of stored crops, brutally killing Englishmen. Civilians were not spared.

"Jordan's earned his epithet, *Curse of the Coast* in blood." *Piddling sneak attacks on defenseless fishing villages*, thought Breton. *He murders old men and boys while our fighting men are away in the service of our King.* He looked up at his second in command. "Admiral Warren has learned Jordan slipped past the fleet on a dirty night not a week ago. He suspects the pirate may have his sights on our Channel ports. The Americans feel a direct attack on our heartland will drive our government to concessions in planned peace talks. We have intelligence *Rattlesnake* will water in the Azores." Breton pointed to a set of Atlantic islands on the chart spread out before him, his finger set on an island known for its tall volcanic apex, Pico. "Although this privateer sails under the Hammond flag, unless they provide us with certain intelligence, we shall sink them. I expect to intercept him there. Their *letter of marque* be damned. When I capture this mongrel, I shall hang him. This is what we shall do…"

Colonel Samuel Hammond and his banker Matthew Westerly had met many years before when they were young and hungry for fortune absent the inconvenience of an overburdened conscience. Along the way to prosperity, the colonel had found respectability in society while his banker preferred to remain behind the curtain, strings dangling in his stubby fingers. Despite different approaches to business and life, however, they remained cordial collaborators. As the war drifted, however, and profits shrank, Westerly's former easy-going style changed to an irritating insistence on meeting commitments on their joint investments. Increasingly, Westerly spoke of Geoffrey Morris where Morris' opinions had no obvious place in the matter at hand.

"Mr. Morris thinks that… Mr. Morris observes this…" Westerly repeated with annoying frequency.

Following weeks of dancing around the matter with Westerly, the colonel came to better understand the tight bond his banker had developed with Mr. Morris. At the onset of the war, Hammond had heartily agreed with Morris' professed goals for the new syndicate: a return to peaceful accord with the British. Along with other ship-owners from Newport, Boston, and New York, Hammond had offered a significant slice of his privateering profits to find their way to Westerly's bank, and thus to the syndicate for its rear-door entreaties. In return, he expected the syndicate to deliver a peace treaty that freed his ships from British interference, re-opening the lucrative British market. Hammond was beginning to fear, however, as he listened to Morris at their most recent gathering, that his contributions were not in the most trustworthy of hands.

Matthew Westerly leapt from his carriage at the front entrance to Great Hill with a lightness that surprised, given his ample girth and stubby legs. A man of average height, broad in the shoulders, and although rotund, Westerly could remember his muscles and the days when he could throw a man to the ground and keep him there. He carried his fifty years with unusual grace and nimble step. His puffy, poxed face, however, betrayed unkind years in the company of a bottle. And blotches of pink skin about his cheeks and forehead did little to warm his constant, humorless grin. The colonel took his banker's arm, leading him into the inner sanctum of the manor. Surrounded by oil paintings, they began to discuss their business in private hours before the other syndicate guests would arrive for his daughter's suggested afternoon social gathering on the adjacent veranda. The evening discussion to follow, however, would surely turn steamy.

As a general practice Westerly loaned Hammond the funds necessary to provision ships, returning profits to his bank at an agreed-upon price—far above the usual market returns that were subordinate to the inconveniences of wind, waves, supply, or demand. For near twenty years, they had operated as private lender and preferred customer—the colonel paying higher interest to obviate undue government curiosity. Though he did not consider himself a thief, Colonel Hammond in his dealings with Westerly recognized they operated at the outermost circle of legitimate commerce. Westerly straddled the arc further, however, providing credit to honest firms but also to smugglers and slave traders from Norfolk to the St. Johns River. He twisted as conditions warranted, and although not a seaman like Hammond, knew when to tack to carve out the most advantage of opportunities that dropped into his ample lap. Yet neither man tried to convert the other from their extremes. Westerly considered Hammond a good-hearted family man who repaid his loans most often on time. The colonel, for his part in the dance, kept his banker close at hand, often inviting him to enjoy the comforts of Great Hill.

Matthew Westerly openly admired Great Hill's massive, sloping lawn, its serene pasture bathed in the shade of tall pines and spindly juniper trees. On the portico outside the library's open floor-to-ceiling windows, the syndicate would meet Hammond's privateer officers, enjoy a repast of the colonel's fields and forests before settling down to brass tacks in Hammond's grand dining hall to argue further about how best to acquire and then allocate the additional funds needed to turn the tide in this ruinous conflict.

Westerly took in the colonel's splendid library, as he stuffed his ample backside into a large leather chair. Sipping sherry and complaining to the colonel of the feeble efforts of America's Navy *unable to protect our merchant ships*, he came to the reason he had asked to speak to Colonel Hammond in private.

"Samuel, I saw your brig tied up… looking the worse for wear."

"She took a fat prize, Matthew, though the enemy put up a powerful defense," Hammond answered.

"I saw her injuries. Captain Jordan has her now, has he not?"

"He has—"

"And he has taken how many voyages these past six months? Three?"

"Correct. Raiding along Scottish and Irish shores. Then again to England's west coast. Twice overseas, once off Virginia." The colonel sensed a hint of what was coming.

"And yet after taking… how many ships?"

"Twelve—"

"And yet after taking twelve enemy ships, rich ships, full to their waterlines, our profits are far below what we expected."

"Shipping taken is not the same as shipping sent. We know what cargoes we place aboard our ships. We cannot, however, anticipate the value of what our privateersmen capture."

Westerly pushed his chair back and smiled. "Yet *you* were the one who put a value on what you would deliver to the syndicate."

Hammond did not rattle. Earlier, he had turned it over: the value unloaded at his own pier from his ship appeared far short. Something was amiss.

"I agree, Matthew. I, too, expected more. My captain adheres… How shall I put it? …ruthlessly to his commission for mayhem. Although he successfully discharges his cannon under the bright sun, he could better unleash his knife in the dark. But you cannot instruct a man how to fight, can you? His approach is costly, hence our problem."

"You can afford only one Captain Jordan, then. Is that it?" Westerly let his judgement sit in the air for a moment before he posited, "Do you know a less risky course we might steer this captain, so our returns appreciate to the level required?" Westerly waited, heard nothing, and so continued, "I learned one of your ships ran aground on Matinicus—*Heron*?—and carried an unsigned letter. It appeared intended for our enemy. This letter contains embarrassing information were it to find its way to the press... or Washington. You were lucky friends of mine retrieved it for me." Westerly placed a water-stained canvas envelope with the broken seal on the side table between them.

Hammond made no effort to reach for it. Hammond and Company's private communications had no place in this conversation. *Damn Captain Holmes!* Colonel Hammond ruminated. *If captured, unless you can hand-deliver my letter to a British naval officer, place it in a tarpaulin sack with lead and drop it overboard!*

"Samuel, I must be convinced your loyalty to our cause is without compromise, or else we must have a different conversation." Westerly smirked insidiously, absent a drop of mirth.

"Neither side wants this war, Matthew. You know that." Hammond chose to shift. "And except for my privateers that avoid capture, I enjoy little open commerce. My business is as dry as low tide."

"Which is why we must continue to invest in our syndicate's activities. What do we care, Samuel, if the British expand their territories from their Canada base to the *west*, as long as you and I can expand our trade to the *east*?"

"We are in agreement, Matthew. But I must have free reign to conduct my *letter of marque* cruises as I see fit—"

"So your letter here makes obvious. Clever. But Geoffrey Morris will react with horror if he discovers your private arrangements take precedence over the common needs of your fellow men-of-trade."

"As I told you in April, I am becoming concerned about the direction Geoffrey Morris is leading our group. There is a great difference between funding a private effort to negotiate a peace, and attempting to influence the affairs of government." *Or worse,* Hammond thought, considering Morris' increasingly bullying stance of late.

"My dear Samuel, 'influence' has the brush of intrigue! Morris—"

"I don't trust the man—"

"Morris has deep connections within Washington's corridors of power, people as unhappy with the administration's actions as are we. He also has friends in high office in London able to press the arrangements in our favor—policies Mr. Madison avoids like a quarantined schooner."

"You assured me that my contributions to the syndicate are expressly to gain the ears of sympathetic British government officials," probed Hammond.

"An effort well underway, you have my word. Mr. Morris' people have made great strides though the palms need further lubrication, and hence our shortfall—your shortfall—has thrown plans in disarray. I am here today to ascertain your continued willingness—and ability—to make good on your promises… before we are forced to take more drastic action."

Hammond did not truly believe Westerly wanted his ruin, though his tone had a new edge; they enjoyed refreshment from the same spigot. Ignoring this explicit threat of exposure was like opening one's eyes to a nightmare: it never happened. Three weeks earlier, Samuel Hammond had taken out a mortgage on the Great Hill manor and farm with this very banker whom he believed to be his most trusted ally. Now, however, the curtain had been opened: he was on his own. Instead of acknowledging the threat, the colonel spoke of the future.

"We're planning a cruise to the east. Morris will not be disappointed," said the colonel.

"And where exactly are you sending Captain Jordan and his thugs?"

"I cannot divulge his course. Jordan has asked for our ignorance on these matters, and I heartily agree. Spies are everywhere." Hammond quietly seethed and could not help himself. His eyes shot towards the letter again: authentic—his hand, the Hammond seal. He swallowed hard, avoiding Westerly's narrow smile. He suspected Westerly would relay to Morris what he had said and what Westerly concluded, *Hammond's resolve is weak.*

"What of your triangular trade?" queried Westerly, adding, "You followed my advice and sent out a schooner loaded with molasses and rum. She shall return with cane, I expect, and profits three times over? Will the syndicate receive our share of this voyage?"

Hammond stared: a second surprise in as many minutes. To meet Westerly's harsh demands, the colonel had been forced to use his last ready capital to outfit one of his oldest ships with desperate men dragged from saloons and brothels. He sent the ship, *Windslayer,* southeast then west. His daughter managing his office knew nothing about that voyage, although his wife had made her objections clear and had packed. Nor was the cargo of this voyage listed in any Hammond and Company manifests.

Matthew Westerly had enthusiastically recommended the molasses trade months before when American privateers were being captured with alarming frequency. "Turn some of your fastest schooners south and east," Westerly had said over brandy one late winter evening, "...to Whydah then along the middle passage to St. Kitts or Nevis. Return with cane and molasses for Newport distilleries and your coffers will fill to overflow." The implied, nefarious *middle passage* was never mentioned in polite company, nor even among smugglers and thieves.

Surprised, Hammond stared at Westerly. *He knows. Geoffrey Morris, therefore, also knows.*

"You've invested in my privateer voyages, Matthew. *Rattlesnake* shall either return with the funds the syndicate requires or will find the bottom. My other business is of no concern to the syndicate. You'll get your money." His tone was harsh and reflected a younger spirit when his vision had been clearer, his breathing steady and strong.

Emma Hammond silently slipped into her father's study and kissed her father's head.

"Good day, my dear Miss Hammond!" Westerly brightened and shifted his bulk off the chair, preparing to stand then giving up the effort.

"Good day, to you too, sir. Do not mind me," insisted Emma, placing a tray of crystal glassware alongside a robust bottle of brandy on a small table.

"I shall see you, then, at your *soiree*, Colonel. And you as well, my dear Mary Celeste," Westerly said.

"Everyone calls me Emma these days, Mr. Westerly."

"Oh, but your full name has such a magical ring to it, does it not Samuel?"

"It does, though I agree with my daughter, 'Emma' suits her wonderfully." The colonel and his daughter shared a smile.

Westerly toasted. "To *Emma* then. And *Rattlesnake* and Captain Jordan."

Hammond joined in, sipping from a crystal goblet. He watched Westerly staring back above the rim of a matching goblet crafted on

Ireland's west coast, where six months earlier Captain Cornelius Jordan and his Hammond warship had anchored, stealing what they could not kill.

Chapter Four

Thomas Hammond sat by himself on Great Hill's portico overlooking the rocky point. In the nearshore he watched occasional flashes of silver where juvenile menhaden swirled on the surface, fleeing feeding bass below.

He turned to the guests arriving for Emma's afternoon gathering but feared the tardy captain might not appear. Thom practiced once more how to approach the captain or one of his officers asking to be assigned gun-captain, ordering the crew to load, aim and fire on his command. To fight an empire, the boy reasoned, he must contribute more than spittle and rousing cheers. Pressing his way through the forest of guests in long coats and flowing dresses, he reached the brick walkway. Awed, Thom admired Captain Cornelius Jordan striding into the gathering with his captain's hat resting fore and aft in the modern style. Thom studied him intently, hoping for an opening. Tall and resplendent in the uniform of a naval officer, Captain Jordan quickly passed by the boy, however, with not even a nod. Instead, the captain answered Colonel Hammond's wave to join a throng of well-heeled admirers. Thom followed meekly. He maneuvered through the crowd on the porch where other tall hats and bright uniforms gathered around lemonade, fruits, meats, wine, and sweets. Thom's shoulders sagged as he caught glimpses of *Rattlesnake's* captain making the rounds, first shaking hands with patrons, then a slow bow to Emma. He paused to sample the delectable culinary spread. There, the captain nodded to his officers permitting them to join him in conversation.

"*Now,*" the boy exclaimed under his breath and leapt into the fray. "Good afternoon, sir! Welcome to Great Hill!" Thom shared a noble bow in the direction of the three officers. He hoped his father (or especially his sister) would not interrupt while he and his fellow privateersmen discussed the war.

"Ah, Mr. Hammond, indeed, you set a fine table. Doesn't the lad?" Jordan remarked to Gant and Briggs.

"My sister is the hostess, sir, not I. I'm more of a fighting man. And I was wondering—"

"Mr. Briggs, how goes the refit?" asked the captain. "And Mr. Gant now that you're an officer, I shall expect a daily report on the armaments and powder supply for our next engagements…"

As Captain Jordan spoke, his mouth full of tart, his officers crowded the remaining open space between them, leaving no room even for a Hammond. Thomas slid back in shame. Retreating to the veranda once more, he noticed the captain did not appear to listen to his officers' answers more than he had to Thom's query. Rather, Captain Jordan's gaze followed Emma about the lawn, the portico, and as she slid in and out of the kitchen. *Em looks unusually foolish today*, thought Thom, all fussed-up as if this simple lawn reception was a grand holiday ball. That she and the captain exchanged odd looks was as obvious as it was unsettling to the boy. His captain should be focusing on the *war*, not a girl. And *she* should stay out of it! Thomas eyed another opening. The moment his father guided Captain Jordan to meet new guests, the youth sprang at Gant and Briggs.

"Sirs, do we have our destination?" asked Thomas, intent for the officers to accept him into the private world of privateersmen.

Quartus Gant's new authority rendered him a superior officer to the youngster, who remained a midshipman in naval hierarchy. Even so, on board a merchant ship—even an armed privateer like *Rattlesnake*—Thom was nothing more than a well-dressed cabin boy. As the owner's son, however, Thomas Hammond could not be ill-used. He could, however, be ignored. Gant did not answer. He smirked at Briggs and bid good day. There was much to do on board, he noted aloud, factoring little to gain by coddling the owner's children as Briggs seemed so keen to do. The gunner made his exit to retrieve his horse in the stables behind the manor.

"Come, Thomas, let's enjoy your sister's cake and make plans," said Ben Briggs once Gant's shadow had left them. Smiling, Ben placed his hand gently on the boy's shoulder and guided him back to the table where Emma and her maids had set out sweets and fresh fruit tarts.

The Hammond reception had attracted a disparate group: *Rattlesnake's* three officers, a dozen investors, even a few wealthy neighbors, all men-of-trade. Colonel Hammond and his two children were practiced, gracious hosts, and had hired three local girls who assisted the house servants and brought fresh apple tarts and peaches recently picked. As the sun lowered in the sky, the afternoon slipping away, Ben Briggs felt relieved Quartus Gant had taken his constant brooding elsewhere. For the first time since joining her father's service, Ben made particular notice of the colonel's daughter as she listened intently to conversations about ships and seafaring. Time and again, the young women reappeared from the kitchen with another tray of canapes or small desserts and glided around the veranda. Emma, too, did so to welcome new guests. Some of the colonel's colleagues were expressing controversial positions about the war, Ben observed, opinions that, if not shared among friends, might sound unpatriotic. Emma, too, listened to these pronouncements with such keen attention that Ben wondered if she might be tempted to capture the extreme opinions in some private journal, writing with the same tight script she used to issue commands from her father to Hammond and Company ships' officers. Despite her cheery airs, First Mate Ben Briggs decided he would treat her as warily as he treated her rambunctious brother with affection. Surely Emma would not soon forget the bold remarks and perfunctory boasts spewed earlier by Captain Jordan about how British convoy escorts—undersized frigates and aging brigs—could never out-sail an American privateer. However, when a brig built for the coastal trade like *Rattlesnake* was confronted by the Royal Navy, Briggs knew all too well a privateer had only one recourse: to fly away as fast as possible. Fleeing, however, to save blood and powder was not a tactic that matched the illustrious fighting aura crafted by this captain in his finely-tailored uniform. Jordan was a man clearly hungry for his plate of oysters bathed in sherry and garlic sauce—a man whose roving eye followed Emma's every tack. Briggs noted their silent confederacy. Most eyes on the portico were drawn to the flamboyant captain. So, Emma's silent visual replies to him went largely unnoticed. *Smart,* thought Briggs, *she helps secure his command.* Briggs admired the brazen captain's deliberate moves. As Jordan made his leave, like a politician ending a passionate oration, the captain's departure left the crowd wanting more.

After a few perfunctory comments about his expectations for privateers to turn the tide in America's favor, Captain Cornelius Jordan waved an affected but effective fare-thee-well with his upraised palm. He punctuated his departure with a short bow that capped a successful performance. To a chorus of murmured accolades and wishes for luck, Captain Cornelius Jordan withdrew. As Jordan headed down the front pathway to retrieve his horse, Briggs noted that Emma watched her captain's departure with a soft, expectant smile. Understanding the captain's game, Briggs returned to his own.

"I'm considering a cutting-out expedition when we reach our destination, Thom. Would you like to join me?"

"Sir, of course! In the dark I am quite invisible, but I see very well," young Hammond answered.

"I heard from your father you have eyes like a cat."

"A tiger, sir."

"We will practice our guns' elevation on our way across. You must learn to duck, eh?" Briggs gently slapped the back of Thom's head and they both laughed. "How's your scratch?"

"Ten stiches. A prick, nothing more, sir."

"And the blood around you that morning… it did not disturb you?" Briggs needed to know if the boy could be relied on in a fight.

"It was ghastly, sir. I never saw a man's insides until that day. But we cannot let the empire crush us."

"You are your father's son, Thom," replied Briggs. Thom smiled proudly.

Turning from Thomas and the porch, Briggs caught sight of Captain Jordan riding with purpose away from Great Hill. *Though not into town*, thought Briggs, *He veers to the woods.* Jordan glanced around, as if to check for prying eyes. *Thinks he's far enough along to hide his change of direction,* mused Briggs as Jordan gouged his horse with a stirrup and bolted headlong toward the cove beyond.

"Here, more cake, Mr. Briggs," insisted Thom, breaking Ben's reverie.

"You're too skinny for a gunner and too tall for a top man," countered Ben, gently shoving the cake back at the boy. "We must fatten you up like an officer."

"I hope to serve with distinction," Thom declared between mouthfuls. "*Rattlesnake* can outfight every ship in her class, right sir?"

"Aye Thomas, she can fight. Though any sloop can haul eighteen-pounders onto her deck and slug it out with other floating barges... but to thrust and parry with a heavy Indiaman in her class—ahh, that's a sight! *Rattlesnake* has the square foresails to sail with speed when the wind blows abeam or astern, yet her large mizzen spanker, jibs, and staysails let her sail high to the wind where she can circle around a square-rigger. Her sailing qualities make her a ship to fear. We are lucky to have her."

"She *is* a sight!" The boy's enthusiasm took him away. "My sister says she looks like an osprey, swooping home into a nest high in the trees overlooking the marsh."

"She's a seahawk, indeed, Mr. Hammond... with sharp talons."

Emma Hammond, waited for a quiet moment to make her planned escape. From across the terrace, she had noted her brother alone with the ship's first officer. She approached, slowing as she realized she could not recall the young officer's Christian name. Reaching back in her memory, she considered lists of candidates for a future command, each written in her father's hand. She knew almost every officer candidate by name and port of call, every captain's reputation, successes, and failed voyages. *William? Robert? Brigham? No, something Biblical...*

"Mr. Ebenezer... Briggs, is it?" she offered politely, standing taller than he had remembered as she today wore new two-inch heels.

Her full bosom accented by a tight-pulled waistband, Emma Hammond attracted admiration from men. Vendors, sailing captains, and fellow traders in business regarded her with varying degrees of longing as she went about her duties for the firm. She wore her light brown hair pulled trim but not severely tight, which allowed loose wavy strands to escape her hair band like kelp riding in the tide. Her everyday dress was more refined than many women wore to dine. And even on a routine shopping excursion, as she strolled Newport's sidewalks, shopkeepers and passing folks admired her long satin dresses snug to her waist, high to her neck where a collar rose even further north until it magically drew one's gaze to her lips and into her rich, green eyes. When she smiled, she meant it—her joy of the moment flowing free, embracing her entire face. Her lithe, balanced body moved in an open, accepting manner, her arms and hands reaching out, her cheek available for the customary peck between relatives and close friends.

"A pleasure, Miss Hammond, to meet the kind face behind such stern notes," Ben replied with a small grin. He took Emma's outstretched hand gently. "Ben will suffice."

His discrete squeeze upon her soft palm was enough to be polite, she thought, perhaps a tad more. "I hope you are not educating my brother beyond his maturity in the rough ways of a sailing officer?"

"No, Miss Hammond," assured Briggs. "His imagination is vivid enough."

Briggs gave the boy a nudge to the ribs. Thomas squeaked and both he and Mr. Briggs laughed. Emma thought their interaction was charming—*though… the mirth… a bit too quaint? Perhaps for my benefit?* This young officer was comfortable around young people, a trait to admire yet she could not fathom why her father let her twelve-year-old brother go to sea. Thom had not developed the muscle or the vigor for offshore life. At least privateer cruises lasted only months, not years like many ships departing Newport leaving women and families alone season after empty season.

"Like *your* imagination?" Emma added a bit more mischievously than she intended. The smart officer with his green-blue eyes looked at her somewhat surprised. She scrutinized the mate closely—a fair man with hair that tended reddish pulled tight behind a well-formed head. Although rugged, he could stand a few more home-cooked meals, she thought. Though beside her gangly brother—all branches, no trunk—First Mate Ebenezer Briggs towered. She was glad he had joined the gathering, yet… something was amiss. Was it his singular attention to Thom among a gathering of influential power brokers? Or was it the way he stared at her with more presumed familiarity than his short tenure in her father's employment gave license to? "Be sure you instruct my brother on the important things… like washing his linens. And ducking his head when the enemy shoots. You'll excuse me?"

She smiled and turned to leave them.

"Aye, miss!"

Emma heard Mr. Briggs answer her with a playful cadence to his voice. Her brother giggled at the shared witticism between the two. She kept her own way. She did not look back at the officer, her brother's minder, a young man her father believed had promise. She was mindful to attend her father's other guests, particularly the anxious investors, who, until they had no further need for her service, would prevent her sliding away. These men would remain for a private dinner; a long, often angry meal she had gratefully not been invited to share. She would mind missing their conversation, however; their uncouth company she could do without.

Heads turned as Emma Hammond made her way through the throng, greeting each of her father's investors. Most men did not understand the connection between her naturally graceful movements and her innocent intentions. Some men perceived her keen intelligence; some hoped she might have special, intimate interest in their company. These men presumed her synchronized eyes, smiles, and lips hinted at the possibility of an imminent physical connection. Emma, however, presumed no such thing. Yet she smiled with all the energy in her spirit and dismissed the admiring eyes, brushing off their suggestive remarks as harmless flattery. That said, she knew how to turn heads, and enjoyed it. Soon, the party drifted into repetitive conversations, preludes to the serious talk soon to come. Emma deployed the lull to deftly stand aside from the tall hats and ambitious sailors. Deliberately, she surveilled the food table, and gestured toward a platter, picked clean by her guests.

"Good heavens! An empty platter!" she announced to no one and hoisted it.

Platter in hand, she plucked an empty goblet off a table with the other, then departed into the kitchen. Eyeing herself in a hall mirror, Emma stole away out the back pantry door.

Ben Briggs alone noticed the removed bright silver platter was never replenished. He shook his head and smiled, not a little envious.

Head down as he led his nag along the brick path, Quartus Gant nearly bumped into Emma Hammond leading her horse in his direction. Although having grown up in the same coastal town of Newport, Rhode Island, they never had reason nor opportunity to socialize: he from a working seaman's north-side family; she the daughter of the most successful ship owner in Newport. Emma rode a smart, well-tended horse; Gant admired the rider. His horse, more an extension of himself, was a stable brute, a ride for the day or weeks he sat idle in port between voyages. Emma's steed, like herself, was carefully groomed, delicate, and strong.

"Good afternoon to you, Mr. Gant. And luck for your upcoming cruise and new responsibilities." So close and alone with her for the first time, Gant did not know where to focus his gaze. He found her face and its brilliant smile accenting a kind greeting. Surprising himself, his eyes stared into hers and he relaxed. "My father must have great trust in you. He does not often offer commissions... to, ahh—" She flustered suddenly, intending to say '*men from the lower deck*'. Catching herself, she finished awkwardly, "...to such a *young* man."

Gant's face darkened. Emma immediately regretted her casual comment. She had meant no harm. So, she continued to stare back at him with wide, welcoming eyes and a toothy smile framed by her delicate lips dabbed today with a hint of ruby color.

"Let's hope he don't regret it." Gant stopped her short.

"Why should he regret it, Mr. Gant. Don't you enjoy the privateering life?"

"I like the action, the money. But this ship..." He was about to describe it as *dangerous* but he remembered his pact with Briggs: They must keep their opinion of Captain Cornelius Jordan to themselves, and certainly not share their fears with the owner's daughter.

"'This ship...' *what*?" she probed, sensing Gant's deep, hidden worry. *He neither smiles nor jokes like other young men. Instead, he reeks of life's difficulties.*

Gant checked himself and said nothing. He wanted only to fall into the young woman's eyes, rich and deep as the greenest sea, shining bright like the pastures of his youth. He wanted to swim with her in open waters, never climbing out, never caring if he breathed again. Gant forced himself to look away, and with difficulty, inhaled.

"The ship needs my attention, Miss Hammond." He turned. "Thank you for your wine and cakes."

Surprised at his abruptness, she replied, "Good day, Mr. Gant. And good luck."

She reclaimed her smile, forcing her lips' corners upward. It took her some moments to regain her equilibrium after this chance meeting that left her inexplicably confounded. As Emma turned her horse onto the path toward the bluff, she felt more confused than pleased.

Gant stole a glance her way. *Why's she riding into the woods?* he wondered.

Emma headed away from Great Hill as the late afternoon sun continued to wane. Quartus Gant might have asked her where she was going had they known each other better; he might have escorted her on the lonely path. Instead, he mounted his horse. The two young people rode down separate paths into the last of the day's heat.

Captain Jordan's proposed meeting place was a small clearing nestled at the crest of a hill at the edge of a gentle bluff. There the view cleared, and the bay spread far and wide, dotted with mud flats that turned into small islands at low tide, fishermen's weirs sticking up like a fence snagging baitfish to near-shore live-liners. A narrow sandy path led from the rock ledge into the forest where it meandered at the back of the Hammond estate. Emma cantered through the woods to her clandestine *rendezvous* with Captain Jordan. Her attention was distracted, however, by her chance encounter with Quartus Gant, now riding the other way, his massive, angry hands bridled his straining horse fiercely.

In a thicket, Emma pulled up, looked behind her, and reconsidered.

Ceci, I must dash off a few lines before I sleep. Our girls are still tidying after our successful gathering today. First, I must unburden my angry heart... he was rude and uncouth, Ceci, this Gant fellow. He does not know a thing about the world or care two whits about my brother. Thom told my father and me the battle Captain Jordan fought was a success and returned to us a ship taken despite some minor damage. But Mr. Gant—he's an officer now—he and I spoke in private, the first time he was reticent about what he knew, but I followed his getaway path and caught up to him. Cornered so, he said the most unkind things. When I pressed him, he lost his composure and became angry with me! He said Thom's telling was pure fantasy! The battle at sea was a calamity and that Captain Jordan had put the men—including my precious brother—in grave danger. They could have all been killed! The ship almost sank—cannon balls breached her hull below the waterline. And if not for Gant's and Mr. Briggs' immediate attention by stuffing the holes with sail cloth and hemp, the ship would have been lost!

Can you imagine such an affront to tell me this in private, when to my father and brother he offered not a word of argument on the topic? What am I to believe? Does Thomas face great danger when he ships out in the morning to a voyage East—I know not where, but I believe Captain Jordan will stab at the enemy's bosom—or is my dearest safe with our Captain, while learning the tactics of war from Mr. Briggs?

And let me share a few thoughts about this Mr. Ebenezer Briggs—he thinks he is so clever. He pays Thomas the kindest compliments, especially in front of my father—his intelligence, his contributions—yes, yes, yes, we all know Thom's fine points, he is family after all. My ears fell cold hearing Mr. Briggs' such-obvious flattery. I can guess his purpose. We have other vessels, and my father is always finding fault with our captains. But should not the path to command follow hard work and performance? Not kissing the owner's hand and gloating over his captain's successes? I must stay on my guard with this Mr. Briggs. I will tell Father my thoughts about him when his head does not ache so.

Captain Jordan arrived late to our reception. How I long to spend more time with him! He was dressed in a fine blue coat with white lapels and an officer's hat with a feather. So grand! And Ceci—without a word, he handed me a note to meet him by the bluff after the reception. He said he had much to tell me! And then we met there! Oh, Ceci, the things the captain promised, the islands we shall visit! His words floated like a dream, my dear, a dream I've always imagined. Such dazzling collaborations he proposed, I had not one further thought of Mr. Gant's heinous assertions. But there you are: He has suggested more, far more, and after this next voyage, we shall ride out alone in my father's carriage and visit town together. Ha! Can you imagine the wags and how they will loosen their tongues and prattle about the Colonel's proper daughter carousing with a pirate! Oh, I can hardly wait for his return.

The only cloud remains my father. He was unsteady on his feet again tonight after the cake and the wine. He is worried sorely—this next voyage must bring us success, for he has made large commitments to certain friends of his. But every time these "friends" come to visit, afterwards my father falls into a brooding, silent repose. These people feign friendship but I see only angry, violent looks in their eyes, even as they smile and drink our wine and eat our venison.

Mr. Westerly is one of these visitors, though he's been around for ages. Tonight, another stranger joined their table whom I met for the first time. I did not care for his manners. He was brusque and looked at me with a cold eye as if I had poured scalding tea on his velvet waistcoat. His name was Mr. Geoffrey Morris, a man of some means they say... from Providence, though his pale face turns me cold.

Before I sleep however, I shall dedicate my thoughts and dreams only to Captain Jordan, Cornelius, he commanded I call him, since we are becoming fast friends. But I must leave you now for Father calls me suddenly.

Privateer

Chapter Five

As *Rattlesnake* left Point Judith astern, Thomas Hammond was eager to ask the first mate the question he dared not ask his father. The boy stood near the helm watching the top men drop the topgallant yard, letting the new canvas sail fall. Men on deck trimmed the sheets and with the braces led aft twisted the yardarm so its attached sail held the wind with authority. The boy longed to be up on the yards as topmen moved in practiced synchrony. With the sails trimmed, the ship rose on a roller with an extra jump and Thomas sensed her speed had accelerated past ten knots. Colonel Hammond had proudly told his son that no ship could match *Rattlesnake's* acceleration from a lazy drift to full gallop. Larger ships could not catch her when she sailed close-hauled; smaller ships were quickly left astern on any point of sail.

Rattlesnake, an armed brig of one hundred eighty-seven tons, boasted two enormously tall masts and one hundred twenty feet on her waterline. She carried a massive sailing rig of twenty sails favored amongst "armed merchants" as many owners preferred to call their privateers. She sailed fast downwind, a credit to her large, square sails on both masts, yet was able to sail ten or twenty points higher upwind than any pursuing square rigger such as an enemy frigate; a higher course relative to the direction of the wind meant she would arrive faster at her targeted destination; and, a faster ship had the distinct advantage to initiate battle—or escape.

Entering the Sound, Ben Briggs headed aft to check their bearings when young Thomas grabbed his arm.

"A word, sir? I've been wondering—" Thomas held his thought and led the first mate to the nearby scuttlebutt on the main deck where they shared a drink of water. "Sir, why don't they call us *pirates* and be done with it? What's the difference, *privateer'*, *pirate*? They seem the same, sir. Both steal."

"A large difference, Thom. Pirates operate outside the laws of nations. Privateers, on the other hand, have a *letter of marque*, a license from our elected government that permits us to attack only enemies with whom we are at war."

"But we steal."

"Aye, but privateers return to our owners and investors whatever we take, each man aboard receiving his fair percentage. Pirates have no owners, nor any home port of refuge. And they kill without honor."

The boy pondered the distinction with difficulty. "So, why not just add privateers to our Navy? More help for *Constitution* and *President*?"

"Money, lad. Our Navy, our entire government has not the cash to build more Navy ships. The British have hundreds of man-of-war. We cannot attack a bear with only a stone. But we can sting the King's ships with a hive of angry bees! Hundreds of privateers—all owned by private citizens like your father—can swarm and attack British merchant ships anywhere in the world, places where the English have no idea we lurk nearby. Because the King's Channel and Mediterranean fleets of two-deckers are busy blockading Bonaparte, they cannot chase after hundreds of speedy brigs like our *Rattlesnake*."

Even as he explained this, Briggs thought of the real reason owners sent these ships to attack the enemy: not since the days of revolution had there been such an opportunity to amass great fortunes in such a limited time. This war, however, would not last forever, so the taking was *now*, and the taking now was *good*. Though blood spilled, it was an accepted risk for ambitious privateersmen. Briggs glanced aft as Captain Jordan rose from his cabin for the first time in the many hours since they had unmoored in Newport. This man personified the downside of the privateering life: the dangers inherent in arming men with cannon, cutlass, and knife, sending them out to do their worst without accountability if their worst was in conflict with the laws of the land, the rules of warfare, or the *Commandments* of God. At sea, a ship's captain ruled absolutely with iron authority. Mutiny by underpaid, scurrilous crewmen, nonetheless, was a captain's omnipresent threat. This threat neutralized only if he led successful voyages and gold flowed to the crews who did the fighting and spilled the blood. If a privateer captain were a fair man, the cruise would be remembered for dash, civility, hot action, and gold. Captain Cornelius Jordan, however, steered to his own course and played by his own rules. The captain had ignored Thomas Hammond and his many questions before they left Newport. So, the boy had asked Mr. Gant to divulge their destination, eliciting a cold eye and an angry snarl. Once the sails were set and trimmed to a fine edge, Thom instead waited for a lull and probed Mr. Briggs.

"England, lad. Where they least expect us," answered Briggs. "The Channel fleet remains stationed fifty miles off the coast of Brittany—according to your father. How he knows this I am not sure." Ben thought of the letter in his sea chest hidden under his foul weather tarpaulin. *Does the colonel send out privileged information? Does he receive privileged information in return?* Ben considered the colonel's letter that he himself had been tasked to carry; it might not be unique. Perhaps he was not the colonel's only secret emissary.

"You don't say, sir! England?" Thomas exploded enthusiastically. "Where will we attack the capital?"

"No, Thom." Briggs shushed him, whispering, "Their capital was built far up a river. We wouldn't get within a league. We'll sit off the coast and hide in the weather—fog and squalls this time of year—wait and pounce on unlucky ships. The English presume the Channel is their private walkway. It's not called the Dutch Channel, is it now?"

Delighted, Thom laughed. "We'll surprise them at their front door, sir!" Thomas jumped in excitement. *Captain Jordan is bringing the war to the English! Our ship will fire at their heart and the Empire will demand an end to hostilities.* Thomas imagined himself joining his captain on a platform celebration while the war's-end pronouncement blared fanfare and cheering, its heroes *fêted* by all of Newport. "I cannot wait, sir! When will we see England?"

"Not for weeks, lad. First, we must take on fresh water in the Azores. They are neutral islands owned by the Kingdom of Portugal. The captain doesn't expect to find British ships there. We'll provision with fresh mutton and wine, then sail hard for the Channel. We'll find warm action in those waters, you can be sure."

Captain James Breton of His Majesty's frigate *Fortitude* dismissed all the midshipmen from his great cabin except for one ten-year-old, his nephew, Peter Dawson. For lessons on combined fleet action, the English captain had conveyed to his youngsters how they were practiced in the time of Nelson, when long lines of first-rate ships formed and threw their weight of iron hoping to impair the sailing capabilities of targeted enemy ships. Once maimed—masts, sails, and spars having been shot through and sent crashing to deck—an attacking first-rate would come alongside her opponent and send streams of sailors and marines over the side into a carnage of sulfur-smoked mayhem. Fleet actions like Copenhagen, the Nile, and of course Trafalgar were proven tactics seldom used these days, never mind taught. Breton regretted that. An enemy man-of-war in this American conflict rarely ventured from harbor to meet His Majesty's blockading and patrolling force. The United States Navy could boast of little except for a few scattered, heavily-armed frigates—sturdy, well-built ships he did not deny, however, they were ships with more cannon, better trained and motivated crew, with greater displacement and sailing abilities than Royal Navy frigates of their class. Most British frigates from the last war—like *HMS Fortitude*—were, like her captain, tired. Yet British admirals—still planning for wars fought decades ago—continued to instruct their smaller, older frigates to fight toe-to-toe against the newer Yankee ships. Those ship actions were few but devastating to the nation's pride. *Constitution* had yet to lose a skirmish and was out again. *Bill of Rights* was rumored hunting in the South Atlantic to intercept convoys from India. To His Majesty's navy, orders were given to engage, sink, or capture Yankee men-of-war, their crews imprisoned or impressed, their officers granted parole or humane confinement. Yankee privateers, however, when captured were sailed to port and sold at auction. Their officers, condemned as pirates, were imprisoned without trial. And if their actions warranted, they were summarily hanged.

"How goes your first voyage, Peter?" James Breton smiled at his nephew whose late mother Marie had been the captain's beloved younger sister.

It seemed a lifetime ago now that James and Marie Breton's father had sailed off to war. There he had died in a shipwreck off Brittany. The children's grieving mother had soon taken to her bed with consumption. After months of torment, she succumbed, and James and his sister had been left alone in a great country house with an army of servants, relatives, visitors, and tenants coming and going at all hours. Two older siblings who had already been sent away years earlier to far-away schools paid little attention to their young brother and sister. Over the lonely years, James and Marie grew close, each the other's only true family. When James Breton went to sea as a youngster, the two siblings exchanged regular, enthusiastic letters. When he later wed and letters to his wife were required, he nonetheless took a greater joy writing to his sister who had married a widower of meager means. Marie's fate had been cruel. She died not long after Peter was born, never recovering from labor. Breton paid for his cherished nephew's education. And in time, he arranged for the boy to receive a commission in the service. Fortune followed *Fortitude* in this latest American war, short her complement of midshipmen. Thereby, Captain Breton was happily reunited with his nephew.

"I am very well indeed, uncle, I mean, *sir*. Thank you for my placement."

"We can thank the Admiralty Board, lad. They know the importance of our voyage. We need good men."

"I am not yet a man, sir, the quartermaster reminded us yesterday, as he took the stick to Mr. Simpson for poaching an extra biscuit."

"Stealing on His Majesty's ship is a capital crime, Peter. When will Mr. Simpson be walking again?"

"Perhaps in a week, sir. I changed his bandages myself this last watch."

"Good lad, take care of your friends. And be mindful of American corsairs we encounter. Their guns are deadly accurate and when they close and fire, the life of every man on deck is at risk. Cannon-shot will not likely find you—but if one does, death will follow quickly. A frigate such as *Fortitude* built of old wood will shatter from a cannon ball. They fire with surprising velocity, sending shards in every direction. If splinters hit you, they will pierce your uniform and do you deadly harm. Obey your gun captain and your officers. And when you see smoke from an enemy's broadside, duck, wait, and count to two. Only a captain stands through the onslaught."

"Yes, sir, thank you, sir. I will duck. But can I stand and yell at the enemy after?"

Captain James Breton smiled at his nephew, all of one decade old but as full of fury and fire with his belated mother's charm.

"Yes, Mister Dawson, yell at the Americans until the guards at Hell's gate can hear you. Then we will send these Yankees to the devil himself."

"I'd feel better if we knew what's on the other side of that mountain," Quartus Gant ruminated as he and Briggs stood near the bow rail, watching a distant island rise as they drew ever nearer. Gant had stopped at Horta only briefly, ages back on a return ship to Newport.

After two weeks of hard sailing to reach the mid-Atlantic, *Rattlesnake* approached the archipelago of nine volcanic islands. The captain boasted he did not expect to find English merchant ships in the Azores. This Portuguese port was most often used by eastbound vessels heading from the Americas to the Mediterranean. *Rattlesnake's* officers did not share Captain Jordan's confidence and they advised accordingly. Jordan had earlier dismissed Gant's suggestion that a British man-of-war or several might be patrolling nearby.

"Not a chance, Mr. Gant. Not a chance."

So, neither the *Rattlesnake* nor her languid crew was prepared for action. Looking forward to a short respite ashore, Jordan laughed at his officers when they vigorously expressed their concern.

"Worry about the Channel gentlemen Not these remote islands with nothing but fortified wines and fat sheep!"

Once in Horta, the privateer would provision fresh local mutton, cheese and wine imported from Portugal, and refill empty barrels with fresh water. Many months might pass before they anchored again in a friendly port, having committed to fighting alone in enemy waters where there was no recourse but attack and run. Where they ran to—French ports most likely—and what friends or enemies they met would determine their fate. Every man aboard the privateer knew they fought alone on endless oceans surrounded by the world's largest navy. And so, to attack Britain's home island was like pulling a tooth from the mouth of an angry lion.

"Think we got any prizes in here, Q?" Briggs took his turn with Gant's spyglass as *Rattlesnake* sailed slowly into Horta's harbor.

"Don't know," replied Gant. "I wish he'd first taken a quick pass 'round that headland, and anchor after."

Captain Cornelius Jordan sat dozing near the stern. Not expecting anything unusual, as was his custom, he reveled in the glorious mid-Atlantic sun. The crew trimmed a single jib to maintain steerage. As the Americans rounded the southern point, anchored hulls and masts appeared: whalers, French and Portuguese merchant ships of two and three masts. Two ships, however, off to the far right, lay close together. Men on this pair of ships sped aloft at sighting the Americans.

"British!" Gant roared, noting the two ships' ensigns. Jordan ignored him at first. "Captain—two *British* ships!"

At twenty-seven years, Captain Jordan was in his prime: hearty and ebullient with fight. His eyes lit up at a cannon's concussive bellow, though he customarily ignored daily ship-life when seas were empty and the deck rolled in its natural motion. At Gant's warning, however, Jordan roused and sprinted from one side of the ship to the other and back. He held his telescope tight to his eye lest any detail escape. He quickly glanced at his sails followed by a sharp look up at the wind's motion at the masthead. Looking to shore he sought telltales of approaching wind shifts—all would dictate his approach for attack. On the leeward deck, and seeking an escape route, Briggs also carefully noted the wind direction. Whereas the captain only studied the shore, Ben Briggs looked both inshore and offshore—for escape. The land breeze rising from the nearby mountain would lift *Rattlesnake* and pull her away from the next flood tide—slack now by the motion of anchored ships lying bow-to-bow. The flood should turn north, carrying the ship away from shore defenses or any armed Portuguese soldiers rowing out to deter a fight.

Gant kept his eyes on Jordan. The captain's energetic commands had encouraged the crew's spirits, but mostly, Gant thought, the captain was performing for his officers. He wondered how Jordan pulled it off. How did a poor boy from the north side of Newport learn to masquerade as a renowned naval hero? His lilting diction, his bow, his sly look upwards as his back bent seemed innate, not affected. Jordan's posture communicated status and class, when a false pronunciation might give the game away. *Why didn't Colonel Hammond see through him?* Gant wondered. The owner was no man's fool. The colonel himself had climbed from a lowly candle merchant to a wealthy tradesman—a citizen with a voice. Hammond commanded status as resolutely as barnacles stuck to a beach boulder. *Wealth does that,* thought Gant, *whether from privateering or inheritance.* And the manner of fortune-making made no difference to a man like Gant, who had grown up hungry. Colonel Hammond's Great Hill manor was more than a home, Gant reasoned—it was a statement. Money begat money, and the more you had, the more you displayed it. Like Jordan's beaver-skin hat, fine tailored velvet coats, and the best polished steel sword and pistols prize money could buy, Jordan carefully crafted an image announcing to the world that he was a player in the maelstrom of private wars. Quartus Gant begrudged the captain this skill: men, whether rich or poor, cowardly or heroic, invariably followed the winners. The privateering life fit a man like Jordan—a life about the *taking* more than the *making* of wealth—a simple faith. Even backwards farmhands grasped the principles of the business: a privateersman can build a great fortune by stealing gold, sailing home, then returning to sea... where he could steal more. Great fortunes were built in this war; a war that few men understood. *Rattlesnake's* men and boys captured English ships to which they would have dipped their ensign a few years earlier. Now, Yankees stripped English prizes down to the rusty nails that held the copper plates to the hulls. *Rattlesnake's* fifty-odd sweaty Newport men were prepared to spill buckets of their own blood in the venture. They accepted the pervasive risk of death but expected—and demanded—the hard-earned wealth available from no other toil ashore or at sea. The trick was staying alive long enough to enjoy it.

"Prepare for action, my lads!" Captain Jordan cried as he sprang about. "What I expected... sitting prey!"

Expected? Gant thought. *Moments ago, the fool was dead asleep!* Jordan had not expected an English ship within five hundred miles of Pico. And as a result, *Rattlesnake* did not have cannon balls or powder stacked on deck. Gant cursed and shouted hurried commands to his gun crews. Furiously men ran out the cannon, while others dashed laterally and horizontally gathering shot and opening ports.

"Prepare to board!" Jordan ordered above the din of men armed with pikes and cutlasses. Every man carried a pistol stuck in his belt.

Thomas threw himself into the preparations, scampering below, grabbing bags of powder, returning to deck, and placing the ammunition next to the starboard guns first, larboard after. He paused a moment to stare at the two slow-moving prizes: the English had silently slipped their cables, abandoning anchors. A curious detail also struck him: barrels floated, attached to the dropped cables. *These ships were planning to return to their anchors!*

"Captain, sir…" But Jordan ran past the boy, his sole attention on his gang of boarders.

"Mr. Briggs, sir!" Thomas cried out, "Those ships have barrels attached to their anchor cables, sir. They're coming back!"

"Back…?" Briggs murmured. He stopped for a moment to think despite the commotion on deck, then shouted, "Q, they're not running!"

Stopping short, Gant saw what the boy had noticed. He nodded. After giving a flurry of orders to the boarders, Gant and Briggs met near the starboard rail amidships. What wind existed blew from the northeast as *Rattlesnake* ghosted into the mirrored harbor.

"Look, Q! The inside ship—dropped her topsails."

"Captain!" Gant cried to the stern where Jordan stood, sword drawn, two loaded pistols stuck in his wide leather belt. "They've slipped their moorings! They're trying to escape north. We should fall off and present our broadside."

"No, Mr. Gant, we shall go directly at them! Prepare our larboard guns for a volley into their rigging as soon as they cross. You shall lead one boarding party, I the other." Jordan's eyes were alight like a mooncusser's bonfire.

Gant wanted to scream, *What in God's name are you planning?* Did Jordan mean to fire first or board? Which ship? Gant could not read the captain's intention.

Captain Jordan grinned, rolling up and down on his toes, hands on the starboard rail like an anxious child waiting for a present.

"By the time we're close enough to board, we'll be at the point..." muttered Briggs, his arm straight out.

Gant nodded and finished the thought. "...with no room to maneuver." The officers saw cliffs to the right, a rocky shoal on the left. This left the middle with enough room for only a skiff, not three ships. "Aye. And if anyone lurks to the north, we'll not see'em until they fire on us," Gant reasoned. "He needs to fall off until we know."

Briggs approached the giddy captain. "Captain, we don't know what hides beyond the point. If there are enemy ships to the north, we shall be disadvantaged—"

"There is no British man-of-war within hundreds of miles of Pico, Mr. Briggs. We have leagues of sea room. We shall take those two ships."

"But they intend to retrieve their anchors, sir, they could be leading us—"

"Mr. Briggs!" bellowed Captain Jordan, "They are *leading us* to glory!"

"But Captain—!" Briggs looked to the gunner for support.

Gant, all the while, had not removed the spyglass from his eye. The escaping ships had only hoisted loosely trimmed topsails, braces slack. *In a run for one's life, a ship hoists every damned piece of canvas she carries,* Gant knew. Why didn't these ships?

"Prepare a bow chaser," commanded Jordan, overruling both of his officers. "As the ships cross, I shall make their acquaintance!"

Through his telescope, one of Gant's few family keepsakes always by his side, he counted men on the British ships' yardarms and others climbing ratlines attached to shrouds. There, two. Over there, four more—but no more. Not the entire ship's company. On a ship one hundred-fifty-feet-long fleeing danger of capture or destruction, there should have been twenty or thirty men aloft by now dropping sails and hoisting jibs as fast as hands could fly. All combined, Gant counted only ten men aloft. He turned to the captain... But what could he say? That their prizes sought to escape... *slowly*? Gant trained the glass on the nearest shore, eliminating the impossibilities, considering the improbable. Following the ridge up from the beach along the point, to the peak, and then back down, he stumbled on it... a flag! A solitary man stood on the top of the ridge making signals. *To whom?*

"Captain, we must bear away!" Gant ran past Briggs and put his nose into the captain's face. "There's a man signaling on the ridge—to someone *on the other side.* These fornicating ships are leading us into a trap!"

Jordan looked up at the mountain. He did not ask for the spyglass. He scanned the prizes passing his bow, nearer each moment, within an arm's reach if the arm held a spar. He smiled. To delay would ruin his plan, to turn away... not in his nature.

"You worry too much, Mr. Gant. We shall take our prizes. Then we will investigate if ships lurk beyond. If we do not like what we see, we shall be off with a full press of canvas. Arm yourself and lead our men over the rail and show them our spirit! I shall follow. I intend to take the leeward sloop."

"Aye," replied Gant, unsure if he had been given a compliment or a rebuke. "What about the other ship—?"

"You are my most fearsome fighter," Jordan parried, "Can I rely on you?"

Gant nodded. Jordan turned away, raising his own spyglass. Scowling, Gant followed Briggs to the rail where he leaned in.

"If you see a bowsprit sneaking around that point, steer down and hoist every fuckin' piece'a canvas we got. Aye?"

"Aye," whispered Ben. "You think British ships are lying to the north?"

Gant pointed to the man at the peak of the ridge. "He ain't signaling whales."

Coming to windward of the nearest escaping merchantman, *Rattlesnake* slowed and a few English crewmen armed with muskets pointed at the attacking American privateer. Gant placed twenty men shouldering muskets on the larboard gunwale and on his command silenced the scattered British protest with a well-aimed volley. Two defenders were hit and down: one man in the shoulder and a young man, facing Captain Jordan's smoking pistol, held his hands to his face as he fell.

At the wheel, Briggs skillfully brought *Rattlesnake* close from windward as the two ships collided with a thundering crash, spars on both ships tangling, bulwarks splintering. Over the rails, privateersmen rushed, leaping onto the enemy's deck. A flurry of arms swung heavy blades. Clashing iron rang out, echoing against the hulls. The shouting Yankee swarm outnumbered the defenders by almost two-to-one; within a minute, the fighting stopped suddenly. Jordan secured his triumph and stood at his quarry's wheel. He ordered men to hoist more sails on the captured ship; she quickly fell away, increased speed, and headed toward its escaping companion-ship.

The fool, thought Briggs remaining on *Rattlesnake, he'll try to board the second prize from the deck of the first, yet we can hardly keep our spars clear.* Briggs yelled instructions to the sailors remaining on *Rattlesnake*, "Keep the ships apart! Cut their braces if they snag us!"

A few minutes later, the three ships had reached the far point of land. They lay abeam of each other in the narrowing channel. Jordan, with a battle scream, leapt from the deck of the first captured ship, and with ten Yankee men, the American captain overcame the five Englishmen defending the deck. Her British ensign was hauled down; a battle for two plump prizes culminated successfully; a stupendous victory had been executed lightning fast. The Yankees' celebration, however, was cruelly interrupted by the resonating boom of heavy cannon fire.

Gant, having remained on board the first prize with a squirming captive under his sword, turned toward the explosion. As he did, the man below kicked Gant's leg and tripped him, thereby escaping Gant's blade. The British sailor snatched up his knife that had fallen on deck, and slashed at Gant's shoulder. As the American fell, the knife missed the intended target of a neck vein by mere inches. In pain, Gant dropped his sword. As Gant lay prone, another English sailor jumped on him. With the swift action of a butcher's son, he raised his knife high with the intent to sever Gant's head from his shoulders. But a shot rang out and the attacker's arm lost its motion and turned red as the knife fell and, without harm, bounced off Gant's chest. Gant forced his pelvis upward and, turning in one violent motion, pinned the wounded man to the deck. With no weapon but his hands, Gant pummeled his enemy's face, each blow more decisive, delivering a relentless pounding, one violent punch after another. Nearby sailors heard cheek and jaw break under Gant's viscous beating. Hands redder with each blow, Gant could not stop himself, caught, as he was, in the dizzy air devoid of humanity.

"I believe he's dead, Mr. Gant," advised Jordan from the second ship's deck, his pistol still smoking. The captain gazed across the decks of the three entangled ships and with great reluctance scoured the horizon for the source of cannon fire. "Time to go," he said, as if in a dream-state.

To the north, under a sturdy full press of flaxen sails flew a British Royal Navy squadron of three ships: A frigate followed by two speedy single-mast cutters, each ship rushing under full-sail, fast approached. The British trap closed on the American privateersmen. Gant took in the knowing faces of the beaten British sailors, their treachery revealed.

"*Rattlesnakes!*" yelled Jordan, his voice cracking. "Lads—back to the ship!"

Jordan clambered over one enemy deck, then the other, and finally onto his own quarterdeck. Staring, disbelieving at the scene, his mind raced, *Abandon two captured prizes? Run? Do we have room for maneuver?*

"Hoist jibs, topsails, and spanker!" cried Jordan, as his men ran to their duty.

Gant reclaimed his bloody sword, ignoring the inert body at his feet. He grabbed a loose brace and flung his body over the three feet separating the prize from *'Snake*. He took *Rattlesnake's* helm from Briggs; as the two officers had agreed, Gant would steer in shallows such as here. The ship, however, had stopped dead, its rigging enmeshed with the British prize. They could not outrun the squadron. Nor had they firepower to defend against three men-of-war. *Rattlesnake* had no place to hide and no open course to sail but back into the harbor... and certain capture.

Jordan ran to *Rattlesnake's* wheel and stared at his officers, one bloody and sweating from fight, the other white with tension. Jordan's eyes split wide—*In shock?* thought Gant. The captain swayed, his face ashen. Under a gunpowder-stained coat, his torn shirt revealed his glistening chest drenched in sweat from leaping over ship rails and fighting men to their deaths. Of the three American officers, only Gant remained calm, his eyes on the sails as he spoke.

"If we fall off and try to run west for home," began Gant, "the prizes block our course. We cannot clear their sterns. Or we can tack to starboard and head into the anchorage. Perhaps a few men can make it to the hills. Or—"

"Or?" demanded Jordan, looking in every direction at the same time.

"Or we sail north." Gant's arm indicated a straight course. "Cast off from the prizes and sail past the shallows at the point. The land breeze will lift us below the cliffs. Though we'll face their ugly broadsides until we make our turn."

"Yes, they won't expect that." Jordan quickly grasped Gant's plan; once a portrait was halfway drawn, he had no trouble seeing its shading. Jordan regarded the enemy, and looked at his own deck bristling with men and guns. He counted the distance with his eyes, the elapsed time of two converging courses on gloved fingers.

"Once we clear the shoals and pass the cliff, we'll be in open water," Gant continued, "Perhaps we can rake the frigate's stern once she's passed. The cutters have already sailed too far west to hit us. As long as we sail high and hard..."

Briggs pointed at waves breaking on rocks only one hundred yards offshore to leeward.

"We've got no room to larboard, Q." He turned toward the land. "How much water's in there?" He motioned at the beach.

"I provisioned here years ago," replied Gant, "fishing the narrow channel below the bluffs... deep enough close along the beach."

"We need at least fifteen—"

"Tide's rising," confirmed Gant. "We'll find out." Gant made the decision for them.

Briggs took the glass and saw a narrow bed of still water closest to shore. The squadron would soon reach the far end of the rips of rock standing between them. The British ships could not easily follow *Rattlesnake* if she sailed northerly. An enterprising British officer would have had to have already anticipated the privateer's risky maneuver, squeezing between the rocks and the beach, in order to turn his squadron on its heels and sail hard to an undetermined intersecting battle point many upwind miles away if the English wanted to meet the fleeing American brig in a favorable, windward position. Every second the British maintained their line-of-battle sailing westward, however, the more advantage *Rattlesnake* gained. The Americans had an escape route—unless they hit a rock or bottom.

"Captain?" Gant pressed. "While the tide's with us—?"

"I think not," Jordan countered weakly. "We shall clear the prizes and fall off behind. We shall bring our starboard guns to bear on the lead cutter—"

"—who will tear us apart, Captain! And then the next cutter in line will join him. The frigate will pick up what's left of us with a fishin' net!" Gant roared.

"We must fight..." Jordan's eyes darted fast, back and forth. "We're here to fight the British, not run—" Jordan appeared lost.

Gant raged, "We're here to *capture ships*—ones that don't got a squadron of men-o'-war holdin' their frigging hands!"

Briggs shot a look only a friend can send to a man so incensed. *Shut your mouth! Follow my lead!* Gant gripped the wheel so hard his knuckle bones showed through.

"Captain..." Briggs spoke as a father to a young son. "We can wind our course past the reef to larboard and pass the bluffs to starboard through Mr. Gant's channel. Once clear, we can sail down towards the British frigate with the freedom of open water, undo her with a single, well-aimed broadside into her stern before she can turn her guns on us. We have your best Newport gunners aboard, lathered for a kill. The enemy will retreat to lick their wounds. They must haul their wind, heave to, and repair their damage. This will give us ample time to turn and reclaim our prizes." Gant, hearing Briggs' baited lie buried within their only route of escape, was again impressed with his friend's quick mind. Briggs went on, "But *only* if we hit her stern hard. And we'll only get one pass. If we follow Mr. Gant's suggestion, we must sail towards the cliffs beginning *at this moment*, Captain." He added the last clearly and definitively.

It worked.

"Aye." Sober and resigned, Jordan sat slumped, sword down.

Gant looked at Briggs with a crooked lip—a small satisfaction. *Rattlesnake's* deck obeyed Briggs' orders to trim the mainsail and topgallant, catch the wind's lift off the cliff, and head toward the beach. *Rattlesnake* turned north-northeast. The lead cutter fired a weak broadside at an improbable angle which fell far short. The two smaller enemy ships kept their course and position below the rocks and shoal while the privateer raced away along the beach with all sails trimmed, heeling hard through calm water, wind aloft driving her with urgency. If Gant steered wrong or his memory proved faulty, *Rattlesnake* would run fast aground, most of her crew would drown in the wreckage, her straggling survivors damned as captives destined for prison or execution. Briggs noted Jordan's bloody sword: all the evidence the British would need.

This is the greatest day of my life, thought Thomas Hammond. *Two prizes nearly in hand—Such victory!* The boy felt on top of the world, riding a wave and ready to fight the entire Royal Navy—three ships, spread in a line, ready targets for the sharpshooters from Newport. Thom's captain would soon order his ship to face the enemy line and attack. The boy was ready to do his duty—aim and fire his cannon, crushing masts and yards until the entire fleet was under *Rattlesnake's* command—or die in battle. Relishing the promise of glory, he had neither fear nor any understanding of the pain inherent in a violent death. The boy lived in the moment, and the moment was wondrous.

Rattlesnake, however, made no move to face the superior enemy flotilla, nor did the British expect it. Captain Breton, from his quarterdeck, saw *Rattlesnake's* dire situation: The Yankee could not fall off with the disabled prizes drifting in her way. She was hemmed in by shore to windward, pinched in a funnel's narrowing tube, her world collapsing like a bellows exhausted of oxygen. The Yankee must retreat into the harbor, her men running for the hills like ants; there, Breton's Marines would capture them, beat them, and prepare their bloody necks for his yardarm. Or, Breton considered, the Yankee might yet come into the wind and bring her puny guns to bear on his smaller cutters and hope to rip a few sails. One cutter might suffer an insult, though by the time his second warship gained the range, the American brig would be brutally damaged, easy prey for the full power of *Fortitude.* A single broadside from the frigate upon the lightly-built Yankee hull would end the day. By flag signal, Breton relayed his intent to his two leading ships. His plan set in motion, he admired his nephew, attentive and wide-eyed standing straight near his starboard cannon station that, with luck, would not need exercise today.

Breton trained his spyglass, curious as to why the American had not yet re-treated into the harbor. *Good,* he mused, *I will sink them.* His Marines need not muddy their boots. Yet *Rattlesnake* did not turn into the wind to fight either—at least not yet. British cutters were primed and ready... though now nearly out of range: Captain Breton's van would soon sail past the attack angle. While he had used the reef to hem *Rattlesnake* in, his squadron was likewise constrained from revising their approach. *What's the damned Yankee doing?* He looked at the breaking waves between his squadron and the enemy brig. Aiming at his frigate, her course was toward the rocks and shoal that stood between them where, surely, she would hit and sink! Moments later, however, her sails trimmed tight, *Rattlesnake* turned up and away, her new direction now toward the cliffs at the point. She seemed to be trying to carve an improbable escape route to the north! Did her captain intend to sail her onto shore, wreck the ship, scattering the crew like rats? Breton pondered his next move. Perhaps he ought to lie hove-to, bring his twelve larboard guns to bear and fire... Like the sun shooting through a hole in the clouds, the British captain suddenly realized the American privateer's plan: Where cliffs met ocean, a short, narrow strip of water appeared calmer than minutes before when *Fortitude* had passed. Was this flowing channel deep enough for a coastal brig? *Damn it to bloody hell, there's nothing I can do!* Breton recognized his enemy's resolution.

His second cutter, *Aphrodite,* like his first warship, *Bella,* had sailed past the enemy and was now also out of range. Thus, his two ships in front were too far away to fight or chase the brig. To rejoin the attack, they would have to tack and slowly claw their way upwind. Only *Fortitude* had the weather gauge and remained close enough to engage while *Rattlesnake* continued sailing hard and fast northeast. From Captain Breton's perspective, the Yankee ship appeared to kiss the shore as it slid past with ever more speed. He calculated the enemy's increasing track and height above *Fortitude.* If the privateer brig avoided the rocks beneath her and the beach inland, she would be away free in open ocean. A new and disturbing alternative suddenly occurred to the captain: safe now from shore, with wind and speed to spare, if the privateer scooped down and fired on *Fortitude...* the Yanks would find the undefended stern of the British ship. Nearing panic, Captain Breton looked about. His ship did not have enough sea room to wear ship while still avoiding the rocks. His larboard guns pointed too far south to bear on the enemy sailing high away to the north. His starboard guns faced North America, also useless at this angle. He had no choice but to tack through the wind—a maneuver a full-rigged ship avoided due to possible damage caused by flapping sails and loose sheets. He intended to sail to the north and meet the American before she raked his stern. He watched as shore wind lifted the American higher and faster. She sped past the cliffs at a far greater rate of speed over ground than his squadron sailed in the meandering ocean breeze. *The damned pirate has escaped the narrows!* Breton's heart skipped as the Yankees flew past *Fortitude's* just-traveled wake. But then the Yank's sails suddenly loosened, and her bow turned down—directly at *Fortitude.* The knave was preparing to attack a ship with three times her firepower! Breton's hesitation left him no room to wear ship nor the time to tack away; the marauder approached too fast. His gut heaved knowing full well his pitifully small six-pound stern cannons were no answer for the privateer's full broadside of long guns taking careful aim within fifty yards.

"Stern chasers—prepare to fire!" The English captain was not sure if his command came too late.

Gant carefully threaded the ship through the narrow cut. The channel reminded him of Massachusetts' waters when, as a hungry lad, he had sailed with smugglers through the lovely albeit rock-strewn Elizabeth Islands, where his ship skidded through cuts with only inches under her keel. If *Rattlesnake* was to survive the day, she too needed those inches. He felt his wheel trembling in his hands no matter how hard he gripped due to the pressure of water against the oak rudder and its iron rudder post—firm, steady, and increasing. He looked up at the cliff near enough to spit at: Above, a bright breeze flew at the height of his topsails. If she could catch this wind, *Rattlesnake* could sail even higher, hug the beach while picking up more speed. But did they have the depth?

Gant yelled a command to the captain which Jordan dutifully relayed to the crew, "All hands to trim!"

The men tightened braces and sheets with energy, their eyes on Gant and the frigate. Among privateers during battle, it was understood the most able men led. Embracing common sense and profit over top-down command, privateering was a reasonably democratic service compared to the world's navies, which often promoted incompetence as long as an officer was well-bred and bolstered by connections. Gant was neither, but here and now, he had the ship. He felt the wheel shake from side to side no matter how hard he held it. The ship was losing her grip on the water's force, the rudder shuddering unsteady.

"Mr. Gant!" He heard the cry from the crewman with the logline and lead measuring depth on the leeward side. "By the mark twenty!" Soon the lad followed with, "Fifteen now, Mr. Gant!"

Without warning though not unexpected, *Rattlesnake* slammed into an Azores' sandy bottom with a thundering crash. Her keel scraped along the bottom obscenely. Everyone on deck felt her hit. Not a word was spoken. Yet, the ship continued onward. Built Newburyport-tough, the brig sailed steady, and the wheel tightened again in Gant's hands. He regained control, the helm no longer prisoner to the seabed: The *'Snake* had powered over the sandbar. He steered the ship back to a comfortable trim.

"Give me more tension on our jibs and staysails!" ordered Gant.

The ship heeled, free again from the bottom, Briggs turned his attention to the breaking waves and enemy ships to leeward. He was not sure which frightened him more, sixty British cannon against *Rattlesnake's* twelve, or the rocks below that could split the hull like a clam shell. The men aboard the privateer would be dead within minutes if she struck a rock. To the north beyond the headlands lay the privateer's only escape.

The British had kept to their preordained line-of-battle. Gant noticed t; he had *counted* on it. The enemy might have hauled their wind, come around, and met *Rattlesnake* in open water north of Pico, but had not done so. *Why not?* Gant wondered. As fast as this question came to Gant, he knew the answer: his heeling ship had captured the steady land breeze in their upper-most sails. Of the four combatants, only the Americans had a fresh shore breeze coupled with open ocean sea-room. *Rattlesnake* alone could now dictate the upcoming action.

Rattlesnake turned north and sailed away from the van of British ships, catching clear, clean ocean air sailing ten knots or better in the calm waters protected by the lee of the cliffs. The British, meanwhile, lollygagged in rolling ocean swells and a light wind devoid of the land breeze that rose strong from the heat of a long day.

Rattlesnake made her escape. If she kept this course, stayed with the breeze along the beach, the Americans could be miles away before the enemy reformed their line to pursue. By then, darkness would mask *Rattlesnake's* course. Regaining his attacking spirit, Jordan held his spyglass. He studied the frigate carefully and looked back at the land, eyeing the passing cliffs. Without his war council aware, he made up his mind; new orders came in quick succession with no time for argument. The British frigate's ass-end was right *there!*

"Larboard cannon—prepare to fire on my command!" His eyes incandescent, he waved his sword overhead. "Briggs, ease sheets! Mr. Gant, down thirty degrees."

Falling off, the privateer brig found herself in perfect position to rake the stern of the frigate where, Captain Jordan presumed, only small chasers were likely positioned for defensive fire. Even though the officers of *Rattlesnake* had briefly discussed attacking the frigate, Gant was nonetheless dumbfounded that Jordan chose to actually *do* it rather than escape. Chafing, the gunner obeyed reluctantly. In shared desperation, Briggs hung his head, though he quickly detected Jordan recognized what the mates had earlier discussed and discarded: a rare opportunity to ravage a massively more powerful foe.

"We shall cripple the frigate!" screamed Captain Jordan with a maniacal grin—*Deliver a decisive volley then dash away. Cutters cannot climb back upwind in time to respond.*

Whether madness or brilliance, Briggs knew they must act while the fever ran high, the wind at their backs.

Captain Breton saw the puffs of white smoke from six cannon fired in a well-timed broadside at his exposed stern and naked gun deck. No warning to his unprotected crew would have shielded them—the enemy had come down too fast, turned too sharply, and fired without hesitation. If a daytime raid under a clear sky against a superior force could be called a surprise attack, he was indeed surprised. The British commander stood tall in the onslaught he knew would ruin his ship and refused to join his crew who had dropped to the deck as his steering wheel, stern posts, lanterns, spanker boom, railing, compass, and aft companionway hatch covers splintered in the blast with a tsunami of broken beams, glass, brass fittings, and rope that rained down on men shielded only by thin ship's slops: cotton shirts and breeches. Around him, seamen and officers cried out in anguish, blood spilling from injured torsos and limbs. In a flash from within a billowed cloud of smoke, the American brig skidded past *Fortitude* with a full press of sail, made her turn back upwind, and headed for the horizon.

"Jury-rig a tiller from the orlop, come up thirty degrees!" Breton shouted from his blood-red deck. "Follow the goddamn..." He hesitated, searched through his concussed head and blurred vision looking for his nephew. Was Peter unhurt? Where was his nephew? Breton could not see; blood obscured his vision. "Mr. Dawson!" he cried out. "Report!"

Before he lost his senses, the English captain stared curiously at a sharp, narrow piece of polished stern railing extending from his fleshy thigh and out the back of his shattered leg. He knew painful surgery would be required to cut away infected skin and repair torn muscle, a leather strap between his teeth. Fever and burning delirium would continue weeks after the danger of gangrene lessened. Captain Breton would not sleep or sit without pain for many long months thereafter.

Privateer

Chapter Six

C ramped in Captain Jordan's ill-smelling quarters—more like a storage room with a swinging cot and a chart table—Second Mate Quartus Gant found it difficult to close the door behind himself and First Mate Ebenezer Briggs. *Rattlesnake's* officers had no idea what their captain planned so soon after their improbable escape from *HMS Fortitude*. The *'Snake* enjoyed a healthy head start, thanks to Gant's tight turn after they had unleashed their deadly broadside. The British frigate had thus far been unable to match *Rattlesnake*'s northerly course. The pursuing *Fortitude* lagged by ten miles, though on the high seas, any number of conditions might change the Yanks' advantage.

"Shut the door, Mr. Gant," barked Jordan. "You think I do not see?" Captain Jordan spoke with a grim strength he usually reserved for a thrust of his sword.

First and second mate stood, hats held respectfully behind their backs. The captain had been right: His attack on the stern of the superior British frigate damaged her grievously, giving the privateer a greater window of escape not viable by any other maneuver. Indeed, it was tempting to run north once having rounded the headlands, but the frigate only needed to change course and pursue with the even speedier cutters close behind. The damaged frigate wallowed for hours resetting her damaged rig, and thus provided the head start *Rattlesnake* now enjoyed. Soon, after darkness fell and they were assured of no half-moon betrayal, they would turn on their course and head due south, or perhaps first west for a false read, and then fast to the warmth of the West Indies crawling with British merchant ship targets. Left unsaid:

their voyage to the British Islands had been scuttled. Also absent in this evening's discourse was a question on everyone's lips: *How had the damned English known* Rattlesnake *was coming?*

For a long moment, the captain waited for answers that did not come.

"In attacking the enemy, you think I am mad." Jordan's voice climbed. "I engage in battles where other privateersmen would shit their breeches! You prefer *escape* be our primary course so as to save our powder for a day when we face only women and old men?" Jordan caught his breath. Drained of energy, his eyes bulged, daring his officers to deny his accusations. "You doubt me!"

Tension in the cabin exploded.

Not now, thought Briggs. He turned to Gant.

What's the point? thought Gant. Challenged by the captain's taunt, the mates nevertheless stood silent.

Hearing no defense, the exasperated Jordan blasted accusations, "Don't you think I had a plan? You think I'm a fool?"

Briggs shot a warning glance at Gant: *Q, don't take the bait! He'll throw you in irons!*

"We had our escape, Captain," said Gant in a reasonable tone.

Briggs admired Q's measured retort. *Respectful*, he thought, *and to the point*: *Although the frigate was slowed by our daring attack, they might yet catch us.*

"Do you understand our business, Mr. Gant?" Jordan reached under a cabinet and produced a bottle which he emptied without sharing. "Our enterprise is to attack and kill our enemy. Bring unrelenting pain to the Empire. Their people. Their pride. Their instruments of war. We take what we will and so deny the King's treasury. We sail where we desire and steal what we find. We anchor back home with wealth and glory! Do not suffer my patience and pretend our action falls beneath your standards," Jordan spat out.

Gant had no immediate reply, but his neck muscles flexed. Briggs feared one of those two might not climb onto the deck uninjured. The captain sensed his murderous gunner was lathered up to a violent encounter and so pretended to examine a new course on the charts strewn on his small table.

"Do you boys have any idea of the wealth a privateer captain can steer to his account? Do you? I have little need for our prize winnings as I come from a long line of successful whale oil merchants, yet I put my head in danger every time we take a prize! I do this for our country, for our honor! You two will also earn a fair coin on our most recent voyages—you, Mr. Briggs especially—a three percent cut. Mr. Gant, because of your promotion I arranged," he lied. "...you shall find a similar pay—yet it is a mere pittance compared to one who commands."

Briggs and Gant knew a privateer captain's share of prize money was second only to the ship's owner. And a privateer captain had only to feed himself, as provisions and repairs were the owner's responsibility. Gant, however, bluntly confronted a different truth, one everyone aboard *Rattlesnake* could see.

"You leave the ship before we dock, Captain. On our last two cruises, you've examined our pillage and disembarked with chests before our manifest was verified at the pier."

Jordan was not afraid of this accusation. "You think after earning forty percent, I need to *steal*?" These men could prove nothing. He tacked. "One of you may become a ship's master—perhaps even for Colonel Hammond. He's asked me to rate you. But I see much to fault. A lack of loyalty, for starters. Add to that a timid obedience only after calculated delay. You men have backbones weaker than dried bark..."

Jordan looked at the dark deck beams inches above his head. He closed his eyes, his head swayed back and forth. His lips moved without sound. Then suddenly his hands floated in front of his body, back and forth as if conducting a concert. His voice rose to a whisper, and he spoke a dreamy stanza accompanied by a familiar chanty's tune. As Jordan sang to himself, his words made no apparent sense, but the cabin being small, both officers heard the words clear and would long remember their odd nature:

Though my heart lays still and night falls long
I fear we voyage to where the sea's spent, gone
To where the voyage ends and where the drifters sent
Past shoals of peace, of death intent.
But they rose at night and found the block
They found their way, their light unlock'd
They found their grace though twice returned
To live a day, their past now burned.

Jordan's hands stopped fluttering in the air, and dropped lifeless into his lap. Without explanation for his bizarre oration, he opened his eyes and returned to his chart. After a few moments, the captain regarded his confounded officers.

"Thank you, gentlemen," said Captain Jordan, without looking up. "Call me at first light if the horizon is not clear of enemy sails."

Intending to reconstruct the evening's strange meeting, Gant waited until after the second watch. By then, his head had cleared yet his antipathy growled just below the surface. As dawn approached, Gant climbed onto deck and passed Briggs. His friend gestured him close.

"What was that, Q? An act? whispered Ben. Is he mad?"

"Ain't it obvious? He's *afraid*. We know his ship better'n him. We dare to speak when he talks crazy." Gant had been struggling with this fact since running out their guns to obliterate the aft deck of the British frigate crowded with officers, boys, and bare-chested men. "He means to turn us against each other, Briggs."

Briggs stood upright. "He will fail."

The men clasped each other's arms as a sudden cry leapt from the main-crosstree lookout.

"Sail ho, dead astern!"

Gant and Briggs turned to the rising orange sky. *Rattlesnake* was not alone: The British frigate was bearing down on their southwest course. Gant looked at *Rattlesnake's* sails. Dawn's paltry wind was dying fast. In a few hours, the larger enemy ship would surely catch them.

"Mr. Briggs, sir?" the breathless carpenter and his mate interrupted the officers. Ben had little interest in listening. However, a carpenter running from below deck so soon after an encounter with a shoal portended ill fortune. Two men drenched in seawater stood before him. "When we hit, sir, we must've split a beam and cracked two knees and three planks. They just let go this watch, sir. Forward star'bd side. We got two feet in the bilge. Water's rising fast."

"Can you plug it?" asked Captain Jordan, rising from his hammock long enough to examine where the cold Atlantic water displaced stale air and rats below deck.

The carpenter and his mate had hammered plugs and cordage into the most menacing leaks, slowing but not arresting the inflow. The captain observed the cracked ribs and loosened planks. Pumping furiously in teams of four, all watches worked to decrease the water level in the bilge. Nevertheless, seawater continued to rise. Jordan looked at Gant for fighting options, Briggs for creative ideas, the carpenter for sweat labor.

"A sail over the side, wrapped tight over the damage. If we're able, apply a patch of tar from the inside along the seams." Briggs offered. "Otherwise, we must turn and fight." *And die.*

"Aye, a tight wrap," replied Jordan, as if he had conceived the remedy himself.

Two hours past dawn the following day, the carpenter's mate repeated his report, "Still two feet, Captain, but the rising has slowed. Mr. Briggs' wrap and re-caulked seams are holding."

Jordan did not acknowledge the new information, instead, he looked at his officers. They were not giving him what he needed. His aim was not to merely survive, but to fight, victorious.

Quartus Gant spoke first. "We don't have two thousand miles on a patch, Captain. We have five hundred, perhaps six—barely enough to get us back to Newport. No more."

Reluctantly, Captain Jordan abandoned his audacious plan to attack ships in the English Channel. With the hull severely damaged, *Rattlesnake* had become a slow predator, easily caught or sunk as soon as her exhausted men collapsed at the pumps, allowing seawater to rise unencumbered above the bilge. But instead of the obvious course—sail home, careen *Rattlesnake* on her side where sprung timbers and cracked ribs could be replaced, her seams re-caulked and the ship refloated to her original sea-worthy condition—he burst out with another idea.

"We'll cruise to the West Indies." Jordan's utterance came as more a suggestion than a command. "We'll impress fresh crew off captured prizes, replace tired *Rattlesnake* men, and keep hunting."

No man aboard believed the West Indies presented a viable solution: there lies the heart of Britain's North American empire, vigorously defended by armed fleets patrolling in the trade routes from the islands to the Channel. His officers would not have it. A West Indies expedition in a slow and leaking ship was ludicrous. Briggs stood firm beside his friend.

"Even if we conscript new men, Captain, our damaged timbers will not withstand the concussions of a broadside," first mate Briggs explained with as much patience as he could, clear-headed reasoning his sharpest tool to stay alive. "We can only fire a single gun at a time," continued Briggs, "The pounding, never mind suffering an enemy broadside, will loosen other ribs. If they too fail, our longboats will be floating before we even launch them."

Jordan expected the rational from Briggs; from the gunner, he expected heat.

"Mr. Gant?"

Quartus Gant wanted very much to hunt for prizes. His pockets were near empty and unless their fortunes turned would remain so. He considered Jordan's diminishing options: find a wayward West Indies beach, careen the ship on her side, and make repairs while hoping that no English warship came upon them. If they did, their crew could only escape capture by running into a canopy of trees. Gant hated the jungle.

"Nothing to gain by goin' on." Gant's outlook on life was uncomplicated. "This cruise is damned."

A man was either reviled or respected in Gant's eyes. Hell for the likes of Quartus Gant was a likely outcome for a life of violence, so he might as well live while he breathed. Some men could see through clouds covering a bright sun or anticipate a shining sea from fog not yet lifted. To Gant, however, everything was day or night, light or darkness, *aye* or *nay*. There were no opaque shades or middle ground in his world view. In his short life, he had seen too much pain, too little happiness. And so he voted to live to attack vulnerable British ships another day.

HMS Fortitude still loomed in the distance. Each time the carpenter reported the water rising in the bilge, the sails on the near horizon appeared again, gaining. Jordan realized his ship might not survive another night never mind a voyage of two thousand miles to the West Indies.

Thomas Hammond had finished his navigation tables, instructed by the first mate. The boy's role as a rising master was to learn navigation by the stars, how to trim each sail under any condition, and how to properly command a ship's ornery crew. He sat close by the aft companionway hatch hoping to hear some tidbits of the captain's plans. Without the necessary muscle to contribute to the pumping, Thom did not sympathize nor even comprehend the growing collapse of the men around him. He understood, however, their small crew could not pump, sail, and fight the British all at the same time. He heard the arguments drifting from below deck: The captain argued for the ship to stand and fight! *As would I!* thought the boy. The captain remained resolute. Thomas was sadly disappointed when *Rattlesnake* turned down with the northerly, now abaft, and made a course due west for the Massachusetts coast.

After a long sultry day, a lookout from the masthead bellowed to the deck, "Sirs, the British frigate's still gaining!"

Overnight, the crew had taken turns on the pumps. Off duty, the men collapsed anywhere they could find a few hours' sleep. The two officers hoped to lose their pursuers overnight when the sky merged into the ink of the distant sea. The previous sunset gave cause for relief as Gant steered a careful jog back and forth, changing tacks downwind mile after dark mile. Briggs remained reluctant to place stress on the weakened timbers he had carefully examined. He knew, however, if the wind rose while on a starboard tack, the leak would likely open to violent pounding seas. And so, the jog was more like a fractured rhumb line pointing towards the obvious destination: Massachusetts. The British did not need particular insight to guess where the Yankee's were headed.

On the second day of the chase, both the sunrise and British reappeared in the east. By midday the summer sun punished the crew on the open deck devoid of any shade. Every man on watch glistened, exhausted and weak. Briggs handed the brass spyglass back to Gant who reattached it to his waistband. Jordan had retreated to sulk in his cabin, having lost the latest debate with his officers. In the next four hours, he did not even bother to raise his head above the hatch cover or inquire about the chase. Unlike earlier heated, one-way conferences with their captain, Ben observed Gant had become more thoughtful, listening to Briggs' advice, and, by magic, assembling the best of both their minds into a single, practical plan. Ben was sure Gant did not realize he was doing this—the logic of the sea presented itself to Gant as natural as rolling waves slapping the bow in a steady symmetry, as dependable as a moonrise. He was glad he had found so early in his career at sea a man he could trust with his life and his hopes for fortune. *When I build my fleet, I'll need captains to guide—or plunder—if my business includes cold trade.* He believed Gant could help him pursue his dream and together they would share the profits... and the life. But he wondered what ambition, other than embracing the winning side, did Gant hold close? To query Gant was to encroach, however. Gant's eyes continually warned even his new friend: *Keep your distance.*

During the night, the *Rattlesnake's* downwind jig had been less than a full commitment to an untraceable escape. Their course westward merely followed a loose, lazy curlicue. Gant argued with Briggs to sail hard in one direction for twenty miles then sharply change direction. In the morning, they had hoped to find horizons clear of the enemy. Instead Gant listened to Briggs. *The ship, always the damned ship!*

"Easy goes it," Briggs urged continually with quiet reason. "We must survive the night."

Not surprisingly, the British had guessed the Yankee privateer's approximate course toward the safety of New England. By dawn of the third day of the chase, the British remained looming astern and to weather not ten miles away. Either the English captain was lucky or he noted that the *Rattlesnake's* speed had suffered; a brig that had demonstrated such acceleration escaping along the Azores' cliffs could now only meander when she should have sailed three miles for the frigate's two meant a straight, fast course home would be the Yanks' choice. Briggs thought if he could anticipate the frigate's countermoves, he might find the twenty miles of clear sailing they needed to vanish in a night sky. He was sure the cutters followed the frigate hull-down to the east, perhaps spread miles apart to intercept *Rattlesnake's* expected course change in the night, yet close enough to the frigate to join battle even though the thirty-six-gun flagship did not need assistance to subdue a mere twelve-gun brig. Now as the run rose, the British were indeed closing. Worse, the wind continued to wane.

"What do you make of this, Q?" Briggs pointed to the luffing mainsail, absent its billowed shape.

Gant looked aft and skyward. Although another crewman had the wheel, Gant briefly reached over and steered to feel the currents that were pushing the hull sideways; it told him whatever wind remained no longer drove the hull to the west. He stared at the sails and telltales again then studied the sea's calm surface all the way to the clearing horizon. *Rattlesnake* had nearly stopped.

"We'll be driftin' backwards soon." Gant gestured over his shoulder. "And they got more breeze back there."

Surprising everyone, Captain Jordan suddenly appeared on deck. He smiled, clean-shaven and impeccably groomed with a bare head despite the hot mid-Atlantic sun. He wore a resplendent blue coat that complemented his old-style breeches above newly polished boots. Even a snobby hostess would have welcomed him into the finest ball of the winter season. Jordan did not ask his two officers for an update. He observed the rig with care and politely accepted the offered telescope. He studied the frigate astern, *Rattlesnake* now nearly within range of her bow chasers.

"Loose the sweeps from the bulwarks and lower the boats. We shall both sweep and tow the ship." These orders made sense. He continued, his commands crisp, "We shall toss our cannon overboard. Our ballast as well and all stores but water and salt pork for a few more days. They will have us by then or we'll have raised Race Point." Jordan did not ask for advice nor was any given. Briggs and Gant were relieved he no longer entertained a stand-and-fight suicide finale. "And Mr. Briggs, hoist our petticoat stays'l."

This invention of a new *Rattlesnake* crewman, Andy Crowell of Yarmouth in Massachusetts, had never been hoisted before in such urgent conditions. Larger than three mainsails stitched together (in fact the new sail *was* three mainsails stitched together with a spare staysail added to the luff like a giant hot-air balloon), the massive sail hung from the foremast peak with its clew outboard and aft of the bowsprit. Andy, a bright lad of eighteen had devised a patched combination of two lightweight studding sail booms lashed together holding the foot of the petticoat sail outboard secured to the leeward deck. With any wind at all, high and aft, the petticoat sail would help push the ship downwind.

"She looks smart, hoisted like that, Master Crowell." Briggs nodded his approval to Andy. "I should like to hear more about any new sailing concepts you have."

"My father's from Bass River in Yarmouth, sir." The clever young sailor grinned. "He helped me devise this on a fishing trip back from the Nantucket shoals with the southwesterly abaft and our ketch full of spring bass fast needin' a market."

"You're a smart seaman, Andy. We'll see about a bosun's mate commission for you when we get home. I'll mention you to Colonel Hammond myself."

"Thankee, Mr. Briggs. My family sure would appreciate that. My girl too."

"Eh?"

"Yes, we'll be married once I earn enough from these privateer voyages, sir. One more after this cruise should do it. We've waited so very long, sir, and I'm a-burstin'—"

"I bet you are. Mind your luff, Andy. Keep the petticoat flying 'til we're out of range."

With great effort, sailors heaved and rolled the ship's twelve long cannon from their gun ports to gates on each side of the ship. Ten men pushed, pulled, and slid the massive guns into the Atlantic deep. Briggs thought like an accountant: *Each cannon to replace will cost the colonel fifty dollars*—a year's wage for a sailor, and not including its oak carriage, cannon balls, and powder—*Colonel Hammond will be furious*, thought Ben, *although only if his ship escapes. If we're caught*, Briggs admitted to himself, *no one aboard* Rattlesnake *will give a horse's ass what the colonel thinks. We'll either be dangling from a spar or in chains.*

Briggs heaved vigorously alongside the others. The loss of heavy ballast, the lifted power of the petticoat sail, the long sweeps, and the longboats rowing the ship with no small urgency made a moderate difference. Each hour they gained a few hundred yards. Gant studied the captain whose entire being concentrated on all things speed and not a moment's thought to his suffering men. Jordan jerked himself from the rail and issued a new command.

"Wet the sails! Start with the stay'sls, jibs, and stun'sls," Jordan commanded Briggs and Gant. Crewmen climbed aloft and heavy buckets of sea water were hoisted to douse every sail. To the men at their tasks, Jordan roared, "Lads, once clear of these ratbags, there's another bottle for each of you and an extra pouch of silver once we're home free! That's the Captain Jordan way for you, right my lads. But we'll keep that to ourselves, eh?" The men of *Rattlesnake* gave a hearty cheer though exhausted and fearful of a coming disaster if the captain's tactics failed. *An old trick*, Gant grunted muted appreciation.

For an hour, men climbed the rig hoisting heavy buckets, the deck splashed again and again. A wet sail captured whatever wind motion remained aloft. If the sail retained a loose shape—versus a drooping, sloppy mess like a washerwoman's hanging linen—it would transfer its energy to the ship's hull. With the logline dropped over the side, the measure told of their improved speed through the swells as did the steady formation of the stern wake. Soon, they got the answer they prayed for: one extra knot of speed! *Rattlesnake* crept ahead. Gant looked aft at the British frigate losing ground. A few bow cannon shots fired at the privateer fell wide and short, so the enemy gave up. The air stilled. Briggs strode from the bow and spoke to the captain admiring the growing gap twixt hunter and prey.

"Captain, our boatmen near collapse. Ten hours at the sweeps after a night at the pumps."

Even Gant and Briggs had taken a turn pumping and were ready to seize an oar, having lost so many men to fits of fainting and fatigue. Jordan, however, had no thoughts of respite: if men collapsed at oars and pumps, soon they'd be chained, suffering below deck on a British warship. He did not respond to Briggs, nor issued a command for the boats to rest. Instead, he focused forward on a late afternoon cloud, high and dark off the starboard bow, perhaps three miles in the distance. On the surface edge the bright cloud appeared light, sponge-like, its top rising high into the late afternoon heat. A cloud like this most often delivered a torrent of rain, and with rain, wind, thunder, or perhaps a squall. Jordan decided, however, not this particular cloud: The light was wrong—neither angry nor threatening; most likely empty of gathered water, energy ready-to-be-loosed. The cloud served only to blot the setting sun. Nevertheless, a powerful, though short, gust might appear along its front edge, he surmised.

"Steer to that cloud, Crowell." Jordan pointed for his Cape Cod helmsman to witness.

Quick with mathematics and a knack for navigation, Andy Crowell turned the wheel ten degrees starboard, responding simply, "Aye, sir!"

"Briggs. Gant," This time Jordan offered up his thinking in advance, "The frigate watches every maneuver we make. They will think we expect a lift when the sky lets go and a squall arises. We're closer to the disturbance. They will assume we can determine the cloud's power. Too much risen wind, with all our sails hoisted, they'll expect we shall fall over and lose speed. Perhaps they think we'll lose a spar or a sail. However, they know we're a capable ship. They will see us reef in preparation for the blow. So, they will do the same."

Gant nodded. "You want our sails—?"

"Only *loosely* furled. Make it look ragged and rushed, Mr. Gant. Tie release-lines to every buntline. The moment a new breeze catches us, we'll loose them all in unison and trim with urgency. If the frigate copies us..."

Gant understood. A navy frigate with three times as many sails as *Rattlesnake* will take time to reef them in a tight Bristol fashion, secured and ready for the anticipated heavy weather. Jordan counted on it. Briggs also nodded his agreement but worried. He ordered the boats brought aboard doling out extra water and hardtack to the exhausted sailors who staggered onto the deck. He too studied the fast-approaching clouds. If the wind was not as benign as Jordan expected, with full sails they would risk a squall line's high initial gusts and a possible dismasting, ending the chase and their lives as free men. Commands were given to reef *Rattlesnake's* square sails, but not in normal fashion; each had a slip knot securing it with an extra line run to the deck. Her stays'ls received a single reef, making them smaller by a third. Men stood ready with halyards in hand to raise the spanker gaffs and staysails when ordered. Under reduced sail, *Rattlesnake* slowed. They entered the shadow of the tall, dark cloud. Jordan ran from one side of the deck to the other, first staring at the British, then up at the cloud. Minutes earlier, the frigate followed in the same fashion and sail trim—she reefed her courses and topsails and dropped her jibs and staysails. The British captain sailed under reefed topgallants alone anticipating Jordan's squall.

Every man aboard *Rattlesnake* surveyed the sky. The frigate gained. She fired her bow chasers, and the first lethal shot came near alongside and splashed. Gant cursed the obvious: They had fallen back into range! Through the heat of the day, they had out-sailed and out-pulled the English—for this? To drop back *by choice* on a thin hope they might outsmart the enemy? He shot a *'what-in-all-life-is-this?'* expression at Briggs. Jordan wetted his index finger and poked up into the air. He felt air cooling the hairs on his hand and wrist. Pressure was building—another breath, a bit stronger. He saw the first ripple on the water coming from the direction he expected. He told the crew to prepare the braces, yards, and booms pre-trimmed to catch the wind angle he had factored to maximum advantage. Gant and Briggs relayed his commands. Their looks to each other confirmed they were ready to take the ship here and now if necessary if Jordan's crazed antic failed. They must not lose the ship.

"NOW!" Jordan screamed.

Every man acted as instructed: they yanked lines together from all points on the deck and every sail flew open at the exact same moment and grabbed the breeze that rose fast from a whisper to a steady wind. *Rattlesnake* sped ahead, bearing down hard into the wind. Gant saw the shrouds strain on the starboard side as the masts leaned to leeward and the ship leapt from her laggard track. He and another man jumped onto the wheel to lend assistance to the unfortunate helmsman who had not anticipated the force of fresh wind in every sail and nearly lost his grip. Without comment, Jordan looked over his shoulder toward near catastrophe.

In the strengthening wind, *Rattlesnake* quickly left the British ship far behind. The privateer curled around and under the cloud formation and increased speed as she snatched the brunt of the down-spiral draft. The British ship with alacrity, but with no forethought or precision, let her sails fall as fast as her sailors could release them. However, the heavy ship had already lost the initial thrust of wind that had so propelled the lighter *Rattlesnake* as if from a cannon. The frigate wallowed with some sails full, others backwinded, her helm unresponsive. The frigate's headway took many long minutes to regain even a modicum of forward tracking. If she had dropped anchor, she could have hardly sailed slower. *Rattlesnake's* crew watched the danger dissipate like a thundercloud melting into a calm evening's horizon. They marveled at the incompetence of the other ship's captain. *Perhaps*, Briggs considered, *he did not survive our full broadside in Horta*. Within two hours, the disappearing amber sun revealed a clear view seen from both ships' deck—a rippled white-capped horizon, empty of enemies to kill.

Chapter Seven

E mma perched at the edge of Colonel Hammond's expansive feather bed in the master suite with its grand windows overlooking miles of Newport Harbor and the bay beyond.

"If you can hear me, Father, squeeze my hand."

She wiped her cheek with one hand and, with the other, felt for even the tiniest motion from her father's hand. For two days she had sat. The doctor came and went, deducing it was not the colonel's heart.

"It pumps steady and strong, but his brain—a seizure."

Emma demanded that no mention be made of Colonel Hammond's condition; the doctor agreed, given Emma's hope that a quick awakening should soon follow. The preceding days and weeks of the colonel's headaches had been a warning, ringing like a ship's bell, dizziness; yet the colonel had fought it. He had conducted his affairs, though without his typical quick resolutions to problems large or small.

"Your father has been a vigorous man, Emma," the doctor had told her.

It was true. The colonel had indeed enjoyed robust meals of fresh-caught fowl and fish and the best wines. Living in his grand manor he had relished the time spent with his loving children and a revered spouse, until he had erred and Caroline Hammond issued an ultimatum he disregarded. He lost her because of it. That had led to this sickbed.

The doctor stressed to Emma that the brain was a complex machine and recalled patients who had recovered similar collapses. "After recuperating, some of my patients remarked they heard bedside voices, though they themselves were not able to contribute to the conversation."

"So, talk to him?" Emma asked.

"Yes, Miss Hammond," instructed the doctor, "speak to him often. Ask him challenging questions to keep his mind active. The colonel may react better to emotional stimulation with you than from his prodding physician."

Emma therefore spoke to her father often throughout each day: while she changed his sheets, his nightclothes and bedpan; as she attempted to feed him soup or juice from fruit; as she gently sponge-dripped small quantities of water between his lips. He had no fever; he just slept. His hand did not respond to her touch; his lips did not move to any request. His eyes remained closed and dry, even as her wet cheeks caressed his. Emma kept her father's condition a secret, at first to avoid questions where no answers were available. To keep Thomas in the dark, she knew, would prove difficult, however. Perhaps their father might wake before Thomas' return. *Perhaps, meet the ship at the pier, and welcome the officers to Great Hill for a grand dinner of cod, clams, buttered lobster, and cellar-chilled wines.* In the meantime, Emma prepared for the next scheduled meeting of the colonel's partners at Great Hill. *Rattlesnake's* voyage to the English Channel should return the valuable prize monies Mr. Westerly demanded. That was the very worry she suspected had caused her father's collapse. But the ship was weeks from returning, so Emma was her father's last and only defense. In the days following the onset of his illness, she had redoubled her activity in the business: She sent coastal packets to New York, Boston, and Down East past British patrols and blockades. She paid off crews on their return. She ransomed officers taken by the enemy near Halifax, and wrote to the insurance company for claims against the loss of the ships taken and sold by the British. She wrote to her mother, a tight letter that stuck to the facts. She made no mention of the pain and hurt her father had felt when he had read her mother's recent letter informing of her glorious tour of the ancient peninsula with her special friend and escort, a Mr. Pemberley, and his daughter. Mrs. Hammond's sister, Emma's Aunt Helen-Louise Courtney of London and Oxfordshire, was to accompany the troupe. Their tour's itinerary made little impression on her poor father, however. He *knew.*

How could Mother be so cruel, Ceci? In their life together, I was aware they had battles, but in my memory, voices were never raised. We have all we need, why does Mother want more? Why is not a comfortable life of family and home enough for her? Why must passion and adventure play such an important part in Mother's life? I am sorry, my dear, again I prattle. Yes, Father is ill, although our doctor is encouraging. I have by necessity assumed additional responsibilities for our business affairs. Thankfully, I had sat at his elbow in recent years and understand the details of trade. In fact, this morning, I forced the price of New Hampshire lumber to be reduced by twenty cents for one hundred cord by a supplier we have used for many years. The cad!

I sleep poorly. The ospreys sit in a nest by the woods outside my window. Their young have hatched and do nothing but eat. They make a racket every hour and it distresses me even though I marvel at the adults' majestic flight, their soaring, but mostly how they dive from on high and hit the water with their talons coming up with a poor menhaden or alewife to deposit into the hungry beaks of their young who tear it apart as it wriggles in desperation. I feel like that poor fish these days—everyone picking at me, digging into my sides. On my word, I cannot wait for the moment Rattlesnake *appears off the reef and a pilot brings her dockside...*

Quartus Gant and Ebenezer Briggs secreted a few moments alone on deck as the Newport brig slid past Brenton Reef, a nasty outcrop of rock and currents where flocks of terns rested on a white, odorous glaze. Throughout the journey home, Briggs had fretted about what to report at Great Hill to account for the disastrous voyage: the unwise risks taken, the empty hold, the avoidable damage. The two mates had also discussed their lives after the war.

"We can profit famously in lumber and granite from Down East—to Boston and New York, Q," offered Briggs.

"Aye, and face the Cape's outer beaches in every nor'easter?" cautioned Gant, "There's a thousand ships rotting off Wellfleet. The turn southerly is dangerous, especially when lines are frozen and the flood and gales drive you onto the beach."

"Then we'll deliver manufactured goods and raw materials to England and the Continent."

"With them fightin' each other all the time? We'll be taken by their privateers. But listen to us, we sound like old hags. We can make our fortune in the cold trade—"

"You know my thinking," Briggs answered.

"The colonel didn't build his mansion by selling *lumber*! We'll go to him, offer our services to run the trade he don't talk about. We can expand it for him while keepin' our mouths shut," Gant pressed.

Tempted by Gant's suggestion, Briggs replied, "Many die in the cold trade, Q."

"You don't cower at cannon fire! I've seen you rally men as we take a prize!"

"War's different, Q. Cold trade is... a criminal business."

"Aye, and in this *honorable* war we seen lyin', stealin', and murder. We'll see more of it before a treaty. Even so, all this bloodshed ain't kept you hidin' on the beach. Trade—cold or honest—'tis all the same, Ben. Whatever makes up a ship's cargo, makes no difference to me. Cargo's cargo."

The triangular trade, thought Ben with trepidation. For many watches on deck over the past months, Ben considered Gant's words: *Cargo's cargo*. Gant sensed his friend's reticence.

"Smuggling then. Listen, Briggs, at night, when the water's calm and the moon hides our ship, bonfires light the shore in protected coves where our people wait. We send in our boats and return with spirits or goods. We run past any cutter's blockade. Clean and simple."

Smuggling, Ben thought. A time-honored New England occupation for seamen formerly employed in war; a life suited to men hungry for danger, conveying ill-gotten goods across invisible borders, avoiding tariffs while reaching thirsty, ready markets that make a man rich. *But have I the stomach for a smuggler's life?* Briggs wanted to command a fleet of water-borne chariots chasing records across the oceans, not drive floating oxcarts sneaking into shallow coves on moonless nights. He and Gant had agreed on one thing, however: the first thing to do was to buy a fast ship. After, they would decide its cargo: cold trade or honest work. *When the peace comes and markets reopen*, they both could agree, a noted privateersman with a fast ship would have many attractive options.

The gunner interrupted Briggs' conflicted thoughts, "You'll stand with me, Ben. You'll follow the smell of gold."

"You don't understand what you'd be in for, staying with Jordan," replied Ben. "He tells us he's from a wealthy Connecticut family, whale oil he says, but I—"

"You were aboard with Jordan in the spring," Gant pointed out.

"Aye, my first cruise on a privateer, Q."

"He took the war to the English."

"It's not a memory I'm proud to revisit," Briggs answered weakly.

"I must know his way," countered Gant, "if we're to stay alive. Tell me."

Ben Briggs reluctantly agreed. The deck was theirs. He spoke slow and low, "Jordan mentioned a village on the English coast, Porth Diana, was a holding ground for merchantmen loading goods, preparing a run to Dublin then the West Indies. 'Easy pickings,' says he. We stood off a mile and a half and with my spyglass I searched the harbor and the town. I saw no garrison, no corvettes or armed cutters neither. Through the haze I could see two moored ships."

"He planned to cut 'em out?"

"What I thought, Q, but no, Jordan had other ideas. We lowered three boats and filled two with men, the third we towed behind, empty."

"Empty?"

"For what he intended to bring back."

"Go on."

"I was in the first launch and with oars wrapped tight in sail cloth. We slipped into the harbor. We had a still night. A slight mist fell leaving everything wet and our sounds were muffled by the heavy night. Jordan led in the first boat, I the second. He motioned for us to follow his lead and he came up to the first ship moored on a barrel a few hundred feet out. The other was tied to the quay. He held his hand for our boat to sit back as he and a few men climbed aboard the moored ship, a small brig of no more than five hundred tons, high in the water, clearly empty. He went for her anyways. I could hear a scuffle from the cabin. Then a woman's screamin' followed by a clash of metal, a fight that didn't last long. Jordan appeared at the rail and threw a sack which jingled with coin into his boat. Jordan, with blood on his blouse, motioned us to follow him to the quay where he conducted a similar assault on the docked schooner. A middle-aged matron whose bodice was ripped and her hair torn asunder raged at him, a sad sight. The captain struck her in the face with his balled fist and she lay quiet, sobbing. We then made our way down the quay to the village."

"And?" Gant listened.

"It was a small village with a close-packed group of shops along the harbor-way, shut tight in the dark, only a few lamps still lit. A single tavern showed life inside. Jordan brought small casks of gunpowder that he set against the door of the tavern. He crashed a lantern against the door and the building blew up in flames. A moment later, both ships behind us also blew up in flames—Jordan had set similar caches afire in each. The screams from the tavern were a horror I'll not soon forget. Armed old men acting as local militia came running down the hill as burning men escaped the tavern out the back door. Jordan and two crewmen broke into a few stores, grabbed chests and barrels of liquor, and escaped as we set down covering fire from behind three wagons. We lost two boys to enemy muskets but dropped a dozen Englishmen."

"How many perished in the tavern?" Gant asked.

"I cannot say. Jordan meanwhile broke into a lodge near the tavern and came out with a young woman in her nightclothes—screaming, fighting, spitting mad. Two of our men took the woman bodily intending to drag her into our empty longboat."

"Did you make an objection to Captain Jordan's savagery?"

"I was a new officer, an inexperienced privateersman," replied Briggs, "I took orders and at first thought the captain's behavior was according to the ways of war. But when I realized he meant to kidnap the poor lass, I distracted him with a shout about regulars approaching fast from a side path. I fired my musket at a phantom attacker and Jordan followed my lead."

"And the woman?"

"A bald, elderly gentleman grabbed her, his daughter, I assume. He ripped her from our men's grasp as they took to shooting the darkness along with me and the captain. The girl ran screaming back into the house and the man lunged at the captain with his knife. Jordan cried out, 'Damn your King!' as the two met each other, blade against blade. It didn't take long. Captain Jordan is a skilled swordsman."

"And the others?"

"He left our two lads to their dying breaths on the quay. We scurried back to the boats and made the ship with only a few stray musket balls hitting our hulls and one man's shoulder. Once back on board with our loot, the captain ordered a full broadside against what was left of the village. As an offshore breeze took us into the offing, we could see the entire town in flames and both ships burning to their waterlines."

"And you sailed again with this man?" Gant asked not without reason.

"He attacked our enemy... and he, ahh, showed great spirit—"

"Jordan pays his crews extra, don't he? With stolen gold. He binds their tongues?"

"Aye," Briggs answered quietly. "With gold and silver coin he pilfers from Colonel Hammond. Jordan spilled the proceeds of the night's assault onto the foredeck. Each man was given an equal share. He opened oak barrels and every crewman drank his belly-full of English rum and whiskey until most could no longer stand. *Rattlesnake's* crew earned more in that one raid than in six months at sea. The English papers called Jordan a murderous pirate—'*The Curse of the Coast*'."

"He buys loyalty with blood money, Briggs." Gant watched Ben stare out at the Aquidneck Island shore, faintly visible in the sunrise.

"He does. But once the colonel's son joined us on our last cruise, this mayhem ceased. Jordan's returned to attacking only legitimate prizes. For now." Briggs shifted his weight and looked into his friend's eyes. "So, Q, now you know the man."

"Aye, now I know the man."

That same evening *Rattlesnake* made port and tied alongside Hammond Pier—a massive granite structure that reached two hundred feet into Newport's inner harbor. Emma sent word to the docked ship inviting the captain and his two officers to a meal at Great Hill. Briggs and Gant expected to suffer the wrath of *Rattlesnake's* owner. Thomas Hammond looked forward to his father's warm embrace. Emma appeared drained when she welcomed the men as they stepped inside Great Hill's grand foyer in the early evening.

Hooking arms with her brother, she whispered in his ear, "Thom, father sends his love, but is indisposed this evening. I will explain to you once our guests have departed."

"But, Em, I must tell Father about the action—"

"Hush now, Thomas, please, for my sake." Her tired smile coupled with Thom's new-found privateersman pride made his acquiescence feel more like a temporary deferment than a retreat.

Assembled and seated in Great Hill's glistening dining room, the two mates and the boy sat on their hands in a desperate attempt at calm while Captain Jordan remained blithely indifferent to the splendid surroundings. His indifference included Emma's rich-green silk dress, particularly tight to the waist this evening, accenting her shape. Gant and Briggs, however, soaked it all in; after weeks at sea, a table of bountiful, fresh food overseen by a comely young woman was an enticing reprieve.

"Please enjoy your chowder, gentlemen." Setting the tureen on the table, Emma smiled. "We made it especially for your return. It's filled with quahogs and harbor scup, a few tail pieces of the lobsters the cook picked from the beach, potatoes fried in hog's fat and swirling in fresh milk from Great Hill's dairy."

"And Emma's special touch," Thom added, "Fresh dillweed from our mother's garden."

"It distinguishes your marvelous dish..." injected Jordan, rising suddenly from his daze, "...from the workman's runny soup one might find in a Northside tavern."

Captain Jordan leaned toward Gant who ignored the taunt. Instead, Gant admired the hearty chunks of bacon adrift in a fine porcelain bowl, luxuries he had never enjoyed as a child. The dill, however, smelled of grass from a field, the sort of pasture. He ate gratefully. No longer out hundreds of leagues at sea, he could smell the young woman's sweet perfume, watch her tongue wetting her lips each time she took a gentle breath. He savored her proximity.

Seated at the head of the colonel's long dining table, Jordan appreciated the scene: his officers to his left, the family to his right, everyone attending but the owner. He accepted Emma's explanation for the colonel's absence. Today Jordan could avoid explaining why the ship had returned empty, her hull breached, her valuable cannon over the sides. Relieved by this delay, he focused on the girl who was talking so *very* fast. He sat quiet, idly admiring her dancing eyes.

"Are you *listening* to me, Captain Jordan?" Emma's voice broke Jordan's lazy train. "Or have I caught you exhausted from your recent exertions?" Jordan realized she had been speaking to *him*. Answers were required. She asked detailed questions about the voyage, about his management of the ship's business... *odd, coming from a girl...* "I suppose cannon blasts can injure one's hearing," remarked Emma to the officers, concerned Captain Jordan did not provide ready answers. She pressed him on many fronts about the voyage. *Why has he not prepared a response?* Emma wondered. *I'm asking for a simple report, not a great philosophical debate!*

Hoping to enlighten his sister and defend his captain, Thomas offered, "Em, the ship nearly sank! If not for Mr. Gant and Mr. Briggs' quick action getting her into our new Boston dry dock—"

"The expensive pier our men shut tight with lumber and then pump water in and out manually?"

"Aye, Em. Without it, *Rattlesnake* would have sunk at the pier!"

"Apparently, you saved the ship," replied Emma nodding to Gant and Briggs. "I thank you. But do I understand she remains grievously damaged below the water line?" Again, Emma turned her gaze to the captain. "What happened, Captain?"

The privateersmen around the table inspected their bowls, though after a tense interlude Thomas spoke again. "Em, the action was marvelous, our captain, he—"

"Thomas," Emma cut him off, "Your captain can speak for himself."

"But Em, he nearly defeated an entire enemy squadron! Let me tell you the high points!"

High points? thought Gant with a raised eyebrow to Briggs. *This'll be rich.*

"Captain Jordan?" Emma asked, no longer hiding her annoyance. "I am not asking for fanciful tales of warm action fought bravely, only why *my* ship has returned without spoils?"

At length, Emma realized Captain Jordan had no inclination to bestow his account to a young woman standing in for the ship-owner. Quiet as a tomb, Jordan continued to nurse his chowder, his eyes cast downward. *The boy's whimsy might work in my favor with the girl,* he thought. The colonel, however, would be a different reckoning. Jordan saved his dry powder.

Emma turned to her brother. "So *you* tell us, Thomas," she said dryly.

"We charged into port at Pico. A port with two British ships, large and powerful Indiamen."

"You took two ships?" Emma interrupted hopefully.

"Not exactly, Em. They made to escape."

"Does Thomas describe the action as you saw it, Cap—?" Emma doubted Jordan had even heard Thomas. She turned to the first mate. "Mr. Briggs?" Her look was hopeful, though not entirely friendly.

"Aye, Miss Hammond," Briggs answered truthfully without embellishment. "We came upon two Indiamen. They sailed off. We pursued." He looked at Jordan, hoping the captain would assume the narrative before they became ensnared in a tall tale absent a manly retreat.

Instead, Thomas continued the narrative, "Captain Jordan brought us alongside the nearest ship. He was first to board, Sister! He ran their sailing master through with his sword—"

"Did he not ask for their surrender first, Thomas?"

"I could not see the fight actually, only the body lying on the deck," answered Thom, "Captain Jordan made sure he did not rise."

Gant winced. He remembered the unarmed English officer with his hands and arms in the air as Captain Jordan had lunged with fire in his eyes. The gunner found it hard to look at the murderous fool sitting at the table's head, loudly slurping in a chunk of quahog.

"Continue. If any of you wish to contribute to my brother's... *recollection*." Emma's scorn suggested "fiction" though she did not suffer from the skeptical disposition of one whose intuition rushed ahead of a story.

"It was a clear, decisive boarding, Miss Hammond," Briggs spoke up, attempting to save the ship's collapsing reputation. "Our men were brave. Mr. Gant was first over the rail."

"I thought Thomas said Captain Jordan was first over the rail?"

Thom broke in, "And then he ordered a volley of musket fire that raked their deck and before you could say *two shakes*, Captain Jordan took the helm and spun the wheel to leeward. The first ship came up hard against the second and they crashed into each other! Captain

Jordan with a score of men leapt over and secured the second ship killing several enemy fighters..."

Again, Emma looked to Brigg—the only man not inspecting the scalloped edges of the fried potatoes floating in warmed cream.

"We lost none of our men—a complete victory, Miss," Briggs struggled to recount truth, "Only Mr. Gant suffered a wound."

"You are injured, sir?" Emma turned her entire attention to Quartus Gant for the first time.

Caught in her luminous gaze, Gant sat flummoxed. His wounded shoulder wrapped tight to his chest was now curiously pounding. Emma had worked hard to command the table, to ask the right questions—and fend off her brother's fantastic recollections—to get the truth. Was *Rattlesnake* a ship of fools or the most volatile one hundred twenty feet of havoc on the Atlantic Ocean?

"Mr. Gant fell on the enemy deck," Briggs interjected since he no longer trusted Thomas' telling. "An English sailor with a knife swiped at Mr. Gant's shoulder, jumped on his stomach, and was about to slit his throat when our captain shot him."

And then, I beat him dead, Gant recollected to himself.

Emma looked at Gant with a bright smile, her first genuine expression of pleasure during the awkward meal. He met her gaze straight-on and held it tight. He nodded without further expression of any kind, basking in her full attention, her eyes warming him like a mid-morning burst of sun.

"Thanks to our captain, Mr. Gant is alive!" Thomas declared.

"Your shoulder, Mr. Gant?"

"Cook sewed me up, Miss. Good as new."

"I congratulate you, sir. Well done." She turned her smile to Jordan who remained eyes-down. *Perhaps this will raise him from his stupor.* "We must patch our injured men and feed them well, Captain Jordan. Brave men like Mr. Gant are hard to find."

With a spark of light in her eyes, she turned her full gaze back to Gant. His eyes in response murmured, *I am glad I'm alive so I can look upon your lovely face once again.* Emma stifled a quiet gasp recognizing the gunner's intensity, and reluctantly withdrew her gaze.

For an hour or more, as additional courses graced the table, Thomas chewed fast while recounting the battle with meticulous, though exaggerated detail: escape (by mere inches), cliffs (one thousand feet high!), narrow channels (with jagged rocks sharp as a razor), a grounding (both masts swinging wildly)—each danger skillfully minimized by their captain's clever maneuvers. The account capped off with a broadside that mauled a powerful British man-of-war! And after, *Rattlesnake* sailed clean-away. Her brother described a great chase and yet another clever escape (he himself had helped pump!). Was there ever a more determined sailing pursuit in this war when at last *Rattlesnake* found an empty horizon.

"*Rattlesnake* didn't suffer any damage we can't repair, Em," Thom added.

"I am happy you all returned safely," she forced herself to say kindly, but then thought of her Providence bankers. *Rattlesnake has not delivered gold, no captured prizes to be sold, no relief to our pressing demands,* Emma complained to herself, the only one present who understood her father's suffocating burdens. *No wonder the poor man collapsed.* This cruise had been her father's best hope. *What now?* Emma recognized she must repair and provision the ship and send it back to sea immediately. Mr. Westerly expected an accounting and after today's new information it would take all her guile to hide the events of the disastrous voyage. The ship must be away before Westerly confronted her again with his insidious grinning face. She had little time, her father no help. Which of these men at her table could she trust with the Hammonds' destiny? She realized from their chance meeting weeks earlier on the cliff that although Mr. Gant spoke with few, often sharp-tongued words, he spoke true. She might not like what he said, but she could act on his words.

"Mr. Gant. My father's ship?"

"Broke two ribs, Miss. Five starboard planks gotta come off. Re-planking can be done in a few days. The ribs and knees though... I don't know..."

Gant looked to Jordan for help. *Nothing.* The captain, deep in his bowl, floated someplace far away. Briggs rescued the captain.

"I know a master carpenter in Rochester, Miss," Briggs interjected, "I'll send word with a rider tonight and he can get here with his tools and in three days we can replace the ribs. The supporting knees must be inspected—"

"Replaced? Or cut-in?" Gant asked Briggs.

"We don't have much time," his friend answered.

"She must withstand firing a full broadside," stated Gant, thinking ahead. He wanted the ribs out, but could live with half-measures. *Next time Jordan will likely sink the ship, so what's the difference?*

"Aye…" To everyone's surprise, Captain Jordan suddenly spoke, his energy recharged, "We'll fire our broadside and sink them! We'll sink them all! Replace the entire ribs, Mr. Gant, and I want impenetrable Georgia live-oak for the knees. We shall not lose her to a puny twelve-pounder while I command." Wherever Jordan had been, he now returned. Everyone stared at a man resurrected: His face transformed, stoic and firm as marble, his drooped features somehow raised from lost to total command. *Rattlesnake's* captain smiled graciously, as if his silence during Emma's inquisition had never occurred. "We have the best privateer brig in America, and I intend to set her loose. My dear Miss Hammond, turn your best men to her refit and upon my soul, these fine men and I shall return to you so many prizes, this harbor will proclaim our victories with wild admiration! You have my honor-bound pledge." Incredibly, he bowed his head.

Here was the man Emma needed! At last!

Thomas sat transfixed. Holding his fork and knife upright like two lances at a medieval joust, he slapped the table, applauding the man he would follow to the gates of Hell. *My God,* thought Ben Briggs, *the captain has captured the moment.* Emma sat back, relieved. Despite the disastrous cruise to the Azores, she decided she would give this captain another command. She smiled broadly at Jordan who accepted it with the grace of a knight astride an armored mount.

"We agree gentlemen, back to sea!" Emma said with cheer. "To Captain Jordan and *Rattlesnake*! I toast you shall find fair winds and prizes. I thank you from my heart!"

Emma smiled at the room. All but one smiled back: Quartus Gant. Frowning, he almost spoke his mind. Earlier in the day he had convinced Briggs that Captain Jordan was not particularly smart. Gant reconsidered as the table erupted in cheers echoing the clinks of crystal glasses of port. *This girl will do whatever Jordan asks. And he'll probably get us all killed.*

Ceci, you are wrong, my dear. I have absolute faith in our Captain. He is not what you suspect—all seamen are not knaves. I do not believe you are unkind by recounting what your brother told you about our Captain's visit to Mystic last summer. Cousin Alfred must be mistaken. I am sorry for the poor girl's unfortunate condition, but Captain Jordan could not have committed his heart to me while in the arms of another woman. I believe him. I am not a fool, Ceci, even though one of our other officers had a grim look on his face when I agreed to sponsor another cruise. I reminded the table that my father has full confidence in our Captain... I am with my father each day. I know his mind and though he could not meet with your father, everything is fine, Ceci! Please assure my Aunt and Uncle the Newport Hammonds are as well as can be during these unsettling times. We will meet you soon for a grand bake on our beach with all the fruits of the sea for us to enjoy together!

Emma Hammond would not be enjoying fruit or anything else unless one of her ships returned soon with the stolen cargoes her father needed. Yesterday's visit with Mr. Westerly upset her so much her stomach had prevented a single bite. Westerly had discovered, wandering around their shipyard busy with chatty workers, that *Rattlesnake* received an expensive refit after a calamitous Atlantic cruise. The banker probed Emma for explanations. She answered him true. She explained the cost of eluding not one but three Royal Navy warships, noting the painful expense to replace her twelve eighteen-pound cannon. Such weapons of heavy iron were hard to come by during a war where access to British foundries had been severed. Emma emphasized that she was, however, thankful to report that a ship her father had commissioned recently—one of the few whose course or destination Emma had not been privy to—was returning presently with profits expected to be sufficient to reset Hammond finances. One returning ship would save her this month while another schooner was leaving on the evening tide. She explained to Mr. Westerly it was the best she could manage. His slender grin above his ample girth gave her the distinct impression he was neither happy with her account nor had any solutions to offer. He left Great Hill in his carriage, forgetting to tip his hat.

Emma held to only a glimmer of hope as she sat by her father's bed that evening. "Squeeze my hand, dear Father. Can you hear me? Please?"

Privateer

Chapter Eight

A few days after her encounter with Mr. Westerly, as *Rattlesnake* bent new sails and hoisted cannon commandeered from other Hammond ships onto her deck, from her father's office Emma watched a black topsail schooner catch the flood tide and enter Newport's inner harbor. Silent crewmen threw lines onto the Hammond Pier where waiting dock-men secured the ship on the wooden pier's iron cleats. Emma faintly remembered this ship—a schooner not particularly fast, elegant, or noteworthy. Her father often sent it to gather shipments of nails, coal, lumber, or the odd cargo of mixed manufactured goods, she believed. Colonel Hammond had conveyed nothing to his daughter about this most recent voyage. She knew neither where the ship had gone nor what cargo she had carried. Emma waited for the sailing master to appear with his manifest and profits. She expected a warm smile and a tip of his cap. *Curious*, she wondered, *why is this ship not listed on the office's master manifest?* Checking a private journal in her father's locked desk, Emma discovered that the schooner had disembarked nine weeks earlier with a cargo of molasses bound for an unnamed port. There was no other information noted, only the ship's name: *Windslayer*. Her captain was a Mr. George McManus. Emma decided she would go dockside and meet this Captain McManus.

Clapping steadily down the wooden stairs, she strode briskly from Hammond and Company and, rounding the building, confidently approached the pier. But before she arrived within three dozen yards of the schooner, she noticed an uncomfortable stillness around her. Among the workers, the usual dock-side activity had stopped.

Stevedores who typically lugged stores and cargo stood aside like cats warily watching a hungry hound. Carrying sea bags, *Windslayer's* crewmen walked briskly down the boarding plank and melted into the morning without the usual friendly farewells to each other. As she drew closer, Emma's nose detected unspoken truth: An overpowering stench arose from the ship. *Windslayer* seemed an apt name; her latest cargo left a reek that hung about the ship. The foul odor was made worse with no breeze to freshen the morning. Emma's discomfort increasing, she gagged, breathing with difficulty. From her quarterdeck, *Windslayer's* captain saw the smartly dressed young woman approach his ship. Captain McManus presumed she came for him. He grabbed his personal satchel and instructed a deckhand to ship his chest to an up-island lodge. McManus placed the ship's cargo manifest into his satchel and picked up a heavy sack with the monies owed Hammond and Company. On the manifest, he had carefully listed numbers—not descriptions or losses or even a beginning count—only the stark quantity of cargo delivered and sold. Per his owner's instructions, he did not record the port of delivery. The count of owed coin in the sack was correct. He had taken out his cut, reflecting on the words that would end his career with Hammond and Company. Captain McManus had returned *Windslayer* safely to Newport from which she had three months earlier disembarked. She had skirted the British blockade that would likely have sunk her, sending him to Mill Prison. This was the most Captain McManus could say for the voyage. Were *Windslayer* his own vessel, he might have scuttled her in deep water off Block Island and ridden to shore in her longboat. But the schooner belonged to Hammond, an owner he had sailed for the past dozen years. But never again.

"Captain McManus?" Emma greeted the seasoned captain tentatively.

Her father had once told her he did not care for the man, though McManus always returned his ship. She remembered a comment her father had made months earlier coupling McManus' name with straw. *A short straw*, Emma recalled.

"Aye, Miss Hammond. I've seen your portrait in the colonel's office. Can I speak to him?"

"He is ill, Captain. I have come for your manifest and our return."

McManus was painfully familiar with illness. He thought of the ship's owner in a comfortable bed in his great manse with surgeons' herbs and medicines by his side. On *Windslayer*, there were no curative measures—only the finality of sliding through an outboard gate. Silently, Captain McManus followed the girl to the Hammond office, a building at the end of the pier. Along the quay, she led the way. His tense stare indicated he would likely refuse any hospitality she might offer so she made none—not biscuits, not tea, nor strong drink—though she knew he must want it very much.

She peeked into the canvas bag he handed her: It was heavy. She whistled softly to herself and set the bag on her father's desk.

"You return a healthy profit, sir. We thank you."

He did not accept her thanks, comment on her good looks, nor ask to sit. He stared at her with empty eyes. From the moment they met, McManus' awkwardness was not something she could assign to shyness (she understood she looked fair and was used to the lingering gazes from men long at sea). Nor was their awkward discourse due to the beginning stage of an argument; they had no tense business discussion about terms or money before them. His grey, dull eyes told her something else, a look she had never seen before. He projected more than displeasure, unhappiness, or even severe disappointment.

He *hated* her.

A man she had never met, now ashore for the first time after three months in one of her father's ships, whose voyage was curiously absent of all the usual detail—and he *hated* her? *How strange! Does he hate Father, too?* She must make herself understand. One man might hate another for past fights or the memory of an injury long suffered. *But what have I done?* Then she remembered: He had been living on that ship with its foul stench. A stench uncannily... human.

"You have ya' gold, Miss. Me'n m'boys will be off now."

She had questions, so many questions but all she could utter was normal discourse.

"Are you available for your next voyage, sir?"

"Nay, I think not, Miss. Not for double. Your father trades the triangular. I've sailed the last time for him. The triangle is the devil's trade, Miss. I hope you can sleep. Bloody hell knows I cannot."

He turned on her and stiffly left the office not bothering to close the door. Stunned, she stared at the bag of gold and silver coin. She had heard about the nefarious triangular trade, but never did its unfathomable cruelty land in her lap until this moment. Before, she had been aware it existed; now, more than involved, she was responsible. Criminally, sinfully she knew, *I stand at the rotten root of all that is evil.*

A sudden sharp breeze blew the truth of *Windslayer* indoors through her fine lace and tight-woven fabrics draped at the windows. The reek and misery of the voyage filled her office. She slammed the window shut and picked up the heavy canvas bag of gold. The coin itself reeked, as well. She cried and threw the bag to the floor where it split open, spilling dollar coins like pebbles rushing to shore on a winter's wave.

Before dawn the next morning, Emma hired idle men drinking in the tavern to tow *Windslayer* away before the town's notice rose further. She wrote terse instructions coupled with coins she hoped would be enough.

"Take this ship to Block Island or Cuttyhunk to cleanse the decks and hold. Rip out all deck or cargo deck planking retaining any remaining foul smell."

She read it to three shore-siders whom she detained dockside. Having drunk their last pay, they eagerly undertook her assignment. She also decided, on her own authority, that this ship would never return to Newport.

"Paint its topsides white! Paint its new name bright and bold on the stern."

"What's her name to be, Miss?"

"*Atoned.*"

Through steamy days and nights under torches, repairs were made to *Rattlesnake's* hull. After two weeks, she refloated. Tied snug at the far end of Hammond Pier, dockworkers loaded stores, water, hardtack biscuit, salted cod, and beef. A rough privateering crew came aboard. Provisioning for sea the same day *Windslayer* had docked, *Rattlesnake* was well-armed to attack ships unable to defend themselves. At the pier, a sleepless Emma still could not put Captain McManus' hatred and *Windslayer* out of her thoughts. Walking in her direction, she noticed *Rattlesnake's* second mate.

"Mr. Gant?"

"G'day, Miss."

He looked over, and for a moment Emma thought she detected a hint of a smile forming on his lips.

"I expect you'll sail with the tide?"

"We will, Miss."

"Ah, Mr. Gant, you know I am learning through trial and error the ways of our 'gamesters' hope' as my father calls privateering. And as Father remains... you understand, ill disposed... I would be in your debt if you could explain some things for me."

Gant nodded reluctantly. *Why bother striking up a conversation with a woman that could not lead to a warm bed?*

"This trade, Mr. Gant...?" Emma shrugged in the direction of *Windslayer's* recent brief berth. "How are the legs of the triangular trade... conducted?"

"Investors in this State are a squeamish lot, Miss." Gant had noticed her slave ship arrive and quickly depart. He set down his heavy canvas sea bag. The girl was too young to understand that sordid world, yet too mature to remain so blithely oblivious. "They like their gold, but they don't like it when a slaver ranks the port like your *Windslayer*. Rich men make an initial investment, a clean one they claim over cigars and brandy. They buy rum from local distilleries here in Newport town. Their ships full of fine New England liquors run past the British patrols on a moonless night, make the Atlantic passage and sell the rum to the thirsty English or Dutch. Their captains set aside thirty percent of the profits. They sail south, buy cargo on the West African coast, and return to the Indies along what is called the *middle passage*."

"The *middle passage*, Mr. Gant? Near Bermuda?"

He stifled an impulse to laugh. "Nay, it's a passage of steady trade winds between the West Coast of Africa and the West Indies, Miss. In Africa the slavers buy human cargo, men, women, and a few healthy young'ns, natives captured in tribal wars and sold to the beach-traders. Slaver captains pack'em tight below deck, stack'em like logs of wood. The ship sails hard and fast along the middle passage for the West Indies where the cane fields suffer from a want of willing workers. There, *unwilling* workers are found a place."

"Fast ships are therefore required for this trade?"

"Aye, Miss."

"To get their passengers transported quickly, I assume, for a minimum of discomfort?"

Gant stood numb and looked at Emma's striking green eyes.

"To deliver them quick-like before they're all dead, Miss." Gant waited for Emma's reaction. He yearned to see her face awaken to the reality of the stink that still wafted above the piers. She covered her face with her long fingers enveloped in delicate, dark gloves. Gant enjoyed her distress. He displayed his anger of her utter ignorance with a cold lesson. "Slave cargo sold is pure profit." Quartus Gant's eyes narrowed as a slender rope, "More fortunes're made from triangular trade than anything this side of lyin' in wait for a Spanish treasure fleet."

"Go on?"

There it is! Gant realized, *The heart of this young woman runs cold but comes alive with the prospect of gold.*

"When they unload Africans still breathing and sell them to the Island's sugar cane plantations, the initial profit from the rum doubles. The ships emptied of slaves then load raw cane sugar, cotton, or molasses, and carry it back to New England for a third tidy windfall. The locals 'round here distill rum from the 'cane and the triangular trade starts all over. One ship, one voyage, three fat profits. A clever arrangement, Miss, the triangular trade."

Emma said nothing.

Gant sensed she wanted more, more information, more of everything. He continued, "Our fine New England Christians, our upstanding ship owners who pay the crews and make the initial unsoiled investments, they never see the misery of the middle passage, Miss. They don't see the heartless slave markets when men and women are displayed naked, like slabs of beef. They don't feel the heat and petulance of the cane fields. They have their profits and buy silk dresses for their womenfolk and build fine homes along the shore. They plow their slaving profits into building new ships, like yours, Miss."

Gant noticed the girl had steeled. Her eyes revealed she was devoid of remorse. Even he had been repulsed on his first slave voyage, although he numbed to the suffering after the first week with the help of the bottle. He watched the girl's perfect mouth open. But Emma held back what she was about to say.

To hell with her cool detachment—Gant could not resist a final jab, "Most slavers're more careful than your father. Nay, most owners clean their returning rigs bright-like before they tie-up in home ports." Cold silence crept into the space between them. Masking his delight, Gant continued, "The genteel folks living up North don't want to smell the stink of the middle passage. They don't want to know the truth."

Emma took a deep breath and two steps back. "Good day, Mr. Gant. You answered my questions. Though I don't mind saying, I find fault with your tone. Your accusations of my father and our family." His biting comments shook her to her heels, shoving away any lingering thoughts of warm, intense looks previously shared between them. "I might ask myself why you should be honored with a new commission aboard our ship. But I shall let it pass. For now."

The turned floodtide left precious little time for extended goodbyes. Emma ignored the gunner and gathered her beloved brother in a long embrace. Thomas promised to obey her many requests: to stay below when cannon fired, no going aloft in a gale.

"You're not an officer, Thom. You have much to learn. Your education is the only reason father allowed you to go on board—to watch and learn. And the only reason I countenance his wishes while he convalesces."

"Why don't you let me see him, Em? Is he ugly? Disfigured? I've seen worse—"

"He asks this. I am sorry, Thom. He so misses you, and he has told me so many, many times. I know his door remains locked, but Thom I must confide in you—our father has enemies. You are best far away. When you return with gold, he will be mighty pleased."

Thomas listened, not satisfied. "Have you heard from Mother? Why doesn't she come home to care for him?"

"I will not lie. She is..." Emma searched for the right term a twelve-year-old boy might understand. A *free bird*? Too romantic. *Spirited*? No. *Fanciful*? Never. *Wayward*? Too dramatic. *Loose and despicable*? Accurate, though not appropriate for a boy to hear of his mother. "Mother is *lost*, Thomas. So, my dearest, you must be strong for us, for Father and I, until she returns to us. I shall keep you close to my heart. Think of me often? Off you go."

The boy skipped up the boarding plank, waving to his mates, joyful for his life and ready for the horizons and the adventures beyond. Emma caught sight of Gant staring at her from the deck. He raised his hand in a muted goodbye, an attempt at apology. He withdrew when she did not acknowledge him; she thought it one of the saddest farewells she had ever seen. She surveyed *Rattlesnake's* quarterdeck for Captain Jordan. Waving, she smiled brightly at him. He looked past her, however, perturbed, as if he watched a threat appearing on the horizon. She wondered if her captain would fulfill his pledge and someday sail her to the lands of her imagination, to places of ancient cities and lost islands. Waving at him with giddy enthusiasm, she persisted until he belatedly acknowledged her presence and walked slowly down the gangway to the pier. Absently, he took her offered hand.

"Good morning, Miss Hammond." His former warmth curiously missing when he spoke.

Emma rose to her full stature. "Do manage to bring our ship home with all her ribs this time, Captain Jordan?" His eyes twitched and he stammered fragments of a haphazard reply. She noted he seemed a bit absent again and so changed tacks. "I had a locksmith build a new magazine lock. Here is a brass plate key to match the old iron key. The gunner told me the old one is cracked, liable to break-off in the keyhole."

"Thank you, Miss."

"Captain. I did not want my brother to ship with you, yet I leave him in your hands. I charge you… you must keep him safe!" Jordan did not respond in the usual confident manner she had expected. She pressed, "Captain, if an American privateer is captured in this war… what becomes of her people?"

"I assure you, Miss Hammond, it will not come to that."

"I understand, but please accommodate my curiosity."

"The able-body seamen will be given a choice of impressment into Royal Navy service or thrown into Mill Prison. Most accept the former, though my hearty lads would unlikely submit to such a tawdry degradation."

"What of her officers?"

"Paroled if they were fortunate, arrested otherwise until a ransom is paid. If caught without a *letter of marque*, however, their fate is most unhealthy."

"A cabin boy?"

"Gone along with the crew. Though I've heard of situations involving a trade between captains."

"Go on," insisted Emma, breathing faster.

"An officer's freedom surrendered for the lad might be arranged."

"And the boy?"

"Sent home, if the commanding officers were both honorable."

"And what would happen to the arrested officer?"

"Ransom paid by the owner would bring him home in due time."

"I see. Thank you, Captain."

"I do not expect such a tragic occurrence."

"But you must assure me you will dedicate your attention to Thom's well-being!"

Cornelius Jordan tipped his cap and whiffed a sort of kiss onto her outstretched hand. As sudden as a thieving gull, he climbed back aboard.

Inside, Emma felt empty. Thankfully, Ben Briggs approached from the wharf-side street. She wished he had some of the captain's flair or the gunner's intensity.

"Mr. Briggs." Although she called him "Mr. Briggs" she thought of him more as "Ben"—a straightforward name, appropriate for a man who played it straight. Even so, she remained ambivalent about him.

"Miss Hammond, good morning. Thank you for seeing us away."

"Yes, yes, and please call me Emma. A word?" She motioned to a quiet side of the pier.

"Miss?"

"You and Mr. Gant share a low opinion of our captain."

"I'm a loyal officer, Miss."

"Shush, please, we have little time. I told Mr. Gant he was wrong to be concerned about the captain's judgment—"

"Q *said* this?"

"Perhaps not his precise words, though I am a keen reader of a man's meaning. I can tell he's worried. He fears no man, but has ill feelings about this voyage." *He has also revealed his ill feelings about me and my kind*, she thought. "Mr. Gant will not commit to a declaration of any sort, of course, other than a professional, affected loyalty to Captain Jordan. I nevertheless got from him what I needed. I don't expect you to confess more, but promise me one thing..."

"Miss...?"

"Thomas. Protect him, Ben."

"I shall."

"I also asked Captain Jordan to promise, no matter what happens, to do everything in his power to bring our ship home. My father and I cannot afford to lose *Rattlesnake*." Emma stood straight, yet unsure if she could say the rest. She looked at the deck and heard laughter from a crowd of young men ready for adventure. By now, she owned Ben Briggs' attention, the intelligence she hoped for; his future decisions must be her ally. "In two recent voyages, we have almost lost the ship. If *Rattlesnake* is captured, I understand the enemy will arrest her officers."

"That is so," Ben answered, curious about her line of questioning as much as her tentative tone so uncharacteristic of her.

"I need Thomas returned home, safe and without wounds. Can you see to it that if the ship is taken through some unfortunate event, that one of our officer's freedom is forfeited in such a manner as to provide passage home for Thom?"

"An officer? We only have three, Miss."

"I understand. But Captain Jordan will not fare well in British confinement and I have plans for you, here, at my side, when this war is over. You both must come home."

"Q?"

"I know he is your friend, but he is a strong man, more capable than most men of surviving temporary confinement. I don't want to lose any of my people, of course, but my heart will surely break if I learn I have lost my ship and my brother!"

"But Q is a good privateersman, my friend as you said, Miss. I cannot in good faith—"

"Speak of this to Captain Jordan in the privacy of his cabin. Let him make the decision. Arrange a trade or whatever opposing ship captains can arrange between them. Do whatever you must do to bring Thom home to me!" Emma's eyes welled and although it was not intentional, she could tell from the look on Ben's face he was not buying it. "I fear this captain will put you all in harm's way." She quickly added.

"That is our calling, Miss, as privateersmen."

"I understand, and I thank you for your... bravery. But sometimes sacrifices must be made. Thom is the only family I have left."

"Is the captain aware of your *suggestion*?"

"He explained to me how a trade, in lieu of parole, might be accomplished."

"I see. Let us pray it does not come to that. I would not wish Mill Prison on any man or boy in this world. You don't understand what you are asking."

A trade? thought Briggs, stunned. An officer for a cabin boy? He knew that arrested privateer officers were often punished cruelly by the British, charged with serious crimes against the Crown, summarily hanged as pirates. Some were imprisoned in depraved floating hulks or dank Plymouth jails. Only the most fortunate privateersmen, even those officers surrendering official *letters of marque*, were granted parole. Most imprisoned privateersmen—returned for ransom paid—appeared as beaten skeletons, barely alive. *If* they returned.

"I am confident the situation will never arise," added Emma, afraid she had overstepped. "You are a Hammond man. My father depends on you. I can confide, Ben, your future with us is very promising. Keep my brother safe. Return with him and our ship. I implore you. And I'll be waiting." Emma reached out to take Ben's hand in hers, but he pulled away, walking briskly toward the gangplank. She caught up with him.

He stopped, turned back, and asked her angrily, "What other secrets have you arranged, Miss Hammond?"

A fair question, she thought. "Good day, Mr. Briggs. Be blessed with fair winds."

Book Two

Betrayed

Privateer

Chapter Nine

...is that not what you wanted since adolescence, Ceci? To wed a man of means like Mr. Broussard? A man of wealth, with children, yes, from his marriage to that fair young Gould woman who died so young. He is still capable of love, is he not? And he will provide. On that count, you can be sure, given her fortune left to him upon her passing. The comforts you have enjoyed these nineteen years, you will enjoy with Mr. Broussard and his little ones. You have confided in me often how your skin bristles by your father's heavy hand directing your education, manners, dress, and speech. Now you have succeeded and captured the heart of a good and capable man. You complain of his lack of adventure, and of your yearning for love and passion, but you cannot have it all, my dear, none of us can.

Even the wife of a merchant with shops along the Connecticut shore can live quite well without adventure or romance. You and I enjoy luxuries desired by every woman—though our indulgences come with a cost. We sit on our divans in our fine silks imported from Canton, our brocades and whalebone corsets... and look out to sea... Who will materialize beyond the horizon? Who will return to us and love us? Will he be kind?

Emma lay her pen to the table, recalling Captain Jordan climb the gangway to his ship. *My ship!*—she corrected herself. *Why have I trouble making that distinction?* He had been so abysmally rude at her table. At the dock, she had needled him, expecting at least a small, wry smile. Then, without warning, his eyes had sparked with life and profound sincerity. *Is the captain playing me?* She had returned him to the command of *Rattlesnake*——*her* choice now—not her father's. The colonel had always favored someone more dependable—Mr. Briggs was one possibility—for future command. *Or perhaps we should see what our new second mate can accomplish?* The night before her father fell ill, after her confounding encounter with Gant by the stable path, she had proposed her father might consider Mr. Gant as a shipmaster. Emma recalled Colonel Hammond's quiet admonition:

"The Gant kin are north-side people, Em—a hard-working clan. Brutal, fighting men. Their boys grow fast, offshore by seven or eight years if a packet will take them for cabin boys or a man-of-war needing powder monkeys. They don't learn to read Cicero, if they read at all. Most Gants eventually become smugglers. They don't farm or set up homesteads. They do marry, though. They take wives." He paused. "They think anything worth having must be *taken*. To them life is one battle after another... I knew the old man. We fought in the mud in Brooklyn and New Jersey in the Independence War. Over many long winter weeks, we survived by stealing shoes off frozen dead men and sucking the hides of butchered cattle, horses, and dogs. And whenever I see Quartus Gant's face, I see a mean courage. T'was the same in his father. There is a great deal to admire in such men, but there is also much to fear. I intend to watch Young Gant closely and aim his anger against our enemies. That is what we do, Emma—we corral stallions like the Gants, harness them, drive them, and reward them."

She recalled what had brought on her father's lecture—her innocent comment that if she did not find a suitably wealthy husband, she might succumb to the earthy gunner instead. The colonel had looked at her severely, rubbed his temples, then poured an ample glass of brandy before he added, "Mr. Gant's eyes don't smile. He never reveals his thinking, Emma. And he relishes his hardness. He'll marry a country girl to warm his bed on the few nights each month he returns from sea with bloody trousers to mend and wounds to stitch. He'll raise little fighters, brave lads, and we shall hire them too. That is not a bad thing. We need men who will risk their lives for our way of life. But we do not reward their harsh behavior with soft hearts. And they will never love us in return..." Colonel Hammond had trailed off to confront his demons.

Who 's worse? Emma wondered, *Thief or Master?*

Emma picked up her pen again.

...And so, Ceci, this is our fate, yours and mine. The men we covet may not be the men standing before us.

Gant held his tarnished brass telescope tight to his eye. He had stolen it long ago from his father's sea chest and kept it close through many voyages over many leagues. No cherished memories of his upbringing or his father could Quartus Gant recall, yet his old man's spyglass remained a comfort, a trophy reminding Quartus that he had somehow survived a tormented childhood. *It's hard to determine your location far out at sea without stars and a sextant*, he knew. And the glass for him was therefore a stake in the ground, even where the ground lay thousands of fathoms below, among only the fish and the dead.

"She struggles to keep up, Captain," Gant said to Jordan.

Gant dropped the glass. With a naked eye he gauged a dawdling ship. He handed the instrument to Captain Jordan summoned from his isolation below. Jordan eagerly joined his officers on deck anytime a target prize was sighted. Otherwise, he left the ship's business to Briggs and Gant. Jordan said nothing at first, though a smile grew slowly on his tight face. He rocked from side to side, opposite the rocking of the ship—a natural sway, Gant observed, as if Jordan could anticipate the deck's roll before it happened, as if he could out-maneuver the sea itself. The captain's clarity of vision and decision-making agility was critical to *Rattlesnake's* success—and the pockets of every man aboard. So, any indication of slippage was noted. Unlike a man-of-war's captain, privateer masters were held to an ultimate standard of competence, not mere rank. More than one private ship had been known to lose its captain over a lonely quarterdeck rail on a dirty night. Men like Gant noted Jordan's every behavior nuance, every misstep, every miscalculation of the odds.

The brig had sailed southward from New England, heading for the British islands east of the Spanish strongholds where they hoped to find and capture laden British merchant ships, London-bound. And here, well east of any island, they found a lonely ship separated from its convoy by storm or laggard sailing—an easy capture for an anxious predator hungering for action. Jordan issued a few sailing commands to his officers, unnecessary since the brig was already beating upwind to cut off the slower ship. Gant positioned his gun crews, including Thomas, not expecting to use them, given that boarding was the practiced method of taking an unarmed merchant.

"Q, if we risk action, Master Hammond had best go below decks," Briggs reminded Gant.

"Mr. Hammond!" Gant called to the lad. "Prepare wads in the magazine for quick delivery to the deck. Remain there—"

"But, sir, I—"

"Until we finish our business." Gant's cold look could stop a shark.

Thomas retreated below, chin to chest.

Paying no attention to the details of the battle preparation, Captain Jordan doffed his hat to enjoy the warmth of the fine day. With a piece of sail cloth, he polished his two pistols so fiercely as if to wipe away not only oil, salt, and grime, but the responsibility for its steely wrath. He never harbored regrets, his focus exclusively on a fine finish. Absentmindedly the captain ambled to the taffrail and settled in comfortably on a coil of rope. Gant smirked at Briggs. This capture was theirs to conduct.

The British ship, a square-rigged vessel with three masts, ran for her life as *Rattlesnake* came upon her. No cannon were visible either on deck or through closed gun ports, which appeared to be only outlines, painted white as an often-used ruse that seldom fooled a privateer. Briggs took the wheel as Gant walked the forward deck inspecting the starboard cannon for the prime angle of elevation and sturdiness of their recoil lines. Rubbing his shoulder injury, as he looked along the deck, then to the helm, he nodded to the first mate. Briggs turned the wheel and steered the brig aggressively to intercept the enemy ship. Their target must either hove-to or risk collision. Briggs assumed his overt move would force the other ship to haul their wind, drop their colors, and accept their fate. Depending on the attacking privateer, surrendering could be deadly or reasoned. Privateers stole everything of value—cargo, coin, food, rum, personal effects—and arrested a ship's officers or captain paroled. Then, with an armed American prize crew aboard, the captured ship would sail to the nearest neutral port. If the British ship was lucky, if the attacking American had too few men to spare for a prize crew, they might issue a memorandum of ownership: Once captured, the prize ship owed monies payable to the American ship who took her. All based on a "gentleman's promise" that the defeated merchant captain would immediately divert to port for auction, her crew and officers free to find their way home. However, on a few occasions, the honor system was ignored. And woe to any ship caught a second time who had not followed the code of a privateer's mercy.

As they closed on the British ship, Captain Jordan reappeared next to the wheel, his hand hard on Briggs' shoulder. "Why are we headed to cross his course, Mr. Briggs? Do you not see their cannon?"

"Sir, their gun ports are painted. The ship is unarmed. We can take her by forcing her to haul her wind—"

"By God, she is not unarmed—I know her! We took her last spring—*Victor of Wentworth*. I paroled her officers! But the ship was never sold and her proceeds never appeared on my account! Damn, he has crossed us, the scoundrel!"

Gant heard the commotion by the wheel, saw the concerned face of Briggs and ran aft.

"Captain?"

"Mr. Gant, prepare our larboard guns to open fire!"

"Sir, we have her now. See, she hauls her wind, her men are on deck without weapons. She carries no cannon—"

"Cannot you see their deception, their trickery? I know them!"

The captain gazed upon the men on deck paying close mind to another hot disagreement. Gant backed down. He turned to his gun crews. *Better to ruin a few sails than blow away skulls and hull,* he reasoned.

"Aim high," he ordered each gun captain that he walked past.

"Men of *Rattlesnake!*" Jordan suddenly called out. "This ship has crossed our path before... do you recall? They fought us without mercy last season. When defeated—at a loss of two of our own boys—we granted their officers the honor of parole. But the ship was never auctioned! Our prize money was stolen from us. Will we stand for this treachery? Will we fall for tomfoolery a second time? *I* shall not. Men, aim at their decks! I want them to feel our vengeance. Fire!"

If ever a broadside from a warship sounded uncommitted to her mission, this was one. *Rattlesnake's* cannon did not explode in unison, only spat-out one by one. Gant could only watch: One shot carried through the merchantman's main course caused no damage except a sailmaker's curse. A second shot hit the hull, however, crashing through planks, slicing anyone on the mid-deck with deadly sharp debris. The third and fourth cannon followed the captain's orders: Cannon balls hit the main deck, splitting apart rails, shrouds, masts... and shoulders, arms, heads, and guts. Men's screams shattered the air, and even from *Rattlesnake's* deck, the Americans could see blood pooling out the scuppers from the enemy's deck. British Union Jack colors were already on deck as *Rattlesnake's* volley stained its design of a red cross and white *X*. The men aboard *Rattlesnake* moved slowly. They glanced at the maimed ship with her maimed men crouching about her smashed deck while others lay crying out in pain.

"Well done, lads! She's ours!" Captain Jordan was visibly unmoved by the suffering across the way; instead, his eyes brimmed with fury. "Mr. Gant, take a boat and accept their surrender. Take your toughest lads, put a prize crew aboard and send the ship to Martinique. Clasp their captain in irons—"

"No parole for the officers?" asked Gant.

"None! Pay the French in gold so these scoundrels disappear into South American prisons and never see the sun again!"

"'*Clasp their captain in irons,*' Jordan screamed at me, but I couldn't put shackles around the man's legs, 'cause he had nothin' below his knees," explained Gant as he downed his daily ration of whiskey.

Briggs and Gant shared their mess on the main deck sitting on barrels by the scuttlebutt water-barrel.

"Q, what did you find on deck?" Briggs asked out of Jordan's earshot.

"Like a coyote that broke into a chicken coop," replied Gant crunching a mouthful of biscuit. "The wounded were dragged below, the decks showing their bloody trail. If those men could've killed me with their eyes, I'd be dead a hundred times over."

"Did you find cannon?" Gant's cross stare, his only answer. Briggs feared Gant was now and forever hard against the captain. "We're out here to take ships, Q. Jordan had reason to suspect their worst—"

"He's a bloody killer, Briggs."

Briggs understood. *Although... who would Colonel Hammond blame if his most successful captain returned home in irons, a victim of mutiny?*

"Q, I'm not sure—" Ben broke off; an excited call from deck interrupted them.

"A sail, above our port bow, ten points to the north!"

Briggs and Gant raced onto deck. Jordan nowhere about, had abandoned his watch for a bottle. *Rattlesnake* had quietly entered the channel named for Drake, the famous adventurer, pirate, admiral, lover, scoundrel—history provides one with a choice. After a quiet night, *Rattlesnake* had approached islands where the colonel's earlier instructions directed them to hunt: "Find unescorted English ships while their protective navy patrols are reported hundreds of miles to the north. Drake Channel is ours," the colonel had so informed *Rattlesnake's* first mate. And now, in the quiet of the Drake Channel, before a gentle breeze, sailed a large British merchant ship.

"Q, this one appears armed," Briggs advised. On this, the two mates quickly agreed.

From the companionway hatch leading from his quarters, Jordan joined his officers at the wheel. His demeanor had changed again—sober, direct.

"An English prize, gentlemen?" He made no move to take the glass. "So... what is our best course of action?"

As he answered, Briggs glanced to Gant for confirmation, "She's armed, Captain. We count eight ports. We'll approach from windward, sir, fire a warning shot, see if she defends herself. Then, we'll sail under her lee and send a broadside into her stern if she does not lower her colors."

A reasonable plan, thought Gant, whose eyes never left Jordan's face.

"Splendid. Carry on," replied the captain.

The American brig fired a single cannon. It splashed twenty feet in front of the British ship. Watching for a response, they could see eight long cannon protruding through open ports—guns that would come to bear on *Rattlesnake* if the merchant ship turned to larboard and set up for ship-to-ship combat. Or... she could loosen her sheets, let the wind escape from her sails, drop her British ensign, and wait for the enemy to board. Which they did.

"Well done, Mr. Briggs!" declared Captain Jordan, who then turned his fiery gaze on the owner's son. "Thomas Hammond, do you see how I wage war? Sometimes it takes courage and daring, and sometimes the gods favor tactical restraint."

Thomas beamed. During the previous day's attack, second mate Quartus Gant had forced him to sequester below decks. Resourcefully, the boy had kept apprised of the action through mess mates who told him of the captain's disagreement with the "cowardly Mr. Gant who had tried to weasel out of an armed engagement" yet afterwards, even when pressed, not even his mates would talk about the bloody result. The crew after the action, however, had walked slowly through their duties, eyes avoiding each other, their mess quiet and without the usual energy after a successful capture. After taking this newest prize, Thom would ask Mr. Briggs what was amiss aboard *Rattlesnake*.

After this latest English surrender—Captain Jordan stood, sword in hand, in the bow of the longboat returning with captured British officers—after this orderly capitulation, a quiet satisfaction sifted among *Rattlesnake's* privateersmen. Hunkered in corners, sailors quickly devoured a midday meal, speaking to each other in low voices: They had done well—Captain Jordan had captured two valuable ships in as many days. *The crew should be celebrating. Why aren't they,* Thom wondered?

While Gant had the watch, Briggs sat in the captain's cabin with Jordan selecting crew to transport the new captured prize to a French or Dutch port.

"Well done, Mr. Briggs. In my report to the colonel, I shall note your planning as a great part of our success."

"Thank you, Captain." Briggs bit into a piece of hardtack soaked these past minutes with tepid water, yet still not enough to return it from the dead.

"Our gunner, however, I have concerns about his temperament," Jordan confided.

"He won't fail us, sir."

"He, fail '*us*'? Yes, you may be correct. It's not '*us*' I'm worried about."

"Captain!" A seaman scrambled down the ladder and burst into the cabin. "New ships from the north—British we think, sir! Looks like the same squadron from Pico!"

Jordan flew up the ladder and pressed a telescope to his eye.

"Yes! Yes! Yes, by God!" he cried. "Mr. Gant!" Gant approached anticipating the worst. "Mr. Gant, take two lads over to the prize and set a charge in their magazine." He pointed to the captured ship. "Mr. Briggs, remove their crew and lock them below deck, if you please." He turned to Gant. "Here we go—the squadron will come down… they must pass the Indiaman. And when they do, you shall time your fuse so when she blows, she takes the frigate with her!"

"They'll come for us first, Captain, not their own merchantman." Gant pointed out the obvious. Briggs agreed.

The captain frowned at his officer's lack of imagination. "Not if they believe we are unable to escape!" Jordan answered with eyes bright, darting from officer to officer. "Can you not see it, gentlemen? Our opportunity? Have you not heard of a *ruse de guerre*? I shall explain."

Thus engineered reluctantly by the gunner, the Indiaman would explode without warning. If Jordan was correct, the explosion would also burn and sink the frigate, something *Rattlesnake* could never do by itself. Briggs thought through the sequence and looked carefully all around; they must act quickly. His eyes told Gant that Jordan's ruse might work. The captain, often rash, might this time save their skin. Gant shook his head not agreeing with the reckless plan but kept silent. He selected two men and heavy barrels of fresh black powder; crewmen loosened the davits and dropped the captain's longboat into the water.

"I believe I shall join you!" Jordan bounded over the side into the boat with Gant.

Briggs followed in another boat and returned to the privateer with the rest of the English ship's crew of ten Englishmen and boys all looking fearfully at the notorious Yankees. Jordan and Gant—with crewmen in tow carrying the powder—scrambled aft on the merchant ship and found the magazine. Gant split the barrel open and led a steady trickle of escaping powder to the locked magazine. He anticipated how long a fuse-line he would need. More than once, he went above to watch the squadron's slow progress: Steady and smooth they came, sailing four knots in a dying breeze.

"Mr. Gant, I will have you set the charge carefully timed so when the frigate comes near alongside, the prize explodes in their face. Do you understand?" Gant grunted, working the powder in a direct line. "Thank you, Mr. Gant. Lads, return to deck and I shall light the fuse myself!" Jordan crouched, looking up with a smile like a setter awaiting a fresh bone.

Gant stewed; he wagered his plan would work. *Most likely, Jordan won't follow the trail of powder that I redirected,* he mused. *We can still escape the frigate without killing three hundred men.*

Moments later Jordan climbed over the side and into their waiting boat. The privateers rowed furiously back to *Rattlesnake*. The ship ready, they sailed downwind to the reef Jordan had spotted. Jordan ordered her sails loosened with enough trim to catch the wind for a quick escape as they had done at Horta; he ordered ballast moved from larboard to starboard: portside cannon moved leeward, every man to the far side. He commanded an anchor be dropped off windward stern, and it grabbed the sandy bottom. The ship lurched to a sudden stop, toppling onto her beam; her rail nearly in the water leaned hard to leeward. *Rattlesnake* was free to sail away as soon as they cut her anchor cable and trimmed her courses. From the approaching British ship, however, the Yankee privateer appeared hard aground.

"Captain Breton, they've hit a reef!"

The British captain observed the scene from *Fortitude's* foredeck, walking gingerly, still in great pain from his encounter with this same damned American privateer of two months prior.

"Mr. Dawson, if you please!" The word passed and the young midshipman approached his uncle, saluting, hand to his forehead as trained. "Your first command, Mr. Dawson! Take a boat of able-bodied men and six marines. Mr. Clarke will accompany you." He looked over at the young lieutenant who smiled at the boy. "You shall take command of the Indiaman and place your sailors in their proper stations and bring the ship into our line as we pass. We shall take this Yankee. Their prisoners will be placed aboard your command."

"Yes, sir, my command! Aye, sir, bring the ship in line..." The boy was about to repeat the entire set of orders. His uncle coughed and men scurried over the deck to their positions.

"Mr. Clarke, I suspect the Yankee took the Indiaman's crew aboard their brig. They will have a prize crew aboard but I am confident the frigate's naked guns will keep them in line. Keep an eye for our mid, though allow the lad freedom of command, if you will. I do not expect we shall bring the Indiaman's cannon to bear, but see that they are primed and loaded. Take your place in line aft our cutters. This bloody pirate will not escape me a second time."

Captain Breton watched his nephew, deliriously happy in command of sailors and marines, as they rowed over to the nearby ship. He thought of his dear sister—*If only she had lived to see her son this day!*

From their slanted deck, Gant watched the frigate slowly approach the merchantman prize they had abandoned. He had expected his charge to fire the merchantman by now. The ten-minute countdown he set had passed. Nor did the frigate come as near alongside as Captain Jordan expected she might. The frigate stayed astern at a safe distance, her guns threatening any mischief aboard. A longboat filled with British uniforms—sailors, marines, and officers in blue and red with embroidered hats and pigtails—rowing fast from the hove-to frigate toward the merchant ship. Why had the powder magazine not exploded yet? Gant froze and turned to the captain who had been observing his gunner's coming understanding. *Damn Jordan to Hell!*

Smiling, Captain Jordan placed himself behind Gant. "Closer, closer..."

"What did you DO?" as loud and clear as any epitaph, Gant screamed, absent the deferential *Captain*. *I will confine this man in irons before the tide turns and after dark, overboard...*

Without a glance at the gunner, the captain asked, "You timed the fuse for twenty minutes as I instructed?" Gant said nothing. "I asked you to fire the ship with a full fury in time for the frigate to arrive alongside." Now, Jordan shoved his face into Gant's. "But the fuse wasn't the agreed twenty minutes, was it, Mr. Gant? Your line of powder had a gap and a clever misdirection, eh? The ship would blow, though only five minutes after we left. Your action would have done no damage to the enemy frigate except perhaps block the channel. Was that your intent, Mr. Gant, to sink the prize in the channel where the squadron must pass? You sought to save a few enemy lives instead of bringing glory to our cause! I foiled your deception and lengthened the line of powder to its proper length. The Indiaman shall explode just as the frigate comes aside! Our enemies shall burn this day in Hell, Mr. Gant!"

Briggs stared at the captain and Gant, their noses mere inches apart. Blows must surely follow. He had no idea which man the crew would follow. Even the winner might hang once returned to New England. He looked to the prize as the frigate sailed nearer, but then hove-to.

"The flagship has backwinded her sails, Captain. They will not come near alongside the prize!" yelled Briggs, pointing.

Silent, Jordan's face betrayed his surprise and profound disappointment. His lips tightened—the frigate was now free to pursue *Rattlesnake*.

"A boat of twenty men is about to board the merchantman, *Captain*," said Gant, barely containing his ire knowing that imminently two dozen more innocent men who, when the lit fuse met open barrels of black powder nestled in the magazine, would vaporize.

Toward the sitting ship Lieutenant Clarke, ten-year-old Midshipman Dawson, and twenty able-bodied seamen and six armed Marines in red uniforms rowed in *Fortitude's* largest gig.

"Do you think we shall see action today, sir? I so very hope!" said Peter Dawson, concealing nary a modicum of an officer's stoicism.

"The Crown's ships are well represented, young sir," replied the Lieutenant Clark, "We have cutters and a frigate. I don't expect your command shall come into play."

"I suppose. Too bad, she looks like a fighter!"

Captain Breton's nephew was increasingly excited as their longboat reached the drifting prize. Being aboard a warship for these past months had turned his formerly dreary school-day life into one of constant merriment among the men and boys on a ship that never slept. Firing guns, loading cannon, shooting at birds, and running below deck to fetch his uncle's whatnots, sailing was a marvelous blur. He could hardly wait to tell his school chums about life at sea! And now, after only a short time, he had earned a temporary command of a two-hundred-foot-long vessel with masts towering to the sky! She looked immense from his seat in the captain's gig, looking up as his men rowed closer.

"English-built, sir?"

"By her lines, no, I think French, taken in the last war, most likely. Her stern has a flare not seen by our own Indiamen, carvings and bright-work the British East India Company would think excessive."

"But I wager she sails fast, does she not? Look to her fine entry, to her mast rake. Her foretopmast could come back a bit which will help her upwind, do you think, sir?"

"I do, indeed! I had not noticed. Your lessons are going splendidly, the men respect you. You shall make post someday and fly your pennant, upon my mark. Now here, up the sides and mind me. We shall take a look around, and make sure no Yankees are lurking—"

"—or have left us any nasty presents, sir," added Peter Dawson as he followed the sailors up the side of the ship on its footholds.

Indeed! Lieutenant Clarke thought about what the lad said. Reaching the empty deck, he took the marine sergeant aside. "The Yankee's did not have enough time to strip her before they fled, Sergeant."

"Aye, sir. She appears tidy. The Company will pay handsomely for her return!"

"Sergeant, run below. Search the ship for anything... unusual. Quick now."

"Aye, sir."

Lieutenant Clarke rubbed his hand along the wheel and issued commands for the sails to fall, stations taken up. He watched young Dawson make a few commands of his own.

"Steer southeast—you at the helm. Follow the flagship in line," the boy shouted with a firm voice, trying hard not to squeak.

"Aye, sir," answered an able top-man fifteen years the boy senior. The lad smiled at Lieutenant Clarke and felt the morning breeze lighten his step. Today was a grand day to be a young man on a great sailing ship with trained men at his command and an enemy to fight. Lieutenant Clarke was enjoying the sincere smile when a guttural shout spun him around. There, dashing up through the main companionway hatch ran the marine sergeant without musket, hat, or wits.

"Out! Over now!" The man's terror ran ahead of him, his eyes wide, his mouth agape spewing his last anguished screams of dread.

Peter Dawson's morning suddenly exploded and he and Harry Clarke disappeared forever in a cloud of burning hail.

Captain Breton had watched with care as the lieutenant and midshipmen climbed aboard, walked to their post by the helm, and issued orders for sheets trimmed and braces to pull the yards into position. Suddenly in a brilliant flash, his men vanished. Smoke and fire, red, orange, and yellow streaks of hellish fury billowed straight from the center of the ship two hundred feet into the air. Blazing embers from the initial blast clattered down like broken branches and falling leaves, hissing into the cool waters of the Drake Channel. Sails caught fire, and masts crashed into the collapsing cauldron. As the initial smoke cleared, the fire consumed what was left of the hull, and additional explosions from cannon ammunition took every plank, rope, and sail into the depths and gloom. Captain Breton saw uniforms' scraps, red marine cloth and blue seamen's blouses in small unhuman formations floating among the debris. There, minutes before, a proud vessel had sailed. Now, not a shred of evidence of a living ship survived.

Disbelieving, Captain Breton gripped the rail of his warship. He swallowed his life's hopes and stammered commands of despair, "Leave a boat... for survivors... Run out our larboard guns. We shall sink this Yankee devil."

Captain Jordan watched the explosion and jumped almost to the first yardarm in excitement.

"Away! For glory, men, the day is ours! To the west now before they give chase. Slip the cable and trim hard, lads!"

However, Jordan's crew stood motionless, watching months of their own income blow to the heavens. Into a scarred ocean, they witnessed the remains of British sailors rain down along with wood, metal, and debris. Death during war between armed combatants was universally accepted, though even the slowest landlubber understood Jordan's action today was wrong. The crew turned and glared at the man responsible for the morally despicable act. In that moment, Captain Jordan recognized he was at risk of mutineers heaving him overboard for the sharks. Quartus Gant unsheathed his blade and raised it menacingly as he approached Captain Jordan. The gunner headed for a fight to the death with a madman. Who might win hung in the balance. Gant had a knife, Jordan two aimed pistols and a cutlass waiting to release an arm from a shoulder or a head from its neck. With a crooked smile, Jordan glared at Gant, egging on the gunner's mutinous attack.

"Wait!" yelled Briggs and grabbed Gant's blade-wielding arm.

Jordan gloated. His officers once again yielded to his will. What a glorious day! He turned and looked at *Rattlesnake's* course, free and clear; they would sail away to the open ocean where no frigate in this NW breeze had the upwind speed to catch them.

"Not now, Q," Briggs whispered to save his friend, "The men will be with you, with *us*. We must find a better way. Once we escape the squadron, we'll call a ship's council. I will represent the owner's interest, you the crew's. I have Colonel Hammond's confidence..."

Gant looked at Briggs. *This* was new information. "Not another day will pass—"

"Calm yourself, we need to make our escape first, or we'll all swing from a British yardarm at sunset."

As clouds parted and the afternoon sun spread across a tall island to their south, the canvas and hull of a seventy-four-gun British second-rate ship-of-the-line sailed into view. The massive two-deck ship with dark sides and yellow stripes separating two rows of deadly thirty-two-pound cannon sailed within range to hit *Rattlesnake* the moment she had appeared from her hiding place in the lee of the nearby island. With a single broadside from either deck, fired in unison, she could split *Rattlesnake* into a thousand small pieces.

The silent crew of the American privateer stood dumbfounded. The massive British warship took their bow, cut off escape, and ended their war.

Chapter Ten

Emma wrapped her fingers tight around her father's limp hands. "Father, I need you. You *must* wake and tell me what to do! Your supposed friend Mr. Morris demands to speak to you. He will come today, uninvited, and I cannot stop him unless I flee or call the constable." She watched, hoping for any indication of recognition. "Father, how much money do we really owe Mr. Morris? Have you other funds hidden?"

She put her ear to his chest. His heart pulsed slowly. His breathing steady had not weakened like the doctor had cautioned weeks before: "*Sometimes a coma represents a prelude to a long, slow slide. At times, though, it can be corrected by rest or the grace of our Almighty. No one knows precisely. No one understands the intricate workings of the brain, or how the blood flows, bringing oxygen to and fro.*"

So, she sat, talked, and asked her dear father questions. No answers came.

Rattlesnake had been gone two weeks. Another two would pass before she might hear word of success or failure from an incoming packet. She did her best with the Hammond merchant fleet: Two ships were repurchased at auction with the remaining funds she withdrew from the Providence Bank (on whose board sat her father's so-called friend, Mr. Westerly). Two other small schooners had recently returned. After provisioning, she sent them Down East to retrieve cargoes much in demand in Southern New England: timber, granite, and fresh cod for salting. Regardless of her feverous work to trade, barter, or negotiate lower prices, profits hindered by the war without *Rattlesnake's* expected bounty were insufficient to satisfy the angry demand note she received in the morning post. *"Fifteen thousand dollars to be paid in full"* or a guard would be set up around Great Hill, constables sent to the docks with writs for possession of Hammond ships and chandleries. A second note bearing an elegant, embossed header was hand-delivered:

Mr. Geoffrey Morris of Providence and New York will appear at three o'clock in the afternoon to speak with Colonel Hammond, or if he remains indisposed, with his daughter.'

Uncertain, Emma considered, *Should I hide? Scurry away in a carriage to visit Ceci, leaving Father alone with the servants? What if he wakes, calls for me, his mind clearer, able to provide the direction I desperately need?* She looked again at the repugnant note. *No, I'll not abandon Father nor run from Great Hill. I'll talk to Mr. Morris. After all, he is only a man.*

The two Providence men enjoyed their bourbon but only one felt sated as they sat at the dining table ensconced in the comfort of an upstairs private booth. The more corpulent of the two men thought about nothing but returning ships brimming with what was owed him.

"Your star has risen appreciably, I understand, Geoffrey," Matthew Westerly said as they relaxed after dinner at The Providence Arms.

"Eh?" Geoffrey Morris retorted, deep in thought.

"My associates in New York and Washington mention your name often these days, as a man to reckon."

"They're all fools. Governors. Senators. Judges. These people started this absurd war. I mean to finish it." Geoffrey Morris stared into his glass. "We attacked Canada—to what end?" he groused, "So what if we lose a few seamen to British impressment—ship owners have those losses covered tenfold by insurance—*if* we trade freely! Was it wise to anger an empire whose territories surround our pitiful Republic? Why war with a nation whose ambitions conflict directly with our own?"

"You refer to the fertile western territories? Ah, indeed, the English might strike out from their Canada strongholds or take New Orleans and fortify the river," said Matthew Westerly, adding, "Others I've spoken to think they mean to limit our States to the coast."

"And Madison is foolish enough to agree to their terms in a treaty. I agree that the English want the riches of the west, mountains heavy with ore, silver, and gold. Let them have the plains and the deserts, I say. Yet instead of protecting the rights of us and our friends, Madison sends out a handful of frigates to annoy their armadas. Our men-of-war are out-numbered by no fewer than thirty-to-one! What do the fools in the capital expect? These ship-actions and shore skirmishes have been embellished by the press as if it they were Trafalgar or Austerlitz. They only serve to distract the damned public!"

Matthew Westerly was not surprised at Geoffrey Morris' outburst—it was accurate. The pressures of his grand *Purpose* must be eating at his soul. Indeed, such a bold endeavor would eat away at any man's soul, in addition to his conscience, and not to mention his reputation. Unless his grand *Purpose* succeeded.

"Is it word of the incoming Hammond privateer that has you so in turmoil, my friend?" Westerly asked, hoping he did not sound overly accommodating.

"I need commitments made, delivered as promised. Our banks are not a charity-house."

"Indeed no, we have been generous to the colonel for some years."

When Hammond ships needed capital for provisioning crew or cargo, Westerly well knew, Morris approved all requests. Westerly's modest bank only disbursed the funds needed for Hammond's trade or privateering. It was a useful ruse to keep the true power anonymous behind a web of banks and counting houses that Morris alone controlled.

"Geoffrey, I have been clear with the colonel that we must deny further outlays if commitments made do not fulfill the terms."

Morris looked askance at Westerly. *Tell me something I do not know.* "Matthew, we have an opportunity before us that will never come again in our lifetime. The time to strike is *before* the United States signs a peace treaty with Britain, while the English continue to delay, waiting for advantage, an avenue to extract territorial concessions they foolishly forfeited many years ago. Now—and *not* during peacetime—is the only time the British government might listen to our generous proposition."

"Indeed—"

"But all that is at risk if we do not have the ready funds for our friends." Morris stared at Westerly as if he was the root of the insufficient funds rather than the singular conspirator who had raised the most for the cause. Westerly filed the threat away, useful someday perhaps when he was free from the vice in which he found himself squeezed. Morris continued to fume, "I need an elevated platform from which to negotiate. A banker, or a governor, even a senator has woefully inadequate leverage to deal with a crowned head! I own banks. I issue orders to governors!"

"Geoffrey, you have the Southern States in our sphere, as it were," said Westerly hopefully.

"Yes, our most promising path. Which is why I need Hammond's damned money that you fail to deliver!"

Westerly took umbrage but offered no defense. Morris swirled his glass. Morris had made great progress with the leaders in the South whom he so assiduously harvested. With their extraordinary wealth, their vast plantations absent any punishing labor costs to inhibit unbridled profits, these men and their Washington representatives had the unique power to raise him. They needed Morris as much he needed them. He had recently agreed to help them expand their *peculiar* institution. The triangular routes to the West Indies plantations and slave markets would not remain open forever, costs might rise on the West African coast, and the *misguided* abolitionist movement might attract ambitious, rabblerousing politicians. Morris hoped if he acted with speed and dexterity, an opportunity to accelerate the supply of cheap labor remained for the taking. And in return, these Southern confederates would raise him to a position where he could make the necessary arrangements with the Crown. Only then would like-minded men-of-trade enjoy unfettered access to trade wherever their ships ventured. The power of politics would unleash extraordinary wealth to the few men bold enough to take the reins.

"Your visit today to Great Hill has therefore great weight, my dear sir," Westerly said smoothly. "The girl has kept me from speaking to the Colonel. I am confident you can apply your unique persuasive talents and shake him from his hiding place. You will stiffen the backbone of a man who, despite his purported illness, is the cornerstone of assured, steady, and untraceable funds we need for our syndicate's operation, crafted by your vision, of course."

"Of course." Morris eyed his man curiously, trying to decipher how much flattery Westerly could vomit in a single sitting. "Which brings me to a question I have been meaning to ask. Enlighten me, if you will, Matthew, how it is that your friend, Colonel Hammond, has become the most successful privateer owner on this or any coast? Yet he cannot fulfill his obligations? Does he live for Sunday services perhaps?"

Westerly failed to be evasive. "His manner of operation is what makes him so valuable to us. He has confided in me, of course, and has asked that I honor his confidences—"

"Damn his confidences! Either you empty your closet of perfunctory secrets or I will be forced to find another banker for our syndicate's transactions. And do not forget the promissory notes I alone hold—"

"My dear sir, at no time did I intend to withhold from you any—"

"Spill it man! What is Hammond about!"

"Well, it seems he trades in confidences..." Westerly stalled. "...like a fishmonger negotiates bait in return for bushels of fresh catches."

"Go on."

"It involves certain items we discuss at our meetings at Great Hill. Bits and pieces only, of course, though mixed with some genuine intelligence of our plans. Some are intentionally left vague and misleading, hoping to hook them later, if you will suffer my piscatorial references. All of which are beneficial to our great cause, however. The British are led to believe our efforts are moving even faster than we are."

"And in return to this secret sharing?"

"Ah, it seems he is provided with the locations where Royal Navy ships, whether on patrol or on blockade, might be found, so that—"

"His privateers are able to avoid those oceans, hunting where unarmed merchantmen have no Royal Navy protection!"

"That is my understanding, yes."

"And does he know you are privy to his way?"

"Geoffrey, he does know. Though he is not privy to my indebtedness to you."

Morris smiled. "So, your revelations this evening would disrupt his dealings? Hurt his trade?"

"He would be disappointed. We have been partners for many a year."

"I see." Morris indeed saw opportunities where most men saw foreclosure. "Hammond turns forbidden information into bounty, then commits those same funds back to our cause. The she-wolf feeding on her own den, as it were."

"Yes, that is the way of it, though he is late this quarter."

"You damned well know I am sensitive to that! What do you plan to do to fix this, Mathew?"

"Well, we can start with the daughter. She is craftier than her handsome appearance and lovely eyes would lead one to believe."

"Handsome is not it, my man. She's a stunning beauty and she knows it! Let us talk on this. Does she understand her father's double-dealing ways?"

"I doubt it. She was only recently made aware of his fondness for the triangular trade. I do not believe she has yet learned how he plays both sides against the middle."

"He may have admitted it to her."

"Possible, Geoffrey, but she does not speak like one holding back a great secret, one that would send her father to the gallows."

"Whose gallows—ours or theirs?" Morris smirked at his own wit. He enjoyed it alone as Westerly squirmed in his chair. "To the girl," Morris continued, "I agree she could be an asset unless she turns against us. At which point, she may fall as a *victime de guerre*."

After Geoffrey Morris bade goodnight to Matthew Westerly, his thoughts turned carnal, despite the favors both men had just enjoyed behind the curtains in *The Providence Arms* upper supper rooms. His imminent visit to Great Hill offered the potential for a pleasant diversion. He had noted Hammond's striking daughter at the summer reception. Her inviting smile pretended modesty though he suspected it was merely a ruse of her sex to gain advantage. The predator unleashed in him wanted to find out how sincere had been her invitation to *visit Great Hill again, and soon.*

Emma Hammond's maid answered her visitor's imperious knock and led him into the parlor. There, the colonel's daughter greeted her loathsome guest with an indistinguishable bow.

"How do you do, Mr. Morris." Emma disliked the angular man's brooding manner, his dark complexion, and a gloomy appearance that matched his menacing countenance. Geoffrey Morris was ill-groomed for a supposed gentleman, his unshaved black stubble two or more days old. She recoiled at his confident, aggressive manners.

"Miss Hammond."

He, too, bowed his head slightly, and took the seat opposite Emma though she had not yet invited him to sit. The banker's eyes bore deep as if he had appointed himself judge. He was no jurist, of course, though he paid handsomely for their favorable opinions. Even before his first words gave away the intent of his peremptory visit, he calculated every datum he encountered—the size, smell, and cleanliness of the parlor at Great Hill, the dress of the young woman (*to impress? to deter?*), the richness of the proffered food and wine.

"I came to speak to Colonel Hammond who has not returned my letters."

"As I wrote to Mr. Westerly, my father remains ill-disposed, sir. He is not taking visitors. Since you insisted on a visit, however, I have made myself available. I know my father holds you and his other Providence friends in high regard."

You lying sack of honey. Your father is not sure he trusts me and would hate me if he knew how I'm playing him on a puppet string. "I learned of his illness only recently. Is he able to conduct his affairs?"

"His mind remains sharp," Emma responded as prepared. "Thank our Lord, he keeps our enterprise running." Emma forced herself not to stammer.

Lies! You have emptied your accounts in my banks. When you tell me your first lie, I know everything that follows is the same...

"I pray for his recovery. I congratulate him, that he has kept this enterprise thriving. My associate, your father's dear friend, Matthew

Westerly, tells me, however, your finances are stretched." Morris made a sweeping look around the grand parlor, looking at the oils, the wainscoting, the coffered ceiling in gold and silver leaf, the imported walnut chairs, rugs from far reaches of the East. "This fine room looks quite respectable. How do you afford this, when your privateers return damaged and empty of spoils?" He pointed an erect, obscene finger.

Is he accusing me of stealing? "I am not quite sure what you imply, sir. Great Hill was appointed her fine furnishings long before the war was thrust upon us."

"Stop insulting me, young woman! You well understand my meaning!" Morris exploded. "The last voyages of your privateer fleet have been disasters! You are lucky you have a ship still afloat. Two were recently captured, total losses." He paused and stroked his whiskered chin. "I have also come to learn your father's particular trade, one he would, I am sure, prefer to keep from your awareness." Emma's thoughts turned immediately to *Windslayer*. Morris continued, insinuation turned to accusation, "How he corresponds with our enemies!"

This revelation surprised Emma. "I do not follow, Mr. Morris, what—?"

"Miss, your eyes betray you. Colonel Hammond learns of the movements of the British fleets in the North Atlantic and West Indies. With this information he positions his privateers so as to avoid convoys sailing with Royal Navy protection. It is a smart play. And his action is acceptable, admirable in fact—if his gain, and my own, along with our country's best interest, are one and the same. However, if he employs extra-territorial enterprises to singularly bolster the fortunes of Great Hill at the expense of his agreed upon commitments to our cause, my dear, that is a different situation." Morris paused to study Emma's face for any reaction to implicate her complicity. "And of course I know about his triangular trade. Since the year '08, as you know, that trade is a business illegal in these United States. Your father is engaged in the illicit trade of Africans *and* through his communications with our enemies, is guilty of treason as well..." Morris devoured Emma with his cold eyes. "Yet he still loses money? Miss Hammond... these are serious transgressions."

Emma had anticipated he might confront her with the truth of her father's triangular trade. But allegation of conspiracy and treason were beyond her ability to counter with anything but honest shock. Her face telegraphed panic. Geoffrey Morris rose and approached her chair. Standing too close above where she sat, he stared down. Her face came eye to eye with his gleaming belt buckle, inches away, and she was forced to look up awkwardly.

"Your father's payments to our group are overdue, my dear. He owes fifteen thousand dollars, and your accounts are dry in Providence, New London, and Boston... all of them! The war siphons off Great Hill just as it sucks dry the fortunes of my many shipping friends. My position remains... to save our fortunes, we must redirect our diplomatic efforts so new wealth can grow. And for monies owed to the efforts of my friends and I, the institutions I manage charge twenty-percent interest for outstanding debts." He lay a hand on her cheek as if to reassure her, but his cold touch appalled her. Frightened, Emma turned quickly away. He grabbed her chin harshly and spun her face back and leaned in close. "You will make those interest payments, my dear." Gesturing around at the well-appointed parlor, he added, "You obviously have the means."

"Leave here at once!" Emma kicked at his legs and tried to stand.

Morris pushed her back into her chair. She screamed. The cook came running from the kitchen. The upstairs maid appeared running from the top of the stairway gripping her broom handle like a musket. Morris looked down at Emma and smiled.

"'*Payment is due at the settlement date or interest accrues.*' These are the terms the colonel agreed to. However, I will give you and your father another way out. If his accounts are indeed empty, and he is unable to pay, you yourself, my dear, can still help settle the debt."

She couldn't help herself, "Or *what*?"

"Or sometimes a man taken ill does not recover. Sometimes his breathing is restricted naturally or by a mysterious malevolent force. Or perhaps a fire erupts with no warning in a grand estate like yours taking it to the ground. Multiple misfortunes might fall on a moonless night like tonight." Morris stepped away abruptly, as the cook and maid held their protective stance. "Good afternoon, Miss Hammond. Mr. Westerly will follow up to discuss the accelerated payment schedule we've just agreed to. You have my address in Providence, in the event you change your mind about paying down your debt—in person."

Privateer

Chapter Eleven

Precious few minutes of freedom remained. Captain Jordan worked fast.

"Haul our colors, Mister Crowell!" he cried to Andy, nearest the ensign halyards. "We can still escape!" Gant pointed out the narrowing gap.

The slow-approaching frigate astern would close their escape route east if the crossing battleship did not do so first from the west. Briggs too estimated their slim chances. Was there enough depth in the shallows to clear the two-decker astern? *Perhaps.* But if Gant and he erred, the two warships would blow *Rattlesnake* out of the water—a quick death from two British broadsides. Briggs knew he would die someday, just not in the next ten minutes.

"Q, there's another way," Briggs whispered hoarsely. "I have a... a... Trust me. If I can speak to a British captain, I might save... some of us."

Gant glanced at Captain Jordan, just out of earshot. "The English will hang him. He knows it," muttered Gant, not moving his lips.

"The crew did nothing wrong, Q," Briggs whispered. "Prison or slavery, yes, likely. But the ship can't escape—they got the range. This isn't Pico."

"Jordan's a bloody murderer!" hissed Gant.

"Aye, he is. But focus on our lives. We must ask for quarter."

Gant walked to the rail. He grabbed the ensign's halyard, all the while staring at Jordan who stood in a daze, mute. Gant hauled the Stars and Stripes to the deck, fist-over-fist, arm-over-arm, yanking with unrelenting passion, straining his healing shoulder. His war was over, leaving only one last chore that honor compelled him to finish. A hand on Gant's shoulder spun him around.

"He's a dead man, Q, leave him be. Help me save the ship!" Briggs stayed Gant's ready knife.

Jordan was no longer grinning or admiring the carnage he had wrought. His eyes no longer flashed wide with crazed excitement. His look darted from one closing British ship to the other. Each lowered gigs crowded with angry Marines carrying muskets. Their bayonets shone in the sun, resembling bait fish darting through the shallows. Captain Jordan looked at his officers, one poised to kill him, the other trying to avoid bloodshed. Jordan knew the approaching British marines were not his most immediate danger.

"Men of *Rattlesnake!*" Jordan cried to the terrified men on deck. "We fought bravely this day. We brought glory to our country! You are steely men but I need to ask one last service. You know the many ships we captured over these past two years. I succeeded beyond reason and have accumulated a great wealth, safely stored where no man can recover it without my help. As you know, the British execute privateer captains who bring war to England's shores. They aim to hang me, lads. Prevent this! Protect me! Brothers, hide me amongst yourselves. I will change into the blouse of a man before the mast. No man here shall call me by my name or rank. If we're imprisoned, and I survive, I will share my accumulated bounty with each of you. You'll enjoy a life of wealth beyond your dreams. You know I speak the truth—you understand my peril. What say you, lads?" The deck remained unconvinced. The British were as near alongside as Jordan was to panic. "Again mates, to each man here, I pledge an even share of my fortune. You are smart lads: factor forty ships taken—my cut, untouched I swear to the angels, thirty-three percent times the total. I am wealthy, my friends. And I will split it all among you—but only if I survive this day..."

Gant reluctantly admired Jordan's desperate self-serving drivel. His short speech might save his worthless carcass today. Though Gant preferred to kill him now and deprive the British their vengeance. A vision of a brighter future summoned, however—a ship under his command, perhaps, freedom from land altogether, and hearty men to lead into a fight. A wealthy girl with green eyes to meet him on his return... For this manner of freedom, in some future time, he shall have needed to make his fortune. He turned his back on Jordan.

"Aye," Gant said in a measured tone for all to hear. The first man to respond to the captain's plea, Quartus Gant gazed along the deck at each and every man, defying them to do otherwise while Captain Cornelius Jordan stepped backwards, shrinking among his men.

"Aye," the crew responded slowly one by one, then in hushed groups.

Without a nod of thanks or even recognition to Gant, Jordan raced below returning moments later wearing a sailor's simple homespun clothes, his uniform having been hastily sent to the bottom wrapped in a cannon ball. Hidden in his palm, however, was something identifying only two of fifty men on board.

Sword in hand, a British marine sergeant climbed aboard *Rattlesnake* and barked, "Fall in line for Captain James Breton of His Majesty's ship *Fortitude!*"

Once on deck, the sergeant drew his pistol pointing it at the first face he met: Briggs. The first mate froze, his lips parched. He looked down a loaded muzzle and thought of *Scepter*, another day he had feared would be his last. He suddenly imagined Newport's serene harbor in the early summer where the lilacs' scent carried from shore aloft the afternoon southwesterly breeze. A foolish ambition had sent him privateering, here to his probable death on a morning as thick and dry as his mouth. The sergeant's trigger finger did not flinch. Briggs did not move. *HMS Fortitude's* surviving Marines flowed through the gate followed by their captain. The heavily armed soldiers took positions facing the Americans—shoving with sharp bayonets any man who did not move in the right direction fast enough. One crewman—Stephen Crosby from Yarmouth in Massachusetts—tripped over his own feet, jostling for safety. A popular young man of eighteen, Stephen was a top man whom Briggs had recently rated able-body because of his willingness to climb to the peak even in the dirtiest weather. Briggs had taken a shine to Stephen and often thought of where he might be placed on a Hammond or future Briggs-flagged vessel. Stephen had helped Andy Crowell, another Cape Codder, to rig the petticoat sail on the *'Snake's* last cruise, saving the ship. Because of Stephen's sudden stumble, the leading Marine lost his balance as well due to the throng's sudden shift aside and aft. With momentum he did not fully control, he thrust his bayonet into Stephen's gut. The steel blade protruded obscenely out the lad's back before the soldier quickly removed it. The boy screamed in anguish, and dropped to the deck, his blood quickly spreading.

"Mr. Briggs, sir! It hurts… so bad…" Young Crosby faded away.

The men of *Rattlesnake* stared in horror. Indifferent, Captain Breton watched. His careless soldier expected a harsh reprimand for the murderous action. Grievous, Briggs regarded the dying boy near his feet.

"Who is master of this vessel? Present yourself!" Captain Breton spoke.

When there was no immediate response, Breton nodded to his sergeant who approached the next nearest sailor in the ragged line, Connor Muther of Aquidneck Island, a seasoned deckhand, fearless in a fight, a good man to have on your side. He had been first to follow Gant onto the first prize in Horta. The sergeant, without hesitation, thrust his sword deep into Muther's chest. The violence of the angry marine's thrust pinned the unsuspecting sailor hard against the mainmast. In disbelief, Muther's eyes bulged. His pain wrought sickening sounds from him. Muther remained upright as he bled out. Pooling, the life of two men flowed out the larboard scupper.

"I will hang every Yankee criminal on this ship before midday if I do not have your master. Where is he?" raged Breton, spittle flying from his lips.

Shifting foot-to-foot, each '*Snake* man had to choose between betrayal of their captain or the low odds they might someday taste his promised fortune. A common rational hit each man in a different manner, but it added up the same: fortunes came seldom in this life, yet a privateersman risked death on every cruise. Briggs heard the crew's wavering silence, loud and clear. He realized he was probably the only man—aside from Jordan—able to prevent more death. He glanced at Thomas Hammond standing wide-eyed near Gant, so young, so resolute. So defenseless. The situation dire: A seventy-four-gun ship loomed above *Rattlesnake* to windward and a thirty-two-gun frigate sat close along their other side. They were surrounded by enraged British marines who needed neither orders nor excuses to kill his men. His Newport crew had no hope unless he took charge.

"Captain, a… word, sir?" Ben Briggs stammered.

Rattlesnake's first mate took one step forward toward Captain Breton. His calm voice was a respectful attempt to assuage Breton's flailing ferocity. Breton limped around the bodies of the two dying Americans, Stephen Crosby, his eyes mercifully closed still lay twitching on the planks, his blood sticking to Briggs' shoes. Briggs wanted to comfort the lad in his final moments but could not bear to look. Nauseated by the heat, dizzy from the oppressive stress and confusion, Ben waited warily for the British captain to answer.

He's not the captain, thought Breton. *A mate likely.* "Name?" *I shall listen. Then perhaps run him through myself.*

"Briggs, sir, Ebenezer, First Mate. I ask that you and I speak in private. I have information for you." Briggs knew his words would likely have no effect on a man so obscenely injured. If so, he hoped to die quickly, unlike his two murdered crewmen. He added, lowering his tone, "Important information."

Gant tried to catch Briggs' eye. *What bloody information?* In the time it took a solitary gannet to swoop low around the three clustered ships and soar upwards on a graceful lift, Quartus Gant pivoted from trusting Ben Briggs with his soul to a feeling of abject distrust. Captain Breton's first impulse was to point the Marine sergeant's lethal sword in the direction of the impetuous first mate. He had demanded the identity of the captain, not *information*! Instead, he remembered his standing orders. He yanked his head toward the companionway ladder and the sergeant herded Briggs below with a butt-end blow to his ribs. Captain Breton followed.

"What?" Breton demanded as they stood in Jordan's cramped quarters.

Briggs reached into his pants where he kept the letter entrusted to him by Colonel Hammond. *Either it'll have some effect today or I'll be the next corpse.* Without prelude, he presented the letter.

"What is this?" demanded Breton, hesitating at first to accept it, as if the act itself could indicate some form of acquiescence, when all he wanted to do was scuttle the Yankee brig in one hundred fathoms, the entire crew chained below deck.

"Those who wrote the letter asked me to deliver it to a British Officer if our ship was captured."

"Do you know what this says?"

"I do not, sir."

"It won't save your miserable life."

"Sir, I am following orders. I was simply asked to deliver the letter to a British officer. You will decide if I live or not."

Credit him with balls, Breton thought, as he broke the seal and read. Finished, he crumpled the letter and threw it to the cabin floor and yelled, "Damn you Yankees, all of you!" He stewed, not sure if he should return to the deck or sit in the dim light of the small cabin and collect his thoughts. Breton stooped in pain from his recent injury inflicted by this very ship. He retrieved the letter. Sitting at Jordan's desk, he rummaged for paper, a quill, and ink. He scratched out a few sentences.

"Present your *letter of marque*," Captain Breton demanded, not looking up.

Briggs had not expected this, but he should have. With a *letter of marque*, captured privateers were granted a modicum of protection under the rules of a declared war. Without it, however, *Rattlesnake* and her men were nothing more than lawless pirates—criminals and murderers caught in a bloody act, without protection from any sovereign nation.

"I, I do not have it." This was true. Briggs had no idea where Jordan kept it. "The captain kept the *marque* close, hidden. I can hunt for it."

"He can deliver it himself, damn you! Give him up!" In the shadows, Briggs could see the British officer flushed red with fury. "Identify your captain or I will execute the next crewman I see on deck." Briggs remembered Thom. *Damn!* He stood unsure, searching for strength. The letter had had an impact, though he could not gauge if he was in any position to negotiate. "Without a *letter of marque* and having attacked a British ship," Breton continued, "you and every man aboard have committed crimes of piracy against His Majesty. Britain hangs pirates. Clearing the sea of vermin such as you is an essential duty. Give... me... his—!"

"He's overboard, sir. We took the ship after he fired on our prize."

"You're telling me you've mutinied?"

"He's dead. We were not of his mind in this kind of action. We regret—"

"You'll regret my noose, damn you! And you're lying! You're no more a mutineer than Lady Hamilton. He lives. He's here among you. Give him up—you don't owe him your life!"

After a long wait, Breton realized the mate's story of justified mutiny was going to stick. Even an Admiralty inquiry would show a modicum of forbearance in such an extreme situation. He imagined how the dailies would cry, *"Curse of the Coast Killed by His Own Men."* No, these men will never give up their captain. Was it loyalty? Honor among thieves? Doubtful. And he could not execute such a vital messenger. His squadron had been cut from the larger patrolling fleet to specifically seek out intelligence agents like this man, on these ships, with back-door communiques his government sought assiduously. Captain Breton had not expected or foreseen such capacity for violence from such a scraggly group of privateersmen.

"You may come to regret your misplaced loyalty," Breton added with a coldness in his voice that stood Briggs upright.

Captain Jordan correctly anticipated his captured crew would be split into groups. Assuming the British did not hang everyone, a few guarded privateersmen would be needed to sail *Rattlesnake* into a British port, where they would be imprisoned. That he could endure. The remainder of the crew, however, would be sold to the Dutch, forced into the sugarcane fields where a man might live a few miserable months before disease or hunger killed him. Several very lucky captives—usually limited to officers—might be granted parole, their freedom in exchange for a promise to lay down arms for the duration of hostilities. Men accused of war crimes, however, would land in English prisons, notorious for squalor. Jordan looked at the faces of the British Marines standing erect: red uniforms, feathers in hats, muskets with sharp bayonets pointed, ready. He looked into their eyes and remembered the violence he had inflicted on their mates, violent deaths these men had witnessed this very day.

There will be no parole, he reasoned.

Quickly, Cornelius Jordan considered his remaining options: Slide into one of the two groups—assuming no one betrayed him first. His bargain with the crew was weak, he knew: Life as a poor seaman, despite Jordan's passionate promise of wealth, was a better alternative than hanging from a frigate's yardarm on a hot afternoon. His fingers felt inside his pocket for the final deception. Unnoticed, he slid slowly to the center of the deck, away from the rail where the men condemned to slavery would likely descend first. He sidled up close to Thomas and Gant (who had been relieved of his knife by a Marine). Positioned centerline, they stood by the mainmast still dripping blood from the murdered sailor, the young man's body in a crooked mass at their feet. Jordan noted Gant's shirt had stains of spilled gunpowder similar to his own shirt before he had thrown it into the Drake Channel. He also noticed, unlike most sailors who went barefoot for better footing, Quartus wore his customary gunner slippers, soft sheepskin shoes that prevented a wayward spark from prematurely igniting powder during battle. A plan came to Jordan in the time it took a spark to find soft, dry tinder.

"You're fortunate," Captain Breton remarked as he handed his folded letter to Ben Briggs. "Deliver this. It requires an answer. And while we wait, your crew will suffer in my orlop chained to the hull. Know that when I learn who gave the order to fire that ship, I will hang him and leave his corpse to rot until his flesh falls into the sea. Is that clear?"

"Aye, Captain," replied Ben Briggs respectfully.

"My men will deliver your worthless skin to Jamaica, where you can find your way home. Deliver my message to your masters. This is the last time I will enquire—where is your captain hiding?"

"If you were in my place, sir, would you betray your captain? You can hang me, but then I could not deliver your message, sir."

I have other ways to find him, Breton reasoned.

The two traded looks, sizing up character and motive, factoring the effects of their next actions. For Briggs, a simple equation: certain death or an ignoble escape; for Captain Breton, censure if he showed poor judgement or perhaps promotion if his decision helped end the war.

"Do you understand the stakes?" Breton held up Briggs' letter.

"I do not, sir."

"You're a liar! They would not trust this message to paper alone. You know what the Crown wants. But your leaders are divided." Captain Breton paused and thought of the near future. "As I said, we shall require an answer. Do you know Boston Long Wharf?"

"I do, sir."

"On the third Wednesday of each month I shall have one of my officers find his way ashore. Meet him at a tavern on the wharf, *The Fishmonger*. He is missing an arm. And while I wait, your men shall suffer. Only after I hear from your leaders, will your men be released." The captain's voice dripped with profound hate. He handed his own letter to Briggs.

Briggs understood and could not counter what this man felt. Breton's face carried otherworldly weight, dragging Briggs' spirit down with it. He might have felt compassion, but then he remembered Stephen Crosby's body on the deck.

"I understand." Briggs made a failed attempt at connecting.

"Get out!"

Briggs nodded, and then spoke, tentative, unsure if the captain would change his mind. "I made a promise to our owner. His son, an innocent lad of twelve, sails as our cabin boy. He will make neither a productive captive nor a worthy top man in His Majesty's Service. Let him escort me home. My report will note your accommodation."

"His name?"

"Thomas, sir. Thomas Hammond."

Breton looked at the crumpled letter. He nodded.

Breton connected some of the many dots his admiral had failed to share. Hammond, the very same house the Service had allowed free transit, be it their merchant ships or slavers. Hammond, also the owner of this heinous privateer that had so long haunted British shipping and the tranquility of the home islands. Hammond's commercial interests might survive this war due to the man's duplicitous machinations, but Captain Breton swore a silent oath, *Hammond's infamous privateer captain and his ship shall not!*

"Sergeant, please tell Mr. Hammond to step aside for my inspection."

"Thank you, Captain," replied Briggs.

"You'll not be thanking me."

Briggs' heart missed a beat. He stared at the feral look from the British captain. Untethered hate bubbled from Breton's chest soon to explode in repercussive violence. Briggs realized the British captain intended biblical justice to fall on the owner's innocent son! He recalled how the captain did not flinch when his soldier killed two innocent young men whose only crime was standing in the wrong place. Additional killings might satisfy his thirst for revenge and momentarily replace his frustration, unable to hang the privateer captain. Briggs risked throwing his life to the wind. *This man had lost young officers in the explosion.*

"If your aim is revenge, take me instead, Captain. Let the boy return with your message," Briggs said unable to hide his shaking hands.

Breton jumped out of his chair, screaming, "My midshipman was a lad of *ten years,* Mr. Briggs! His body was split open into a thousand small pieces! *Ten years!* What chance did *he* receive? *He* will not return home! He *too* was only a boy... and you expect me to save your filthy owner's bastard, and send him home fat and fed?" Breton turned from the American. He wiped under his eye. He could not help his despair or thoughts of a visit to an empty country manor, once filled with his sister's love and her fine little fellow, now an empty manse, cold and dreary forever. "No. I shall not send him home in your place. You alone shall carry word of your vile crimes and cowardly capitulation. The boy will remain my prisoner. Rest assured he will not enjoy the privilege he has enjoyed on his father's scow." The British captain continued, his nerves steadied, his voice measured, "If you do not give up the man responsible, another officer will suffer in his place. An innocent man will feel the sting of my cat and the misery of an English prison. It is your choice. Give up your treacherous captain or condemn an innocent man."

Ben remembered Emma's instructions on the pier: *If our captain falls... and another officer... must be held accountable for our action, I need you to return home... another officer must take your place. No,* he thought. *I will not betray Q! My knees may tremble facing an enemy's cannon, but I am not that kind of coward.*

"Sir, I cannot make that decision—"

"Pray then, an innocent man does not come for you in the night. I would. I will hold one of your officers responsible—by his order or his direct action—for the firing of that ship, and the murder of my men. I do not believe it was you." He had learned that a man's eyes often admit his guilt. "But I will find a man responsible, mark my word."

Breton turned and with great difficulty climbed to the deck. Briggs followed, his legs near collapse.

"Line up!" commanded the marine sergeant.

Fortitude's red-coated professionals shoved, prodded, and pushed until two lines of American sailors stood facing the captain. Thomas Hammond shadowed Captain Jordan, hoping for safety. In the confusion and noise, Jordan bumped awkwardly into Gant who sneered at him. Thomas watched as Jordan's clenched hand move toward the gunner. With interest, Thom eyed the shiny bronze object protruding from Captain Jordan's grip. Thom continued to observe as Jordan carefully dropped it into the gunner's loose trouser pocket. The gunner seemed oblivious to the faint metallic sound that Thom's young ears easily heard. *Odd*, thought Thom. *What was that? Did the gunner not know it?* Gant, however, was focused on the bloody bayonet a British Marine brandished in his face.

Briggs stood apart from the crew, alone by the companionway ladder—the only American left unguarded. The men of *Rattlesnake* stared at him with harsh, unblinking eyes. *My God, my men think I've turned!* Worse, he realized, Breton appeared ready to strike Thom dead! Three innocent deaths—Briggs' fault! *I should've listened to Q and seized command of the ship when we had the chance. I should give up Jordan to the noose, now. Damn his promised wealth! Damn the dishonor of betraying one's captain.* Perhaps, he hoped, another crewman would weaken first and point an accusing finger. Events were moving too fast! Ben Briggs had saved his own life, and perhaps he might still save others—the boy, Gant? Instead, he realized his clumsy words may have instead *killed* the boy, subjecting him to an ugly public execution. *The colonel—and Emma!—will never forgive me!* Breathless, Briggs watched as Captain Breton limped along the line of sailors, staring into each trembling man's eyes, the murderous sergeant close behind with his bayonet. Breton moved past the men—some with knees buckling near collapse with fear.

"Look at me dammit, you coward!" the captain shouted at men whose eyes could not stand the examination. Staring into the eyes of each prisoner, he searched for a man he could turn. Lusting for a man to sacrifice in revenge, he came to Thomas Hammond. As ordered, the boy stood apart. Breton looked at the slender lad, his skinny arms, soft cheeks, and hair wild in the wind. Unlike every other man on deck, however, Thomas Hammond did not shake. He did not look away from Breton's condemning eyes.

"Are you Hammond?"

"Aye, sir," Thom chirped without hesitation. *Come what may*, he thought.

The sergeant's sword lifted, pointed inches away from the boy's chest. Breton stared. Thomas stared back, acknowledging his likely executioner with respect. He faced his fate and did not cower. *If this be my first and only act of defiance in the face of our enemy, I will die bravely,* Thomas told himself. *I will not cry.*

Breton looked to find traces of his nephew hidden in the face of the Yankee child: some evidence of the joy of life at sea he enjoyed with friends on a noble voyage. All he saw, however, was a boy who, though he might be brave, was not worth the fatal punishment for another man's sordid crime. Part of him wanted to gut the owner's son and splay his insides across the deck if doing so would settle his own soul. The captain stared at the boy for a long minute. Midshipman Peter Dawson, RN, however, was not sailing home. Captain James Breton, RN, after having sent his own nephew to his death, would allow this stolid lad to live. He moved on to inspect the next man as Thomas warily glanced at Briggs. Along the line of privateersmen, Breton came to Cornelius Jordan. Had the commanding British officer been more aware, and not dulled from the shock and confusion of the morning, he might have sensed the collective inaudible gasp from the American crew. He stood nose to nose with the guilty man he sought. But he only saw the furtive eyes of a nervous seaman of no note, a man with vapid eyes and twitching head indicating a scattered intelligence, not the cunning of an officer or the brutality of his guilty minion.

Captain Breton moved then to a large, swarthy man. *This* man's eyes did not cower nor did he make any effort to hide his hatred. Gant appeared as angry as he was capable of great violence. Breton took hold of the gunner's soiled shirt and ripped off a sleeve and put it to his nose: *Gunpowder*—graded *X* for the quickest burn. He also noted a sag in the man's trouser pocket. Promptly, Captain Breton reached in and grasped a brass key—likely to the ship's locked magazine of powder. He had found the gunner who had set the powder and lit the match! In failing to discover the man who gave the order, he had instead found the perpetrator of the fatal act. Captain Breton held up the shiny brass key, visible to all. For today's bloody business, they must be one and the same. Gant stared at the key, momentarily confused. He assembled the disparate pieces and the vile conspiracy against him.

Breton yelled, "Sergeant, take this man!

"You buggers!" howled Gant, first looking to Briggs standing alone, free, and blanched.

Gant turned to Jordan, realizing his scheme. But Jordan had already slipped to the row behind, and as Gant continued to bellow, intending to finger the guilty man, the butt end of a British musket struck his mouth. Gant staggered back.

"He shall be transported to Mill Prison to rot until they hang him," announced Captain Breton. "He will first feel the cat—Mr. Karp, two dozen with enthusiasm. If he's still breathing after—lay on another dozen!"

Gant struggled against two Marines holding his neck in a suffocating grip. One slammed the butt end of his musket first into his belly, then again into his bleeding face. Gant's fury was undiminished. But now dazed, he was unable to speak coherently. They dragged him off *Rattlesnake's* deck. His fellow Americans, although sympathetic, were relieved they had avoided similar punishment. The British had their man, perhaps the crew might now enjoy a reprieve. As Gant was lowered into a waiting longboat, he reclaimed some clarity. First he looked to Briggs, then spotted Jordan, head downcast, a sailor among sailors.

"You betrayed me, y'sons of whores! I'll never forget this. I'll come for you, Jord—"

Another blow to his head and Gant fell limp to the boat's floorboards, unable to implicate the man he craved to see hanged. On deck, Jordan willed himself invisible, away from this place, apart from the guilt of the day. He refused to acknowledge Gant's accusations or even look at him, which could only end with his own beaten body swinging by the neck in the Tortola breeze.

"Q No! You don't understand!" Ben cried out. Unlike Thom, Briggs had not seen Jordan's insidious sleight-of-hand with the magazine key.

"What was your price, Briggs?" Gant shouted, momentarily lucid as the boat moved off.

The angry marine who had lost half his men in the explosion cracked Gant's face once again. Blood gushed from his nose and mouth. His face a victim of multiple blows, he said no more.

Breton walked to the companionway where Briggs stood unsteady. The British officer dangled the brass key he had taken from the gunner. He dropped it on the deck.

"Yours?"

Briggs looked at the magazine key. Odd, it was shiny bronze. Q's magazine key was made of simple iron.

"Captain Breton, the man you've taken... he's only the gunner. He was following orders—"

"Then give up your damned captain!"

Briggs imagined what would happen next if he identified Jordan: the crew, coveting their promised fortune might put up a fierce, futile struggle to keep their captain from arrest. After they were beaten down, however, the ship's company and their British captors would watch Captain Cornelius Jordan's execution. Briggs knew nothing good would result of anything he might say or do. He had presented a plausible mutiny scenario that might come to work in their favor. American privateersmen—guilty or innocent—would die for nothing if he changed tune now. Betraying a countryman only to satisfy the bloodlust of a man so incensed, had no purpose; the British captain had a right to his vengeance. So, Ben Briggs remained silent.

"Get out of my sight, before someone slips a blade between your ribs. I believe a score of men on this deck would oblige," said Captain Breton, his voice so cold it might have been the breath of a corpse.

Briggs looked at the key again: such keys only he or the captain controlled—safely away until an engagement when the gunner required access to the magazine. He heard Q's muffled oaths and groans as his friend was man-handled up the side of the British ship.

The sergeant approached Briggs and set his sword blade hard against his chest. His hot voice said what fifty men were thinking, "Ain't no one likes a Judas."

Captain Breton counted ten men, the last, Jordan, whom Thomas stood beside.

"Mr. McGilvery!"

"Sir?"

Speaking slowly, Captain Breton looked at Briggs, "Take six Marines and five able-bodied crewmen and deliver these prisoners and their ship into Kingston."

"Aye, sir."

"Sell them to the Dutch." Breton turned to Briggs. "Those men shall feel the sting of the cane fields. They'll spend their last days as plantation slaves on Nevis." Breton raged for Briggs' benefit, his voice dripping with the venom of unrequited hate. "Those men will toil without hat or shirt. They will drink an ounce of putrid water once a day, until they collapse. Eat garbage so spoiled as to repulse a rat. Even in the heat of noon, they will hack and cut the cane until their hands and feet bleed. Their wounds will turn green. If they are lucky, a handler will hack off a rotted limb and they may live a few more days, until the fever takes them. Delirious, they'll beg for the sharp end of a machete. This, Mr. Briggs, is the fate of these men, condemned to die in the cane fields. And yet even in that Hell on earth, your boys will have a better chance to survive than my brave lads had when they stepped onto your bloody trap. Relay *that* message to your Hammond in America." He looked pointedly at Thom for a moment before he continued, "The rest of your crew will remain with my squadron, starving and cold until you rendezvous."

Briggs followed a British seaman into a small boat bobbing alongside. As he climbed off *Rattlesnake,* he lost sight of Thomas and Jordan. He could not, however, ignore the sound of a British coxswain on the deck of the frigate lying nearby yelling out numbers followed by the crack of a whip and Quartus Gant's undisguised cries of anguish. Briggs had lost his friend. He had failed to save anyone but himself. He thought he would rather be strapped next to Gant, their bond and future plans still secure. Instead, he heard the whip's slap. Along the deck, fifty faces of *Rattlesnake's* defeated men stared—hateful faces that would haunt him forever. The promise of Jordan's stolen gold had sealed their lips. They had saved a man whom many would have given up if they had heard even a word of encouragement from an officer they trusted. Such as Quartus Gant, who was stripped to the waist, enduring leather straps strung with iron balls. Briggs' world toppled upside down. The searing weight of the West Indies air choked his every breath. As he was squired away in the small boat, he sought to catch the gaze of Jordan but all he found were vacant eyes watching the flight of mosquitos and terns above.

Chapter Twelve

B en Briggs found a berth on a Dutch packet bound for Boston. After ten days he disembarked, hired a seat on the Middleboro coach, then a livery horse for Aquidneck Island and Newport. Arriving exhausted at Great Hill, Ben considered the colonel would either dismiss him on the spot or agree he had acted in the company's best interests. The colonel's daughter, however, did not appreciate his efforts or even hear him out.

"No, Mr. Briggs, you cannot speak with him! Where's Thomas?"

"Taken prisoner, Miss. With the rest of the crew. The ship captured."

"No! Was my brother injured?"

"Not when I saw him last. I cannot speak for his captivity. I presume it is grim."

Emma did not hide her eyes exploding in anger and fear of the worst of fates pressed upon a tender boy.

"It cannot be."

She turned away from yet another man who failed her. She listened, however, as Briggs detailed Jordan's blind passion to attack the lonely Indiaman with no regard for another possible trap. Emma accepted his narrative, if not his diminished regard for Jordan's approach.

"The captain followed my father's instructions to capture enemy ships. He took one and now you tell me it was his fault the British did not take kindly to it?"

"Miss, there were other ways—"

"Mr. Briggs, when you command a ship of fifty men, I am sure you will make all the proper decisions. I asked you to watch over Thomas and return our ship! Yet, you alone have returned! With only *messages*…What *good* are you?" she spat unconcealed disgust. "What of Captain Jordan?"

"He, along with Thomas and a skeleton prize crew will be sold in the Dutch islands."

"*Sold*?" she asked finding the mercy of a nearby chair. "The gunner?"

"Arrested, charged with war crimes on account of our action. Transported to prison in England. He'll probably hang."

Emma sank further into her father's soft leather chair. Bad enough her brother was a captive. Her letter offering a rich ransom would ride on the next post to Halifax and a copy to sail on every neutral ship leaving American ports from New York to Salem. Worse, Hammond and Company's most successful privateer captain had been taken prisoner. Almost as foul, she lost her proud brig, her last hope to pay her father's debt owed to the Providence men. Each week Hammond and Company fell further behind on the payments owed Mr. Westerly's bank. The engine that drove the family's lucrative privateering enterprise had been lost; the health of the family's entire estate was collapsing. Again that morning, her father had failed to respond to her squeeze of his hand, despite the sighs she heard escape his cracked lips. *How would he react to news of this latest disaster?* Everything she had tried had failed! Might the pain of his family's impending misery register and cause a rift in his slumber? Emma wanted to cry and escape to her privacy, dismiss this disappointment of an officer, and send him away forever.

"I don't think you knew, but your father…" On Emma's desk, Ben placed the letter that Captain Breton had written. "…gave me a letter. Along with instructions to deliver it to the British if our ship was captured. The English captain who took *Rattlesnake* read your father's letter and wrote a reply—to your father. Apparently, his squadron has been hunting *Rattlesnake* due to our captain's action against the English coast."

"The seal appears broken," Emma noted, making no move to pick it up.

"It is," replied Ben. "I read it, Emma. In order to free the rest of *Rattlesnake's* crew this letter requires an answer."

"Well, since my father is not able, you might approach his banker, you met him at our spring gathering, Matthew Westerly."

"Read the letter, Emma. I think *you* should reply."

For a long moment neither Ben nor Emma made a move or a sound. The letter lay there. She picked it up and read it carefully, and again. Her vivid green eyes opened to their widest, wild brilliance.

"My father... could this be true, Ben?"

"Your father's letter made an immediate impact on the British captain. Whatever your father wrote in his letter saved my life. And every crewman on *Rattlesnake*." *Except Q,* he thought. "I'll meet with Westerly, find out what he knows."

"He'll know you've read this."

"He doesn't know *you* have," replied Ben.

"I suppose. Are there to be ongoing communications? This letter implicates... my father, and others, in a serious crime! Is it right to call this treason?"

"Indeed. I surmise there are multiple correspondents on both sides. Hammond ships were simply a conveyance. I expect your father—or Westerly—has something more to say."

"Or Geoffrey Morris..." she mused quietly. She retreated to her own intense method of thinking through the myriad details and facts that clouded the air. Ben wisely let her be, fast realizing the depth of her perceptions. He guessed Emma saw through layer upon layer, while he had mostly examined the oily surface. Handing the letter back to Briggs, Emma presented her thoughts. "Approach Westerly. Apprise me of his reply. And... no one else can know of this."

The father's daughter, Ben Briggs thought. While sympathetic to Emma's misery he noted a quiet strength that appealed to his heart. For now, he determined, he must help her work through the disasters of the lost ship, captain, and crew. He did not expect to see Thomas, Gant, or Jordan again in this life though he would not admit that to her. She seemed resolutely turned against him; so first he must regain her confidence.

"Your father has two ships alongside the pier. The small brig, *Caroline,* and a topsail schooner."

"What about them?" Emma asked, distracted.

"We can outfit them with cannon. Send them out with new *letters of marque.*"

"We could. But we haven't any cannon."

"I can procure ten from smugglers I know in New Bedford. Whalers are buying heavy guns as British privateers are hunting them in the Pacific."

Emma turned to him. "Do it. Buy as many cannon as you can find. You may operate as my father's agent. He will appreciate your assistance."

"Thank you, Miss Ha—"

"Emma," she corrected. The tall, young man with sunset hair was not an injury to her eyes. Although the message he had delivered was painful, she knew she needed good captains, fighting captains—intelligent captains. She smothered her anger at the men who had failed her. *I need a man of action and cunning.* "You are our employee, not a servant," she added.

He replied softly, "I'll take that as a kindness."

"Do not be smart with me, Mr. Briggs! I have no time for frivolous young men. My father believes you have potential. Someone who can help us in our time of—" She stopped and selected a better word not dripping in self-pity. "...*challenges*. If this war comes to a quick end, we won't have the time to fulfill our immediate commitments. Mr. Briggs, I need privateers to capture enemy ships. If you help find these ships, arm them, and send them out, you will assist me greatly while my father lies ill. And I should also be grateful."

"Am I to command?"

"You've lost my brother, my ship, and an entire crew! And you ask that I reward you with a command?" She glared at him, surprised he remained calm as she flashed open bitterness. The brave men of her dreams were probably dead along with her only sibling. It suddenly occurred to her that perhaps it was not brave seamen with wild eyes and passionate words she needed. "Perhaps our next brig. We are laying a new keel. Find me cannon... then we shall see." Seeing a morose face where she needed to see confidence, she knew she must either turn Ben Briggs away forever or lean on him as timbers are built upon granite. "...please?" she added with the promise of a smile.

In another time and place, Emma Hammond might have flashed her luminous face sending him along with a skip. Today she only felt shock at the loss of her brother, her ship, and her heroic captain. She also felt an empty longing in her belly realizing she would probably never see Quartus Gant's face again. She was running out of men.

'Pastor' A despicable name for a sailing ship. Even a glorious two-decker with brass fixtures polished like a High Mass chalice and wood varnished to the gleam of an altar rail would be disgraced having been burdened with such a name. Ship names are important. They should reflect higher purposes: 'Victory', 'Undying', and even 'Fortitude'. But 'Pastor'? The floating sewer of tar, human waste, and fetid water sloshing over a body had no right to a churchman's name. Even from the perspective of Quartus Gant's squalid upbringing, this ship was Hell on the high seas, ferrying the condemned, squired by Satan's turnkeys, seamen too incompetent for even the Crown's most unsavory naval services. Gant wished he had died under the lash. His ribs and back were now a festered hash of minced skin and torn muscle. *I should've butchered Jordan with my knife,* he ruminated. Instead, Gant had listened to Briggs whine, *'Not now, not here,'* blah, blah... *You cost us the damned ship,* Gant accused a vague image of Briggs in his delirium. *Or did you conspire to steal it? What did you tell His Majesty's Captain when you slithered below like a river rat down a hole? What did you trade for your life? You promised to safeguard the boy, yet you protected nothing and nobody—now Thom's likely dead in the cane fields where the young and weak perish first. You traded him for your wretched skin, didn't you? An owner's son could have brought a fair ransom. How had you not managed even that simple bargain? And because I fired the prize, you had your convenient dupe, didn't you? Handing me over for slaughter while you return home to bed the girl! And as for me, I don't expect to live another fortnight. At least I'll fade into eternity relishing the hope Jordan does not survive Britain's justice. The girl's yours, Briggs. The ships are yours. Your cup of ambition now filled to overflow. But go, run, and pray to your God that I do not find you in this world or the next. Pray my hand does not fall on your head, because my hammer will be heavy, my blade sharp, and my thrust into your guts deep. I promise to carve out your*

innards and display their bloody mass to your face as you choke, gag, and die. Amen.

In the bilge, Gant rolled onto his good side, lacerated, bleeding still. He tried to hitch higher onto the cold, wet planks away from the bilge water where he had been lying. His wounds were raw—*Fortitude's* bos'un had laid on two dozen, five after he lost consciousness, his sides about to split open, revealed crushed ribs. Even Breton would stop senseless torture. Firing an entire merchant ship, however, swarming with a complement of British Naval Officers and Marines in full sight of His Majesty's frigate before two hundred witnesses had settled Gant's fate. Whether the transport crew kept him alive or not, provided medical attention, comfort, or nothing at all, was of no concern to his majesty's government or *Pastor's* crew. Grimacing, Gant recalled having seen transported slaves treated better than himself—*that human cargo had value*, he thought.

One morning, someone left a bandage. Gant wrapped his bloody body. After another empty day, he found a bowl with food scraps and a slosh of water that he gulped in two desperate, sloppy chugs. By the third day—*or was it the sixth?*—his fever had run its course. A sympathetic English sailor had placed a lice-coated blanket over Gant's shaking body, first considering to jam a wad of sailcloth down his throat to stop his screams of delirium. If a man lost his mind aboard a transport ship lulling its way to England across the Atlantic, even in the dark of the prisoner's cages below deck, he must conform to the vessel's fellowship. He must not scream all night.

Most mornings Gant woke with frost on his breath. One morning a thin coat of ice caked his cheeks. Lice crept into openings his defenses could not prevent. Even so, one guard, an older man having lost two brothers in 1776 near Trenton and thus loathing everything American—their slang, flat accents, lack of decency and dress, lack of King or honor—took special satisfaction ensuring his prisoner enjoyed no sleep. For days, on the hour every hour, even off watch, the guard or a mate descended into the bilge to find the prisoner wallowing in fever or the vague outline of sleep. If the American's eyes were closed, a foot aimed hard would slam into Gant's blood-soaked bandages. If curled up like a dog, the guard rammed his boot into the prisoner's face, breaking his nose more than once in the fifteen days they journeyed together. Gant's cries of anguish and hatred were interspersed with threats of lethal retribution.

"If only my hands were not chained, I would rip out your eyes and stuff them up your arse until they found their way backwards into your eye sockets, soiled and blind!"

"Ha, mate, you don't scare me. Be polite now..." The wheezing guard stood over his prisoner and slowly aimed, letting his flow splash. "...lest your next bowl be not what you expect!"

Gant recoiled in disgust, restrained by chains. The gunner decided he must stay alive, somehow, to kill this man, to kill all the rest. To keep his mind focused or at least intact, he remembered his vow to extract revenge. For his remaining days, he promised to keep the memory alive of this unrelenting pain, intense misery, and purposed suffering of His Majesty's condemned. If he lived, both Jordan and Briggs would suffer for causing his incalculable torment. Until then, Quartus Gant determined to simply endure.

With no small relief, Emma Hammond learned that Captain Jordan's former first mate demonstrated great talent for the business of trade. Ben Briggs ably secured the promised cannon—and at a fair price, from smugglers, no less! He directed dock hands to place the two-thousand-five-hundred-pound carronades on the deck of the Hammond topsail schooner, *Marian C.* While interviewing prospective captains, Ben had been especially careful to confirm their skill with sail trim and navigation. Delighted to find two candidates who also boasted past successful captures, he recommended them to Emma. One had served under Stephen Decatur in '98. The other, on a homebound downwind leg, was a Newburyport privateersman whose overfilled ship unfortunately foundered off the Gloucester rocks. Her decks swamped, his captured goods were lost along with the ship.

"I know neither man, Mr. Briggs. Nor do you." Emma tightened her bottom lip. "What more have you?"

"One man is a former Naval officer. He obeys orders."

"The other understands our business though."

"I lean toward the service. You can trust them... unlike Jordan."

"What do you mean by that?" she countered, "Captain Jordan has returned from many successful voyages." Her annoyance with Briggs roused again.

"Yes. And he lost your ship and your brother—" Ben momentarily considered revealing Jordan's habit of stealing gold and silver on every voyage, monies due his owner, monies that had been shared by the entire crew, Briggs included.

Emma clapped her ledger shut and stood. "I know you dislike Captain Jordan. He did well for us... until recently. I solemnly pray for his return."

"Not likely, Emma."

"*Miss Hammond*," she corrected. "I think, based on the tone of this conversation. Cornelius must return. And Thom. What will become of our gunner?"

"Q...?" Briggs looked away. He dreaded her knowing the truth of all that had happened in Tortola. How his attempt to salvage events had so disastrously failed. How Gant suffered the result. That morning had sped past: the sudden violence, young men he knew well suffering in agony as they died, bleeding to death at his feet, he unable to offer even a tender final condolence or a respectful burial at sea. In the heat of the suffocating cabin facing Captain Breton, Ben had felt ill, unsure, and slow-witted, thereby putting Thomas in imminent danger of being gutted with a cutlass because Briggs had foolishly surrendered the boy's name to a man intent on vengeance. "Many prisoners don't survive English transport, Em—*Miss*."

"Mr. Gant is strong. If anyone can withstand an unkind confinement, it is he."

"They are more than unkind. They will torture a man to death who has killed the King's officers. Have you received any answers about ransom for Thomas?"

"Three port officers wrote. Pay them first. They'll search after."

"And you did not pay?"

"Only if they can convince me that Thom is alive. From what you say, a man rarely survives the cane fields."

Never mind a gentle dreamer nurtured in luxury at Great Hill, thought Ben.

November gales turned to icy December winds, and each day Emma Hammond and Ben Briggs sat side-by-side. In a pantry office at Great Hill or in her father's pier-side office, together they worked schedules for voyages and cargoes of the slow-growing Hammond fleet. She admired Benn's competence: Outfitting ships and crews for war, selecting ideal islands and shipping lanes for privateers to hunt with minimum danger of capture, identifying the quantity of stores brought aboard and at a favorable price. While Briggs focused on the fleet, Emma tallied their returns, made purchases, and established new, increased lines of credit. With Ben Briggs flanking her, she grew in confidence. And she pushed back on Westerly's threats from his sponsor—the Providence man's name seldom spoken, though a name Emma often heard in her nightmares. Not a day passed without her hearing his vile threats replayed in her head. She thought herself safer, now that Mr. Briggs enjoyed a very public position of trust inside Hammond and Company's management office. She hoped his presence might dissuade another unwelcome visit from Geoffrey Morris. Struggling to remain calm, Emma squeezed her father's hand each morning and noon and again before bed. Questions she had formerly whispered into Colonel Hammond's ear, questions that had remained unanswered, these she now asked Mr. Briggs—and he answered with conviction. Thus, the Hammond accounts began to spike, allowing her to approach Mr. Westerly with a proposed payment schedule.

"You admire *Rattlesnake,* Ben. Do you miss being aboard?" Emma asked one morning as she pondered her lost brig. "Thomas loved that ship—as if it breathed. He spoke of it most every day."

"She was a fine brig, Miss," replied Ben, stoking the coal fire in the drafty office.

"Why was she special? I heard men talk about her like she was their paramour. I saw only wood and canvas." *And profits*, Emma neglected to mention. "What did I miss?"

Ben smiled, recalling, "I remember the first time I saw *Rattlesnake* round Brenton Point under full sail, bearing hard into the wind, heeling with grace. Her fine lines followed a long, graceful sheer. Designed sharp at the bow, she eased into the sea as she parted the waves. Her wide beam kept her cargo safe and dry. With extra-tall masts and a huge spread of canvas, she danced with speed no square rigger could equal."

He answers my question a bit too poetically, Emma mused. "You describe a belle at holiday ball, Ben." Emma smiled. She was after something else.

"I have no influence on the appearances of a young woman. I admit my dreams are filled with designing the perfect ship."

"Yet does not someone of my sex also have 'fine lines' and a 'delicate sheer'? Or are seamen all lost in fantasies of wood, tar, and gun smoke?"

"Ship design is a balance, Emma, between the heart and the mind." Unsure how to answer, Ben ploughed along, not realizing he was losing her with every saw-cut and iron fitting. "Don't you see? I hope to design ships that take the aesthetics into account as well as the hard business of the sea. My dreams indeed are filled with the mysteries of wood and water. How remarkable it is to me that from draft lines on paper appear sturdy keels, smooth hulls, and fast, record-breaking cruises. A designer must understand the degree to which deep troughs rise to become wind-slapped whitecaps so that he builds a hull that can withstand such violence. He must envision green, cold ocean water rushing madly over a deck so that his bulwarks can withstand the onslaught and save men caught unaware from a certain death if they slipped over the sides. A proper designer of this new century must build ships with inch-thick planks on oak knees supported by a thick keelson upon which the *entre* rig and all her people must depend. I can see new hulls rising from a shipyard, *your* shipyard, Emma, like a renewed forest bursting from long-ago-burnt desolation. I intend to build a ship that will shatter all oceanic records and deliver unfathomable speed and comfort for her passengers. A ship with paltry spars and masts without tops will never conquer the ocean and deliver the speed the future will demand."

"I see," Emma replied, meaning it, astonished to find herself near to breathless as well.

She recognized the profit in Ben's dream. She stared long and hard at her employee, a man whose previously dormant passions suddenly shone like beach sand fresh from a gentle out-going tide. *If these same passions could be redirected...* she considered for a moment. She surmised sailors looked at their ships with affected hearts; although she had never seen nor felt it, she knew seamen talked about their ships as living creatures, a mechanical device with a soul hidden beneath timber and caulking. Sailors left their loving women on shore and crowded together on cold, wet ships on lonely oceans for many months. *At some point, does a ship become a passionate partner*, she wondered, *replacing feminine flesh men must miss, a form of mystical conjoining that no two people together can experience?* Was there attraction to life at sea that she did not understand? Living for months in cramped quarters below a rolling, leaking deck had to be miserable. Yet men jostled for a berth when a privateer such as *Rattlesnake* made ready for a cruise. *What do men find admirable about my ship, or any ship, for that matter?* Was there something beyond a life ashore with its rigid rules, beyond fortune-making, a more attractive shared adventure with other daring young men?

Nonetheless, the floating castle that had been her *Rattlesnake*, with or without her fighting crewmen, was lost forever. Whether it remained a sailing treasure-ship or a sunken hulk, *Rattlesnake* could no longer help Hammond and Company meet its steep obligations. She dared not share with Briggs her father's unwise commitments that had resulted in her darkest fears and her banker's threats. At night, with only the roar of winter storms slamming the shore near Great Hill Point, her guilt often overcame her. She lay awake thinking about her sweet brother, likely dead, her father unresponsive. She saw an image of the man her family's shipping empire had condemned to hell's fate, suffering, sure to die unless she secured his freedom.

In the early fall the sea hawks flew south from Aquidneck Island and the Northeast. And without their constant company, she felt dependent on men she alternately cursed and dreamed about. As she rode alone to Providence, Emma Hammond knew she must succumb to the worst of them, enduring guilt's sharp talons.

"Here's a spot of loverly bread and cool rainwater for ya." The British jailor chucked putrid remains of old food across the floor at Gant and four other hungry prisoners.

Each prisoner crouched, sat, or lay on filthy straw in Plymouth's Mill Prison. None could stand upright without bashing his head against dungeon rafters in the dank basement below the main prison floor, a crawlspace less than five feet in height. In Mill Prison's subterranean cells, inmates were forced to crab-walk or move about on hands and knees to any destination within the vile confinement. This included reaching the foul-smelling hole in one corner that emptied into a meandering stream below, or to gather near the door when what passed for meals were thrown once a day directly onto the dirt. Gant watched, still dazed, weak and bloody from the cold Atlantic voyage on which he had endured continual beatings to festering wounds. A low half-door opened. It was large enough for a rat, yet too small for a man's shoulder. Through it shot a few bones from an animal butchered long ago and a black bundle of stale bread. The prisoners pounced. The guards' game began. Through the grates on the upper door, the head jailor and his mate peered; odds were counted, and the turnkeys pointed to their favorites. The five prisoners were accustomed to the daily savagery: not enough food for five men to survive on, the jailors threw provisions for only four. One ragged prisoner, once tall and strong, swung a clubbed paw and sent a younger man across the cell where he crashed dully into a wet wall. The ragged prisoner grabbed the bread and inhaled what he could before another man ripped the piece from his mouth. The last combatant dove for the small bowl of water, casually left just inside the door. He swallowed one gulp before the first prisoner stuck a finger in his eye and grabbed the bowl, finishing it. The bone was left for last. Gant watched with interest as the two losers jumped on the larger man and clawed their way to a hold on the bone. Gant did not move. He noted his fellow prisoners' bloodied eyes, faces, fingers caught in others' mouths aiming to forcibly remove bread not yet swallowed; most of the water spilled. *Feral dogs in a gambling pit fight each other with more grace*, Gant thought. After the fighting over remnants of food, the stronger man, licking a bone and digging for marrow with his filthy fingernails looked at Gant. Still unsmiling, the gunner stared back.

"You ain't gonna play their li'l game, eh, mister?"

Gant did not answer. He turned his attention to the turnkeys outside the cell. One announced the winner; losers paid off their bets.

"More for us'n," the prisoner continued, "We're used to our daily romp, ain't we, lads?' The voice turned to the other sad, black-and-blue faces. One man's nose, newly broken. Another's front tooth snapped off, loose jagged edges left in his open mouth, gasping air after his hard-won victory: he swallowed not one—but two—half-mouthfuls of the sawdust-textured bread, weeks past edible. "You'll join the romp, friend. Tomorrow your belly will ache. We'll hear ya all night, or what we call night in 'ere, ain't no light down here that we call 'lower deck'. But we ain't in a hulk, thankee the devil for that. Down here, we reckon when the sun sets only by how cold we gets. You'll join us, sure now. A few of us will beat on you. You'll beat on a few o'us. You look like you was a strong lad, but the transport done ya, eh? We all took a one-way ride from one hell t'here. Me mum never told us children about the different hells, only the one with the Satan angel who'd burn ya every day. Our hell in this Mill Prison is worse'n that: We burn, we freeze, and we hurt each other—and after fightin' all through the pitiful, cold night, we hold another man tight for the only warmth we get. This place ain't human. But you'll see. You'll join in the romp tomorrow."

"I will not fight," Gant rasped. "It won't be necessary."

"Aye? You'll try to divvy up our feast nice and equal, eh? As long as I have my strength, I'll make sure that never happens."

"Come morning, there'll be one less mouth t'feed," replied the privateersman.

The soiled man in rags laughed with the wicked bark of a diseased dog. "A blessing, that'd be, I say." He leaned back on the wall built like one lining the gutters of an ancient city, a boundary thick with phlegm from the hacks of tuberculosis and spittle flying onto the ramparts, dripping as time crept by, one hoarse breath tentatively followed by another.

When a slice of light showed the next day—only enough to discern faces—the prisoners saw that the tall man who had commanded the romp wore a face as grey as the prison walls. His head rested haphazardly on a neck twisted sideways. At the opposite end of the cell sat Gant, awake, staring straight. The door opened; a jailor saw the corpse and with a musket brandished to keep the prisoners in their squalid place, his mate dragged the dead man away. He returned with only enough food for the remaining four—now, less one. After the cell door was again locked, the prisoners sat in a circle and looked to Gant who moved toward the moldy bread. He split it into four even pieces and handed the cup of water to each man to drink one mouthful before passing the cup carefully to the next thirsty man. Gant drank last. Tolerating this rare sign of civilized society, at the next feeding the guards abandoned their game. They had many other cells for entertainment.

Many weeks after Emma Hammond dispatched *Windslayer* from Newport to Cuttyhunk, the schooner returned cleaned, painted anew. Renamed *Atoned*, she was ready for sea. From Hammond and Company's office window, Emma watched the ship tie up at Hammond Pier. Beyond, however, approaching the outer harbor she suddenly noted an unfamiliar vessel limp into Newport. The ship's three untidy masts caused Emma's stomach to rise to her throat; she suspected it might be another of her father's middle passage transports, home to unload molasses or sugar cane. As the ship drew closer, however, Emma saw her decks were awash with people, fair-skinned folk with all manner of cloaks and shawls. Pilgrims, Emma presumed, displaced with their own dreams, arriving on these shores to seek a future far from their country of birth.

The beleaguered ship tied at Long Wharf, two piers to the north of Hammond's. Emma quickly found her way to the ship's rickety gangplank where passengers were carefully negotiating their way down without the benefit of a railing. Awkward men and bundled women carting babes in arms alongside terrified toddlers crushed the narrow board and tumbled out onto the wharf like a school of bunker entering a narrow gap between river rocks.

"What ship?" Emma asked a dock worker she recognized.

"This'n packet's the *James R. Hardwick*, from Cork City, Miss Hammond. Them first down the side, they be the lucky ones. There's a hold-full of sick'n dyin' folk. *Coffin ships*, we call'em on account of some passengers are already near t'the grave before they even stepped aboard. Many folks never make it across to our shores."

Emma thanked the man though it did nothing to ease her conscience. She lived in a grand manor estate with four score rooms, while these unwanted souls would be lucky to find a small unheated hovel along Newport's poorer waterfront buildings. If one immigrant in a family of ten was lucky and found a job, the family might survive the long winter. If not, they had no choice but to trek into the cold darkness, heading to New York's tenement slums, Pennsylvania's rocky fields, or the barren wilderness of the Ohio territories.

She studied the crowd of desperate souls. Searching the faces, Emma sought one person with whom she might connect. She hoped to single out one. Angry men bore dark expressions, ready to bark at her. Their women in colorless hats wrapped in scarves and large shapeless shawls appeared dazed, barely able to see the possibilities of their new homeland. They appeared more amazed than grateful that they had miraculously survived the storm-tossed passage. Several stooped down to collect a first handful of North America pebbles and dirt; this brought a smile to each exhausted face. To Emma, one pair of eyes stood out—a handsome red-haired woman. Not more than eighteen, she disembarked alone. Her radiant green eyes shone with hope and smiled at the grey day that did not return the favor. A younger girl stumbled behind her as they walked down the wobbly gang plank. Instinctively, the red-headed woman caught the youngster's arm and kept her afoot.

The child's mother gushed with gratitude, her own arms burdened by twins and a tied bundle of belongings. *Strange*, thought Emma, observing that the reflexive rescue was immediately followed by an eruption of emotion: the red-headed woman nearly wept, her hands to her mouth, as if the unsteady child reminded her of a recent sadness.

"My dear, how do you do? Welcome to America." Emma's own green eyes squinted in a pretty smile rivaled by few. She reached up and took the young woman's arm.

"Pleased, ma'am." The red-headed young woman dropped a slight curtsy. "Claire's the name me mother gave me. Claire Shortell."

"Do you have family hereabouts, dear?" asked Emma, leading the girl away from the throng.

"Nay, no one. My parents put me on the ship in Cork City with my little sister. She was only eight—there was a fever rampant aboard—" Claire held back tears, wondering how she would ever to write the letter to Ma.

"I, too, have a sibling, my brother of twelve years—"

The two women regarded one another with an unspoken understanding forming an immediate bond. Emma decided she would do what she could to help Claire who was her parents' best hope for the family's future, now cast ashore and so terribly alone.

"There is a respectable boarding house down Thames Street. Number twenty. Run by a kind woman, Mrs. Hunter. She'll offer you a clean bed for at least a few nights. Do you have any skills—for employment?"

"I bake a fine loaf and sweet muffins so the gulls hover over my stove on a wet morn. Biscuits and cornbread, too, bread pudding and the like, Ma'am. My father was a baker, when we had flour, that is." Claire explained as they walked away from the pier, arm in arm.

"Then it is settled. I know Mr. Grandy, our local baker. I'll ask him to take you in as an apprentice. I provision many ships from his store. Come, dear, this way."

"Ma'am, how do I thank you enough? Who are you?"

"My name is Mary Cel—call me Emma. My family owns ships of trade. I run our business now, for a time that is."

As the red-headed beauty walked briskly down the street to the lodgings Emma had indicated, Emma turned away, her spirits bolstered by the encounter. With new-found purpose, she returned to her father's office. After a quiet hour with Ben seated at her back, she heard a commotion down on the docks. Ben and she looked up hearing a worker from the pier below cry out in glee:

"Miss Hammond, Mr. Briggs, she's back!"

Emma and Ben rushed to the window. Rounding the old fort, a brig came nearer flying the Hammond banner from the truck on her mainmast.

"It's *Rattlesnake!*"

Minutes later, Emma's ship tied up to Hammond Pier. Thomas flew down the gangplank into his sister's arms followed by Captain Jordan. Laughing and crying, Emma swung Thom around and around, lifting the boy as they danced.

"My dear Miss Hammond, how lovely you look on this bracing afternoon!" Captain Jordan stood tall, rested and again in fine dress and groomed handsomely. He nodded to his loyal first mate. "Mr. Briggs, I'm pleased to see you made it home."

"Captain—" Briggs answered, hardly believing his sight.

Within the hour, the happy group had settled around the dining table at Great Hill, enjoying a hot meal. Jordan, without asking after Colonel Hammond, assumed the seat at the head, the boy and his former mate to his left, the young woman to his right, his good side. Thomas talked fast as was his manner, his words tripping over themselves.

"Two days out from our capture, Emma, Captain Jordan and I, well, we talked of nothing but escape. We waited until the ship neared Nevis—Captain knows the port well, there's a beam of rock off the East end as we rounded—and he told me we could slip the deck and swim for it, then steal away on a packet. The captain thought I should try the currents first, since I am the more able swimmer—"

"You jumped off the ship, Thom?" Emma asked.

"He was right behind me, about to follow. Weren't you, Captain?"

"Aye. The boy and I make for a devilish team."

"You followed him into the water?" Briggs asked.

Jordan turned soberly to Briggs, though he said nothing. *Let the boy tell the story,* his face said as clear as a sunrise.

"The currents took me, Em, I could not make headway. Captain Jordan threw me a line. Only with great effort did he haul me back aboard, Sister. He saved me!"

Emma looked at the captain and gave him a smile with her profound appreciation. Unlike Briggs who reserved comment.

"So, you came into the Dutch Island, after all?" she asked.

"No, that i - what saved us! The ship lost her wind, our headway stopped. And with the tide on the ebb, we could not enter the channel. Without a pilot, the *'Snake* drifted a half mile, heading east. The English officer said we must wait for the flood. So, we hove-to, and spent a rolling night—"

"Until the dawn delivered us," exclaimed Thom at whom Captain Jordan beamed "Emma, the *Bill of Rights*—our own American frigate with forty-four guns, sister-ship to *Constitution*, was east above us, sailing hard. She saw our British ensign, but her officers recognized *Rattlesnake* and figured we'd been captured."

"And so, after a few shots through our sails, our captors struck their colors and surrendered," recounted a rejuvenated Jordan. "*Bill of Rights* came alongside to windward. Upon a thorough examination of our people, they determined we were fit to sail her home. The Navy Department will submit a prize claim for *Rattlesnake* in New York. They took the British crew and marines under guard. And well, here we are!"

"They cannot claim *Rattlesnake* as a prize! She's not a British ship." Briggs argued, factoring the lost capital, while hoping to end the boy's retelling of what was likely another fantasy. No small wonder his shore-bound sister's head was filled with such absurd understanding of life offshore!

"Mr. Briggs, they can and have done so," the captain answered firmly. "The *Snake* was under enemy colors and therefore a British ship. Once taken back, her value is owed to the account of the captain of *Bill of Rights*, at three-twentieths of her value. Colonel Hammond may wish to re-purchase her at auction," Jordan added casually.

Except we do not have enough money to buy our own ship back, thought Emma as she responded neutrally, "I see. Nonetheless, this is a day for celebration! My captain, my brother, *my* ship all returned safe!

We shall find a way to make her ours again and then, Captain, you must weigh anchor right away. We have work to accomplish important work. We depend on you!"

Emma Hammond raised a glass, shimmering with the sun's early winter low-hanging orange filtering through the windows. Ben Briggs, Captain Cornelius Jordan, and Thomas Hammond obediently raised their crystal glasses. Jordan's eyes caught Briggs' glare over his uplifted rim. Briggs emptied his wine quickly and poured himself another.

...Mr. Briggs assists me in a manner I did not expect, Ceci. I understand my father's methods—the process of trade, the fitting out of ships and crew; hiring, ledgers, letters, accounts; tallies and balances. I understand all this though I am not as creative as Mr. Briggs. We must decide if a voyage will turn to misadventure or success with little or no advance intelligence. Will a gale blow a ship off course and miss her shipment of perishable fruits? Can we trust the captains we hire? How best to avoid the patrols of those belligerent British! I understand from friends of my father that our American trade has been nearly annihilated by this war, a war so unnecessary, everyone in Town says. And yet those Republicans, that Virginia dynasty, keep our merchantmen either blockaded or taken if they venture offshore by insisting the British relinquish their impressment of our sailors. I do hate to lose people, but is that not a cost of doing trade in the open seas?

My father can match cargoes with ships, ships with men to sail them and return without theft, to find buyers willing to pay a price that exceeds our costs, all that and more... I am gratified Mr. Briggs can accomplish the same. He does not share his techniques though neither does he boast. He seldom makes me feel small or inadequate, Ceci. Rather he intuitively moves his knight down two and over one, blocking an invading rook. Mr. Briggs confidently makes his move and then defers to me. That part is still a bit unsettling. Is it deference to my position as the acting head of our firm, or does he legitimately trust my intelligence? Does he recognize his limits and understand I too have strengths?

Father very often treats me like a child, each day a new lesson. With Ben, the orders, writs, and bank drafts are in my name, but the plan as we grow our trade becomes ours together. The spirit of our business, its direction and timing, I feel is shared. He takes the risks—'Easy,' I can hear you say, 'when it is with Hammond money that he gambles.'—but he intuitively knows the game of trade. Ours is a strange dance, Ceci.

I wish, however, that Mr. Briggs had a bit more of the dash I see in other men. Why is my world so full of incomplete puzzles with gaps in the center that ruin the entire evening's efforts? Why is it not clear which man to follow, whom to trust with my heart, or from whom I must run with alacrity? Mr. Briggs is either shy or uninterested in those of our sex. He stands apart when he could walk nearer and brush my dress as we pass in the stairs or in the office. He has had many such opportunities… but, I trust I bore you.

I hope your engagement party was grand. I do wonder about the speed with which you approach your great day. During times of war, however, I have learned a short engagement is not uncommon. We have such little time alone with our men… I regret I cannot attend your party. I cannot leave Father, you understand, I am sure…

Chapter Thirteen

An indeterminate length of time had passed since Quartus Gant had been thrown into Mill Prison. It felt like more than a few months, though less than a year. Gant had stopped counting daily meals. During that time, in addition to the man who suffered the crooked neck, another prisoner had died of fever—a pestilence from the air or perhaps the putrid water. Soon after the latter's death, a new prisoner, a young sailor, was kicked into their midst. Gant said little to the newcomer though he looked at him with interest: *Did he bring news about the war?* The new arrival, however, kept his tongue. *A spy,* Gant reasoned. It was plausible the lad had been placed among the privateersmen to encourage confessions of misdeeds, or inquire about battles or the fate of captured ships for recall in court against Americans. *Ha, what a sick comedy,* thought Gant. *We were condemned the moment we landed in this place. We suffer misery on the 'lower deck' followed by the kindness of a rope. A trial is only for the public. 'See, we treat pirates with justice. Then apply the King's judgment.'* All the same, he wanted to hear what the young man might have to offer. During the scrawny lad's first week, Gant ran interference from the blows often delivered to newcomers. One evening after the prisoners ate their morsels, the young man ventured a few words to Gant.

"Name's Will Doyle," the boy whispered respectfully. "Your ship, sir?"

"*Rattlesnake*, Newport. Quartus Gant, second mate." He shook the boy's slender, dirty hand. "You know the ship?"

"Aye, I do. Not a happy story, Mr. Gant."

"What then?"

"I was aboard a brig headed from Martinique when a British patrol came upon us. I was pressed. There were other Yanks aboard. We shopped what we knew." Gant looked at him for more. He was younger than Gant had first thought—the bruises and filth masked a fair face that had not yet seen a razor. "There was talk of *Rattlesnake*. How her gunner had turned on his captain."

Gant clenched his fist. "That's what they say? How could they know?"

"The story is true enough, sir—the *'Snake* was recaptured by an American frigate, the *Bill of Rights*. The Yank delivery crew left aboard told of their capture off Tortola."

"What became of the first mate?"

"He was rewarded, sir, as was her captain. Seems they conspired to save the ship and the owner's son. To do this, they had to sacrifice the crew. Some of them poor souls were sold into slavery." Gant looked away. "You were aboard, sir?" Will guessed correctly.

"Aye." *And I shall keep this close to my heart. If I die in this place, it will be my final thought, my final oath wishing death and misery on those who sent me here.* "Your wrists, son. They're raw with open sores. They bound you tight, eh? Dragging you down here?" Gant asked with accustomed sympathy the boy's suffering.

"Aye, sir. They trussed me up like a wild turkey, but I fooled'em good." Will grinned.

"Eh?"

"So that I could free my hands—I'm always looking at ways to escape, to jump off the wagon, you see—I'd need my hands free. So when they began to tie'em together, I fought them without them seeing what I was doing. I forced my palms apart and extended my hands full, my arms muscled hard to their strongest width as the ropes were wrapped and tied. I fought the pressure with all my livin' strength, sir, while I looked all sad and defeated. The pressure pushing my wrists apart and their lashin'em together cut my skin raw, you see, but when they let me be, I found a bit of room to wiggle some. I worked my hands free of the ropes, but before I could jump free, they threw me in here."

Gant nodded. *Boy's got pluck.* He stored what would likely be a useless tip. Perhaps he'd free his own hands and make a final obscene gesture to a Plymouth hanging-day crowd as they led him to the scaffold.

Bearing Captain Breton's letter, Ben Briggs sat across from Matthew Westerly in the banker's Providence home built in the popular Greek Revival style. Its false portals evoked flattened ancient columns perpendicular to wide clapboards of painted oak that gave a formal touch to the front of the home while the sides and rear wore economically prudent weathered cedar shingles. High on a hill, the home nestled near other elegant homes and the square where Mr. Geoffrey Morris' grandfather, with generous proceeds from the family triangular trade, had, fifty-eight years earlier, helped build a college to rival the riverfront school in Cambridge. Westerly, curious, had agreed to meet with one Ebenezer Briggs who sailed for Colonel Hammond. Surprisingly, the lad had recently abandoned the privateering life and, according to sources, had become a force in the Hammond office aside the colonel's daughter. Westerly and Briggs had only spoken briefly at the colonel's reception in summer. In that social setting, the young man from Massachusetts had not impressed; all guests' attention had remained on the flamboyant Captain Cornelius Jordan, now miraculously returned from capture. Ben Briggs' business quickly became clear.

"On our last voyage, I carried a letter from the colonel," Ben offered. Westerly smiled, revealing neither surprise nor any particular interest in the letter's contents. Ben leaned in. "And as Colonel Hammond had instructed, I showed it to the British captain who captured us. The captain read it with interest. He wrote a return message for me to carry back."

"And do you have this letter?" asked Westerly, his curiosity piqued.

Briggs held back. "He meant it for the colonel."

"So why not give it to him?"

"I believe you know Colonel Hammond is ill. He does not receive visitors."

"Then why come to me?"

Why indeed? Briggs considered. Because he had been shamed by the girl. She had asked on that fateful day when he had returned to Newport alone, *"What good are you?"* After weeks close by her side, he had hoped to win her over or at least mollify her antipathy, yet she still regarded him as something less than a man. The letter entrusted to him by the English captain implicated her father with serious crimes; indeed, it implicated the entire Hammond and Company. Perhaps too, its banker. Ben Briggs' crew's deliverance hung in the balance. Resented by *Rattlesnake's* men, injured by Emma's poorly disguised disdain, Briggs came to Westerly seeking more than a response for the British. He came looking for redemption. If Westerly had the power to arrange for the release of his hostage crew, he must beg his help and deliver a proper response to the British. He came to Providence to end interrupted sleep, to extinguish recurring nightmares of a ship raining debris of flaming wood, torn sailcloth, and the scorched remains of young men; Briggs came to Providence to erase the mistake he made when he had stopped Gant's knife from plunging deep into Jordan's chest. Briggs now here in Providence, debased honor and pride in an attempt to calm his own suffocating guilt. And he came because Emma Hammond showed no inclination to award Ben Briggs with command of a Hammond ship, now or any time soon. The Bay had other ship owners.

He spoke slowly. "You and the colonel are partners, Mr. Westerly. Whatever he wrote to the enemy, I expect you know about. I'm guessing you and others have made secret, friendly overtures to the British. The letter I have brought today is the English captain's response. It asks about a place and time. It requires an answer presently. And while they wait, my crewmates remain captive on one of their frigates that is blockading Boston."

"Did you read Colonel Hammond's letter?"

"No."

"The British reply?" Westerly smiled. "Eh?"

"I don't owe the enemy." Ben's temper rose.

"So, tell me what you think—"

"Mr. Westerly, what I *think* does not matter. I am here to give you Captain Breton's letter and deliver your answer, not to play games."

"Very well. I shall be straight with you, young man." Irritated, Westerly stood from the chair. "How dare you storm in with vile accusations about my friends? I bled for this country while the likes of you drifted across the ocean and found a soft marsh to build your homes. You know nothing about war! Do you see the scars upon my face—the pox? In the War for Independence, I nearly died—twice! I had not a full meal for an entire winter. I saw soldiers beg for a piece of leather just to suck out a faint taste of horsemeat. *I,* play games?"

Calmly, Briggs placed Captain Breton's letter on the table between them. As he had practiced, he turned to leave.

"If I was mistaken to approach you, my apologies. Good day, sir." Westerly regained composure. "Are you leaving this letter?"

"The letter is unaddressed and unsigned. I'm the only person who saw who wrote it. The only one who knows who wrote the original from Colonel Hammond that it answers. Only you and I know I left this letter with you. An answer to the British captain—any answer for all I care—is required in order to free my men. His frigate patrols off Boston, waiting for me."

"Calm down, son. Sit," instructed Westerly, clapping a hand on his shoulder. "We are all over-wrought because of this war. You have convinced me you are in communication with people we hold in high esteem. We indeed wish to keep open... what do they call it? A 'back channel'. The colonel's ships, as well as others, on occasion are stopped, and in a spirit of anticipated reconciliation between former friends divided by an ocean, information is exchanged. Everyone wants peace. I see you sympathize with the necessary efforts to draw the antagonists together. If so, we could use a seafaring man willing to approach the enemy beyond the sight of land. Such a man must glean intelligence while delivering the same from our people. Agents often ask for assurances, or favors, or some advancement for their part in what is by necessity not only hazardous but a potentially deadly undertaking. Both sides, you see, would hang a man for such an intermediary role, were he caught. So what is your price? Speak plainly, son."

"Command of a privateer, Mr. Westerly."

"Ah.. Let me speak to the others. Yours is not an unreasonable request. I know Colonel Hammond thinks highly of your mariner skills, though I am sure he would be devastated to learn you have left his service." Ben waited for a firmer commitment he felt was on Westerly's tongue. At last, Westerly continued, "And Miss Hammond? How would she respond once she learns you had taken a captain's commission from another house? I hear, with her father's illness, she depends on you."

"Cornelius Jordan has recently returned. He's the best privateersman on the coast. I'd like my own commission while the war is on and the taking is hot," replied Ben.

"Your own ship… Miss Hammond has not been accommodating in that regard, has she?" Westerly knew Ben had been cast ashore, now at the mercy of an heiress' whims. Despite the vaguely implied offer, Ben felt ill at ease. He wisely made no response. Matthew Westerly closely examined his young petitioner. "We need men of good conscience and strong backs with a seaman's skills to penetrate blockades while avoiding patrols of British men-of-war, Mr. Briggs. Due to time and distance between our governments, we are challenged to communicate our thoughts about the war directly. Communiques through Canada take far too much time. You appear to appreciate the political rhumb line. I agree to read the British captain's letter and will prepare an appropriate response. It is up to you to find a way to deliver it. Have you made arrangements to meet with this British ship offshore?"

"If I had command of a privateer to cruise the New England coast, yes, I would do so. He gave me coordinates." *Alternately,* Ben reminded himself, *Captain Breton had suggested an on-shore rendezvous in Boston.* The time set for that fast approached.

"Ah, acts of espionage and intrigue—how very exciting, Mr. Briggs. Very well then, I believe we have an agreement. Are you familiar with Mr. Morris' square-rigged heavy privateer *Raptor*? She has recently lost her captain."

For her visit to Geoffrey Morris, Emma Hammond's first mistake was to wear a blue satin dress off-the-shoulder in the style of daring New York women. Emma had wanted her father's creditor to regard her as a woman of the world, not a provincial girl. She hired a fine city carriage and driver. Unfortunately, her delicate features had been tanned by the sun these past weeks, having ridden through Great Hill's snowy fields during her morning rides. Thus, her fair complexion on this evening more resembled a workingman's daughter, despite a dusting of cornstarch and rouge newly applied to her cheeks. Geoffrey Morris' stark-white home on one of Providence's most prestigious streets boasted ceilings of great height yet a *décor* studiously devoid of earthy charm. She felt small in his grand parlor reeking of tobacco that clung to the damask drapes and upholstery like sap oozing from a pine tree.

"My dear, what a pleasure," Morris declared, "You reconsidered my offer."

"Mr. Morris, I should like to re-negotiate my father's obligations." Emma sat erect and spoke with a confidence more practiced than felt. "I fear he was not of sound mind when he made those commitments, as we can see by his ensuing illness."

"Miss Hammond, whether made by a sound mind or a raving Bedlam inmate, his contribution to our cause is absolutely necessary."

"We are able to fulfill our mortgage obligations to Mr. Westerly's bank—our new managing director has made considerable improvements in our privateering trade despite the war's effect on our merchantmen. To pay additional funds to you, however, we need time for our ships to return. It is these unexpected funds for your cause, payable from privateering cruises, as I understand the agreement, that has caused us to slip in arrears—"

"Impossible! Payments are absolutely necessary to a schedule neither man nor beast can alter! All patriots must dance to the same tune." Morris' eyes never blinked.

Emma understood that Morris did not care how Hammond and Company got the funds he demanded—smuggling, privateering, slaving, or honest trade. However, the newest source of Hammond trading profits, she had only recently discovered, was tainted with shame. She remembered Captain McManus' disgust: He would accept *no more cruises on a Hammond ship.* No other captain had ever abandoned Hammond and Company. Her father had, essentially, left her barefoot and alone on a muddy flat with broken shells and barnacles preventing progress forward or back. She fidgeted in her seat and turned the conversation to a more benign request.

"Perhaps, Mr. Morris, we can discuss an advance?" She tried to sound business-like. "In order to recoup profits from... a particular trade. It is the only commerce able to deliver to you the full contribution in the short time you require."

"Impossible!" Morris repeated again. "...unless, of course, *you* provide additional collateral."

"You mean Great Hill?"

"Among other charming assets at your discretion."

Emma felt exposed. She sat low on a padded, satin bench seat, he towering high above in a wingback. His needling grey eyes voyaged over her bare shoulders and heaving bosom, never once addressing her eyes. His naked insinuation drew crimson to her cheeks. She wrapped her shawl deliberately, revealing only a hint. Refusing to lose composure and crawl to the door, she sat ever straighter. She turned, then, to the other reason for this humiliating visit, the reason behind the blue dress, the hired coach of a rich Beacon Hill matron, and the extra color applied to her lips and cheeks. She must save an innocent man from execution, a man for whom she felt responsible.

"You have many friends, Mr. Morris... *powerful* friends, I gather."

"Your information is correct," he replied neutrally.

"Including friends in government... in England?"

"My business often takes me there. Why do you ask?"

"There is a charity in England... in Plymouth called the *Commission for Sick and Hurt Seamen.* They sympathize with the dire straits faced by captured seamen, American privateersmen in particular. My father reached out to them last year to help us with a captain fallen seriously ill. If your friends could contact them..."

Morris was about to quash this innocuous request, then realized it might hold more sway over her than threats of financial ruin.

"And what would you have them do for *us*?"

"One of my father's most able officers, his name is Quartus Gant—you met him at Great Hill, a tall man—was arrested when one of our privateers was captured in the West Indies. He is imprisoned in Mill Prison."

"A cesspool. He's likely starved to death if they've not hanged him already."

"He is an innocent man, Mr. Morris," she exclaimed, newly shocked by Morris' condemning prognostication.

"All prisoners proclaim their innocence, my dear," he mocked.

"My Father and I are agreeable to remitting a generous payment for our officer's parole."

"What you suggest, Miss Hammond, has some risk for me. I would have to lower myself and plead for the unlawful release of a common thief, some privateersman you've lost."

"Second Mate Gant is no thief. You can assure your friends."

Morris looked into Emma's captivating green eyes. "My friends would wonder why it would trouble *me* if a man I did not know had made a nuisance of himself and managed to get himself captured? Such an incompetent as he I would happily be rid of."

"True friends would not question *your* motives. Are they unable to do you even a small favor?"

Morris gathered himself. "There are a few debts I can call in, though my gain must be commensurate with my risk, dear girl—"

Emma interrupted, placing a weighty leather satchel in front of him. "Mr. Morris…"

"Ah, the colonel's gold," he said admiring the weight of *Windslayer's* coin. "I'd been expecting this month's overdue contribution."

Emma recalled an older, trusty schooner she had recently sold to maintain an illusion of untethered financial capability; the vessel had been one of her father's favorites, known for speed. Desperate, Emma would never admit to Morris the thin fortunes of Hammond and Company, nor the secreted dwindling stash remaining from *Atoned*.

"I told you," Emma cordially continued, "our promised installment to your cause will come once another of our overdue ships returns. The coin in this purse is expressly for our officer's safe release and transport home."

Morris considered the gold, and her request—the gold was timely. A simple letter and a generous draft from his London bank would send the wretch Quartus Gant home—or his corpse for interment. Had Emma been a plain girl, he might not feel an urge to amplify the stakes with urgency. However, there she sat, close at hand, alluring—a sweet pastry for his evening's ribald enjoyment and perhaps to add to his delights on other future nights.

"My father," Abruptly, the girl trespassed on his salacious daydream. "shall require proof of your generous efforts on our behalf for our accounts. Hammond bookkeeping is exceedingly strict," Emma added quickly, trying to divert Morris' stare from her chest by reminding him he was dealing not only with her, but also with the south coast's most famous man-of-trade who would rise from his sickbed if necessary and strike down any man who infringed upon the honor of his daughter. An afterthought tumbled out, "And I shall remain ignorant regarding your other *arrangements* with the British, as you and my father call it."

"*Arrangement?*" Morris did not conceal his shock. "The Colonel, despite his obligation for discretion, has shared with *you* our group's private business discussions? That is all they are, Miss Hammond, *discussions* between old friends and partners. Nevertheless, I wish he had not done so. That knowledge places you in jeopardy, you see. Unfortunately, this revelation goes beyond your simple request to spring a seaman from jail."

Emma realized she had mis-stepped. She had no physical proof, beyond Ben's report and Breton's letter. She had only heard disparate, ominous sounding words, "arrangements" and "purpose" and "syndicate" as she had listened to her father's friends argue late into the night at Great Hill. She did not fully understand the depth of the deceitful group's treachery. But in this moment, she began to sense the weight of the matter as Morris's eyes bulged. She had thought referring to his mysterious undertaking might improve the cards she had been dealt. Incentivize him. Here in Morris' lair, however, her allusion to Morris's political machinations had precarious weight, obviously more serious than mere chicanery. She did not know where to maneuver next nor how—like struggling to aim a musket too heavy to hold, never mind shoot. Emma scolded herself, *I should have known what sort of response I'd get before bringing up their damned political intrigues!*

"Sir, it is not an issue among friends," she heard herself say confidently. She stood, smiling cordially.

Calmed, Morris returned to her last request. "Rest assured, Miss Hammond, a directive will travel by my next speedy packet in regard to Mr. Gant. If they find him alive, my associates in London will send you a message upon his safe release." Morris leaned too close to her cheek, pausing to gauge the jagged movements of her ribcage. He breathed in her scent, so close now, near to tasting. "Ah. Lavender. A prudish scent, Miss Hammond." He chuckled, and held his position, inhaling slowly again. "You shall receive notice that our shipment of 'lavender' has been released from 'the Mill' by way of Calais. Will that suffice?"

She gulped. "Thank you."

"Splendid." Morris continued to gaze at her. She squirmed, her tight corset compressing her on all sides. *Has whalebone no give at all?* she scolded herself. He ignored her discomfort. "So, Miss Hammond, you have what you came for. And you brought this other matter to my attention. To protect the integrity of the group I am fortunate to lead, I must ask exactly how much you know about our activities. Your anxiety is visible upon your lovely face."

She granted him an amused sniff before she spoke. "Let me assure you, sir, since you agreed to help release our officer, any other matters you have discussed in the privacy of Great Hill are forgotten. They are of no concern to me. I have a trading company to run... if you'll excuse me—"

"But, Miss Hammond, I must be sure I can count on your discretion. You appear faint. You must be hungry and it is fast becoming late. I trust a dinner at *The Providence Arms* will restore you. We can converse on the cost of discretion and trust... it will also help speed my instructions about Mr. Gant to its destination. Surely, every day a condemned man spends in wretched British incarceration is a day closer to his demise."

Rather than hope against hope, Emma Hammond had approached Morris to save a troubled man. She had available to her only that one last, distasteful resort. Her intuition and low-cut blue dress, with some good fortune she had hoped, would bring Quartus Gant safely home while buying time to settle her father's loan obligations. Unfortunately, she had never considered the possibility of a late-night romp behind the insalubrious curtains of *The Providence Arms. Damn!*

"Send out the missive now, before dinner, Mr. Morris, and I shall join you."

Emma's memory of that painfully long evening would linger like a kernel of autumn corn stuck between one's back teeth until a toothpick must stab it free. Upstairs at *The Providence Arms*, wine flowed, and Emma excused her abstinence on account of a fierce stomach disorder. Nevertheless, Morris' hands sought purchase of her person anywhere and everywhere. As he drank an imported claret, she heard revealing suggestions about his unmarried status and his freedom to soon select a partner for life. As Morris' slurring increased, he proclaimed that this fortunate woman would occupy that favorable position.

"A daughter of Great Hill will find," he promised as the curtain parted discreetly and an extended arm deposited an open bottle of a coveted Petrus with the first remove, "a life of comfort and status."

Emma *already* possessed a life of both comfort and status. Desperately, she scouted an opportunity to escape his insipid ardor. After the rabbit stew and again before the tender pheasant with wine and rosemary and sage, she conspired to douse his passion by affecting first a series of gentle burps followed by deep, rich belches and incessant hiccups signifying her inevitable, oncoming distress. Drenched by decanters of claret, then port came and vanished into Geoffrey Morris, then magically a steward replenished the lot. To Emma's advantage, Morris slid into the abyss of a drunken stupor. She marveled at the quantity of libations he consumed. She recognized his desire to ravish her right there behind the curtain in the *Arms'* leather-bound private booth where the server had enough experience to wait for the master's bell before peering in at an amorous entanglement, willingly engaged by both parties or otherwise consummated. Perhaps later such a hateful encounter might be required to save Hammond and Company, she reasoned, if it comes to that—but certainly not here and not in this manner! She leaned forward and smiled at Morris' slurred witticism and then quickly retreated to her flatware and small bites. *All this duplicity for Quartus*, she reminded herself—*Why?* The gunner and she were not lovers, barely friendly acquaintances, in fact. And after all this time, he was likely hanged. Would her sullied coin even find its way to the right people of influence? If it did not, if she had been deceived and the mate never returned, she promised herself Morris would never get within an arm's reach of her or her money again. However, if he arranged for Gant's ransom, then came for his full due... such a distasteful prospect might somehow be deferred. Perhaps if she were married...

As the night wore her down, Emma endured Morris' garbled words, boasts of planning done, actions near to happen. *Perhaps if I listen, I can learn more... He babbles so... I will encourage his tongue with one more bottle...* She poured. And she pieced his ramblings together with conversations, shouts, and accusations she had heard when her father's associates had argued downstairs at Great Hill. She thought of what she had read in the British captain's letter. It began to make sense. Astounding, yet credible. As her mind raced, she took sober notice of her dining companion's descent into what could only be called a drunken stupor: his eyes red, his braying a mix of boasts and compliments. Emma kept her arms pinched at her side, her shawl tightly draped over her bosom, which loosened inadvertently when she forced herself to chuckle gamely at some lame witticism he offered. At such moments, he leaned over and tried to kiss her—his passion fueled by the red wine of grand reputation. She withstood his amorous suggestions with a practiced smile. Other women would have either succumbed to the wine—and roving hands—or run off into the night. Instead, Emma steadied herself and let his anticipation continue to build. Dinner nearing at an end, Morris showed obvious signs of needing to answer nature's calling.

"You'll forgive me, my dear, as I dash off for a moment."

Wide-eyed, Emma nodded. Morris stood, clutching the curtain to their private booth for balance, then he fell flat on his red nose. She lost no time and instructed the hovering server.

"Sir, this gentleman needs your assistance! And I shall pay you accordingly if you do my bidding. Here, take this." Emma handed the serving master two dollars in gold which he pocketed faster than a gambler's sleight-of-hand. His eyes beamed knowingly; he had worked the upstairs room for many years. "Get help to carry my friend to one of your beds upstairs. Undress him and slide him between the sheets. And here..." Emma bent over, unlaced her shoes and removed first one, then another of her fine-woven cotton stockings, necessary on a cold December night out and about. The server looked down wickedly, admiring her bare legs. "Place one of these nearside the bed and the other draped on the bedpost. Or in his fist. And..." She tugged at a few loose strands of hair. "Place these on the pillow next to the gentleman." By now, the master server was well-tuned to Emma's game, and he became hers. She looked around and then applied more red to her lips and bent over the unconscious Morris, no longer a feared power broker but a despicable drunk. She rubbed her lips on his shirt collar and the nape of his neck, redolent with French civet.

"And when he rises, madame?" The server smiled. "What will he discern has happened?"

She gave him another gold coin. "Paper, please, pen and ink." When she finished a tight note, she gave it to her confidant. "Place this against the oil lamp next to the bed. Please make sure he sees it."

"He is not of a custom to waking alone, however, madame."

"He'll get used to it," Emma Hammond said with a smile as she left for her waiting carriage.

The night air was cruel; Emma missed her stockings. She laughed blithely knowing they now served more usefully as decoys about the bed chamber of the loathsome Geoffrey Morris. She enjoyed a newfound sense of control that warmed her through to her soul. *Battle requires a warrior*, she told herself.

Weeks that dragged into months in the bowels of Mill Prison. Gant fell into a cold brain fog. Day and night blended: Doze, wake, doze; roll over in pain to whichever side had the least festered injury. Having seen many wounds at sea, he knew to live he had to keep his gashes clean. Despite his attempts to do so, the wounds from his flogging refused to close. To cleanse them, he had sacrificed much of his drinking water—his small swallow of a cup the prisoners on the lower deck shared. The water itself was unclean. He resorted to letting the stale prison air reach his open wounds, allowing them to breathe and dry clear. Slowly, over time, the worst had tightened. All the while, his fever persisted. He hallucinated he might live to repay his great injustice in vivid, bloody imagery of two men ripped apart by his bare hands.

The newcomer, Will, was already terribly weakened when they threw him among the ragged prisoners. From a semblance of youthful health, the shriveled boy disintegrated into a spindly mass of legs and arms attached to a mop of ratted hair covering darting eyes. Gant discovered, however, a kind, intelligent lad underneath. Newly fifteen, William Doyle had shipped on a privateer from Salem, Massachusetts these past two years, he recounted, feeding his family with his earnings. There had been good voyages, though he did not always receive his promised share, due to the owner's excessive expenses. With determination and the hope of youth, he had signed on with the next brig at the Salem pier and shipped out again, with scant hugs and tears from his mother, young brothers, and tiny sisters left behind. William had sailed from the North Shore, leaving his mother with his meager earnings, so the family might eat throughout winter and spring until the field beyond their house grew enough root vegetables for a stew or broth to accompany a chicken wrung or a pheasant shot. On those mornings, he remembered how his pointer Zeke and he used to tromp together on the marshes by the Merrimack's mouth when the air was clean, and he could hear every step in the bristles and hard grasses. William's musket cracked through the still morning and Zeke retrieved the fallen fowl like Pap and he had done so many times before the war, before his Pap had shipped out on a privateer from Salem with promises of a quick cruise. That had been nine months earlier when January's winds threatened the warmth of their hearth. William Doyle's spritely sisters and brothers smiled every time his dog and he returned with a fresh kill. As they ate the family meal he had provided, they prayed, waited, and hoped for their father's return. William Doyle chose action over waiting any longer ashore; in the spring he had set out on the Salem privateer *Fast*—hazardous duty for a lad with a frail build and a weak chest. Despite his agility, he had more trouble aloft than the stronger boys. They could lean over the spar and grip cold, wet sails of cotton and bring them up to the yard where, with buntlines hung for this purpose, they could tie and stuff the sails hard against the yardarm. Will Doyle could not. And *Fast,* unfortunately, proved otherwise. Taken by an English brig-of-war off Long Island's south coast, Doyle was separated from *Fast's* survivors and ended up in a dark bilge, then a wagon ride in the rain. At journey's end, he was thrown into this deep hole reserved for the worst enemies of the Crown. Thankfully, here he met Quartus Gant, though a rough sort. William felt lucky to meet a privateersman from the renowned *Rattlesnake*. Notorious to the enemy, she was so admired among the brotherhood of armed private sailors. Reportedly, *Rattlesnake* had been hunted these past many months with purpose by an entire squadron cut out from the British blockading fleet.

The man and the boy sat side by side during frigid prison days and came to shelter one another on the bitter cold nights. No blankets were assigned to pirate prisoners except to heave a corpse on its final journey over the riverbank into the outgoing tide. Quartus Gant and William Doyle forged friendship. Doyle offered to clean Mr. Gant's back-wounds—dozens and dozens where the lashes had cut across earlier strips, and the metal balls at the end of the tails had made deep bruises and welts against muscle and bone. The young man saved a few swallows of his own daily water ration to wash the worst of Gant's wounds; as he did, he felt the large man suck in his breath, never uttering a grunt. They often talked about sailing and of the prizes they had captured, of the lives they would live once peace came and prisoners wandered home. But Gant knew better. Marked as a criminal and murderer, his future offered only a brief show trial and a hanging. Torture first, perhaps. He harbored no illusions. Nonetheless he feared he might outlive the boy.

"Your cough's getting worse, Will. You hot in the head?"

"Aye, Mr. Gant, a bit."

He had seen the look of it in the West Indies: Pallid skin, coughs from deep within, fits at night, shaking limbs. *A week? A month?* He figured the boy did not have much more. Gant wanted to make Doyle's last days less painful. He felt a taste of compassion for this lad and would extend to him any vestiges of friendship. Hate for his betrayers had kept him alive as much as the heat from the boy's body at night or the putrid water dripping down his throat. Hate had made him strong, as his long days lingered with dark thoughts instead of ending in peaceful sleep as they should. Of late, the boy's talk became less animated; his stories of a happy home fewer, and his loving memories of hunting with Zeke the dog, and of his family grew fainter at each telling.

"Where does your mind go to, Mr. Gant? Each day when we sit with nothing to attend?" Will asked of a man not known for conversation.

"A cabin. At sea. Next to a coal stove."

"Aye, sir, a *hot* coal stove! In my mind, sir, I go home to my sisters and cousins and our little ones who come scooting around our hearth, laughing and singing. I go home, sir."

"You'll go home, son, as soon as the bloody peace comes," Gant assured him. He turned and looked at his young friend. "You'll go back to sea?"

"Oh no, Mr. Gant! I've done my time offshore. My father, too, sails somewhere out there. I pray he's still alive. No, I have dodged a great danger. I will not put my neck in the noose again. I shall leave this place, regain my health, and clear land for a farm. I'll find a girl, Mr. Gant, with blue eyes and bonny, curly hair. Aye, it's the clean, green land for me, not the sea. It's a dirty life at sea."

A farm and a girl. Ain't nothing wrong with that. Gant thought as he listened to the boy wheeze. Will had survived transport and their underground Hell. He could not run away fast enough, however, to escape confinement's trailing curse.

"The sea can offer a good life, son. Many choose it," Gant whispered, closing his eyes.

Some weeks later, Gant woke before his four cellmates. One of the prisoners had once been an officer on a packet, mistaken for a privateer, though he had claimed they were cotton traders. The hidden twelve-pound cannon, loaded and primed with grapeshot, however, was all the evidence their British captors required to send him to Mill. Gant's instruction to split the food had provided a calm order, like repairs done mechanically each day at sea on a well-managed vessel. He had also assigned each man to a corner for sleep on passable mats of straw. Every prisoner had been required in turn to clean the latrine in the corner, near which no man was forced to sleep. Gant had meagerly improved their squalid existence. And after a time, eyes smiled back at him in thanks. Even the packet man with broken teeth, Caddy Melbourne, soon talked like a man with a small measure of hope.

"Psst. Gant. No guards at the door. Or in the corridor," Caddy whispered.

"So?" Gant was staring into the wall, then glanced at the grate.

"Dunno. Any change is worth noting."

Gant caught his meaning. *Caddy may be a dog in a world without rules,* thought Gant, *but with command established here on the lower deck he shows clear thinking.* Gant crawled over to the door and looked through the small opening. He knew full well the risk he was taking. A guard might throw a pail of human waste at him, or worse. Once, a bucket of scalding water burned the face of a hungry cellmate who dared peer out of the hole in search of their overdue scraps. Gant saw no guards dozing in the nearby cot nor did he see other turnkeys on the chair along a near wall.

"Guards're gone," muttered Gant. "Darker in the passageway than normal."

Gant turned to William's coughing. The boy had hacked constantly during the sleeping hours. *If the gloom was night, less gloom must be morning.* Without thinking, Gant put his hand on the door and pushed gently. It opened a crack. No one inside the cell noticed. *A trap most likely,* thought Gant, *'Shot while escaping.' Why bother? I blew British naval officers to hell. They'll hang me. Why would they lead me to death in the corridor?*

A shadow appeared.

"Looking for a Mr. Gant," whispered a voice in the darkness.

"I…"

"I am a friend. Follow me if you wish to leave this place."

"There are others."

"One—to help you. My fee covers only two. Quick now, she cannot hold them off for long."

"Will, come! Not a noise," whispered Gant.

The boy's eyes widened, and his hand covered a cough. Gant saw the boy had trouble moving with the spirit and energy escape required. Nevertheless, he would not leave him to die.

"Caddy. On your feet. Help the boy."

Gant turned to the shadow. "Three will leave here. You'll be paid."

The shadow regarded a man obviously comfortable with command. "Agreed."

The other two prisoners awoke. One had not moved for days and lay in his own excrement and piss, and would probably not last another day. He flashed a weak smile. The other man was confused.

He asked, "The peace? Release? Trial? Or does a hanging await this morning?"

Gant had nothing for him. He and Caddy dragged the youth out the door and down the corridor following their mysterious savior. As they moved along down the passageway, they heard a woman's low grunts and means coming from an empty cell. In great pain, the prisoners—unused to standing erect—hobbled as fast as they could. The four came to a corner where lamps shone dimly. Gant looked into the kindly face of the man he had blindly followed. *Is he leading us to our death?* The man recognized the question in Gant's eyes.

"Buckley's the name. I represent the *Commission for the Sick*. We arrange provisions, early releases. When special arrangements are made, we can arrange for unscheduled paroles for officers. There's a boat on the river with a man and muffled oars. It will take you past the gunships and across the channel. A Dutch packet in Calais waits with berths for you. Passage to North America has been paid."

"By whom?" asked Gant, his words eclipsed by William's coughing.

"I do not know, good sir. Hurry, this next passageway is the most dangerous. Distracting your guards was the easy part. Boy… quiet—not another sound or you'll die!"

Gant looked at Will whose face was red and about to explode with the need to exhale his chest and let go the building phlegm. The threat of the boy coughing terrified Gant as they moved down the corridor. They stopped near a small alcove where they heard muffled sounds from within. A crossing passageway ahead appeared untended. Buckley pointed.

"Straight up there's a crossroad. Beyond, this passage continues. Guards may be at the corridor to the left, we must slip by without a sound…"

Buckley's face flickering in the dim light showed fear. Even when the boy did not cough out loud, his muffled resistance deep in his chest bounced across the walls and ceilings like thunder heard from under a pillow. Perhaps, Gant reasoned, the sound of William's sickness blends with the hundreds of sick and dying prisoners whose miserable coughs, hacks, and struggles to breathe echoed off the corridor walls every night. But no, he cursed, the boy's coughs indeed echoed freely outside thick cell walls. His sickness rang of death. Caddy brought up the rear. He grabbed one of Will's weak arms, and Gant the other. Buckley put his finger to his lips. Guards hovered around a small lamp down the left corridor. The prisoners and Buckley stood where the two corridors intersected.

"We need to go forward, all the way across," he whispered to Gant. "Those guards were not there a minute ago…" The prisoners needed to enter the crossroad, pass through the light, and continue straight to an unlocked door leading to the river. Buckley looked at Gant with a new concern. Obviously, this was how he entered—but before these new guards had arrived. Gant remembered the woman's noises in the alcove they had just passed—sacrifices for a few earned coins, expressly for his escape. He would not betray these people.

Caddy whispered in his ear, "You gotta muzzle his mouth!"

Gant knew it was the truth. He could not look at the boy but put his large, open hand tight over William's gasping mouth and the night noises became still. The boy's chest heaved though no sounds escaped. He struggled and convulsed as Gant's massive paw pressed tighter. Buckley peeked around the corner and saw the guards stir. He timed their escape: Caddy first. The boy, carried by Gant, would take too long and make too much noise. Caddy crouched and darted without a sound. Laughter raged and guards' spittle flew into the air. Drunken guards were good for prisoners' escape. Buckley motioned: Wait, *wait!* The boy heaved and his body shook. Gant gripped him with all the strength he had left and poised for the dash: Their lives at risk in a matter of feet. Buckley's hand went down, and Gant dashed ten feet through the light. As Gant disappeared, a guard half-turned, not interested enough in the faint sounds to stand and investigate. Buckley slipped into the turnkey's familiar company.

"Ah, Mr. Buckley, what you got for us t'night?"

Buckley dropped the satchel from his shoulder and opened it.

"Ale for you boys! We're visiting the sick in the south corridor. But I've decided you need fresh bread and cheese from Montaigne more than those scum!"

"Ha, Doctor Buckley, you do us an honor, sir, by my word. And does the lovely Mrs. Crouch accompany you on your rounds this week...?"

Gant ran behind Caddy, his hand still tight on the boy's face. They reached the end of the corridor and saw a door. Gant let go of Will. The boy collapsed onto the cold stone floor. Will's face was blue.

"Will!"

Gant slapped the boy's cheeks. He hit him again and again. The boy did not stir, the noise of the blow echoing obscenely. He felt Will's neck; only the chill of the dead met his fingers. Caddy looked at Gant, aghast.

"You suffocated the boy—"

"I did not mean for this!"

Gant knelt. They had kept each other alive. Only one of them, however, would leave Mill Prison. He gently let the lad's body fall limp, but then changed his mind.

"I'll take him."

"Gant, impossible—"

"He will leave this place. We will bury him at sea—as a privateersman."

Later that fogbound night, halfway to France and certain they no longer trespassed in English waters, Gant and Caddy mumbled what fragments of prayers they could remember. Gant held William Doyle's chest and Caddy his feet and slid him over the gunwales into the cold water. Gant hoped the weights he had pilfered were enough to rest the boy on the bottom. He watched as Will's body disappeared. And despite his newfound freedom, Quartus Gant felt an iron door slam shut on the possibility of a life warmed by sunlight. A deep, dark sadness that he knew would never leave heightened his rage and strengthened his determination for revenge. He knew this sadness would never leave him; bolstered with anger, it choked him with bile he could never swallow.

Privateer

Chapter Fourteen

After their celebratory dinner at Great Hill, Thomas Hammond left the table and stood by the pantry door. The boy intended to leave the house and enjoy the delights of the rousing night air. Instead, his attention was drawn to a gently seductive gesture his captain made toward Emma. Thom watched Jordan and Emma talking quietly in the corner by the large window of the grand dining hall. He did not like how his sister smiled at the captain, appearing pliant. The captain should be focusing on the war, Thomas glowered The boy still had troubling questions about the action in Tortola. For weeks after their escape his mind had raced and he desperately needed his father to explain what his eyes had seen, but the colonel's bedroom door remained locked. And his sister alone retained the key... another key... another disturbing unknown. The lad's mind returned to Tortola. Perhaps the first mate could explain.

"Mr. Briggs. A word, sir?" Thom asked the officer as the two left the house and stood for a moment on the portico taking in the harbor view with its many idle ships.

"Thomas, you look well despite your adventures—let us recall your escapades: Captured. Enslaved. Nearly drowned. And then recaptured by our side and returned home without a splinter in your cheek this time. That's what I call an adventure!"

Thomas smiled tentatively at the compliment, *Aye*, he told himself. *An adventure.* The boy remembered how the first mate in Tortola had disappeared below *Rattlesnake's* deck with the brutal enemy captain. Every man on deck could guess what had been said: Mr. Briggs had bargained for his life. Thomas, however, before sidling up to Captain

Jordan, had stood closer to the companionway hatch than any other crewmen. He had heard snippets of the negotiations; the two men were decidedly unfriendly. The more Thomas thought about it, the more he became confused. The crew claimed Mr. Briggs had turned traitor. But it had not sounded that way to Thom. He sucked in his stomach and told Mr. Briggs what he had seen.

"About Captain Jordan," Thomas whispered. "I hesitate to say anything unkind, you understand. But I saw him do something odd."

"*Our* Captain Jordan? *Odd?*"

To his surprise the boy did not smile. Thom's looked concerned; his eyebrows squeezed tight like the colonel's. "In Tortola, sir, on deck. I saw the captain bump hard into Mr. Gant right before the British captain came down the line to inspect us. He did this just as all the men had looked your way…"

Briggs recalled the confusion. Most of the men, including Gant, had been staring at him waiting for an announcement, perchance a reprieve. Instead, Briggs had offered no good news and the murderous Captain Breton had selected whom to punish for the unleashed desecration that had slaughtered his men. Briggs had seen Captain Jordan stumble past Gant as they fell into formation at the centerline, a coward trying to sneak his way to the gate.

"Aye. I recall. What of it, Thomas?" asked Briggs.

"Well, sir, when he bumped into Mr. Gant, the captain slipped his hand near to Mr. Gant's trouser pocket."

"What was in his hand, Thom?"

"A shiny brass key, sir."

The magazine key! Ben realized. By planting it on the gunner, Jordan had identified Gant as an officer—the man responsible for firing the prize and killing English sailors! *But Gant thinks it is I who betrayed him! That I was in cahoots with Jordan. That the two of us conspired to make sure Gant would be the only officer arrested. He thinks I made a deal with the British captain when I went below. That I bargained away Gant, the ship, and her crew in return for my own freedom. The crew thinks this as well. Only Jordan knows the truth. And now… so does Thomas Hammond and so do I. But if I accuse the captain with no proof, do I forfeit my place forever? The girl remains besotted with the man; I have no ground to stand upon.* Dismayed,

Briggs watched Emma as she and Captain Jordan ambled slowly in the direction of the door out to the portico for a full moon rising.

"You don't say, son," whispered Briggs, "Let's keep this to ourselves. I may ask for your recollection in the future."

"But don't you think I should tell Em? She should be warned—"

"No, your recollection may upset her. She was fond of Mr. Gant. I will talk to her."

"But sir, because the British captain found the key on Mr. Gant, he thought—"

"Thomas, events did not follow as you think." Briggs' mind raced: he could set Emma against the captain, for good, now. And perhaps fill a newly vacant captain's cabin. He thought this evening of joyful celebration, however, was not the right moment to shatter her false impressions of a man without honor. *If we hear of Q's execution... her heart and mind will be more open to the truth. And Thomas will support my testimony. Gant would advise otherwise, but I feel I must wait.*

Ben glanced at the couple nearing the doors out to the portico. How could he sail under Jordan knowing that the captain's cowardice and duplicity had wrongly incarcerated Q? Ben and Thom looked at Emma who took Jordan's arm. Sailing under Jordan again would be the straightest, most direct course to building Ben's fortune; leading to his own beautifully designed sailing ships he had imagined down to the last plank and oak knees. The boy, the young woman, even the scurrilous captain, would help him achieve this dream as long as future privateering cruises returned him with both the gold needed for shipbuilding and the good health to see it through. Betrayed and imprisoned, Gant, however, remained a dangerous cog. An unknown. *If Q survives and returns, will he follow when he is told I played no role in his arrest? Or will Q's violent demons extract revenge?* Ben reconciled the sad truth: the gunner would kill him, the truth unheard. As a result, Ben Briggs watched his ceiling at night with a nagging fear of the unknown, fear of a man coming in the black of night, cornering him in an abandoned back alley. Gant, a man of intense acrimony, would forever blame Briggs for his arrest and never believe otherwise. *Yet he might be dead.*

All smiles, Captain Jordan and Emma Hammond stepped out of the house, politely disbanding Briggs and Thomas. Briggs excused himself from the happy reunion to return to his lodgings, and Thomas to his warm bed to read histories of Cochran and Nelson. Thus, Emma was left coy behind her teacup to fend off her captain's unusually ardent advances which had increased as the bottle of port drained. A hero bathed in glory, Cornelius Jordan had returned without the gold Hammond and Company needed. And as the minutes passed, the fair captain was fast losing his charm. To Emma, Jordan appeared a changed man. She wished Briggs had not bid his goodnight as much for his reassuring company and warm looks as for the protection his very presence assured. With increased passion, Jordan pressed her. She tried to conclude their awkward conversation with the excuse she must retire, when suddenly Jordan changed tacks.

"Your father's dead, isn't he?"

"What? No, Cornelius, he's sick in his bed—"

"You said he cannot take visitors, yet *you* see him," Jordan accused.

"I must—"

"*I must* speak to him. Or at least look at his face. I must know when I sail under his pennant, I am following *his* orders." Jordan's meaning was evident.

"I *told* you," Emma replied coldly. "Father's health does not permit visitors. So, I speak for him. If instructions from a woman do not sit well with you, perhaps another command might suit you better." She turned away toward the door, then added, "…if a Hammond ship no longer can satisfy your passions." Truth hung in the air.

He recognized she understood him better than he thought. Cornelius Jordan hungered for cannon fire more than her bosom, more than what any woman might offer in the soft night. He thirsted for the sweat of the fight, when his pistol took a body down, or his sword cut deep into a fleeing combatant. The beauty of battle fire's orange and yellow hues, air pungent with sulfur, and angry cries filled him like no other pleasure: Not wine, not venison cooked in juices and spices, not a port whore where fulfillment lasted sweet moments quenching nothing, and not his deep, powerful urge to kill. Emma, he admitted to himself, represented both a temporary pleasure and a needed distraction. She was fair, smart, no doubt, though an unskilled liar. If she were a woman taken by his sword, his blade to her throat, she would readily give up everything she knew, what she had hidden in her blouse or below her berth in a secret compartment; she would give herself to him and he would take her, use her, discard her, and perhaps let her live to tell of his mastery. Or perhaps he would run her through to see her shock as she realized her great and final misjudgment. In the confusion of taking an English prize, a worthy privateersman had no place for conscience, pity, or forgiveness. Only the taking mattered. Sailing under instructions from this girl had shifted a delicate balance within Jordan's breast. At sea in the employ of a successful man-of-trade, he could bend the colonel's orders to his will without worry his passion might be misconstrued or condemned. The girl, however, now holds the purse—or the keys to it at the very least—and he had refused to face her insidious inquisitions and her double-guessing of his every point of sail. He must endeavor to rise above her like warmer water coats the surface, where deeper, the currents run cold and true, according to the laws of the sea.

Besides, he knew where the colonel slept, if it came to that.

"I regret my forward words, Miss Hammond. You *are* your father's voice. I accept your authority." He smiled and bowed in a grandiose manner that if performed by a seasoned stage actor would have looked foolish. Jordan, however, complemented his bent back with a graceful sweep of his sword arm and gave her a knowing look from a supplicant's angle which she accepted gracefully although with little of the warmth she had shown him earlier. "I await your instructions, Miss Hammond," he said, aware the sparkle from her eyes was missing as she held his gaze. "The Navy will sell your ship in the next few days. Four or five thousand dollars, I believe, should buy *Rattlesnake* from auction. If you do not have the ready capital, please let me know how I might assist."

She stifled an angry retort to his offer to buy her ship back, then caught herself. *I bet you can assist, Cornelius,* Emma recalled her father's complaints, suspecting purloined booty, cravenly stolen by the man in command.

"Goodnight, Captain Jordan. I am glad for your safe return."

She forced herself to perform a decorous if not warm dismissal. *Let him save face.* Jordan bowed again. If her father was correct and Captain Jordan had been pilfering a fortune out of what he owed to Hammond and Company, then damn the imprudent man! He should buy the damned ship he lost and deliver it to her on the next tide! But she let this pass in that moment. There were other lonely merchantmen with money—any man her father had invited to their *soiree* would do. Her father's banker and creditor, Westerly, was her first target... tomorrow. She convinced herself how unwise and unseemly it would be to borrow money from an employee, even if much of Jordan's purported estate was rightfully hers. She might not trust Matthew Westerly, but his long-standing investments in her father's trade had made both men rich. She could understand the banker's motives; he was not a complicated man; his motive was clear. What drove Captain Cornelius Jordan, on the other hand, was a deepening mystery. Once bought back at auction, she was determined *Rattlesnake* must sail by month's end.

As Jordan's horse galloped down the drive from the manor, Emma decided she must find a safeguard. If Thom were to sail again under this captain, she needed an honest man to watch the boy. Although she wanted to keep Briggs in the office, she decided to send him once again to sea, for Thom's sake. They had danced around the subject of a future command; both saw the arrangement through a looking glass of self-interest.

After negotiations with Matthew Westerly for a credit extension, Captain Jordan, First Mate Ben Briggs, and the armed *letter of marque* brig *Rattlesnake* once again from her mainmast proudly flew the blue-and-red pennant of *HL Hammond and Co*. Refitted with new cordage and sails, she set out from Newport into the Atlantic on a hard upwind beat. After two days she crossed the frothy Gulf Stream current, skirting Bermuda to the east. After ten days' hard sailing to intercept any British merchant ships crossing from the West Indies to England, nearing British Barbados, the brig chanced upon a welcomed sight: a convoy—six ships hull down at first light.

Ben Briggs engaged Captain Jordan for his battle plan. But the captain refused to rise from his stupor below. Failing this, Briggs determined his own approach: a speedy downwind attack with the sun striking from dead-astern. Unfortunately, perpendicular to *Rattlesnake's* course, and to windward, the man aloft spied a twenty-gun British Royal Navy brig trailing the six-ship convoy. *An unfortunate sight,* thought Briggs. *No captures today.* Any other privateer would have recognized the dangerous superiority of the more powerfully armed enemy ship and immediately run. Captain Jordan, however, staggered on deck, stared out, and smiled. While he knew with one well-aimed British broadside from close quarters *Rattlesnake* could be sunk, that reality did nothing to quell his lust for honor so soon after his humiliations—not only in Tortola, but worse, at Great Hill acquiescing to the impudent girl. Perhaps some tragic sacrifice would be worth it, Jordan told himself, if he could see her anguished face at the news of his valor. But, then again, a rash move might cost him his skin which he very much valued... so he perished the thought, holding to his first steely impulse.

Briggs watched the captain mull over the options. He had begun to understand how Jordan operated: could he best a Royal Navy ship with only a pitifully small, light privateer, thus bolstering his feared reputation on both sides of the Atlantic? A merchant brig hastily converted into a fighting privateer, however, could not fight a man-of-war broadside-to-broadside. *Rattlesnake* did have one great advantage though—she carried over fifty men thirsty for prizes and enjoyed the nimbleness of both sail and hull to lay alongside any vessel and send over a hoard to kill and take control. The key to *Rattlesnake's* success was, therefore, before any boarding attempt, the enemy must be effectively raked by broadsides of grapeshot to disable her rig and small arms fire to decimate her gunners manning cannon on her open gun deck. The enemy's crew injured and dying would make for an easier capitulation. *Rattlesnake* had won numerous skirmishes against unarmed sailors on slow merchantmen—a vastly different scenario than taking on a seasoned warship with British Royal Marine sharpshooters above in the tops. That said, Briggs convinced himself, there was at least a fair chance that their motivated armed privateersmen, in a surprise maneuver, might come alongside a damaged ship, board, and overcome one hundred or more unhappy pressed men of varied nations, colors, and tongues. If *Rattlesnake* successfully captured the enemy two master, Captain Jordan could corral the entire British convoy and lead it back into Charleston—making it the largest privateer haul and greatest Yankee victory in this war—eclipsing even *Constitution*'s mauling of *Java* and *Guerriere.*

As insane as their prospect appeared, Jordan could not resist the opportunity. Briggs realized that without Gant at his side, he himself lacked the backbone to stand up to Captain Jordan, hard set on a direct attack. Feeling ill, Briggs looked along the deck at the crewmen in this command, mostly new to *Rattlesnake.* Her seasoned, murderous veterans—more used to Jordan's maniacal ways—had been captured in Tortola and were now either toiling in the cane fields or chained in *Fortitude's* orlop. Those captured privateersmen were waiting for the letter from Matthew Westerly that Ben had sewn into his inner jacket pocket, stitched tight in the event he might come upon Captain Breton at sea or find a way to rendezvous off Boston or ashore in the designated tavern. He planned to send any captured British merchant sailors into Kingston with a message for the Royal Navy that he would meet their agent or designated ship off Boston later in the month. But first the American privateer must do the unthinkable—overcome a heavily armed British man-of-war.

"Orders, Captain?" Briggs looked to Jordan.

Eyes beaming, the captain set down his glass, his smile rich with pleasure. "He shall not expect a direct attack, of course. So, we shall aim straight at his broadside, as if we plan to come alongside and board," Jordan announced calmly.

"We shall suffer great damage, sir."

"They shall miss. Look at our course of sail. Consider the rising sun. We shall blind them," countered Jordan. Briggs turned toward the dawn. "Let their cannon fire one broadside. After, we'll trim fast, head up hard."

"Up? We'll be near alongside. And with our speed, a bit ahead of her course—" Briggs argued each of Jordan's planned steps.

"Aye. And then we'll wear ship and cross her bow. They will have no bow chasers set and won't have the time to ready one. Our cannon will rake their gun deck while their larboard guns are reloading," Jordan explained. Briggs recognized the well-crafted design. "I want every sail set and trimmed for maximum speed. We enjoy a freshening breeze. We'll ride in on the easterly swells. Even if they hit us, they'll aim too high, or else shoot low into the sea. Only a lucky shot will land. Thomas Hammond!" cried Jordan. The captain pondered how his authority of command might sound across Emma's forest of fine crystal decanters and stemware. *She won't like my next orders...*

Thomas huffed to the taffrail and put his fist to his forehead. "Captain, sir?"

"I need a good man on the bow to call our turn. I want you to—"

"Ah, Captain, Mr. Hammond's place during action is below deck, you recall our promise to—" Ben made a flaccid attempt to comply with Emma's request.

"Damn the girl! I shall take the convoy and audacious Mr. Hammond here will do his duty like any brave privateersman! Won't you, lad?"

"Aye, sir." Thomas obeyed the captain ignoring Briggs' suggestion but catching the mate's eye, recalling their private conversation that night at Great Hill regarding the captain's erratic decision-making.

"But, Captain—"

"His eyes are better than any man on board, Mr. Briggs. Timing the turn is the key to our advantage! Mr. Hammond, I order you to disappear beneath the bulwarks the moment you call the turn!"

"Aye, sir!" came the youngster's retort.

"Mr. Briggs?"

Briggs sighed, conceding. He glanced over his shoulder yearning to see Gant—two brothers against one to talk sense. Briggs stood alone. "Thomas, the captain has... an interesting plan." His hand on Thomas' shoulder, he advised, "Watch for their cannon smoke then count 'one thousand one'. We shall be close to her broadside and if their shot hits our bow... you must find space below the bowsprit bulkhead where a shot will unlikely injure you. Your sister shall tar my pale skin if we return you with stiches in your cheek. Be a good lad and stay alive, eh?"

"Yes, sir. Do you think—?"

"Follow your orders. Your eyes *are* better than any on board. Yell as loud as you can. We may find it difficult to hear."

"Aye, sir!"

"God bless you, stay low." Briggs smiled weakly, feeling nauseous.

His hands were damp with sweat—this enemy displayed far more peril than a lightly-gunned West Indiaman. He did not trust the captain, once again sending the ship straight into a thousand-weight of deadly metal. He stared at the trim British ship: ten larboard cannon were run out. A single shot fired to find *Rattlesnake's* range, but like the captain surmised, landed short into a rising swell. The British sails backwinded, thus slowed her forward speed, steadying her deck against rolling swells for a more accurate fire. The enemy was ready for ship-to-ship battle as the sky flashed with the sunrise's deadly greeting.

"Do it! Do it! Do it—*now!*" Jordan yelled, encouraging his enemy to fire prematurely as *Rattlesnake* dipped into a deep swell.

The captain considered the elements as the enemy would—he timed the rolling swells, anticipated the ball's flight, factored the deep troughs, watched for gusts and shifts, anticipated the resistance of the downwind pressure against twelve-pound long-cannon balls flung through humid morning air, calculated distance by a careful reading of the sextant—each could alter a fired projectile's flight. Jordan gauged it all in careful detail as he hoped the enemy gunner would not, until ten angry British guns suddenly fired as one: Clearly, the brig was newer-built with ribs able to withstand the synchronous violence of a broadside that would spring open seams in an older vessel. The enemy's volley was well-timed, well-aimed. The British hit *Rattlesnake* with the ferocity of a professional navy. The American privateer absorbed a crushing injury of shots purposely aimed high: spars split and broke, sails ripped and holed, the foretopmast shot through teetered, held in place by only shrouds and backstays. *Rattlesnake's* deck fell into chaos under the raining debris.

Thomas Hammond crouched on *Rattlesnake's* forward deck; he watched the ensuing fury instead of ducking behind the bulkhead as ordered. His critical job came next. Thomas recognized his crafty captain's plan. *Rattlesnake* enjoyed superior downwind speed and had room to maneuver to either side of the man-of-war, attack the enemy's stern if she fell away or at her bow as the privateer enjoyed enough speed to bear up, overtaking the slower ship. The boy noted the significant damage hanging above his head caused by the British broadside. He focused on his job, however, peered through the enemy cannon smoke and admired *Rattlesnake's* speed despite her damaged rigging. The captain ordered all sails trimmed. The helm turned sharply up-wind. The privateer and her more powerful enemy were suddenly abeam each other, the Yankees, however sailing considerably faster.

Thom, watching the *'Snake* pass the British ship, counted, *one, two, three*.

"Ahoy the quarterdeck! We're clear to cross! Turn NOW!" screamed Thom.

The boy could not be sure if his shrill adolescent screeching carried the length of the deck with all its intended urgency though he heard it repeated along the way. Thom trusted his ability to gauge the enemy's course and speed, having taken into account the man-of-war's long sprit and its even longer sprit boom that, when coupled with forward motion, might have impeded the privateer's crossing action if he had called the turn prematurely. He had accomplished his mission. Then, Thom heard a crack far above his head. He looked up.

"Tack!" screamed Jordan, and *Rattlesnake's* spars and staysails flew across the deck as her rudder caught the force of the water. Spars and booms crashed from the larboard tack across the ship to their new settings on a starboard tack. The ship turned sharply nearly ninety degrees on the compass, headed up, and slid by the enemy's long sprit boom. *Rattlesnake*, on her new course, her guns ready, faced the enemy's unarmed bow.

"We should fire into her rig and stop her dead, Captain—" Briggs screamed at Jordan, who was now a bloody mass from his right shoulder and arm.

"Nay, aim at her gun deck! Kill them!" cried Jordan. "Fire!" he commanded moments after the change of course.

Every heart jumped. *Rattlesnake's* well-aimed eighteen-pounders sent their discharge of grape—canisters of small, lethal iron balls, nails, and broken pieces of glass—directly at the exposed gun deck of the British brig where her massed deck crew looked on in horror. At point blank range, grapeshot does not miss. Jordan's broadside tore into men stripped to their waist. The powerful pellets of death shredded arms and legs, and wrought unimaginable damage to bodies, eyes, and faces. The blood of one man splattered his neighbor, body parts and gore splayed on deck and bulwarks. Black powder in their canisters sitting idly next to the hot and still-smoking cannon caught fire and spread more explosions unleashing additional terror on the British ship. The enemy deck was strewn with screaming injured, silent dead, and cannon unable to point at their American foe unless their course abruptly pivoted.

Rattlesnake's deck was hidden in sulfur-tinged clouds of smoke as Jordan's second command rang out, "Wear ship, mates! Hard over! Crack on the braces! All hands to the larboard cannon!"

Briggs saw Jordan's mouth move, knowing the plan as he spun the heavy wheel its full turn, but his reeling head could not hear the words. The sails caught the breeze and *Rattlesnake* turned on its keel. *Has an enemy projectile crushed my skull?* Ben wondered. He wiped blood from his eyes and realized his vision was blurred, yet he still moved to the command of the man who might yet kill them all. The English man-of-war had only to come about and aim her powerful starboard broadside at *Rattlesnake*'s thin hull, the battle lost. But the British did not change course. *Why? Have they not enough crew,* Briggs considered? Her larboard cannon primed and loaded, on her new tack *Rattlesnake*'s gun crews aimed at the enemy's unprotected foc's'le. Minutes earlier the British brig had shot a deadly volley at the Americans but it had not been deadly enough. When the privateer crossed the British ship's bow, the Yankees' initial fire dealt a murderous blow: British crewmen, dazed and injured, many of whom had been pressed from merchantmen or dragged from the fields, ran about the decks following officers' conflicting orders: '*You, trim topgallant star'bd braces! Gun crews, reload!*' The man-of-war's deck fell into a wreck of bleeding bodies cluttered with fallen sails, lines, and splintered wood—madness and fury bleeding into the West Indies Sea.

"Kill their people, protect the prize! Fire!" crying out, Jordan waved his sword with his left hand.

Once again Jordan's privateer delivered devastating results. *Rattlesnake* unleashed her second crippling volley at the unprotected bow of the enemy. The Americans' second broadside hit true—again with the murderous effect of grapeshot. As the American cannon fired in unison, the sudden violent vibration brought *Rattlesnake*'s injured sails, broken spars, and foretopmast crashing to the foredeck. Jordan held his sword and waved it high—now they could board and take the enemy ship while her decks bled. *Man against man, the only way to fight and die! What glory!* The Southern States from New Orleans to Norfolk, despite the blockade, would open their ports to his returning ship, their charming belles warmly welcoming his drunken celebration for weeks. His employer in her mansion would read about his bold feat when news traveled north. She would taste none of the accolades, however, only the spoils come her due when *Rattlesnake* sauntered into Newport after the revelry in welcoming ports had sated his unbridled desires.

Tragically, the British captain's initial strategy failed. His Majesty's ship had attempted to slow the charging privateer by sending a larboard volley into her rig, debilitating her sailing abilities. The pirates had come at him faster than expected, however, hardened up and crossed the 'T'. As he lay on his quarterdeck bathed in blood, his feet and legs no longer moving to his command, he saw the cursed Yankee brig prepare to cross his bow for a second pass, having tacked with astonishing dexterity for an injured ship.

"Helm up thirty degrees! Starboard guns, once in range, fire at will!" screamed the captain, his coarse voice fading.

"The brig's already about, sir. Coming back to rake our bow again!"

The startled British captain had belatedly recognized the privateer's intention to cross. His ship's point-blank broadside had failed to stop *Rattlesnake*; she still had speed. He hoped to bring his starboard cannon into the battle and was about to give orders to come about when he saw the Americans bearing down. His eyes wide, he blessed himself as the enemy fired their larboard cannon armed with grape, if aimed low as now, intended to rip his men apart. The Yankee cannon flung their ruthless, deadly loads down the long, unprotected deck of his warship. He watched as men, already in distress from the initial volley, disappeared in red cloudbursts of skin, teeth, and shredded uniforms. Nevertheless, the British captain retained his wits. He was desperately undermanned on this convoy home with only one hundred men to both send aloft and fire cannon, eight men to a gun. To fight another warship and sail his two-mast square-rigger in close maneuver at the same time was not possible. His plan for battle, therefore, had favored the one move that presented him with clear advantage: an initial, full-throated, unanswered broadside into the brig's naked bow. It had failed to slow the Yankee, however. His mangled warship ship was now a cruelly injured casualty of war.

As the unfortunate captain passed out, he ordered the Union Jack be lowered, "…before they murder us all."

Dazed, Briggs stared ahead. What were these black blotches in his eyes—blood? Shrapnel? A wound? Was his brain in pieces due to an injury he could not feel? And then, echoing in their wake, he heard the distinct menace of cannon shot from a distant, new direction.

"What?!" Jordan too looked to the west. He had heard the same cannon. A British squadron, coming up hard had been following the convoy and the covering brig at a safe distance just over the horizon hoping to lure a privateer's attack. *Was it the same relentless squadron from the Azores and Tortola?* Jordan asked himself. *How… how could that be? In this entire ocean, am I never to be free of them?* "Damn him to Hell-fire! Briggs!" Jordan cried out.

"Ahhh, yeah, Capt—?" Bleeding and weak, Briggs hung onto the wheel, faint voices reaching him at last.

"Does the helm respond?"

Briggs looked up and as far as he could tell, their lower fore course was in full trim and powering the ship despite the damage to the mast above it. Their mainmast carried all her sails and spars—holed sails were many—though they still enjoyed reasonable speed and maneuverability.

"Aye…"

Jordan watched the waves, waiting for gusts topping off each rolling crest. He needed the sea's support in unison for his next move. He waited and took a deep breath.

"Wear ship!" cried the captain.

Rattlesnake obeyed and found a new course to the north. They might yet escape. The approaching squadron was too far west and south to catch them in this breeze. The wounded British brig drifted, limping and groaning with the agony of fifty bloodied men, confused and dying. She too, was out of the chase. Focusing with great effort Briggs recognized Jordan was badly wounded, his right arm and shoulder a mass of bloody skin and tendons hanging loose. His face black with powder, streaked with the blood of another crewman who had stood nearby when a shot hit his mid-section, killing him in an instant. *Rattlesnake* sailed back on her original course. The escaping British convoy remained safe and unharmed, all sails hard-trimmed for England. The privateer must abandon the attack to return home, her crew cut to pieces, the ship hanging on for life: men, gripping each other to stand, searching for bandages to wrap wounds, to stop the bleeding, holding bones inside broken bodies.

Briggs ignored Jordan's momentary intention to return to the stricken enemy man-of-war, to a battle that would end with *Rattlesnake's* sinking once the squadron came up. Instead, the first mate steered straight away from the enemy. The squadron would likely cut away and pursue; *Rattlesnake* might yet be caught. After calculating the speed of both pursuer and distance, he thought not. Men already were high aloft to jury rig a stun'sl boom in place of the foretopmast which had crashed to the foredeck...

"The foredeck, Thomas!" Briggs grabbed a nearby crewman and threw him at the wheel, ordering, "Steer!"

Jordan, in shock, continued to shout nonsense. Briggs stepped over pieces of men and cannon, climbed around a ripped sail that had collapsed, and passed crewmen struggling to reset sails. He surveyed the damage aloft and the carnage below: the fore royal yardarm, along with its blocks and rigging had fallen into a heap on the foredeck. Sticking out from the debris he noticed skinny legs. With help from two crewmen shoving aside the weight of a fallen spar Ben found beneath a mass of blood and shattered bones.

"Thomas! Can you speak?"

The boy gazed up at the bloody face hovering above him in the smoke. *Who are you? The Devil? I cannot move my legs or my body. Nothing moves to my command! I will cry out and yell my epitaph that will reach the deepest part of his black kingdom and curse and rain hatred on every soul trapped there.* Thomas Hammond's blurred vision cleared for a moment.

"Mr. Briggs! Did we win?" Thom mouthed the words. *Why does he not respond? Will Mr. Briggs save me from this monster? No, he is the monster. Help me, Mr. Briggs! My legs hurt, they hurt so bad, I cannot move and I cannot cry out. Where's the captain? Oh, my Lord, sweet Jesus, I cannot bear this! Mother, help me, my sweet Lord in Heaven...*

Briggs held the boy as blood of his own head wound dripped onto Thom's face. Briggs wiped the boy's face with a burnt hand. The spar had crushed Thomas Hammond's spine. His hip was twisted in a way it was not meant to turn. His hands were already cold. From his leg wounds poured blood faster than any tourniquet could arrest. The boy had precious moments left.

Briggs whispered into his ear, "You saved the ship, Thom. You called the turn. Rest now, sweet lad." He held the boy's hand and felt a firm squeeze moments before Thom's terrified eyes stared back at him for all time.

Chapter Fifteen

Captain Breton's squadron pursued the Yankee privateer for two days. Again, the chase proved futile—the brig, though damaged, sailed faster than *Fortitude*. Although Breton flew every stuns'l she carried, the pursuing British gained little ground. In the Indies, the Yankee ship had appeared like an Irish ghost trespassing over a bog, even though months earlier Breton had watched it sail from Tortola for Kingston with a British ensign and an able Navy prize crew. It occurred to him the hunter may himself have become hunted: An American forty-four-gun frigate was rumored south of the Carolinas. Quite by accident his squadron had come upon the privateer's attack on the brig assigned to a convoy, not a planned ambush as before in Horta. His report, however, took credit for saving the unfortunate *Palfrey*—a disgraceful action that would cost her wounded master his command: A twelve-gun brig, a privateer no less, disabled one of His Majesty's warships? *Fortitude* and his two trailing cutters passed *Palfrey* and the escaping convoy, not offering to take their wounded. *War has a cost,* Breton rationalized as his own injuries continued to torture him.

Captain Breton gave up the chase when, after a night of winter squalls, his lookout lost sight of the American brig. He anchored close by Admiral Warren's fleet of frigates and line-of-battle ships blockading New York Harbor and the Connecticut coast where a small squadron of an American warship and consorts were blockaded in New London. He signaled the flagship, went aboard, and made his unfortunate report. The interview did not take long. Breton had been assigned his squadron with a clear directive: *Find the American privateer* Rattlesnake *and sink her, damn bloody Hell, sink her! And yet, this pirate brig has thrice escaped your superior force?* Breton made his leave as soon as the admiral had flayed his pride, hearing one final command. *Yes, by all means, if she carries any communiques for His Majesty's Government, bring them here immediately!*

He took on water from the flagship, made repairs to rigging and sails, procured at high cost in the form of further debasement from the admiral, "Indeed, the fleet is in desperate need of supplies ourselves, Captain. Take only what I am able to spare and assure me this *'Snake* will darken Hell before you darken my cabin again!"

Captain Breton set a course north—to New England, *Rattlesnake's* home—following the admiral's final order, one not committed to paper in his sealed packet: *'Wait there until you rendezvous with representatives of the friendly forces in Boston.'* The squadron sailed past Long Island, Nantucket's shoals, Pollock Rip, rounded Wellfleet, and halfway between the Stellwagen Bank and the mainland, hove to and waited. Fog on the banks started to lift. The British squadron drifted at the designated longitude and latitude. A few hours later, on the appointed day, a schooner dutifully appeared, though her topmasts were not set. No warship, only a fishing workboat plying the banks for cod and halibut. A longboat lowered from her side and a man in a heavy cloak was rowed by crewmen three hundred feet across to *Fortitude.* The man climbed aboard the frigate with an easy effort, surprising for a man of his bulk.

In the cabin, no names were offered. Breton kept to himself on his side of the great cabin, with its China service, crystal clarets, and rum decanters. Marines guarded the door. Mates kept the crew busy aloft tarring the shrouds. On board *Fortitude*, at this late date in her nearly twenty years of European wars, sailed a crew of loyal Englishmen, as well as impressed colonists: white and black, from the West Indies, Far East, India, and Canton, and a few captured French sailors who chose the harshness of the English navy over the unsure reception they might face at home. Few of the men on the lower deck were trusted by their officers; the worst, twenty sailors who claimed American birth but who had been impressed from Yankee ships over the past eighteen months of open war and many years of open harassment prior. More than a few dragooned Yankee men had not seen the North American coast or their families for over five years. Many American ears strained to hear even a snippet of the conversation taking place below deck.

"Plans are underway," the cloaked stranger said.

Breton spoke deliberately. "We have done our part. Your slavers have been granted passage."

"And their owners are most grateful," the stranger confirmed. "The cotton export to your mills will accelerate by two hundred percent in '16." Breton grunted and waited; he had no gift for economics though he knew of his country's desperate need for imported raw cotton to drive their cotton mills, export the woven fabrics, and gather foreign currency. "And so, our friends sent me to inquire about the other matter." *The man was direct like all cursed Americans,* thought Breton shifting his weight to his uninjured leg. He was not sure he wanted to provide an answer.

"You refer to a landing?" Breton clarified.

"I do. Your troops to come ashore again, but with overpowering force this time. As agreed. Here..." The man took out a rough drawn map of the Virginia coast, up the bay near the river. "...and led by your Iron Duke with the full force of His Majesty's combined Army and Navy. Our troops shall join you."

"Do your friends anticipate a major engagement?"

"No. In fact our plans are moving ahead as expected—the flow of monies to men we influence is nearly complete. Their votes will promote a great friend of our cause into high office."

"And what of your standing army? And States' militias?"

"The militias are called away to the West and the North—another feint against Canada and far from your landing."

"If His Majesty's troops meet massed American forces in battle..." Breton's secret orders were to make this point extraordinarily clear. He looked out his aft windows to the calm, cold waters of Stellwagen Bank. He repeated, slowly, "If we come to a major battle, His Majesty's officers will show no quarter. Yankee leaders who profess to be our friends and leaders who do not will be treated alike—without consideration for mercy, rank, or privilege. If English blood spills, we shall do what we should have done in 1776 on Long Island. Like we did at Culloden. We will crush you and your armed peasant farmers and throw your leaders into Mill Prison to keep your pirates company."

Breton's injured leg throbbed; the subsiding dose of opium made him more irritable than usual. He thought of his nephew, Peter, cut to the quick having savored only a single decade of life. Perhaps he would fire the schooner and watch the American traitors drown like he had watched his own men disappear under the blue of the Sir Francis Drake Channel. The cloaked, heavy-set man opposite did not flinch, however. The British captain recalled a final question his admiral had instructed him to ask. "What do we call you people, once we have secured our landing?"

"Our agreement is we remain free to govern within each of our states. His Majesty will have free access west of the Ohio and the Mississippi rivers. Bonaparte's former territory will be sold to the Crown at the price already negotiated, less the commission due our syndicate, of course. We shall remain unto ourselves—The United Atlantic States." ...*of America*, he conspicuously left unsaid.

They can't have returned so soon! Something is wrong... Emma was startled by the news *Rattlesnake* had been sighted picking up a pilot off Point Judith. This time, she decided she would not rush to the dock—*Let the captain come to me with his report.* She feared the worst, however: a privateer returned early would likely carry only more pathetic excuses. *What stories this time? 'Your empty cargo hold, Captain?' 'The repaired ribs did not hold!' 'You abandoned your prize?' 'The blasted Royal Navy appeared in force...'* She allowed herself to drift... *What would Father do with a captain who returned with a damaged ship and deaths while bereft of spoils in multiple voyages? A man who surrendered his ship, and whose crew largely remains in prison. Should I scuttle him before he scuttles Hammond and Company? Who do I have to replace him?* She considered Ben Briggs again, but quickly discounted the notion. *More valuable ashore.* Ben was a sailor—but not a stealthy privateersman. His intellect best suited trade, whereas a privateersman must frequently unsheathe his sword. Before this last cruise, Ben Briggs had successfully purchased replacement cannon from a smuggler as he had promised, proving his estimable value. She must find someone else to replace Captain Jordan. For a moment, her thoughts turned to Quartus Gant. The handsome, angry Mr. Gant had the particular fortitude necessary for offshore trade. He would accept dangerous cruises that other men refuse. His darkness of personality matched the lack of light that engulfed privateering. If he had a heart, he hid it. As she thought about him, a deep sadness overcame her. His unblinking stare had shaken her to the core on their first meeting, and it infected her. The silence of his tart answers had conveyed a great deal more; a turn of his head when he looked at her made her stomach jump—so much left unsaid. What was becoming clear, *he* was the privateersman she needed. Why had Morris not yet informed her of success freeing Gant from Mill Prison? Had his intervention failed? Did Morris expect her to crawl to him once again? She must wait him out. Sitting alone in her father's study, Emma intended to confront Captain Jordan within the hour, her cherished brother beside her to fortify her courage. Unless *Rattlesnake's* return so quickly was due to an overflow of success, multiple ships taken in quick order and sent to auction, she intended to end Cornelius Jordan's service with the Hammond Company. She would ask Mr. Briggs to help her select a new captain... after his expected objections to her change of mind had subsided.

An hour passed. No riders appeared at Great Hill's gate. No dashing captain on horseback, no grinning Thomas, no First Mate Briggs to calm her nerves. Alarmed, Emma could wait no longer on decorum and rank. She readied her chaise herself and whipped her fine mare along the road until *Rattlesnake* stood before her: her sails only loosely furled, many ripped and tattered. Her fore topmast was missing, while her long bowsprit boom was snapped like a twig. The ship's starboard forward gunnels—even from a distance—showed the great violence the ship had suffered. Injured crewmen in blood-soaked bandages staggered past Emma, silent as death as they limped toward mercy nurses who would do their best. By the mangled hands and arms she saw, odds for many were not good. These men—*her* men, *her* crew—barely had the strength to acknowledge her. Only a few raised an eye or pretended to smile at her. Most who looked at her had the long faces of the defeated, limping on their silent way. Into the harsh sun, Ben finally emerged.

"Mr. Briggs!" cried Emma as she jumped off the wagon and approached the gangway, emptying of all who could walk on their own.

Briggs appeared confused by the young woman's voice. With trouble, he recognized Emma; his vision had not yet cleared. His skull still rang; pounding down whiskey had done little to soothe it. Bandages around his head, brown from dried blood, bore fresh red blotches from new leakage. He found his way to the gangway plank, and with the assistance of a strong, young crewman, reached Emma.

"Briggs, where's Thomas?" she cried, terrified.

He looked at her, focusing on her flushed face. *Where to start?* He had only a few moments of energy to both talk and stand, to absorb the anguish he knew would soon fill the morning. He wanted to slink away leaving Jordan to speak of his ship's fate.

"Ahh... he's ahh—"

"Tell me, Briggs, what's happened? The ship's in tatters!"

"We attacked a convoy... a British man-of-war, a heavy brig protecting five ships—"

"You attacked an English man-of-war?" she spat out, incredulous.

"We could have taken them... but a squadron hidden in the haze trailed. The same ships from Pico... and Tortola. Tracking us..."

Emma looked toward the ship's deck, and then all around her at the pier.

"Has Captain Jordan run off to his *dying mother* once again?"

Briggs stared at her. "He's alive. Though he'll need to learn to fight left-handed." Emma put her hands to her mouth. She eyed the deck again, expecting to see Jordan waving. "However, Thom—" Briggs murmured.

He looked directly at her. The right words refused to flow. The obvious connection between the ship's carnage and her brother's absence cruelly collided. Emma nearly collapsed on the wharf held up only by Brigg's catching her under her arms.

"No! No, no, no... it cannot be!" She screamed with a savagery that rent her thin ribcage.

Briggs held her as tenderly as he had held Thomas's bloody, broken body.

Men with drawn, lost faces circled away from Emma Hammond and her anguished crying.

Several days alone at Great Hill in her upstairs bedroom, Emma sat in her alcove. Tending only to her sleeping father in the next room, she allowed herself little private grief. From here on, all her days would be without Thomas and his innocent mirth. Slowly, she came to accept that. She stiffened, rode into the port, and sent word, instructing *Rattlesnake's* two officers to meet with her in her father's office. Before they arrived, she placed two plain, stiff chairs to face her seat behind Colonel Hammond's desk. When her father's officers arrived, awkward and hesitant, they sat at her command and stared at her, dressed in black, tight to her neck and loose at the waist, her habitual smile firmly locked away.

"Which of you thought my instructions included attacking a British *warship*?"

Captain Jordan displayed none of his former luster. He was, in fact, quite ill. His severely wounded arm had become infected; the local surgeon proposed amputation above the elbow for as soon as that same afternoon. Face pale and taut, cut in many places from splinters, Cornelius Jordan made no attempt to smile. Although he was a rich man—one of the richest in Rhode Island by now, or so he claimed—he looked like he fell off a cart on the way to a charity house. Jordan's eyes refused to meet Emma's. In fact, had Briggs not dragged him out of his stupor from his berth on *Rattlesnake*, doused him with water, and helped him dress in fresh linens, breeches, and a clean shirt, Captain Jordan would not have made the appointment with his employer. He had arrived, however—his presence all he had to offer. It was apparent the captain felt no need to explain his manner of fighting. Sullenly, his eyes rose toward the haughty girl—his unbridled contempt burned openly at her insolence. She hadn't *been there*. She didn't *understand* the heat of battle. Here sat a spoiled, arrogant woman—while he, for her father, had waged bloody war against the Empire. Emma recognized Jordan had no intention to explain himself.

"Your wound?" she asked as if it was a mere scrape and he no longer a respected captain.

"Arm's coming off, Miss Hammond. They'll strap me down and gag my mouth so my screams don't scare the neighborhood children... They'll cut skin and muscle to the bone, then saw it off—" Jordan intended to make a bad morning worse.

"I see," she interrupted, resisting her inclination to point out that the fool had brought this upon himself.

Ben was grateful for her intercession. He began to recount the disaster carefully, knowing his own future hung in air. "We came upon five ships, Miss Hammond—five prizes at dawn—a once-in-a-lifetime opportunity. We could see the sixth, an escorting warship, meandering, her movements not service-like. Thus, clearly under-manned, unable to operate both her long guns and maneuver at the same time. *Rattlesnake* had the wind and the breaking sun at our back, and the advantage of speed."

"But in the heat of your once-in-a-lifetime opportunity," she said dryly, "you didn't keep your wits about you, did you? You missed seeing an *entire squadron* of British ships coming down on you as you stepped into their trap?"

Briggs looked at Jordan who wiped his nose with the sleeve of his working arm.

"Aye, but you see, in battle... the smoke—" Briggs answered tentatively.

"I don't care about the *damned* smoke—didn't you keep a lookout atop the mast!"

"Their first broadside shot away our forepeak, Miss."

"Go on. I shouldn't have to pull words from your mouth. I expect a frank exchange."

"The lookout went over the side, Miss, when the mast collapsed. The wreckage crashed onto the deck. Three men were caught beneath. Including Thomas..."

She put her finger to her eye and wiped it before they noticed—a swipe to steal away the mate's words before they were uttered. *If he didn't say those words, perhaps Thom didn't die.*

"And who allowed my brother to remain on deck during this carnage?" Silence followed. "I see. Mr. Briggs, did my brother have any... final words?"

"He asked if we won," Ben replied.

A silent memory of her brave brother stopped the inquisition. Its soft deafness crept from the window to the desk to the chairs and back around again, abused by another of Jordan's prolonged sniffs and a wipe on his good sleeve. Disgusted, she turned away from her officers and spoke in short, clipped words.

"Thank you for your past services to our family, Captain Jordan. However, you have failed me grievously. I instructed, no... *pleaded* with you to keep my brother safe. Yet, you chose not to. I can never forgive you. I honor Hammond and Company's commitment to pay you for this disastrous cruise." Emma reached into her drawer and tossed a small, heavy pouch deliberately in front of Jordan's right side where his wounded arm in its sling could not reach for it. She wanted to see him grovel. "You are, however, relieved of command. Good day."

She stared at the broken man and expecting his anger to rise. Jordan looked at the pouch, slowly realizing it was a pittance for the price he paid with an arm. Staring at her, he reached awkwardly with his good arm, scoffed, and stuffed the money into his jacket. Indifferent, Emma turned her gaze to Ben.

"Mr Briggs, please remain, if you will."

Captain Jordan looked once more at her. *Bitch!* He regained his posture and stood. With his left arm, he waved low, bending forward in a final, obscene gesture, his hateful gaze pouring over her. She glanced at him as he staggered out the door and down the stairs, whistling. Emma stood. She grabbed her chair-back in a tight grip as her eyes shifted angrily at the view out her window. She regarded the men working furiously to get her warship back to the war. Her demeanor softened a degree though her voice retained a hard edge of antipathy that Ben had never heard from her.

"Mr Briggs," she whispered without turning to face him, "I have a proposition for you."

Privateer

Chapter Sixteen

F irst Mate Ben Briggs carefully considered his next move. "I am eager to hear it, Emma," said Briggs softly, watching her stare out at her sad, injured warship docked at the wharf.

By the time Cornelius Jordan's insolent whistling faded, Emma reconciled a chapter of her life had ended. Remorseful, yet resolute, she turned the page.

"Mr. Gant's warnings were warranted," she murmured with a chill.

That she spoke of Q at this moment stung Ben. He had hoped she might consider himself as her only hope, present and at the ready. Instead, she pined for the imprisoned gunner.

Briggs answered neutrally, "Q saw Jordan clearly."

"I need men who see clearly." Emma let her comment float in the air, a declaration that did not require a reply. She made sure her carefully selected words had time to register, then sat, sighed, and looked straight at Ben. "Briggs, whom can I trust? My father trusted me. You trusted Quartus. I once trusted Cornelius Jor—" She stopped before her eyes became wet. After a pause and a deep breath, she continued, "Things are different now. I have enemies."

"For sure you cannot trust your father's friends," said Ben disingenuously, as he continued to carry the bankers' instructions tightly sewn in his jacket.

She straightened. In this hazy war, although the enemy was British, the Providence men might be more dangerous.

"I need the Providence bankers, Ben. I have to finance three ships for war—hire men, buy provisions and gunpowder. On top of the five thousand I spent to buy back my own ship at auction it's cost me five hundred dollars to return her to sea. And now, she's come home wrecked! How much did the new cannon cost?" He took a paper from his satchel and showed her. She inspected the paper more carefully than the sparse invoice required. She struggled to think of ways to raise more money—a great deal more. Would Ben serve her needs? "Based on recent history, three merchant ships set sail, yet only one returns. We need to send out more privateers, Ben. Only privateers can evade the blockade and increase our position. Can you help me find them?"

"Your accounts are low—"

"I will get the money—" Her tone sharpened, peeved that he too questioned her resources, and angry at the truth. "Can you find more ships, yes or no?"

"I can. Emma." She looked at him and anticipated another of his questions she did not want to answer. "Captain Jordan's finished. Q's not coming home. And even if he does, he's more for smuggling than honest trade—"

"Quartus is a stout privateersman," she countered.

"He lacks a certain quality. He cannot lead men. His courage in battle... was not what you may think." *Hammond ships are my fleet to build now, my ships to command. I sit next to you each day. Not Gant.* Ben would not accept second place to a distant, fading memory. Emma sighed, not surprised at Briggs' words. They revealed more about him than Quartus. She knew Gant had faults, but lack of spirit was hardly one of them. Nevertheless, Briggs clarified her thinking. Respectfully, she listened as Briggs continued, "You have all you need in front of you. With your father's and *your* permission, I'll command *Rattlesnake* and work our other ships into a privateer squadron." Emma bridled at *our*, but let him continue. "I'll keep my ships within signal range and cover fifty or more miles of open water. One ship will find a prize, signal the others, and converge as a swarmed fleet. We'll build a veil of protection and avoid enemy warships—"

"Mr. Briggs, even a woman knows one cannot apply naval tactics to run-and-gun warfare! We don't have line-of-battle ships! Ours are small coastal brigs and schooners. We can only capture weaker, slower ships!"

"But Emma, you are missing—"

"I am only missing men with good sense!" Her cold fury, heretofore reserved for the likes of Jordan, froze him out. Before her father fell ill, before Thomas died, before Jordan's wrecked body slithered out her door, she had presented to the world a kind and gracious young woman. Now flames seared within her vivid green eyes. She calmed herself, remonstrating, *Have I overplayed a weak hand? I mustn't chase away my last hope.* First, she must tell him what he would not want to hear. "I'm not giving you command of *Rattlesnake.* I've changed my mind."

She folded her hands and watched for his reaction: If he exploded in a violent outburst, she would be left utterly alone. She played her hand well. Though surprised and unhappy, Ben thought about a different kind of future.

"We agreed the next command was to be mine." Ben's voice remained flat.

"We did. I do not run from my change of heart. What is best for you, for me, for my family is that you stay ashore with me. If you were lost..." She gave him a small sliver of a smile and hoped it hinted at more. But Briggs saw through her. He sat unmoved and showed his dismay without words. He folded his arms: *Flattery not accepted.* Emma ignored the rejection. "Please remain by my side, Ben, as Company Director. That is my proposition. I need someone to stand in my father's place managing our cruises, setting down keels, and buying ships at auction. I have decided our fortunes are too thin for trade in commodities as long as the British blockade our southern ports and with their pervasive patrols choke us. And we're at the mercy of powerful men who will try to take advantage..." She thought of her visit to Morris. "I've decided we either retreat from the privateering enterprise and become shopkeepers or farmers... or we build a fleet of the largest, most powerful armed ships in the state, the largest fleet on this coast. I cannot manage this worthy endeavor alone."

Emma Hammond has her own heady ambitions! Briggs thought before he offered a neutral rejoinder, "Interesting..."

She saw him smile. *Good.* She leaned in, her voice low, and explained, "Our most pressing challenge remains how to raise a great deal of money in a short period of time. Only a fleet of successful privateers can do this, acting on their own best individual tactics—not in a fleet. Our ships must sneak out in the pitch black and surprise the unwary ships on their way to England with valuable cargoes, returning here without blood-loss. To build these ships we must either borrow heavily from men we would otherwise avoid or consider a different, perhaps more risky option." She paused, as if adding figures in her head.

Intrigued by her suggestion, Ben admired her obvious daring. He watched her angry eyes and the corners of her mouth where in a happier time a smile might have escaped. The privateer mate turned man-of-trade sensed she was hiding with every muscle in her face the excitement of a new idea. Ben realized Emma Hammond was raising the stakes.

"And...?"

"Rumors abound at the docks that Captain Jordan boasts he has amassed a great fortune while in my father's service."

"He has. Much of it stolen from your father."

"I intend to steal it back."

Chapter Seventeen

Two well-dressed men sat opposite each other in high-back chairs bolstered by firm cushions and garnished with elaborate carved handrails. Polished claw feet nestled into a deep pile Persian rug. Its brilliant turquoise fringed with silk tassels provided the sole hue anchoring Geoffrey Morris' otherwise austere library. The bankers spoke economically, hushed with self-importance. Thick cigar smoke rose directly over their heads indicating an airless room; with neither door nor window open, their secret plans had no obvious means of escape. Matthew Westerly smiled weakly at his colleague. Along with the independent thinking and bold initiative he must impart to ensure his own survival, Matthew Westerly hoped to convey the proper balance of respect and deference that Geoffrey Morris' ego required.

"What did he say, Matthew?" demanded Morris, interrupting again.

Westerly ignored the affront with more indifference than he felt. "He noted the location. I made clear our people would join their disembarked force."

Morris probed, "Is Wellesley committed?" Westerly looked down. Morris spat out, "So, what exactly *did* you accomplish?"

"They understand we are serious men." Westerly sat straighter. "I explained our private arrangement. Their captain has a squadron cut out from blockade duty to receive further communiques. He's to remain off the coast of Boston with orders to sink privateers."

"*My* privateers, damn him!"

"To be honest, he was more interested in Hammond's ship. This Captain Jordan has gained a certain notoriety among the English public. They call him *The Curse of the Coast*, after his scathing voyage last spring. He attacked English fishing villages with unfettered violence. They say Jordan's a barbarian."

"A thug—with feathers in his hat. I met him last spring at Hammond's."

"He took many prizes."

"He wreaks havoc. And now he comes begging for a new commission?"

"Yes. The Hammond girl dismissed him. He lost an arm to the British and has been in a fever ever since. Could be useful… if he lives. We might unleash him aboard *Raptor*."

"We might." Morris welcomed the news. "I thought you already found a new captain for *Raptor*."

"I have made no commitments I cannot undo, especially if events move in our direction." Westerly, thinking he had successfully steered the conversation, moved closer to his true purpose of their meeting. "Captain Jordan has other assets our cause could use. As you know, monies promised by Colonel Hammond have fallen far short—"

"Damn, you know I do! And he sleeps all day. Have you checked under his mattress?"

"I understand your frustration, Geoffrey. Let us return to Captain Jordan. If my sources are accurate, he has hoarded a massive fortune over these past few years. Including his profits from smuggling in the years before the war."

"How much?"

"Near one hundred thousand dollars—Spanish silver. Sterling, too."

"*How* much?"

"At least one hundred thousand, my friend: Forty, perhaps fifty ships taken, his contracted share—one sixteenth of the total value of prizes sold at auction—plus… *extra*." Geoffrey Morris puffed, exhaled, and stared up at the smoke rising to the coffered ceiling, as Westerly continued, "*Rattlesnake,* you may recall, captured a fat West Indiaman earlier in the year. She was transporting Aztec plunder the British took from a large Spanish packet—silver mostly, gold nuggets as well."

"Let me guess. No Spanish chests were seen coming ashore in Newport?"

"Correct. And Captain Jordan has an odd habit. When his ship approaches the Bay, he often meets a coastal packet near offshore, southeast of Block Island. From there, he sails up to Bristol—alone."

"Do you know where he stores what he steals?" asked Morris.

"No— in *my* bank." The other man nodded. *Not in any bank.* "But if Captain Jordan sailed for us... keeping our enemies close so to speak—"

"Do it," instructed Morris. "I will think how to encourage his cooperation." He quickly plotted, a skill that had brought him far in this world, a new republic with few hard-and-fast rules: its laws mostly untested, its new leaders few and weak. *An admiral's pennant perhaps in my new service?* "I hear he is not driven solely by gold. I understand that kind of man. We will need men motivated by higher *ideals*. Move quickly, the vote approaches. We lack enough committed senators."

"Ah, Geoffrey," Westerly remembered, "the English captain asked about our proposed naming convention. How will we refer to your new... role?"

"*Governor*," answered Morris without hesitation.

"*Governor* Morris. I see..." Westerly mused calmly, masking his discomfort with Morris' self-crowned title; its sinister undertones startled Westerly.

"I have simple tastes," replied Morris, instructing, "Tell our friends that only *I* speak for the new administration. Assure them there will be no confusion. We will have no elected officials to be meddlesome, once we pay them. The Secretary of War—an incompetent. Our generals—feeble and still fighting the Long Island debacle as if this were still 1776. Our Navy Secretary—a drunkard like his admirals. I will wash them all ashore! Permanently."

Did I offer my idea to commandeer Jordan's fortune prematurely? Matthew Westerly was deeply concerned. *Is the power of our syndicate slipping away from the many into Morris' hands alone?* Their consortium—men he himself with Hammond had recruited into a syndicate bound by mutual self-interest—would blanch if they heard this new, unguarded *Governor* Morris. Westerly knew he alone must speak to the colonel before events devolved into anarchy or a coup and disunion. Westerly stammered a new question, "Have we heard anything about Gallatin's negotiations in Ghent?"

"No. Why should I care what the Treasury Secretary thinks?" asked Morris.

"He's spreading fear among our negotiators. Gallatin claims if the United States continues its animosity against Britain, New England might seek a return to a benevolent, forgiving Crown... leaving the rest of our States—"

"—in shambles!" exclaimed Morris. "Open for Spain and France to pick at the carcass. What of Adams the junior and Speaker Clay?" Privately, Morris was pleased that he had successfully stoked raging chaos from within.

"The men in the capital appear to place all their hopes on Jackson if our most recent concessions fail and the British continue the war. If he fights the British army to a draw, or heaven forbid beats them, our people in Brussels feel our negotiating position improves dramatically," said Westerly. "Perry's success in the Lake action has had a positive impact."

"It is critically important, therefore, we keep our British friends far from the Kentucky madman. He's proven efficient at killing savages. We don't want him decimating Wellington's best if they land in peace," replied Morris, not expecting an argument. "Where *is* the damned Indian killer and his sharpshooters these days?"

"Pensacola, in the Spanish Territory."

"Good. That leaves Virginia undefended?"

"It does, Geoffrey. Our final message to our friends will direct them there at the time and date you select. Also, one of Hammond's officers came to see me recently," said Westerly through thickening cigar smoke.

"The Hammond girl has lost *another* one?" Morris scoffed.

"No, well, yes, the *HMS Fortitude* arrested one of their officers in the action off Tortola, last June. The man's name is Gant. Captain Jordan had demonstrated a most aggressive style of action—"

"That disaster almost cost us two years of planning..." Morris interrupted, having felt the renewed distrust and enmity of a foreign power he was trying to impress.

"This officer, a Mr. Gant, had been blamed for the ferocity of the action, though he has been fortunate. Certain friends have secured his freedom from Mill Prison. He does not know who paid for his release. He assumes it was due to the influence of our syndicate, however. In appreciation for his ransom, therefore, he has offered his services. He has great insight into Hammond's operations having sailed as gunner under Captain Jordan last summer. I first met him at the colonel's reception at Great Hill in June. Do you recall him, Geoffrey? Tall with a mean appearance... a surly man. I'm told he has a keen intellect, though he appears a changed man as a result of his harsh confinement at Mill. He is determined to make his fortune while privateering remains so profitable. He is ambitious, dangerously so. And like Captain Jordan, he could be an asset. We might reacquaint the two aboard *Raptor*."

"To what purpose, exactly?" asked Morris, never mentioning his own aide to free Gant.

"With Mr. Gant as our trusted man, he, side by side with Captain Jordan, may help us find what we need."

"Jordan's money... Why would Gant work on *our* behalf?"

"I'll promise him command of *Raptor* and a gunner's share of Jordan's fortune—*if* he does our bidding. I heard a sad tale that he was betrayed by Jordan for a crime he did not commit. I suspect therefore, he has planned a warm conversation with his captain. It is easier to manipulate a man driven by vengeance than by morals. He could be ours if we aim him toward the target."

The two sat back in their fine chairs smugly pondering their own next steps.

After a short while, Morris said, "We have only weeks before Congress votes on our proposal. Once we pay the rest of those people, events will move with haste. I need you to commission Gant and tell him to learn where Jordan has hidden his stolen wealth. Tell him to steal it back! Either that or wring Hammond's neck for what he owes us! Pin his daughter in a corner, she'll squeal. And Matthew, send out every privateer we own and attack any ship they find—English, American, French, Dutch—I don't care."

Privateer

Chapter Eighteen

Ceci, time goes so slowly! Every day is filled with pain. Thomas' dear face never leaves me. I see him sometimes as I walk through the town amidst a gang of boys off ships. I turn to greet him, but he is gone... I fear I am losing my equilibrium in my sorrow. For over a decade my happiest family memories have included this dear boy, the only one to comfort me since my father closeted himself in his work and my mother dashed off to one adventure or another. Now my brother is gone, though his face is everywhere! It is unnerving. I fear the dark when he comes to me. I fear the light when I think I've found him again, smiling at me, joyful and so very much alive... I apologize, I must gather myself. I thank you, sweet cousin, for your condolences and your kind letters. And I will look forward to your visit, but you must wait until my father improves. The news of my brother's death was a cruel blow for such an ill man. We speak each morning. He regains some strength. I carry out his orders; that is my life now.

I must rely on rough men in the yard. I try to manage our accounts as best I can with our dwindling resources. We have enough to get by, though my soul yearns for the day when war that forces us to capture men and ships is finally over. This cursed conflict hovers over me like a fog that refuses to lift. But we do enjoy random good days. In fact, I sent two sloops with letters of marque *off to the Maritimes looking to take British ships unwarily coming into Halifax. I have great hopes for quick engagements that will refill our accounts. Our flagship, the stout* Rattlesnake*, sits in dock nearly ready for sea. I need to find the rare man to command her, however, and send her back to a war where bloodshed must be avoided if the captain had such a notion. Of course,* *those men are not easy to find when valor is published, and great fortunes are only built by men who wear the bloodstains of our enemies.*

Emma read at her words again. They built on each other until she could not untangle truth from fiction, dreams from reality—from men who stood in her visions and the man who sat with her hour after hour fashioning an armada from driftwood. She lay her pen down. Turning in her chair, she rejoined an earlier conversation she was having with Ben who sat hunched over a ledger on a small desk behind her.

"Our next steps, Ben..." Her look bordered on a kind of intimacy shared by committed couples, not employer to employee. "Remind me... the verses Captain Jordan sang aboard ship?"

Odd request, thought Ben. Moments passed before he replied, "Jordan is a strange man, Emma. Sometimes he ranted, screamed, and yelled. And at other times, he recited verse like an orator at the Boston Common... his eyes boring into me as if we were having a private conversation." Briggs had patiently waited for some days to hear from Emma some inkling of how she thought they might steal Jordan's fortune, gained in large part by the trusted captain's sticky fingers. Briggs suspected Jordan's odd verses held clues. Emma accepted Q's jaundiced view of her departed captain. *Does Emma now suspect Jordan's odd verses hold clues to the whereabouts of his fortune?*

"I never heard Cornelius *rant*. Perhaps you imagined it?" posed Emma, surprised at her defense of the indefensible. Or was it the memory of her poor choice of *beaux* that made her obstinate still? Either way, her hardening heart challenged Briggs. "You never liked him, admit it, Mr. Briggs." Briggs' silence caused her to soften. "I did, on occasion, notice a far-away look in his eyes, as if he were someplace else entirely. And I too have heard him recite verse. He claimed the words were his own invention. I never believed him."

"His verses we heard at sea, I believe, were his own," countered Ben. "Did any of it make sense to you, Emma?"

"At first, no. Gibberish, I thought. Sometimes I wondered if he was trying to tease me. Or perhaps he was playing a child's trick, gaming me to guess his secrets." The shipping heiress chose to confide no more. "I suppose Captain Jordan sought to confound people, dazzle them with his poetic brilliance because he so desperately needed to be admired, to hold power over his officers, his crew—"

"His suitors—" Ben interjected.

She ignored his remark, then corrected him, "*Sponsors*. And this power of owning private knowledge likely drove him as much as fortune and renown."

The first mate, for his part, also had kept from Emma accounts he captured of Jordan's singing. Bored at sea during weeks of idle cruising, searching for prey, Ben had written on old sailcloth descriptions of men, snippets of conversations... and Jordan's songs. Ben's first mate duties included carefully logging the ship's course in latitude and longitude, speed and weather on the chalk board by the helm. This information Jordan transposed into his own hand in the official logbook below deck. In the event the captain forgot his duty, which he often did when he retired for days at a time into his cabin with his bottle and opium pipe, Briggs updated the ship's log himself and sometimes took the time to transcribe notes he had made on old sailcloth onto precious paper. At first Ben thought the captain's rantings were pieces of disparate verse, reflections of a strange and damaged mind. After rereading the captain's lyrics of late, however, Ben thought he detected a pattern, and perhaps a recurring story.

Emma, too, had committed to paper her recollections; at the time she wrote, it was for the joy of remembering her illustrious captain's rarified words of passion. She recalled Jordan singing after dinner the night he returned home from his miraculous escape. Before that, besotted by his gallantry, Emma had listened to him croon to her alone as they stood together on the bluff overlooking Newport town. He had sung about their shared future, how he saw it unfolding, how he had planned it, and how he could afford it... Recalling happier times, she gazed wistfully out her office window until it occurred to her that Ben was watching her with great interest. Perhaps he knew something she did not.

"I believe Cornelius was bragging..." She had come to trust Ben Briggs, and made a calculated declaration, "...about where one might find the fortune he'd sequestered... I kept a record, Ben, of the captain's bizarre, rambling shanties."

Briggs rose to her remark with an answer he had reworked in his mind while he had sat studying Emma. Beside him lay his leather satchel; he reached inside for his journal. From it, he drew a piece of paper scribbled with verse. Carefully he placed it in front of her. The two looked at each other and Emma slid a chair close beside him to get a better view.

"Maybe, it *does* make sense," said Emma.

With their heads close together, their pulses quickened as a pattern emerged from Captain Jordan's nonsensical lyrics. Each listening to the other's quickening breath, soon they became keenly aware of each other's proximity.

The Geoffrey Morris-owned *Raptor* of six hundred tons showcased large square sails on three masts, armed with eighteen long guns of twenty-four-pound shot, and carronades on her foredeck and stern. She carried her cargo low in the water—a beamy ship with a deep draft of nearly twenty-five feet when provisioned for a long ocean voyage and fully crewed. *Raptor* rarely skirted the coast and its shallow inlets except at anchor; rather, she was built for fast passages across the heavy seas of the North Atlantic Ocean. Formerly a speedy Boston packet in the Liverpool trade, she had been turned into the largest privateer in America after her former owner had been foreclosed upon by Geoffrey Morris. *Raptor* could out-sail any ship except the newest American frigates while easily overpowering any armed British merchant ship she came upon. She carried a narrow entry designed for fast transatlantic voyages with cargoes of sugar, spices, silks, manufactured goods, as well as first-class passengers—for extra profits. The pride of the New England privateer fleets, every eye watched *Raptor* when her black hull glided confidently and silently into Boston, New York, or past the British blockade in daring runs up the Chesapeake. *Raptor* captured British ships large and small, while her impressively tall rig and massive bowsprit out-sailed every ship, save a whippet-fast Baltimore-style topsail schooner. A few months earlier, *Raptor* had attacked a helpless unescorted convoy with only minor damage to her rigging, losing two men to the convoy's twenty dead. She had survived; her captain, however, had not. A new set of officers had therefore come aboard for her latest cruise south to the British shipping lanes.

As spring turned to summer, the longtime crew of hardy Newport men watched their two new officers climb aboard, Captain Cornelius Jordan and First Mate Quartus Gant. Tales and half-truths of *Rattlesnake* flew in the breeze all along the East Coast: *Raptor's* new officers, formerly of the *'Snake*, were known killers, a danger to both the enemy and their own crew. And each other. These officers themselves barely able to stand on the deck due to recent injuries, had surrendered the famous *Rattlesnake* to the British in the West Indies. From her crew of fifty local boys, however, only a few had managed to return home.

Raptor, under full sail, made nine knots past Long Island on her way to British hunting grounds beyond the Bahamas, the British colony nestled in the Lucayan archipelago. Jordan attempted a gallant pose, admiring the trim of his new command, a ship larger and more powerful than any he had previously commanded. His sea legs failed him, however, and the captain was forced to lean against a leeward rail holding on as well as a one-armed man weakened by fever can manage. The illness after the botched amputation had left him fifty pounds weaker, his limbs shriveled. The fate of his sutured stump remained unclear; it emitted an unfortunate odor. His stomach lurched and overboard he heaved the remnants of his whiskey-laced dinner. He wiped his mouth and smirking, looked to Quartus Gant who had the delicacy to mind his trim.

"I wager you look forward to meeting your old friend again, eh?" Captain Jordan said with a humorless smile.

Gant ignored his one-armed superior. After his many months of privation, Gant retained little of his former vitality, though unlike the captain, he still enjoyed the use of all his limbs. The journey from England to France in search of the packet home was a blur. Caddy Melbourne had proved useful and helped Gant when he had thought he would rather dive into the cold, salt ocean than deal with the future. Revenge consumed him, though he knew a man cannot live on hatred alone. He must first regain his strength and when able unload his fury. He wondered if thereafter his life would be as empty and useless as a cup of rancid water spilled on Mill prison's filthy floor? Would he ever find peace or was he doomed to recall a lad's trusting eyes defiled by dark corridors, a blue face and lifeless lips? He convinced himself he might yet enjoy a comfortable life and held fast to his last hope left behind in Newport. It was not for Westerly's promise of command, however, nor for a share of Jordan's stolen wealth. Quartus Gant grasped at the one dim possibility that might refill his cup… help him to survive this voyage… and accomplish his sworn purpose.

"My old friend?" Gant spoke into the wind. "He'll get what he's due."

"Aye. I applaud your patience, my friend. A man betrayed, such as you, would have every reason to storm off the packet into her office and spill Briggs' blood in front of her! They spend their time together—and nights, too, I hear. Aye, I would imagine she'd weep, pressing her hands into your flowing wounds—"

"Enough, Captain."

Captain Cornelius Jordan smirked, a bit surprised the gunner did not bother to hide his hatred. He was not oblivious to the possibility the gunner might turn on him as well—or had Jordan's sleight-of-hand with the keys worked so well that the gunner believed his captain guiltless in his arrest?

Jordan had told Westerly he would not accept command of *Raptor* with Gant aboard as a commissioned officer. His surprise at Westerly's answer was genuine: Gant's commission was not negotiable. Jordan had therefore quietly hired a bowery man, Angus McSweeny, to stay near his side, slinging his hammock near Jordan's aft cabin, with a knife and pistol handy, to watch for any man who might have reason to accost *The Curse of the Coast*. At every opportunity on the voyage south across the Gulf Stream and into the Indies, Jordan stoked the gunner's antipathy toward the former mate—and incrementally away from himself.

"Aye, I expect you dream of vengeance, Mr. Gant. Would you like to know what I dream about? When I laid in a sweat-soaked bed after six weeks of fever and burning skin, interminable days when I knew not day from night? When my cries for help went unanswered? None of my crew came to nurse their generous captain. No one fed me except the kettle girl I'd hired. Lying sick and alone, I dreamed of my wealth, Mr. Gant. My vast wealth—the wealth I promised you and all the men of *Rattlesnake*. And yet, only three scoundrels have come and found me, demanding their share. Of course, in my delirium, I could not satisfy their requests. Two men escaped the English on the *'Snake*. I convinced them to ship with us on *Raptor*—and they are my guests in chains below. A third, bless his soul, found his way from the cane fields. He told me the island hell was worse than the stories—Africans collapse by the score and are dumped into pits as new boatloads replace them each day. The white slaves last not much longer, though the handlers are not as quick with their machetes. Yes, Mr. Gant, I dream of my great wealth. And we shall retrieve it and share it, you and I, after this cruise when we both recover our strength."

Gant remembered Westerly's instructions.

"Retrieve it from *where*, Captain?"

"So... you *can* be a pleasant fellow, eh? When a reward is offered... Pay note, I'll give you a hint. Someday we'll go there together...

Near yet far from walking paths low
A bottle drunk from a stash we've stow'd
We leave our neighbor's ports astern
On our heels by supper we shall return

"I shall match my verse with a shanty tune and sing it to you someday. Perhaps it'll soothe your spirit, so you can sleep without screaming. Oh yes, we hear you."

Gant suspected Jordan revealed more than he intended. He was beginning to understand the captain's game—the power of absolute command, a simple matter compared to the necessity of parsing out concealed knowledge to a hungry, desperate audience. He looked at *Raptor's* helmsmen and grabbed the heavy wheel and felt the ship's trim in his wrists and arms. Weak from months of deprivation, his skin drooped where muscles were once oak-hard. His prison beard was tight to his lips and shielded his cheeks from the wind, now scutherly, taking the ship southwest on a port tack. He repeated Jordan's rhyming madness in his head, with an increasing sensation they were neither mad nor casual. *Time it takes to empty a bottle of rum... paths from low-lying hills, a neighbor: Middletown on Aquidneck Island? Connecticut? Block Island?* Gant shoved those thoughts aside returning to his planned retribution. In prison he had the boy for company. Now, only a drop of humanity remained, and nothing left for casual conversation. He lived each day only to plot his recompense. Briggs would die, and not well—no measured goodbyes to loved ones, no time to settle affairs, only the stark realization his time on this earth was over. In addition, Gant had decided he must shame Ben Briggs, strip him of his pride and steal his reputation. And in the last stage, in Briggs' final moments of consciousness, he would force him to stare directly into the eyes of the man he had so pitilessly betrayed. Today, however, his thoughts of vengeance were more immediate. Cornelius' scorn hard to overlook, Quartus regarded Jordan for a tantalizing moment, considering the lonely taffrail behind his handicapped captain.

"Sail-ho! To the east, hull-down!" the man atop the foremast cried out.

Jordan stepped away from the rail, turning to look back at the horizon, then to Gant. He smiled broadly. "Come up twenty points, Mr. Gant, if you please. We shall introduce ourselves."

Gant's eyes never left Jordan as armed crewmen prepared to board the targeted merchantman. From windward, *Raptor* swept in like her namesake and sent an unannounced broadside into the hull of the other ship. No telling how many lay dead and dying. The English ship had insulted Jordan by having dared to defend herself. As they spotted each other, she had sent two ill-timed cannon shots in *Raptor's* general path; neither found its target. This affront sent Jordan into a frenzied display unlike any Gant remembered from the year before on *Rattlesnake*. The captain's eyes flashed like a rabid beast. Disheveled, his shirt split open to his waist, displaying his glistening chest. His mouth, as wide as the moon, let go primeval screams. To men crouched over cannon nearby, their captain sounded maniacal. Others forward turned back, urgently trying to understand his shouted commands of mispronounced words:

"Fare!" for *fire*, "tic!" for *attack,* "come alive!" for *come alongside!*

Cacophony and confusion erupted on *Raptor's* gun deck. Half the men obeyed what they thought they heard as others stood stupefied. Gant countered Jordan's idiocy with taut, sober instructions sailors understood.

"Loosen the main course sheets, spanker sheets, release the staysails, and prepare to come alongside!" Gant had not learned crewmens' names yet, so he barked, "You, and you, first over, take ten men with cutlasses. Wait 'til we send one more volley into her rigging."

Raptor fired a second broadside high and true into the fleeing merchant ship—yards fell, a topmast hung loose, the deck filled with broken rig and injured men. The Indiaman lowered her ensign,

backwinded her mainsails, and slowed for a boarding. *Raptor* crashed
alongside slamming into the British ship as privateersmen crawled over
the sides like crazed ants. Jordan sprang awkwardly in the lead, never
looking behind to see how many of the crew followed.

Too weak for deadly hand-to-hand combat, Gant remained at the
helm. He waited until Jordan engaged. A clumsy entanglement erupted
as Captain Jordan swung wildly with his good arm, trying to control a
sword with mistimed, left-handed swings. Before the Yankee crew
quickly overpowered the Indiaman's thin crew, her captain without
ceremony released the ensign halyard dropping the British colors to the
quarterdeck. Forward, an ambitious officer fought on, however, with
an active cutlass, unaware his captain had capitulated. The young
Englishman fought with zeal trying to encourage a few gun crews to
fire their cannon into *Raptor's* hull. Jordan though, had seen the flag
drop to the deck and so unleashed his fury when he realized the enemy
officer—*dishonorably*, in Jordan's eyes—fought on.

"*Raptors*—back aboard! We shall fire again!" cried Jordan.

The Yankee sailors scrambled back onto their own deck.

"Babcock, mind the main yard!" Gant yelled to the one man whose
name he knew, a former shipmate known to hate Jordan now frothing
with the fight, though confused by commands coming from both a
crazed captain and his scurrilous second. "Take two men and haul the
braces back so we release from the prize!"

"She'll spring off by herself, mate. I'd mind the wind if I were
you," Babcock spat back at Gant.

Gant turned his helm and separated the ships enough to gain
leverage for the height needed to fire cannon into the enemy rigging.
He watched to see whether Jordan was aware of the fast-widening gap;
the captain however had engaged the enemy officer, distracted and
unaware his own escape from the British ship was threatened. Cornered
between two men, Jordan fought on, his one arm holding a sword,
lacking another arm to push his opponents away. A British sailor swung
at Jordan's shoulder; his blade made a savage slice as Jordan screamed
an oath and fell to his knees, head down, his neck exposed. Jordan
looked across the growing gap between the British deck and *Raptor*.
His eyes found Gant staring back. The two ships shuddered, their
rigging and yards snagged briefly. Suddenly a heaving wave pushed
the hulls farther apart. Jordan felt the release and watched helplessly as

Raptor broke free from the British prize, its deck slippery with blood—his blood. Barely aware of the stinging bitter cold in his left shoulder—he knew the enemy blade had hit bone, severing muscle on its way back out. He felt faint as blood streamed down his remaining arm, now useless as his stump. Still close by *Raptor,* Jordan waived his feeble stump derisively at Gant and struggled to breathe. He spent his remaining energy holding his head high as *Raptor* wrested free. He held Gant's eyes as if in a claw.

"Mr. Gant! Remember the key!" Jordan shouted a final affront. He saw the naked steel inches from his neck. If this was to be his final cruise, best to leave something behind for the gunner to chew on. He ached to see the surprise on Gant's face. Dizzy from blood loss, he did not see his ship veer away.

"Hard over!" Gant yelled.

With breeze in her set courses, *Raptor* fell fast away from the other ship and gained speed in the clear air. Gant watched Jordan collapse in a heap on the deck, blood streaming from his shoulder and face. Two angry British sailors stood over him. They kicked him and raised their weapons to strike. Gant heard Jordan's screams—a madman cursing sky and King. A boot stomped, kicking his useless sword out of his reach. Gant saw the motion of an arm swing high over the captain's head, its sword poised to strike. An unexpected gust forced Gant's eyes to his mainsail before he could relish the sight of a headless Cornelius Jordan falling to the English.

"We shall come over onto the starboard tack!" cried Gant. "Prepare to rake her stern!"

Gant steered to a wide course. However, he had not gauged the wind's inclination as was his custom—it had freshened and the afternoon's grey sky fell suddenly dark as often happens in southern waters. Adding to the growing distance between the two ships, an unseen offshore current caught *Raptor's* heavy hull, pulling her even further from the other ship. Down-course the wind now shifted against them. The result became clear: *Raptor* had lost their prize in a wind-shift, a foul current, and the black curtain of fast-falling darkness. The British prize caught the breeze, and stood away, sailing fast. *Raptor's* captain was left for dead on the enemy's deck.

Recalling the key, Gant lied, "I did everything I could manage." No one cared.

Chapter Nineteen

The unfortunate events of *"shifting winds and foul currents"* appeared on *Raptor's* report to her owner, inked by Mr. Babcock since the captain had perished and the new man, Gant, refused to record the own account. In the weeks after Captain Jordan's loss, Geoffrey Morris recounted to Matthew Westerly the disagreeable encounter he had with the surviving officer when *Raptor* arrived back in Newport.

"The scoundrel was impertinent. He did not hesitate to tell me his mind," exclaimed Morris.

"Did Gant learn anything about Jordan's stashed money before he was killed?" asked Westerly, visibly irritated.

"Drunken verse." Morris' mind worked slowly this morning after a rousing night at *The Arms*. "Gant said Jordan never pointed to any particular location. Foolish to think any intelligent man would fall for such tomfoolery and riddles."

"Do you believe Gant? He might well be withholding what he learned, Geoffrey."

"We need more than a lunatic's ravings. I'm having Gant followed."

"Did you tell Mr. Gant he will not take command of *Raptor*? 'Foul currents' my eye!"

"I did. I told him despite bringing the ship home, he lost our captain. I told him we made other arrangements for *Raptor*."

Westerly thought how Ben Briggs might fill the opening, once he returned from his latest errand, delivering the syndicate's final message to the British.

"And Gant accepted your reasons?"

"Quite the opposite. He threatened me! He had the effrontery to bring two brutes with him who stood outside my parlor door. One scoundrel had apparently kept Gant's company while in prison. The other, a hired ruffian from South Street."

"Well-chosen men for a fight," Westerly observed. The two considered their brandy. Sweet and rich, the fine spirit flowed as smooth as muggy summer air changing to a warm blanket of ground cover, pine needles, and leaves. "So, how did you leave it, Geoffrey?"

"I promised Gant an officer's berth in a future voyage on one of our older ships. He seemed open to the triangular trade," replied Morris, thinking ahead.

"And smuggling, of course, after the peace? We'll need men with such spirit," Westerly reminded Morris, hinting their inner circle of loyal conspirators lacked obedient enforcers.

"Yes, but our problem is now, not after the peace," Morris shot back. "Press the girl. She must deliver whatever funds her father has squirreled away. *Raptor's* latest cruise has added little more to our coffers than *Rattlesnake's*. Since we have no idea where to find Jordan's money, the Hammond girl remains our best recourse. Threaten her that we're about to call in *all* of our loans and will sell her ships." *And I shall foreclose on her fancy manor and settle her father's score with the willing or unwilling compliance of the comely mistress cowering inside.*

Quartus Gant had had great hopes when the men from Providence first dangled the promise of a ship of his own. His stomach had leapt with anticipation as Jordan had limped over the sides of the prize only to fall beneath an executioners' lethal swing. Compared to the many nights he had suffered in prison he wondered had Jordan deserved worse? Gant hoped if there was a judgment beyond his own, the answer was yes. Vengeance, however, would not sate his stomach or lay him on a featherbed with a warm quilt and a woman in front of a cedar-filled hearth. Vengeance would not dress him in a smart woolen suit, nor provide comfortable city shoes, a tall hat nor a carriage. Hate redeemed would not place another tankard of ale in front of him or serve him a meal of goose or turkey that other men nearby enjoyed. Poverty was the price he had paid for retribution, living only for vengeance... and the possibilities with a girl whose eyes never left him alone for long. For the many nights rotting away in Mill Prison, she had appeared in his delirium with her wide smile, her hand to his forehead. He furtively reached out to touch her in a futile embrace, when suddenly the air turned bitter cold and her image faded away. In the short time he had worked for her father many months ago, she had only spoken to him briefly a few dozen times. Those few words of silk and honey, however, were carved into his memory forever. He recalled every word, each syllable with its lilting melody. When her pleasant greetings were paired with a bright, uplifted face mirroring unrehearsed happiness, he wondered how on this wicked earth a woman had the means to speak, sigh, glance, move an eye or a finger, turn a head to invite or reject, in such balanced measure. *Was it deliberate?* Gant wondered. Was she trying to reach him where no else one could, to speak to a part of him hidden by the pain of his father's whip, crushed by a life filled only with disappointment and dashed hopes? He wondered if he had consciously sent her a subtle signal like a sea hawk's chirp to a circling, prospective mate. They were no match, however; Gant knew that. She knew it as well. His place was on a ship's deck, issuing or receiving commands—which one made little difference. A rolling deck with wind in his hair, his eyes stuck on the sail's luff was the only place he felt a complete man. He remarked to himself on the cruel symmetry: a girl with keen eyes who balanced her careful words with intellect and a body's sly declarations, coupled against the sails of a ship, steering him, steered by him. This girl, a creature of the land: he and his ship, of the sea. Both the girl and he had met on a loosely defined neutral shore, at the high-water mark on a perfect patch of sand where the outgoing tide had washed every imperfection and footstep out to sea. He wanted to visit this washed shore again, a safe place for a man like himself, stay there with her, forever perhaps, just past where the rushing tide might force him to make a final declaration for either shore or sea. Could he manage such a dance? And why should a wealthy girl agree to live in this uncertain margin when her fortune allowed she needn't ever compromise? He shook off the gloom of the day and set his mind in order. First, he must settle his account with the remaining Judas. Afterwards, he would come for her. Gant finished his ale and stared into the stained hollow of his mug. Seeking one more gulp, he raised the empty vessel to his lips. Longing for its rich taste, only meager drops dribbled into his mouth. Time was a strange thing, he remonstrated. With one dirty charge remaining to accomplish, Gant had direction, a certain purpose however unpleasant. More accustomed to a timeless existence where nothing was early, no one late, he now had no place to venture, so each day merely began, meaningless hours a blur; existence merely one short breath followed unconsciously by another. He thought of the violence to come... the unbearable hurt, a man begging forgiveness. *As I did with Captain Cornelius Jordan, I am determined to lead Ebenezer Briggs to an untimely death.* At moments like this, Quartus Gant had flashes of another future: had Briggs not been a coward and scoundrel, had he met the girl before she had naively fallen for Jordan... Was there

room for doubt about Briggs' crime in Gant's single-focused drive for vengeance? *Might I be wrong?*

In her father's office, Emma read letters: One from Ceci admonishing Emma for assuming leadership in the affairs of Hammond and Company. *Yes, sit there in New London with your quilts and beau,* thought Emma, dropping her cousin's latest rambling letter on the desk. *I must raise fifteen thousand dollars or I shall end up living in a hovel by the wharf, forced to feed my father porridge from a wooden bowl, while my mother bombs me with letters carping about our empty accounts.* Emma picked up a quill and ink.

Ceci, your most recent letter criticizing your Aunt Caroline, cut me to the quick. While I daresay my mother has caused some confusion, it is not your place to cast such aspersions upon her honor, and by extension, upon our entire family. In fact, I have recently heard from

Mother. Her letter expresses her deep concern for my father. She explained to me things I did not previously understand. I knew she and my father had had a falling out, and she explained why. She could not, and will not, countenance the type of cold trade that he had embarked on. She acted upon her threat and therefore vacated our manor until he should choose to return to his normal, honorable business practices. She and I have reconciled. I understand the nature of her displeasure. Let us just say, my father had entered into a trade that, though legal until eight years ago and still countenanced by our Southern neighbors, is contrary to our Sunday learnings. As a Christian woman, Mother could not abide this activity, even if it was necessary to replenish our accounts due to this war draining our accounts. She admitted she had a weak heart for such a business and chose to leave her husband rather than stay and be judged guilty by association. I have unfortunately inherited my mother's untenable position, though I shall not run away. I am, you see, my father's daughter and will persevere. We Hammonds are blessed with an inner strength. I shall not falter ...

Emma stacked bills in one pile and paid invoices due Hammond and Company in another much smaller stack. She sighed, pushing away a larger third pile, angry letters of demand. *Why do they write these so starkly worded,* she wondered? *Would not affectation of optimism be better, if they intend to cultivate a long and mutual relationship with our house? Or because I am a woman, speaking for her father these past many months, must I prove myself each day, and with each penny spent?* Hammond and Company suppliers and partners must have assumed one of two things, she surmised: either the colonel was dead or had mysteriously run off to sea, perhaps to join his wife. He had left Emma in charge of the Hammond ships, estate, accounts, and many employees on the docks, warehouses, counting houses, and farm. Her words, written in a tight script, were the instructions their partners read—*a woman's hand.* And so, their suppliers barely masked their disrespect: Harsh demands without alternatives, never were options presented or entertained. If her father had read these injurious demands, he would have confronted his trading partners with a sharp retort, an energetic threat of his own to stave off the wolves a bit longer. But her father remained deeply, restlessly asleep, his hand not responding to her daily gentle touch and soft whisper, "If you can hear me, Father, squeeze my hand." Perhaps, his mind was already departed, having forgotten to tell the body the time to die had arrived. Still, the colonel swallowed water and broth Emma spooned between his lips, though most spilled on his chest which she wiped with a hand not bothering to dab at her own eyes. "Father, press my hands with your fingers if you can hear me…" A twice-daily ritual had had no effect for the many months of the colonel's somber sleep. She had no reason to believe today would be different, yet she never considered the alternative.

Emma was more than shocked, however, when on this misty July morning of 1814 when the osprey cried to their mates, an unexpected, though hoped-for stirring took place. At first it was a single wiggle of the Colonel's forefinger, and then the entire hand took hold of hers, and gripped it as tight as she remembered from their many walks along the town streets.

"Father, you're awake!" Emma cried, her two hands seizing his, rubbing and caressing his fingers back to this life. In a few tense moments, his eyes blinked open and Colonel Hammond stared hard into his daughter's eyes. "Father, I am so happy to see you awake! I have many, many questions to ask you, you must help decide so many things, I have been awake each night with worry and concern—"

"My dear Caroline, I am pleased to see you today. How are the children, pray tell, and my hunting dogs?"

"No, Father, it is I, Emma, your daughter, Mary Celeste! Mother is… with her sister. Do you not recall?"

"My daughter? No that cannot be… she is a bundle of pink chemises and ribbons. Have nurse bring her to me, Caroline… if she is awake from her napping… And let me see… my son? He is sure to be—"

As suddenly as her father had re-entered her life, he left once again and fell back into his pillow, his eyes shuttered, his hands fell to the bed. Emma pressed her hands to her mouth and wept openly. *He must return, he must… and Thom too. If Father believes he is alive, then I, too, must have hope. Where is he, really? Over the side, I cannot believe that. He is here, with us, our family in our home…*

That cruel resurrection had been just the day before. Her father newly conscious, her dreams of the tender boy never let her sleep in peace; now she forced her attention to the papers before her on the desk. She picked up a crude note, unsigned and unencumbered by an envelope. It was on coarse canvas, folded and without wax. She read a sailor's letter:

Miss Hammond,

Our former Mate and Gunner Mister Gant did finally return from Capture. He shipped out on Raptor *with Captain Jordan. In battle with the Enemy our Captain was hurt Mortal. Mr. Gant escaped with the Ship and found his way back to New Port. He is weak and has an Evil look. I fear for him. He is found most days at the* Scarecrow *where his credit for Whiskey has run dry. He is a Pitiful sight Miss and I know your father once gave him a commission, so had regard.*

I was on the 'Snake, *Miss, in Tortola. I saw what happened. I knew your Brother and pray for his soul. I hope the Good Lord finds you Healthy. I ship out tomorrow on a Packet for China.*

Your humble servant,

Matthew Edgerly, Carpenter's Mate. Restitution.

As Emma reread the letter, the startling news about the captain registered hard. Jordan had survived the surgeon's saw, escaped a ravenous fever only to die at sea? The young woman Emma had sent to tend to him after his amputation had reported back daily, yet Emma herself had not dared visit the captain. She had longed to see his eyes, if only to find one last dash of charm from a time before his ignoble failings. He had caused her lasting pain. But she believed in her heart she had once loved him and that he in return had cherished her. Someday, she would shed a tear for that brief moment in time, now forever lost.

Emma twisted behind her to the desk where Briggs usually sat. He had gone to the sail loft. She felt relieved to be alone. She forced her thoughts away from Jordan and his sorry fate, and considered the freed Quartus Gant. Some said Q had blown up a valuable prize which sank with many enemy lives unnecessarily lost. His cowardly violence had turned British officers against her ship and crew with such acrimony that many Hammond men had yet to find their way home. Some boys sent to cane fields never would. She had also heard—from Ben—that the events of the day in Tortola were, at best, confusing: Even those amidst the carnage did not agree on all the facts. She also recollected what Thomas had confided to her one morning after his escape. He told her Mr. Briggs had recommended he keep his observations to himself, yet with his sister near and his father not, he broke his promise to the first mate. Thom told her everything about the shiny brass key that he had seen and heard: *Mr. Gant may have misunderstood some of the events of that day.* She stood and collected the small bag she kept near: Coins, a handkerchief, a pencil and notepaper for commands, so her wishes were not misunderstood by the men she employed. Her father had never needed to put his instructions in writing. She called for a boy to hitch the mare to her carriage. As she left her father's office, she glanced at a note just arrived from the yard foreman: As she rode to the *Scarecrow* to find Quartus Gant, she read the message:

"Rattlesnake *is provisioned, ready for sea.*"

Chapter Twenty

Ews of Quartus Gant's escape from English prison traveled fast. No sooner had the gunner stepped ashore in Newport from a neutral packet then he shipped out again on a Providence privateer, *Raptor*. Gant did not visit the Hammond office to collect his backpay. Nor had he spoken to Emma. Instead, he had sailed away on Morris' square-rigger under the new command of the Captain Cornelius Jordan. Many in the town were not surprised when the gunner-turned-mate returned the ship without her captain. Ben Briggs overheard whispers about Newport; seamen had created their own version of the returned vengeful gunner and his Judas first mate. Q's legend grew—a wronged, spiteful man, returning with a hateful heart.

"Gant was only following Jordan's order to set fire to the Indiaman," said one barkeep.

"…but she was packed tight with Brits."

"Nay, Gant argued with the captain, so Jordan gave'im up," gossiped another.

"An' now Jordan's dead. Bettcha *that* weren't no accident," said another, to general agreement.

"Aye, the gunner's a killer…"

And I'm next, Briggs thought, recalling the last time he saw Q, froth and fury threatening deadly retribution, on his way to be flogged. On *Rattlesnake's* deck Briggs had frozen, unable to save his friend, while Captain Jordan had hidden himself in plain sight. It was widely rumored, and grown into an accepted fact, that first mate Ben Briggs had forsaken the crew in order to save his own skin. As a result, Quartus Gant had suffered cruelly. Briggs heard the talk and knew the danger.

More recently at Hammond Pier, Ben boarded *Rattlesnake* as workers were bending on new sails. He selected a pistol from *Rattlesnake's* locked arms cabin with a key Emma did not notice he pinched from the office. He made sure the muzzle was clean, the breech loaded. Tucking the heavy gun into his belt, Ben disembarked from the ship and pulled his jacket closed, a poor attempt at obscuring it. He would not be caught unarmed.

Quartus Gant did not have friends, only former shipmates. A few men spoke with admiration of *Rattlesnake's* daring escape in the Azores and recalled over mugs of ale Gant's adept handling of the helm and that he was first over the ship's side to fight the enemy. Sailors remembered him more violent than brave, more intense than strategic. Careful observations led shipmates to think Gant maneuvered from intuition better than any seaman on the coast. A few former shipmates—likewise between voyages—bought him drink in recognition of his exploits but left him alone. Gant sat in a corner of the dark, back room of the *Scarecrow Tavern*. He inspected his calloused hands. *By now*, he mused, *Briggs knows I'm back. He knows Jordan's dead. He'll assume I'm comin' for'im next. He'll know why, but not when, not how.* Silent, he finalized his plan to act when the ideal opportunity presented itself. As he had learned in his dank basement cell, less can be more. He came to understand a careful man says not what he feels, only what must be said. *Briggs ain't going anywhere.* He refreshed his memory of the prison squalor where he would have joined the violent romp had he remained trapped there much longer. Those memories of a sordid existence helped solidify his determination for what must come next. It was important that the man who sent him to Mill should feel the loneliness and despair of unexpected demise.

Gant glanced up as a figure approached his booth. For a long moment, he questioned his sanity. Emma Hammond stood before him. She came directly to his untended booth bathed in afternoon shadows, engulfed in the rank of spilled beer and unwashed seamen. She did not smile or ask to sit. She sat.

"I heard you'd returned, Mr. Gant." He stared at her, a more astonishing vision than any dream could have fashioned. Her youthful beauty had settled into fully formed adult radiance during the many months since he last saw her; a flinty impatience had overtaken her shy reticence. "You look... different," she said bluntly looking for some reciprocal response.

Gant did appear different: The most obvious was his beard—dark and close to his lips, high on his cheekbones. Untended at the neck, his was unlike the gentlemen of town who shaved their necks, and sometimes their cheeks or their chin below mutton chops to make their beard and facial designs more stylish in high-collared shirts. Gant's beard, however, reflected a simple truth: He had lost his razor and did not intend to look for it. For some time, Gant did not answer Emma. He had no words ready that could convey how he felt seeing her again. His eyes caught hers. She blinked at his intensity and looked away, his silence unnerving her. She wondered if it had been a terrible mistake coming to this tavern filled with deckhands who dulled their pain with drink and muffled conversation. More than one patron elbowed his bar mate to look over his shoulder at the well-dressed Hammond woman hunkered in the corner with a north-side gunner.

"Are you not well, Quartus?" She tried again; perhaps his Christian name might stir him.

"I've not yet regained my strength, Miss Hammond."

"You'll need more than ale."

"It's a start."

"You escaped from the English?"

"Aye." *How* suddenly seemed unimportant.

"Were you long a captive?"

She removed her gloves, one slender finger at a time, unaware that he found even this simple action mesmerizing. His time in the squalid Mill was *past*—only now did he count: eight weeks on the stinking transport, another seven or eight months in the cell, a month or more sailing home on the southwest trades, followed by a week of sleep and drink. And then the short cruise on *Raptor.*

"A year I reckon."

"Well, I am glad you survived your... ordeal. How *did* you... escape?"

He looked at her: He wanted to say *someone paid something to somebody*. Yet he did not know who. That bothered him a great deal; he was not a man comfortable with debts owed another. He must find out. Westerly was one possibility; though he had smugly taken credit, so probably not.

"Someone arranged an open door."

"Who?"

"Someone I owe my life to." Expressionless, he looked for a sign from her, holding out hope she had not given up on him.

Does he think I'm involved? Emma wondered. She was tempted dearly to admit her role, and *Windslayer's* redemption, but wanted to determine first if she had saved a hollow tube of a man or a kindred spirit. She wanted to ask about his captivity, though she feared hearing what he had suffered might be more than she could bear. If he spoke freely, she promised herself she would listen to his account of prison life. She owed him that. Not that he would want to relive it, she presumed. He took another long draught and wiped his whiskers, something he reminded himself he must do now with some decorum in the company of a lady.

"I did not expect to see you again," he said softly.

"You were arrested from one of our ships. I feel responsible. Have you eaten today?" Gant shrugged. She turned to the barman and ordered, "Fowl with potatoes and another draw. Quickly now, this man is ill!" Returning her attention to Gant, she continued, "You sailed on a Morris ship. Why didn't you come to me and my father?"

"There was something I had to do... and, ah... *Raptor* was pushing off. How fares your father?"

"Not well. He breathes, nothing more. Why didn't you let me know you were alive? We owe you for your last voyage with us." Emma placed a small heavy pouch on his side of the table. Gant made no motion to pick it up, though he looked at it with interest. "So, you served under Captain Jordan again," she continued. "I dismissed him, I am sure you know by now. Too much fighting, not enough prizes... You were right." Her eyes fell. "You heard about Thomas?"

"Only when I returned to Newport. I regret his death, Miss. I do."

"Thank you, Mr. Gant. I am finding his loss extremely painful. He was what kept the family—" She stopped and let her anger return to stanch her tears. "I instructed Captain Jordan to capture ships whilst avoiding combat. Cutting out a moored ship in the night, not tearing prizes to pieces with cannon! We need captured ships in good repair for auction! I instructed him—as clear as the nose on my face, Quartus—to keep Thomas below deck during a fight. And do you know what he did?"

Gant looked straight into her eyes. While *Rattlesnake* was at sea fighting, he was huddled in a corner with a stinking man close to one side and a sick boy on the other, and still, they could not find enough warmth for even one hour of restful sleep.

"I do not know. I was not there."

"He placed my brother on the *bow—nearest* the enemy ship's cannon—to call a turn or some rubbish and the tender boy was shattered when the topmast crushed him to death! I told Captain Jordan to his face that he was to blame."

"He spoke ill of you, Miss."

She was unhappy to hear that, though not surprised. Once not long ago, Jordan spoke floral words of endearment. He had painted visions of romance and happy domesticity. *Bunk!*

"Captain Jordan did not take his dismissal well. His arm, you see..." Emma almost surrendered a tear. She coughed instead. "Will you tell me how he died?"

Gant wanted to relate in great detail how Captain Cornelius Jordan met his death. He wanted to brag about how he himself had lured the infuriatingly pompous fool. How he'd made Jordan's death satisfyingly ignoble and himself blameless. For all the good it did him, damn it! He was ashore without a ship, never mind a command, sitting half-drunk accepting sympathy and a free meal from a wealthy young woman. He stopped and looked at her folded, delicate long fingers. He wanted so much more than her sympathy. So, cutting a middle course, he framed a new thought.

"An action, Miss. We took a ship. The captain boarded as was his custom. His sword arm taken off, he fought with his left. He did not fight well."

"I heard you left him to die."

"He thought they had struck their colors. But he was wrong. Some of the enemy fought on. So, he commanded we separate the ships and fire at their rig to subdue them and force a permanent capitulation. But we were caught in a wind shift. It happened fast."

"I see. You followed your orders. Did he say anything, before..."

The truth? Jordan yelling curses, recognizing I intended to break off the ships' engagement, leaving him to die? Admitting in a final insult, his role leading to my arrest in Tortola? A flaccid admission, however: did Jordan think I was an idiot and hadn't felt the weight of the key he had placed in my pocket?

"A key..." Gant paused. "He admitted to why I was arrested."

"I see. Thomas also told me."

"What?"

Emma looked into Gant's eyes, though friendly, she had a look more like a mother cat protecting her litter from a hungry hound prowling nearby.

"Thom told me Mr. Briggs had nothing to do with your arrest, Quartus. Captain Jordan admitted it. My brother would have told you the same. You must trust what I say. I see in your eyes, you intend to confront Ben. Please do not. I need him."

"That turncoat went below... and cut a deal with the enemy." Gant's fury surfaced from deep within.

"He tried to ransom the crew. He carried instructions from my father."

"He told me he had important information for the enemy. Then he went below with the British captain, Miss Hammond. They spoke in private. The British captain returned on deck, walked *directly* to Thomas, inspected Jordan, then stood toe to toe with me. I was arrested. I alone was whipped dozens of lashes and thrown dying into a stinking bilge on a miserable transport while Mr. Ebenezer Briggs was set free! The connection, Miss, is clear."

Emma saw two paths before her. This man was determined, though not yet lost to her.

"I didn't come here to make Mr. Briggs' case for him. You can settle your own differences." She waited then pounced. "I have a problem."

He was not listening yet, only staring at her delicate face that twitched in frustration. He forgot about the fresh ale and fragrant meal newly set down in front of him.

"I need a captain... for *Rattlesnake*," she said.

Never in this life did he expect an offer like hers in this place and time.

"I would make a poor captain. A privateer must be a fighting man. I'm weak. My body's weak. My spirit—" He looked at the plate of food. "…you got Briggs."

"Mr. Briggs has new responsibilities at the firm. We've asked him to increase the size of our armed merchant fleet. We have pressing commitments to our investors that must be met. *Rattlesnake* is repaired. We have crew, good men, fighting boys. But her hold is empty. I need her to capture British ships, Quartus. Briggs dreams of *designing* ships. I need a man who *fights!" And Ben does not look at me like you do*, she thought.

"Jordan told me Briggs has been by your side… day and *night*."

She was startled by his tone, slow, sinister, accusing.

"It's not what you think, Quartus. Ben and I may have a future together, though I don't know what that might look like. I need *you*—"

"*Me* or some other fool with affected charms and flowing locks?"

"No—*you*. I trust you. Other men ignore my wishes and tell me what they think I want to hear. I need an honest fighting man, not a madman. Privateering is not a blood sport, Quartus! It's a business. You understand the difference."

"My cut?"

"Same as Captain Jordan. Twenty-five percent."

Gant smiled, beginning to feel blood in his arms and legs for the first time since she sat.

"He got forty-one percent, Miss. He told the entire crew."

"He *took* forty-one percent, Mr. Gant… He told you of his great fortune, did he not?"

"He told all who would listen of his great fortune."

"If he has such a fortune, why did *I* have to buy my own ship back at auction? Why did I pay his surgeon's bill? Why did *I* hire the girl who tended his bed pan and brought him his meals? *I* paid for his lodging until he was well enough to stagger into the street with a bottle and his remaining arm around an obliging whore. Forty-one percent, bosh! I shall pay you thirty or you can travel back to Providence and plead your case for a ship to Mr. Westerly. Or perhaps you already know his answer."

Gant relaxed and smiled. "I do."

"Do we have an agreement?"

"Aye."

"Good. And I shall expect you to return with the ship to our pier where the manifest will be carefully tallied. The rumors of Cornelius skimming—"

"He more than skimmed, Miss. He amassed a great fortune due your father."

"Do you know where he kept it?"

"Aye." Gant smiled as she looked at him both shocked and thrilled. "Hidden," Gant added with a cruel smile. She did not find the humor to her taste but at least the man demonstrated he could find small ironies in life's meandering curves.

"I see." *Be like that. Another time will come, and I will wring a different answer out of you!* "And a reminder—you shall not harm Mr. Briggs. If he appears in my office wounded, bandaged, or not at all… Do you understand? He remains your friend, Quartus, if you would only listen to him."

Gant took a healthy swallow from his fresh mug, brimming with suds.

"Aye, Miss, if you say so. I'll listen to him." *Then I'll cut him to pieces.*

Chapter Twenty-One

*C*eci, I must have been out of my mind! I wanted to embrace the
poor man and cry in his arms. His soul, so dark and damaged
from the pain of prison. But something else is wrong. His eyes
were welcoming, though his words had an edge, and sent me on my
way upset. Yet I chose him over all other men to command my ship. Mr.
Gant's answers are short and to the business at hand—how much
salted pork and cod I must buy for provisions and the like—but his eyes
express his extreme loneliness. I suspect he needs a kind hand, a gentle
touch, perhaps a woman's kiss. Is it possible a man so hard can speak
to an unanswered desire in my own heart?*

*Oddly, I have found a suitable man who already sits at my side. He
is steady and true, and honestly not without charm. But passion? On
the other hand, Mr. Gant appears ready to explode... All I know is I
must save our enterprise. Our entire fortune is nearly gone. Another
ship was lost this week. Mr. Morris has prepared court papers to
assume our liabilities and take Great Hill and Rattlesnake and all the
rest. But I will not bend to his request for another indiscreet "kindness"
that, should I acquiesce would partially offset our debts. I blush to think
about what he means. He is under a certain hazy memory I left him
with, trying to buy myself time, but all it has done is embolden the man!
I only have one last hope to increase our coffers. To follow that path, I
need more than a ship and the people to sail her. I must harvest
whatever knowledge both Mr. Gant and Mr. Briggs are hiding from me
and form a confederacy to hunt for something that, truth be told, is
rightfully our own. Without their cooperation, however, I face the end...*

Armed with a pistol, Ben Briggs avoided places he would most likely encounter Quartus Gant. *Q's a better shot, a deadly swordsman, and lethal with a knife.* Briggs had seen Gant's fist break a man's face and his elbow knock an enemy senseless. Ben was not anxious to run into him while his fire for vengeance burned red. He returned to the Hammond and Company office, surprised to find Emma's disposition notably lifted.

"Ben, I think you should visit our Boston banker with this deposit. Best you leave today."

Grateful for the timely trip away from Newport, giving Gant time to cool, Ben did not question her instruction. Of equal good fortune, Westerly's sealed letter secure in Ben's bosom could be discretely dealt with at last; Ben could meet the Wednesday double agent at the Long Wharf pub in Boston, and provide the answer the British awaited, that would free his men. The price for its delivery to the enemy: a privateer to command. Ben longed for an opportunity to abandon the Hammond and Company office and return to sea as a privateer captain flying the pennant of Geoffrey Morris. But that, he knew, meant abandoning Emma Hammond forever.

Emma glanced at Briggs and noticed his jacket bulged with a pistol.

"Quartus shall be happy to oblige you, Ben. Then I will be without my partner." She gave a trifling smile, the kind that rarely escaped throughout all the time she had mourned Thom's death. Briggs heard the word he had secretly hoped for—*partner.* "*Rattlesnake's* repairs have been well done, Ben, I thank you."

The ship's broken spars and torn sails had revealed the severity of Jordan's murderous approach. Back in Newport, Briggs and the Hammond yard brought the *'Snake* back to strutting form, her standard rigging tight and tarred, her sides painted, her cannon ready with shot and polish. Her sails were new, as well, recut for greater speed. Her gunnels, reinforced with oak, were rock-solid. Ribs, futtocks, and knees had all been reinforced for battle. Her ballast re-shipped, reduced in weight. In Ben's vision of a fighting machine, speed trumped all else.

"I have something I must tell you, Ben. I have a new captain for *Rattlesnake*."

"Who?"

"Q."

"What?!" shouted Ben.

"We need a fighting man."

"And you think I'm not?"

"Do *you* think you are?"

Briggs recalled the engagement with *Scepter*. He remembered the blood, the deaths in Tortola, the heat of the smoke that blinded him so that he could neither breathe, think, nor stomach the likelihood of future battles. He sighed at the truth and reflected on her accurate analysis of him.

"Do you trust him?" Briggs countered.

"You trusted him."

"Q's been ashore for days and not killed me." Briggs looked at Emma, visualizing suddenly the secret deal that had been made. And although he had not directly participated in its fabrication, it benefited him; it might save his life. Gant in command of *Rattlesnake* would soon sail away. Perhaps time offshore would soothe Gant's need for retribution. If Briggs were away himself until Gant sailed, he would no longer present an easy target. *Is it cowardice to agree with her suggestion?* "What does he say about me, Emma?"

"We haven't spoken about you," she replied, avoiding his eyes.

"I see." He stood to depart. "Hand me the deposits."

She gave him the heavy satchel. "I'm sending Quartus and *Rattlesnake* east, then south. He'll be gone three months. In the meanwhile, please attend to our business in Boston and Providence, and remain close by my side."

"He blames me still for his arrest?"

"I believe he does." She sighed. "Ben, there is nothing more unbecoming than a frightened man with a pistol stuck in his pants." He cringed at her rebuke, too close to the bone. "While you're in Boston," she added as if an afterthought of no great weight, "if you should meet with certain friends..."

Her unexpected suggestion grabbed his full attention. "What are you talking about?" he asked.

"Don't be coy, Ben. You showed me the British captain's letter, meant for certain traitors here in America. I told you to give it to Westerly and tell me what he said in response. I've heard nothing."

"He gave me a letter—"

"Of course he did. Destroy it, please. Take *my* letter in its place."

Like Jordan, Emma Hammond ran adeptly two steps ahead. Briggs stared at her and decided they must conspire together here and now or part forever.

"If I meet a friend..." slowly he repeated her words.

She handed Ben a small, tidy though unsealed envelope. "Much depends on whether the enemy believes *my* letter is genuine."

Ben looked at the folded parchment.

"After you read it, re-write it in your own style. My hand betrays my sex. You've read the other letters—do not tell me otherwise. Be mindful however... If you are found out, either side will hang you."

"How's that?" he asked.

She knew she owed him more, if to do her bidding might condemn him. "Thomas. On his last two voyages... he kept close to you night and day. He heard you and Captain Menton—"

"*Breton*," he corrected.

"Thom overheard you speaking in the cabin. He heard you try— you argued." She looked at him accusingly. "Without success."

"Thom told you—?"

"Everything. Our sibling bond was strong. Later, I heard from my father's investor friends in Providence—Morris and Westerly. They have plans to establish more favorable trading conditions with Britain. Perhaps they are representing just the New England states, perhaps the entire country, I do not know. The price for these new conditions, however, is steep."

"What are you *doing*, Emma?"

"Morris is spreading lies in Washington, Ben. He pretends to be motivated by patriotism, though he merely craves power for himself. I intend to disrupt his plans. This letter may give our people in Belgium leverage."

"Morris—?"

"Is a *traitor*. He'll hang." *And I'll not have to repay my debt.*

"You are aware you're placing the Company *and me* in a very precarious position—"

"Only if your nerves fail me, Ben."

He grabbed her letter and turned to leave. He realized he had neither the power nor the desire to refuse her. By accepting her letter, by trading allegiances, he was forever relinquishing hope for command of a privateer from the Providence men. *Raptor will cruise without me.* He paused and looked back at her, carefully admiring both her allure and her craft; this was a woman to fight for.

"I'll be back in two weeks, Emma." He gave her a thin, nervous smile.

"Good luck," she said with genuine concern.

She watched Ben stride out the door, a man she had trusted to protect Thom. *Might he fail her again?* She sat, thinking about what she had written in her letter designed to mislead, heavy with believable falsehoods, like she had done in her letters to her cousin... just in case her husband got hold of them. Emma took risks, though had no trepidation about her conclusions. She had overheard her father and his friends lavishing praise on the British Empire, enumerating the many opportunities for trade once hostilities ended, even at the cost of the country's independence earned with such bloody determination a generation ago. She recalled sentence fragments about "damned Westerners" and "propped-up knife fights with Indians". In her bedroom above the dining room during last summer's cool evening breezes and fall's gentle nights, open windows had floated the conspirators' voices aloft. She had listened, confused and conflicted about the *Purpose*. But when she met *Windslayer* at the pier with the morning's foul air, she understood it had been newly generated profits from her father's triangular trade that fed the *Purpose*—her father both complicit and trapped.

She too had been trapped, and like her bed-ridden father, she considered a possible escape: the triangular trade. Emma Hammond wrestled with the moral, economic, and practical dilemmas. Should she provision another topsail schooner bound for Whydah? Hire a cold-hearted man to voyage the middle passage? Hire hard men to crew the triangle's rich legs, returning to her a bag heavy enough to sink her soul, yet keep her enterprise afloat? Should she sacrifice innocents she would never come to know or encounter while protecting the wealth that serviced her comfortable life? Save an estimable estate her father had toiled his lifetime to provide? *Cargo is cargo*, she thought coolly. She recalled the bitter morning after her scandalous dinner with Geoffrey Morris. He had liquored up and spilled his wine along with his ego, boasting of a vaunted life in the new world order that he would fashion. She had recoiled as the fool promised that she, sitting next to him, would participate in his position of power, confiding and providing insight—safe within his aura. That sordid transactional exchange, unsurprisingly, made her feel as soiled as she felt the day *Windslayer* befouled the harbor's morning air. But now, in lonely desperation, Emma felt a growing kinship with Gant—understanding how a person could live a life driven by darkness. She intuited how he could go about his business, unforgiving, with a determined purpose. She felt Gant, left alone in his gloom, might choke on his own hate. As Ben departed with her letter, Emma Hammond found herself reenergized with purpose: She would repay Geoffrey Morris for having sullied her. Her time had come to crush him.

Chapter Twenty-Two

C *eci, I write to you late. I am fatigued and may remain absent for a time. I do not have much liberty or ease. Ours has become a hard life. And though I do not despair, I admit I am disillusioned. The men around me shake my confidence. My world is falling apart. I have nothing in Great Hill besides servants and my sleeping father. I limit my travels to shuttling between my office desk and my hearth. Soon, I fear all the men in my life will disappear over one horizon or the other. Even my companions the Ospreys have left for the season. Their noisy juveniles, after weeks of learning to fish and choosing a mate, have left me, too. Their ragged nest high in the tree lies as quiet and desolate as I.*

Gant figured it would take more than a week for Briggs to ride to Boston, conduct his business and return—plenty of time for a wartime courtship. Briggs would return to find his woman stolen, his dreams forsaken, and a knife to his throat before Captain Quartus Gant set sail. While *Rattlesnake* provisioned for a voyage Emma had not charted, Gant engineered deliberate, increasingly intimate encounters with her. At first, they talked about their undertaking at the stone pier, out in the open. Soon thereafter, he invited her to inspect his tidy, snug cabin aboard *Rattlesnake*, with its coal stove and comfortable sleeping berth. She bent over an oil lamp and her delicate finger drew his eyes to ledgers and ship's records he ignored preferring to gaze at her face. She felt his eyes on her as they discussed which men to sign aboard. Within two days of Briggs' departure, they shared simple dinners to discuss his trip, meeting by lamplight in her father's empty office. Gant encouraged her to reconsider the cold trade—smuggling as well as the triangular.

"...and then after, you do know to anchor at Cuttyhunk and cleanse the ship. I do not want her returned here with—"

"Aye, Miss." He was surprised she was suddenly open to the middle passage. Her words sounded casual.

She did not mean to sound heartless, though, to get out of debt, she determined she felt she had no choice but to turn to the abhorrent trade... just long enough to free herself of the predatory bankers. The Providence men knew her father's secret. Their smug looks and veiled shock threatened to make the Hammond slaving operation widely known: *You, too,* Emma thought she might throw back into Morris's face, *trade in the illegal triangle. At least we acknowledge it. You hypocrites keep it a secret!*

"Quartus, is this triangular trade... right for *us*?" Emma asked late one afternoon as Captain Gant stoked the coal stove in *Rattlesnake's* inviting cabin. Her "*us*" was not lost on him.

"Cargo's cargo, Miss. Ten thousand dollars in six weeks' time."

"But... the misery?"

He made no attempt to lessen her guilt. *Let it fester. It should.* He would soothe her spirit once she was wracked with self-doubt and sought the comfort of his shoulder.

"We all suffer, Miss Hammond," he said dully. She watched him stare away, ignoring the ledgers she had asked him to examine and approve. "When I sat alone in Mill, I thought of Newport—of ships and taverns of working men. But what quickened my heart was the memory of your smile."

"Quartus," Emma countered, catching her breath. "You are now employed, well-fed, and have command of a wondrous ship. Yet you remain angry. You lust after retribution for injuries real and imagined. I cannot reconcile how a man with such a cold soul could have feelings for..." She searched for a word, refusing to say "for me" which is what had first come to her mind. "...for what a woman *represents*."

Represents? Quartus chuckled without mirth. "Perhaps I am not a good man for a gentlewoman."

"Or perhaps you'd rather be at sea than with me?" Emma ventured coyly, playing with fire. His silence disappointed. He offered nothing more. She let an immediate rejoinder slip away. In its place, she remembered a question she had once asked Ben. "Quartus, what makes *Rattlesnake* so attractive… to a man?"

The air between them shifted palpably. She had guessed correctly. On *this* he could speak, albeit flatly.

"Her construction is framed solid, her hull sharp-built. Her bottom's coppered and clean so she's fast. She sails well on all points of wind. She'll keep a man alive. And make him rich."

She had not expected such a descriptive answer from a man who spoke with few words. She was pleased she had put her question to him. Briggs had described to her a fantasy—the flighty ships he saw in his dreams, while Gant explained the subtle movements of a ship's mercenary purpose hidden under ribbed planks of viral strength. But did the gunner also understand how a woman's heart reacted to the subtle movements of a man's eyes and the touch of his fingers?

In a house facing a broad street in Providence, angry voices rose.

"So, what about the first mate?" Geoffrey Morris demanded.

"Briggs?" Matthew Westerly answered.

"Yes, get him back to sea, damn it! Tell them it's time for the *rendezvous*!"

"He no longer voyages off-shore, Geoffrey. He manages the Hammond office these days."

"Then go again yourself, damn you! The vote is counted within a fortnight, or sooner. We are short. We need another forty-five thousand." Morris fidgeted, his fingers greasing his glass.

"Sell your ships—"

"We don't have time! What about the suit?"

"Against Hammond? I'm told the Hammonds have made payments to their other creditors. Apparently, this Briggs fellow is clever, perhaps a better man-of-trade than a privateersman. Only our claim remains. And not every Judge is under your influence." Westerly summed up the legal machinations of the past week, each day turning against the syndicate's plans.

"How'd the Hammond girl get enough money?"

"The triangular trade, it appears." Westerly shrugged.

He watched the other man's face drain of color. Geoffrey Morris' ambition for a reconstituted *Atlantic Coast States* dragged him under like a cross current. Westerly was surprised Morris had so readily accepted that *Governor* title he had concocted over brandies months ago. Morris claimed it was easier to recruit senators from the States facing the ocean once they recognized his uninhibited ambition matched their own best interests. These senators represented people within *those* borders, not states fighting natives in the West, or those in the north with their mills and tidal waves of uneducated immigrants.

"Do the British understand our revised design on this continent?" asked Morris.

"After I presented His Majesty's Naval Officer with our new name," replied Westerly, "he seemed to understand the game. He is not a politician but grasps the larger picture." Westerly did not mention the British sailor's antipathy for America. The banker felt his life was in danger until he stepped off the warship and sailed out of range. Morris sat quiet for a rare moment. Westerly came to the reason for his late-night visit. "I do have some good news. I have new reason to believe we might recover Captain Jordan's fortune."

"How? I thought he took his secret to hell with him."

"I've made inquiries and learned of Captain Jordan's unusual day-voyage last spring. I know many seamen, officers who need a friendly banker. My sources also tell me two of the three men who sailed with Jordan on that day met untimely deaths the same week. Apparently, the captain went to murderous extremes to hide his trail. I've determined a few locations within a day's sail where we might send an armed ship to look."

"Go on."

Book Three

A Fortune for Taking

Privateer

Chapter Twenty-Three

*C**eci, have you ever found yourself dreaming about entering a dark room full of potential dangers, a fall, a crouching animal, or some obscure mystery, and you doubt yourself? You know whatever lurks behind the dresser will be appalling. And this clouds your judgment, making even pedestrian decisions fraught. The sweets you want to inhale will disrupt your system for days. The dress you so carefully selected displays way too much décolletage. You will regret it the minute you step into the ballroom and all eyes are upon you, variously leering and disdainful. Yet you cannot show any weakness. You cannot avoid your course or run from its consequences. You curse yourself as you know what the outcome must be, but you hope anyway. You have seen this before in the vague time between daylight and dawn when the images are but outlines and the malignant intent is shallow and confused. It is not that the future is inevitable. Rather it is preferable to cede your own thinking ability rather than be ruined by faltering. So, you peer into the darkness and accept the unknown soon to be unalterably-known and part of your future life. How can I say no? The ospreys will someday return to circle over Great Hill. I wonder if they shall still find me here.*

Ready to unmoor with her new captain, *Rattlesnake* appeared in fine fettle, tethered to Hammond Pier. Briggs had been gone a week and would not be returning for another. Emma Hammond thought about nothing except the price she was willing to pay to continue to engage Hammond and Company in the evil trade. She had managed to pay down debts to smaller creditors, but the sizeable monies owed to Geoffrey Morris remained. Desperation turned to guilt and back again to resignation, then landed in fitful indecision. She had not slept the night before nor the night before that. Tomorrow marked the day of her ship's departure for its odious triangular route, and at last, her mind opened with renewed clarity. The sun shone bright, dazzling the bay. With Gant's apparent lack of remorse to guide her, she planned to expand the despicable trade. That the trade had been illegal since the year '07 was the least of her trepidations. She had fallen asleep reading the notes she and Ben had assembled from their recollection of Captain Jordan's verses they had both heard. Briggs' recollections were drawn from conversations at sea and shanties sung with the boys after a round of whiskey, when Captain Jordan had teasingly confided his secret, childish game. Going over the notes did not provide her a specific location. Emma realized that in her attempt to keep Jordan's money between only herself and Ben, she had overlooked the man who might hold the final piece to Jordan's puzzle. Like Ben Briggs, Quartus Gant had sailed with Captain Jordan for multiple voyages, including Jordan's last. As the captain had dangled stories of his riches for Briggs and her, he had likely done so to torture Quartus as well. *Rattlesnake* was to sail the next day. Gant at the helm. Emma had one last opportunity to pry.

"You'll require this *letter of marque*," Emma informed Gant casually when he appeared in her father's office. He nodded as she handed it to him; in her presence, he did not read the document. "Please, join me this evening at Great Hill for a farewell dinner."

Along with a hint of a smile, the newly commissioned Captain Gant uttered a rare, "Thank you, ma'am."

"Captain 'Q'. May I call you that?" Emma smiled as the two took their seats at the manor dining table. Noticing his grimace she quickly changed course. "Captain Gant then," she corrected herself awkwardly as she filled his glass with her father's best claret. "Cornelius often made mention of his fortune that he had amassed during the war. He said he stored it in a strongbox someplace. He bragged how his fortune could support me and alleviate my family's debts... and on and on. All horse dung! All riddles and rhymes I might decipher were I only as clever as he." Emma waited.

Attentive, Gant sat quietly, enjoying her building irritation at his deliberate non-contributions to her obvious line of reasoning.

"I believe Jordan skimmed great quantities of gold belonging to Hammond and Company... indeed from every ship he captured. He stored this plunder in secret, not in Bristol or Newport, nor in any bank. I checked. I know where a search for it might end. I don't know, however, where to begin. I think you may." Emma recognized Gant hardly breathed as she spoke. *Good. He warms to gold, if not to my smile.*

There: Direct and in the open, Gant thought. *Either tell her or deny all and never speak of it again.* "I'd already have his gold if I knew where it was," he answered with some truth.

Emma smiled. She thought she detected an argumentative flash, not a basic declaration of naught. "You need to trust *someone,* Quartus." But Gant wasn't interested in trust. Her slender neck was far more interesting. It led down from her open face to a silver, closed hook under her chin. *That,* he mused, *will be the first to open and the rest shall follow.* Beyond that latched gate lay warmth and a life without suffocating anger. Sensing her vulnerability and the rate at which she nervously sipped her claret, he continued to hold back his answer. Flushed, Emma's tone turned to exasperation. "Very well, Captain Gant, I will show you what it means to trust someone. Captain Jordan's words to me were wrapped in absurd verses. And he sang shanties around Ben Briggs and the crew. Ben wrote down these verses as carefully as he could recall. And he and I have scrutinized them at length." She reached for a beaded purse she slung on the back of her chair. As she did so, her chest arched back. Gant stared as Emma knew he would. Opening the drawstring of her reticule, she removed a scrap of paper. She looked at the paper and then at Gant, and said, "If I give this to you, I expect something in return."

"Read it to me." She snatched the paper back to her bosom and looked at him curiously. "You assume Jordan was sane, Miss." Gant added.

"Sane or otherwise, he skimmed a fortune—it should be m—*ours*!"

"What of Briggs?"

"This agreement is between *us*…" She watched him. "You and I, Captain Gant."

He stared boldly into her eyes, followed the line of her neck down to linger on her bosom and did not care she knew it. His eyes traced her hands, her delicate, soft fingers holding the paper: Long and smooth, hers were gentle hands. His seaman's hands were clubs, weathered and calloused, curled with frostbite, clutched for an attack. Her hands, however, lay open for his touch. Available.

At last he heard himself whisper, "Offshore."

"Not here in Newport?"

"Aye."

Gant thought about his plan for the next day: Once *Rattlesnake* dropped her dock lines, instead of sailing east he would sail northeast to search for Jordan's fortune. *But had Jordan intended this very thing? Was the man still spewing lies from beyond his watery grave? Did he want Gant convinced he had sufficient clues, only to fail?* Gant knew hundreds of men who would kill for a dollar, never mind a fortune. Men who suspected that Gant had stolen Jordan's fortune from their grasp would hunt him forever. Under that threatening scenario, Gant knew he would never sleep again without a loaded pistol under his pillow. Jordan had perhaps anticipated Emma might join Gant in the search; how he would have laughed with gusto at Gant's dilemma.

"Listen to this, Quartus. Tell me what you think," she instructed. Gant nodded, trying his best to appear less interested than his increased pulse signaled.

But they rose at night and found the block
They found their way, their light unlock'd
They found their grace through twice returned
To live a day, their past now burned…'

"Where's he talking about, Q?"

"You do not know?"

"I wouldn't ask *where* if I knew!" Despite her insistence, Gant remained stoic and promised himself he would not let Jordan win. Impatient when he did not answer, she spoke again. "Very well, don't tell me. Tell me what you *don't* know." She let her exasperation show.

Her logic caught Gant by surprise. With men, tools, and a ship, he would search a particular likely island for Jordan's gold. *But what if he failed? Would the men turn on him, his promise of hearty compensation unfilled, left alone and exposed on a beach with two shots and thirty angry cutthroats looking to do exactly that?* This might have been Jordan's plan all along—to lead him with an evil tease, to get him close—but not close *enough*. Warped. It fit Jordan—insidious and cruel; the dead tyrant *wanted* Gant to try. He *wanted* Gant to fail.

"The *where* is complicated. The *'Snake* can get us close. But not—"

"—to the exact location. I see." Emma interrupted and immediately regretted cutting him short. She suddenly realized Gant might be planning to steal *Rattlesnake*. His cold eyes gave it away. Did he intend to uncover Jordan's hidden fortune himself, sail away, and never return? She recovered her wits, hiding her suspicion. "You and I shall make a pact, Quartus. I have information you need or you'll search forever." She looked down at the paper in front of her. "I have decided *Rattlesnake* will not sail for Africa. You are free to find another privateer command or do whatever you want—*after* we uncover Jordan's money. Tell me now where we must begin to look."

Gant looked at her with a renewed appreciation. Before his confinement, she had fluttered like a butterfly probing a scented lilac. Now she stalked her quarry like a predator, her priority to feed her own. *A treacherous woman,* he mused with a bit of satisfaction at encountering a fair match. He looked again at where her collar met her dress. *Did the hook open to the left or to the right? Was there a hidden button beneath?*

"An island." Quartus Gant spoke. "Not far." He looked at the young woman and smiled, a slender smile that signified, if not a retreat, then a regrouping before a final push against her redoubt. *You win,* his smile said, *but you shall pay.* He continued, "I'll show you on a chart."

Oh my God, what, have I committed to? Emma felt alone, trapped again. Although she had led him to this moment, she felt unsure. *The way he looks at me—indeed, what does he expect in return?*

"His verses led me to think it was a day's sail from Newport… near a neighboring shore—not in Rhode Island. And once beyond this land, one is in the Atlantic, next port of call Liverpool."

"A guess, in other words."

"If you say so, Emma." He smiled, knowing he was willing to risk his thick neck on a guess.

"Are there any structures there?" she asked.

"Two sheds. A few fishing shacks." He hesitated. "And a new lighthouse."

Hearing that, Emma said nothing but looked into his eyes. She slid her paper of verse towards him, its words bloated with new relevance. She watched him carefully; but he only glanced at it.

"Tell me straight." He pushed the sheet of paper back across the tabletop. "I will not play Jordan's games of words."

"I believe Jordan gave to each of us, in his twisted manner, small and obtuse indications of where we should look. I wrote my recollections here. Matching these with your guess—"

"Ain't no guess."

"We're close, perhaps but we need everything Ben has learned as well. He found a former *Rattlesnake* crewman who helped Jordan hide his loot."

"Tell me what the crewman said," Gant growled, his distrust rising to the surface with his betrayer's name breaking the flow of the evening's otherwise promising conversation.

"I left Ben's notes in my bedroom."

At her neck, he saw it. Through her delicate white skin a blue vein pulsed, quickening. He could see her bosom heave trying to release more breath past the clasp, but it choked her and kept her spirit from reaching her smile and eyes, which looked at him, he was certain, with a question: *I am going upstairs. Will you follow?*

Chapter Twenty-Four

The coach road from Newport to Boston remained muddy from two days of rain. The return was dry and swift, and mercifully came far sooner than Ben Briggs had hoped. He'd thought of nothing but Emma during the long hours on the road. That young woman had blossomed before his eyes: now a driven taskmaster bent on survival and dominance in whatever action she chose next. The yardmen these days snapped to her call. She smiled less frequently, and only if Briggs made great efforts to encourage her former good nature. Briggs worried about her, and he worried about his future. He had ably sourced cannon, crew, and Down East captains for the firm's ships. Designs drawn in ink of new sleek schooners and brigs had risen from his drafting desk over the past months he had worked by her side. When he showed her how his efforts were incrementally reversing the slide of the Hammond fortunes, she gave him a rare smile that came from her heart. One brisk morning during his trek to Boston, he realized he could hardly wait until the next moment he saw her. New emotions influenced his every decision.

He looked at the letter she had entrusted to him. Revised in his hand and now sealed, he had marveled at her sober words. Someday he hoped she would reveal how she had come to learn what surely was known only to a powerful few—men soon at great risk if Ben's trip turned to success. These men had staked their lives for a perverted definition of liberty and volunteered to lead the country on a new path, with far from certain benefits. Emma had determined, through insight and intelligence, she must thwart their ruinous ambition. *Or was it the colonel himself orchestrating this, a feint from his secret lair?* Ben wondered. *No matter, leave politics to the Hammonds. My future's in shipbuilding.* Unless, of course, he was caught tomorrow carrying the forged letter whose possession alone would inevitably condemn him as an intelligence agent. He'd be hanged on a Boston harbor island or perhaps from an English frigate's yardarm—either side would have cause. More for loyalty to the Hammonds—to Emma—and their commercial ambitions than for fealty to free trade or sovereign statehood, he had decided to betray the Providence men. *Their vague promises of a ship can go to the devil,* he told himself. He had turned, now and forever committed to Emma Hammond and her plan, dedicated to a future with her if she would have him. If the young woman's intuition erred, however, he was a dead man.

"Tell your captain the boy he spared in Tortola was killed by a British cannon." As a way of introduction Ben offered an open hand to his British counterpart disguised in homespun civilian clothes. The stranger looked at the hand with contempt and did not take it.

"And this news will encourage him to do what, exactly?" The British agent asked with unmitigated sarcasm. The officer of *HMS Fortitude*, the frigate now patrolling near Stellwagen Bank, between Cape Cod and Boston Harbor, regarded Ben Briggs with the hatred of an enemy, the contempt of an honor-bound man confronting a mutinous traitor.

No patron took notice of the two casually clad men in a booth by a salt-encrusted window flanking Boston's State Street. Weary and uneasy, they sat in the crowded *Fishmonger* tavern. The noisy backroom bar overflowed with men about to board ships that would attempt a run past the British blockade. Thirsty for drink and eager for fresh food, families newly arrived from perilous voyages were jammed inside the establishment. Noisy with languages from myriad foreign lands, the crowded room reeked of unwashed bodies and spilled ale.

"Tell him the American officer from Tortola has kept his promise," continued Ben. "He expects the captain will do the same."

"I know nothing about promises," replied the British lieutenant. "I have come for information."

"I was told the captured crew of our Newport *letter of marque* would be released forthwith upon a continued conversation friendly to the Crown." Ben spoke the bold words he had prepared during his trek north from Aquidneck Island. "Our continued cooperation depends on that arrangement."

"Yes, it is a terrible existence, chained below deck without fresh air, fed only the scraps three hundred men above refuse to touch—"

"Enough! You're in Boston Harbor not Portsmouth. These United States hang enemy spies without trial on that island yonder over your right shoulder."

The British officer winced and controlled the urge to look. He was angry to be here, angry to be fighting these people, angry about his orders to cooperate. His friend Lieutenant Harry Clarke had been incinerated in the ship these degenerates had fired; he missed him terribly. He had obeyed Captain Breton and had come ashore in the fog but would rather be laying his hidden knife into this scab's chest than parrying his words. The stink of the sweaty, hungry masses pressed in on the two men, both accustomed to command, one uncomfortably naked out of uniform. Each man stared at the other coldly, looking for an edge. The British officer knew time was nearly expired for the long-planned expedition to land troops. Great titles likely awaited the officer who effected this scheme if, ultimately, no English blood spilled needlessly. No one in the admiralty would question how the ensuing secret information had been gained. The only thing that mattered now: appropriate land that had been so foolishly lost. The British lieutenant continued to press for what he did not expect, what he himself would never divulge. It bothered him that he sat with his back towards the former King's Street, defaced, renamed State Street.

"We need to know your plans… for our landing," the British officer said.

"Tell the captain I have a message he will warm to," countered Briggs. "But I must have your word as an officer. My crew returns to Long Wharf on the next tide once I fulfill my end."

"Do you have the final arrangements in writing?"

"I do."

Briggs thought about what Emma had written. It was obvious her communique had been inked by a woman, from its lilting, affected turns of pen and ink to its formal punctuation. Therefore, on the prior night, he had sat in his Boston boarding room for hours, rewriting her letter in a steady masculine hand, all the while thinking of the many ways the enemy might kill him: Most likely a club to the head as he exited the tavern, rowed out to a coastal sloop, then ignominiously dumped into the hold of the British frigate alongside the former shipmates who hated him. As he had copied Emma's words, he felt they conveyed a powerful resonance and, in the end, were reassuring and commanding, unlike her deferential style of only months before. Of course, it had only been a little over a year since he had first met the comely young woman. And yet here she described a desolate Louisiana shore in detail, where a British army might land uncontested. She dictated how an invading land force might maneuver despite swamps and bayous she had never visited. As he copied her words, Briggs took a deep breath and gripped his thumb tightly in his fingers recalling the thirty-two-pound cannon *Scepter* had fired point blank. The enemy had been aiming for Jordan's head and Briggs, by standing near, would have been collateral damage. He felt similarly here: Emma's bold ruse placed him in mortal jeopardy.

"There has been a change," Ben advised the British lieutenant who looked alarmed. "Your plans have been compromised."

Briggs stared him down. He must display proof of his sponsor's resolve and yet offer a modicum of sincere retribution for a war few on either side understood. The British lieutenant sat erect and swallowed hard. This *rendezvous* was not going as expected—not at all! His role was to issue commands, not take instructions from a shadow in a tight booth of a dismal tavern. Nonetheless he was startled at news of a change; unknowns in war lead to calamity. His Majesty's massive fleet had been preparing landing craft to be filled to the gunnels with regulars recalled from across the continent, hard-fighting troops although drained by a campaign that carried them from Iberia to Flanders; these men were flush with pride from Wellesley's most recent victories. The lieutenant dreaded meeting with his captain if relaying a new message would entail a last-minute modification of the combined Navy-Army campaign carefully planned thousands of miles from home; a campaign that must take place soon, victoriously, before any treaty was signed.

The British officer faltered. "I beg your pardon?"

"States' militia and Federal regulars are setting redoubts and deep earthworks where your troops originally planned to disembark. American troops will slaughter your men on the Virginia riverside before you bring up your cannon. Your fleet, forced to anchor far downstream, will be unable to lay down supporting fire. The British army will be routed."

"But, how—?"

"Our plan leaked. Madison is taking corrective action. The original landing is doomed."

"Why are you warning us?"

"Because the men who sent me here offer the Crown a safe, alternative landing location. A strategic venue shorn of organized resistance, only snippets of frontiersmen and trappers to contest your regulars. After your landing, after taking the city, you can traverse our great Mississippi unopposed, carry the Shenandoah, and attack the capital from the rear—its undefended rear. You will be in Virginia before the government knows you have even come ashore. You might consider staging a feint, a small landing where they expect, if you choose. But send your strength—your hardened troops, artillery, and fleet—where these United States have no defense."

The British officer had long been besotted with the prospect of the destruction of the new nation; a loose confluence born from rebellion against the King to whom he had sworn allegiance. His manner regained self-assurance. He required no need for further convincing. Nevertheless, his breeding demanded a demonstration of superiority.

"This is all well and good," the English lieutenant observed. "However, if you desire your men's release, show me this so-called revised plan—in writing."

"Disembark here." Briggs slid his tankard across the booth and the officer marveled that he had not seen Briggs place a small envelope underneath it when the ale had been first served.

With one hand, the lieutenant casually dragged the mug closer and caught the letter in his lap. Hidden from view, he cracked the seal and opened it to read the instructions. He stared intently at the final words—*a city of swamp and bayous, where the empire could send a powerful force, control the mighty river entrance, and recover their lost continent.* The British officer leaned back and nodded, even offering a slight smile.

"Your crew," he assured Briggs, "will be run ashore at Nantasket on the next tide."

On his return to Newport, Ben Briggs decided to surprise Emma at Great Hill. He needed—*longed*—to see her face and show her their improved bank balance from the Boston deposits. The Hammond Company, for the moment, stood in a better position to pay down their debt owed Westerly though not enough to satisfy Morris and his syndicate's investors. They either needed Jordan's fortune—or Emma must visit Providence and grovel. Ben firmly believed stealing a dead man's estate was preferable to accepting credit from dishonest men. He thought he could convince her to commission a voyage to search for what Jordan had stashed... somewhere. The precise "somewhere" remained a mystery, of course; the choices impossibly many, although after his latest arduous inquiries, he had whittled down the list. In the weeks since he had learned of Jordan's death, Ben had sought out crewmen from previous *Rattlesnake* voyages hoping to learn of any remote island where Jordan might have anchored, even briefly, while stowing his fortune. Briggs found former crewmen whose ill feelings ran deep about life aboard *Rattlesnake* under Captain Cornelius Jordan. One by one, Ben had listened to these angry men. He bought drinks. Insalubrious stories flowed.

"...We had an English brig under our guns," said one gunner's mate wiping his lips and shaking his greasy hair away from narrow, suspecting eyes. "And took her without firing anything but a warnin' shot. Captain Jordan and me and five other lads rowed over an'faced their people: ten crewmen, including a few Africans, plus the master with his wife and son. 'Why don't you have any gold or silver?' Captain Jordan yells after we come on deck. The English captain' told us his hold's bare and the cabin empty—they's on a homebound lumber run, deposits made already. Ship's got nothin' left to steal... 'I don't believe that, you lying cur!' our captain bellows. With his knife he points at the master. But the wife speaks up for her ship and her husband. 'You filthy Yankee caitiff!' she cries, 'You declared this war on your friends, when you know we're fighting the tyrant!' Then Cap'n Jordan turns to her an'says, 'Filthy?' and he sniffs his armpits. 'I daren't say. I've not bathed these past weeks. Have you, my dear?' Then the captain walks up to the missus, smells her person with his nose right into her bosom, with her husband there next to her who barks dog-like at our captain to get his foul face off his missus. An' before you could say 'two shakes', Capt'n Jordan sticks his knife into the man's gut, and he falls gaspin' and bleedin' to the deck. And Cap'n Jordan says, 'I'll have no blood desecrating my new ship's fine deck.' He looks to one of our mates next to me, and the captain gestures to the water. Mate's seen this before. Knows he's about t'do the damned piece or be done himself. So he grabs the dyin' man, drags him to the rail with his wife thrashing and screaming in tow, and pushes the poor soul up onto the rail. All the while she's a kickin' him and crying for her dyin' husband, but she did no good, Mr. Briggs. The mate got the dyin' man up over the bulwark and pushes him hard over. We all heard the splash, and then more noise and screams as sharks were out. He thrashed and cried for God's mercy. The woman runs at Captain Jordan with her nails out like ten daggers, but he catches her tight and felt her rough-like all over. Then he says, 'I believe, Madam, we're discussing your need for a bath. We must fix that.' And he sends a man below to find soap and when he come up, Cap'n Jordan shoves the soap down her blouse and rubs it all around. Sir, he did this, I swear! Then he pushes her to the side and says, 'To your bath, Madam.' And, with an angry shove, she joined her husband."

Briggs heard other foul stories of Jordan's depravity foisted on his captives: Of mercy allowed, then taken away for the crew's entertainment. Freedom falsely granted, then over the side. Captain Jordan enjoyed the shock of betrayal as much as the lust for bloody death itself. Ben had marveled at Jordan's crazed behavior. Listening to these accounts, however, he realized in his few cruises with Jordan he had never seen the man at his worst. Whether by intuition or foresight, Jordan had tempered his atrocities once Thomas Hammond came aboard. Jordan had played to an image he wished to convey ashore; only the men who sailed with him on earlier voyages knew the truth about *The Curse of the Coast*. Because Cornelius Jordan paid *Rattlesnake's* crew far above the norm, they kept to themselves about his more salacious atrocities at sea. Yet despite the lurid accounts, Ben still knew little more of *where* to look than when he started out.

However, on the day prior to leaving for Boston with Emma's heavy sack in his sea chest, a former sailor named Jeremiah Quigley approached him. The fortuitous encounter occurred after Briggs placed an order for a new heavy weather spanker for *Rattlesnake* at the loft on the hill where the craftsmen stitched double seams to withstand southern oceans' hurricanes. Young Quigley had heard of Briggs' queries and an offer of coin for information about Cornelius Jordan. The lad followed him for two days before approaching Ben striding from the loft. The two men settled under a tree. Yes, the lad had sailed with Jordan. Yes, he had seen the usual: The takings, the fights, the hurt, and the shock of betrayal. Quigley was religious—a Congregationalist, a sect formed of the original settlers' Puritan religion—and no more would he look at blood, no more hear cries of anguish in the night from the captain's cabin when captured women suffered from his worst. The lad had promised himself he would leave the ship as soon as they docked; he would find a skill ashore. One short voyage, however, had been unlike the others: no bounty taken, no ship attacked.

"Only I and two other men joined the captain, not on *Rattlesnake*, but on a loaned cutter, sir," Jeremiah Quigley explained, "She was a fifty-foot ship that three men could manage. The two other crewmen were brutes, strong, mean men not part of *Rattlesnake's* usual crew."

"Why did the captain need you, Mr. Quigley?" Briggs probed.

Jeremiah Quigley paused a moment, recalling proudly, "Why, I was aboard for my local knowledge, sir. Spent my childhood in Chatham waters, fishin'n clammin'. We'd cut up seals too, sir, when the sharks weren't feeding on'em."

"That part of Cape Cod is known for difficult holding ground," Ben noted.

"Aye, sir, but I know all the eddies and the shifting sands. The shallow channels scare off all but the locals. Captain Jordan hired me to guide the cutter up and around the shoals into a small lagoon at the tip of the island. We anchored safely and departed before the next dawn. The curious thing, sir—I was left alone onboard while Jordan and the others went ashore."

"Could you see where they went, Mr. Quigley?" asked Briggs.

"Jordan commanded me to stay below deck after the three lowered a boat. Jordan's order was accompanied by a threat, sir."

"What did he threaten?"

"That my seeing the next dawn was no guarantee if I didn't stay below. I found a corner in the fore cabin and curled under a woolen blanket and slept until one of his brutes kicked me awake some hours later. As ordered, I piloted the ship out to deeper water."

"So you did, in fact, see the next dawn?"

"Thankfully, sir, yes, but then two sets of murderous eyes turned on me. The captain intervened, though. He said I was a good lad, and my services would be needed again. The others backed off. The captain pressed a few coins into my palm, enough to live comfortable for a month. Captain Jordan said he'd come to me someday and I would do as he asked. But of course, I would not. The very day we tied up, I ran off and did not look back.

"And the other two crewmen?"

"I heard one man was found dead the next week behind a tavern outhouse. Whose knife done it no one could say. The other crabber gone overboard off *Rattlesnake's* larboard rail, late at night, sir, far out at sea. Rumor has it, Jordan had the watch that night."

"Tell me, Mr. Quigley, where exactly did you guide Captain Jordan?"

After a surprisingly speedy packet trip from Long Wharf to Barnstable, then by carriage to New Bedford, Briggs caught another packet to Newport.

Running to Great Hill, he entered through the back pantry door. Respecting Emma's standards, he avoided the front parlor with boots filthy from the road. Near the pantry, Emma kept a small, tidy office where the two had often sat studying figures he brought; there she decided which vendor to anger or please with a payment. Most mornings, she would come down from her sleep and as was her custom, take tea and a biscuit, and get to work. Time had begun to soothe her grief from losing her brother; of late, she sometimes even graced Ben with a smile the width of the bay as she offered him ham or porridge from across the table. Working close by her side, he stole as much of her private time as possible. Sometimes he answered her inquires with long and elaborate explanations far exceeding the need or her interest in his level of detail. And although he risked losing her attention, he was able to keep her eyes focused on his, and that pleased him.

Arriving in Newport after a surprisingly speedy packet trip from Long Wharf to Barnstable, then by carriage to New Bedford where Ben Briggs caught another packet to Newport, he entered Great Hill through the back pantry door. Respecting Emma's standards, he avoided the front parlor with boots filthy from the road. Near the pantry, Emma kept a small, tidy office where the two had often sat studying figures he brought; there is where she decided which vendor to anger or please with a payment. On this morning, Ben assumed she would come down from her sleep and, as was her custom, take tea and a biscuit, and get to work. Time had begun to soothe her grief; of late, she sometimes even graced Ben with a smile the width of the bay as she offered him ham or porridge from across the table. Working close by her side, it was his habit to steal as much of her private time as possible. Sometimes he answered her inquiries with long and elaborate explanations far exceeding the need, or her interest, in that level of detail. And although he risked losing her attention, he was able to keep her eyes focused on his own, and that pleased him to no end. Of late, however, she had seemed aware of his shenanigans but curiously let it ride. Was it possible, he had wondered during his trip to Boston and back, that she enjoyed his company, his voice, and their uninterrupted private hours?

This morning, however, Emma appeared starkly different. The cook and maid were in the kitchen off to one side as Emma stepped through the swinging door leading from the dining room. Her look of utter shock caught Ben sitting at her table.

Before he could explain that his trip home had been without adventure; the packet fast under a northerly; the roads clear, though bumpy, and the horses rested; before he could explain his good news of their finances and the decoy letter, Ben Briggs froze: Quartus Gant followed close behind Emma, his hair uncombed. Briggs felt for his pistol and waited. Was Gant armed? *What in damnation is he doing here? And so... early?*

"Ben! Stop! Mr. Gant and I were discussing our next voyage. He has agreed—"

"You... you stayed *here* last night." Ben spoke the obvious, his heart crushed between envy and utter hatred.

Emma recoiled. She whirled 'round to see if Gant too held a weapon. When he had undressed last night by candlelight, she noticed only hideous scars for which she was responsible. On the kitchen sideboard nearby, however, a small armory of butcher knives, was laid out for cleaning.

"Ben, Quartus. Please! There are things you need to understand."

"I understand Tortola."

With one hand, Gant grasped the largest knife from the sideboard, while the other gently pushed Emma's waist aside, opening up a channel direct to the man whose death he had dreamed about for many cold nights. In self-defense, Briggs raised his gun.

"You've just enjoyed your revenge!"

"No! Briggs!" Emma cried. "Quartus, no!"

Briggs and Gant faced each other only three strides apart. At this distance a pistol shot would surely find its target—Q's head for the kill. But if he missed, Ben knew he would feel cold steel deep in his own stomach a moment later. He hesitated. Gant saw the same fear Briggs had shown at sea. He grabbed the table and threw it upwards while he plunged with the kitchen knife. Ben leapt back. Gant repositioned himself, arms wide, wielding his weapon, a possible blade for close combat. Briggs had no choice but to press his finger on the trigger. Gant, having selected the best manner of counterattack, ducked, rolled, and thrust with great force toward Briggs' stomach. Simultaneously, Emma threw the cooking pot at Briggs just as the gun discharged. His only shot rang out, splitting wood and showering the room with cabinet glass. Emma screamed as she fell to the floor. Gant rolled forward and came up on the other side of the overturned table. Briggs, also a veteran of battle on slanted, wet decks, drew his boarding knife from his belt to stop Gant's thrust a moment before it struck home.

"Help *me!*" On the floor, Emma was not screaming anymore, but wept in pain.

Gant glanced her way, while keeping an eye on Briggs' ship knife. Emma's upper arm was dark, seeping wet where she had been struck by shattered glass.

"Do not fight... until... I can speak." She struggled to sit. "Afterwards, go kill yourselves. Both of you… But you *will* listen to me!"

"I'll listen to you once I kill him!" Gant raged. He threw himself at Briggs.

Briggs balanced the smaller of the knives in his hand—strong and sturdy, designed for close fighting, stabbing, and slicing. An arm or hand unprotected was an easy target. Its blade was newly sharpened and intended for one purpose: To kill a man. Gant's weapon, however, a kitchen carving knife, was sharp as well, its edge meant for the fat juicy breast of a wild turkey or a farm chicken; slightly curved at the end, it allowed for a cleaner cut. But this elegant curve when pressed against a straight steel blade lost contact and slipped away. Again, Gant lunged and met Briggs' attack with his knife, but the connection was lost and his weight behind the thrust threw him forward, off balance. Briggs deftly stepped aside. Falling, Gant realized he had lost both blade and footing. Flat on his back he hit hard then felt a stab in his shoulder and screamed with the crazed howl of an injured bear. With his elbow, he struck back forcefully, catching Briggs smack in the mouth. Stunned, Briggs fell back, knife lost in his daze and the two embraced on the kitchen floor, kicking, punching, kneeing, and elbowing the other trying to find advantage. They crashed into cook's table, breaking it apart like the rail of a ship after an enemy broadside. Observing through a gap in the door, the cook and the upstairs maid screamed and ran out another door. They raced down the path crying for help from the workers in the dairy barn. Emma, her arm bleeding, huddled in a corner as she watched three knives skid to far reaches of the floor. The combatants continued to beat on each other like cocks in a pen. Gant, the larger man, although weakened from a year imprisoned, remained a ruthless fighter. He shoved Briggs away and despite his wound, scrambled to his feet. Briggs rolled away and caught his breath. *Hesitating in a fight to the death is fatal*, Gant's early life lesson drove him to grab Briggs' abandoned knife, and he fell on the downed man and put the knife to his neck. Briggs' final breaths imminent—Gant knew from experience where to slice a man's throat so no bandage could arrest his life's flow.

"Stop, you fools! Gant!" Emma begged. He glanced at her. "*I* sent you to prison."

The statement was so absurd, Gant loosened his grip. "What?"

Clutching her bloody arm, Emma realized despite the shards of glass that had cut her, she was the least injured of the three. She stared in horror at the blood-soaked men: her lover and her partner and realized she alone could end the savagery.

"I told Jordan to protect Thomas... do whatever... to bring him home. To protect my ship, bring it back in one piece. Protect the crew. But if the ship were captured, if an officer must be arrested, an officer for parole... that it be you, Quartus."

"I do not believe you," replied Gant, returning to Brigg's throat.

"Jordan acted on my orders," Emma insisted, grimacing more at the pain of her sins.

"Move and you die!" Gant kicked Briggs back into the corner and stood over Emma, hunkered against the wainscoting. "Lies!" he bellowed, towering over her.

"My brother told me what happened that day—he saw the key."

Gant stared at Emma trying to assemble the incredulous news. "*You* had me sent to Mill?"

"I did. Jordan acted on my instructions."

"No *woman* told Jordan to drop the magazine key in my pocket!"

"Do you recall the color of the key?"

"Color—?"

"*Rattlesnake's* old magazine key was iron, was it not? But I had a new lock made, with a new key. Bronze plate. I gave it to Jordan."

Recalling that the British captain had dug deliberately into Gant's trouser pocket and dangled it, shining for all on deck to see, Gant had to admit, "Aye, it sparkled like a binnacle."

"When I gave Cornelius the new key, I told him to do whatever was necessary to bring Thom home alive. He explained how a trade might be offered—"

"*You* put me there..." muttered Gant, amazed, unsure what was real, whether to trust.

"You have a choice, Quartus. Believe me and what your own eyes saw. Or, misled by your angry heart, kill an innocent man. They'll hang you. And I will give witness."

Gant looked at the defeated man at his feet. "You're lying to protect his worthless skin." "There's more, Quartus." Emma spoke quickly. "I believed they'd grant you parole, and send you home, not throw you in a dungeon. I made enquiries. I could not sleep for many weeks. When I learned you were in Mill Prison…" She grunted with the pain of her bloody arm as she staggered to her feet. She stared at the man with a knife whom she had held most intimately that very morning. "I arranged for your escape."

Both Gant's and Briggs' eyes expanded. Briggs recognized her admission, either true or a quick-thinking maneuver that might help him survive the morning. He caught Emma's glance. *No, you fool, stay down!* He sat back, regarding the knife in Gant's hand inches from his face.

"Quartus, I approached Geoffrey Morris," she continued, "I asked how to secure your ransom. He said he had contacts. We owe him… a great deal of money. I was able to barter something else he wanted. He knew the right people. He took my money, the last of *Windslayer*. And here you are." She looked at Gant, then the shattered glass at her feet.

"If I'm to believe that you sent me there," Gant trembled with rage as he spoke softly, "I must hate you for the rest of my life."

"And if you kill Briggs, I shall hate *you* for the rest of *my* life."

Gant looked at Briggs then placed the knife with his own blood still dripping from its blade onto the sideboard. His wound bled but the sharp edge had not struck bone or shoulder tendon. His face contorted, he wrestled with a conundrum; the girl had betrayed him with forethought, and then, racked with guilt, had set him free. But had she saved him? And was Briggs truly blameless? Was this possibly a worse fate, knowing his vengeance might have been wrongly aimed? Had he also foolishly misplaced his heart? She had banished him then released him and yet she took him in her most private spaces knowing all this! Were there more truths she intended to hold over him, sequestered for all time? Like Captain Jordan, this woman with her trove of hidden information kept him off balance. Beautiful, yet, like Jordan, Emma Hammond revealed herself a cruel manipulator interested primarily in her own self-preservation. He stepped over Ben's splayed legs and turned to exit through the swinging door leading out to the front foyer.

"We're not finished here, Quartus," she called. "We have a chance to build our future. I have a ship. Jordan's dead. The gold he stole from my father is out there someplace. And each of us has information about where to find it."

"I thought what you showed me last night was complete." Spitting mad, Gant looked bitterly at Emma, then glanced down at Briggs to make sure he understood. "...before we *retired*."

Emma stared at Gant. "It was not."

Ben realized he was safe, alone on the floor. He gathered his legs and stood shakily.

"She's right," said Ben. "I have critical new information. About where to find it."

"It appears we each kept our own private counsel," Emma interjected with a sharp glance to Ben, then back to Gant. "What we each know is not enough, is it? Jordan intended us to fight each other, you two to the death, rather than provide all the pieces to his puzzle to any one of us. His goal was not for us to *find* his riches—his goal was to destroy us in the effort!" Emma found the one chair not in splinters and sat to gather herself. "But we have everything we need," she continued slowly, "...if we work together... for one last short cruise... just one day." Emma held her arm. Her painful cuts continued to leak through her fingers. Still, she waved away the cook who had arrived with a farmhand armed with a musket. "After that, we shall part forever. Away from all this hatred" She regarded the two men. Bloody and disheveled, she stood, as straight as the flagpole made from a ship's mast on Great Hill's rocky point. "Q, you told me last night Jordan sailed to a sand-spit of an island. Ben, you've admitted you questioned a few of Captain Jordan's shipmates, yet you've just confessed you haven't told me everything he told me. For my part, I admit I have held my final conclusions to myself. I believe I can pin-point an actual location of Jordan's stash once we get near. But I can't find the island without your help Quartus. And you'll dig forever without our clues. I propose we take *Rattlesnake* offshore five miles, hove to, place all our cards on the table and go from there. Otherwise, we'll remain trapped here on shore forever, defeated by the curse of a dead madman... a creature who's laughing at us from the darkness."

She kept firm pressure on her wounded arm while eying the two men who had destroyed her kitchen.

"Do we have a pact?" Emma Hammond asked her new conspirators.

Chapter Twenty-Five

...and yet, I fear him. I fear for him. I gave him my heart, Ceci. He took it in a way you cannot imagine. Well perhaps now that you are married you can, but I had no idea. We had a night of passion mixed with anger. I saw his darkness up close and it scared me. I don't believe he is an evil man, though evil has a deep hold on him. I suppose that doesn't make sense. After, in the darkness of my room, I sensed a kind of escape. I felt that his being, his inner essence had left me briefly, and I feared he would not return to the place we shared. And all the worse, Ben is aware of everything now. How can I know whom to embrace? This is all so new to me. Quartus looks at Ben as if I was a prize pig they fought over at a county fair. Am I a prize? Yes, there is the Hammond wealth, but little is left. So, what am I? Only a simple, former rich girl who took a poor man from the Northside into my bed? Did I give my heart to the wrong man?

I have been bitterly stung.

Emma admitted to herself that a pact based on the rants of a dead man could not last long. Gant wanted to kill Briggs first *then* take his chances searching for Jordan's secret lair. Briggs, knowing this, might take advantage of a low rail in a rough sea. She knew it was now or never again. She also feared the many eyes that would be watching her. If a woman, not known to take sea cruises, set out alone in a small craft with just Briggs and Gant, someone would call their bluff. Gant had convinced her that a hundred Newport men watched the *Rattlesnake's* former officers like a sea hawk watches the shallows. In order to *not* give away their game, she needed to outfox the entire community while avoiding British nearshore patrols. Since her brig was ready for sea, and since a sturdy deck and the privacy of a deep hold was necessary to hide any strongbox they might uncover, she decided to delay *Captain* Gant's first ocean voyage that had been slated for that afternoon's ebbtide. Instead, she, Quartus, and Ben would slip away before dawn aboard *Rattlesnake*.

Rattlesnake's crew assembled under the waning crescent moon. The last of the water casks were rolled up the gangway by able body sailors, directed by Gant's oaths. Emma asked the crew to follow her below where, to their surprise, she announced that aside from two young men, a full crew was no longer needed. For their silence, however, she'd pay them for a full three-month cruise. She left for the aft cabin and Gant informed each departing crewman with an unambiguous threat what would become of their worthless hides if they did not honor Miss Hammond's instructions to the letter.

The two detained able-bodies, Thad Jenkins from Fall River, was a competent sailor, and Andy Crowell, a bright sailor who had been with the past two *Rattlesnake* cruises. The extra coins she pressed into their palms bound them to her; her secrets, she hoped, forever safe.

As they began to cast off from the pier, Emma did not see Gant approach the boys.

"One word about our little cruise to your drinkin' buddies will be the last thing you utter before I cut your throats and bury you in mud."

"Aye, sir."

Gant came only for Emma's promise of a sizable reward, regardless of the outcome of the hunt—enough credit to buy *Rattlesnake* when the cruise ended. Gant saw himself sailing over the horizon in a matter of hours, *alone if need be… my own deck 'neath my feet, my hearty men aboard, makin' havoc on any ocean I chose. I'll write my own future.*

Briggs, however, had tersely asked for a great deal more. For starters, a new sign on the door to the shipping office: *Hammond and Briggs.* Emma took it well though surmising he might have asked for something else. *Unfortunate,* she mused to herself, though entirely unexpected as he had just found her intimately ensconced with a man he feared and now hated. *Quartus, on the other hand, will soon lose himself at sea on my ship. Both men will leave me unspeakably alone.* Emma had promised, nonetheless with little enthusiasm, to deliver what she knew each man desired most. She had begun to understand Gant and how hate presented a clear, guiding light for a future life unencumbered by guilt.

As she sat on board *Rattlesnake* with her pen and ink watching the men cast off dock lines and hoisting a jib, she realized her existence had suddenly gained a single-minded purpose.

Ceci, a short note before I sail this morning long before dawn. At the very moment I thought I had an answer for my life's longing, he spurned me. After the night we shared together and a world opened to me, he looks at me now with unbearable loathing. I must remain near him while we voyage together to reclaim what is mine, while facing danger from men I once trusted with my life. A life bereft of love, however, has little to recommend it, though I cannot regret losing something I only enjoyed for a few fleeting hours.

Once the ship cleared land, with only Block Island to the west barely visible in the dim light, *Rattlesnake's* small crew released her sheets, and with a furl in the spanker, let the ship lie hove-to, immobile in the water. Emma motioned to the aft companionway.

"Let us go below and settle this, gentlemen."

Gant took charge of the deck, instructing, "Andy, you and Jenkins keep a sharp eye for British patrols. They're known to lurk between Holmes Hole and Tarpaulin."

"Aye, Captain," the two crewmen spoke over one another eagerly.

Below decks, the three fortune hunters sat apart from each other in the captain's cabin. Emma spoke first.

"Ben, Quartus believes Jordan has hidden the money on a nearby island. He has yet to provide me with the name or location, however." There was no trace in her voice of fondness for Gant or Briggs. Despite her awkward seduction, Gant had kept his silence during the entire night's embrace. *So be it*, she steadied herself, *I shall know it soon enough*. "So Quartus, to which island do we sail?"

Gant took a deep breath. "Jordan's ramblings about a short sail seemed not far from Newport. Martha's Vineyard, Block, and Nantucket have too many fishermen about. He wouldn't have risked that."

"So, he went west, then, to Montauk—" Ben interjected.

"Nay. He spoke of a shoal, the last one before reaching the Atlantic. His meaning, to a *real* seaman..." Gant's insult stuck in Ben's craw. "...was obvious. Cape Cod has an island that sticks out from Chatham to the south. It's mostly deserted with only a few fishing shacks. The Indians call it Monomoy."

Emma noticed Briggs' eyes brighten.

"What then, Ben?" she asked.

Briggs as well as Gant knew he could lie, mislead the other two, and return later with shovels. He hesitated. Both Gant and Emma knew what he was thinking.

"Lie to us, Briggs," Gant let his coat fall away showing his knife and pistol. "and I'll cut you into slices and make you live in pain until my dying breath."

"Stop it, damn you both!" Emma cried, "Ben if you mislead us, we *all* fail."

"Jordan anchored at Malabar Point, at the tip of Monomoy Island. He took a schooner there last spring with three other men, two of whom were mysteriously killed afterwards, leaving only a young pilot alive. This boy told me he anchored in a small tidal pool that comes and goes with the gales."

"Quartus, does this sound right? Malabar Point?"

Gant hesitated. Briggs had narrowed an impossible search along miles of sand and beach grass to a pinpoint. "Aye, Monomoy Island is where I had it placed."

"Q, you told me there was a lighthouse there? And shacks?"

"Aye."

"Then listen to what he sang to me." In a firm and steady tone, and for the first time presented to either man, Emma read Jordan's dreamy stanzas. Her determined spirit only faintly disguised her excitement.

My tower of sand and milk and stone
Where I climb for fortune and bend for none.
Where I feast on ribbons of water rushed by,
And fingers dig to all come by.

"You see? 'milk' is white, a lighthouse," she said as she continued to read,

Though my heart is still and the night is long,
I fear we voyage to where the sound is gone
To where the voyage ends, the drifters sent
Past the shoals of peace, with death's intent.

They rose at night and found the block,
Felt their way, their light unlock'd
Their grace though not, twice returned
To live a day, their past now burned.

"Quartus, why do you think his verse might point to Malabar Point on Monomoy Island?" she asked.

Gant did not trust her thin smile—the same look he saw in yesterday's first light of a woman pleased at having finished a necessary chore. Her eyes shook him then, as they did now.

"He says '*ribbons of water.*' I wager he's talking about rips flush with feedin' bass. Monomoy's got shoals along the far shore, flats on the bay side."

"That could be any score of fishing holes," Briggs complained.

"Aye, but '*ribbons*' tell his mind. On Monomoy, storms're always shiftin' the sand. What the sea don't move, the trades from southwest do. In the cove, to the west, the sand's got ripples like a desert. He said '*ribbon*' but I think he meant '*ripple*'."

"I don't buy it," said Briggs.

Gant shot back a denigrating look. "Also, men clam on the Monomoy flats. Jordan said, '*fingers dig*'."

319

Emma bolstered Gant's logic. "Monomoy is indeed remote, yet close to shore. He also spoke of '*drifters.*'

"The first English settlers were persecuted, adrift in their lives," added Briggs. "Legend has it they might have been sailing to New Amsterdam, not Massachusetts Bay and tried for days to get past Monomoy Island, but couldn't sail against the currents... '*twice returned*' might refer to that," Briggs concluded.

"Is the lighthouse wood or stone?" Emma asked Gant.

"Stone. Marks the channel for ships entering the Sound westbound," Gant confirmed.

"So did he hide the money in the tower?" Briggs asked.

Gant looked to Emma.

"Likely," she said. "But *where* in the lighthouse? Ben?" Pensively Emma turned to Briggs. "Tell Quartus and me what you heard. *All* of it, please."

Briggs made his critical contribution. "Jordan told me he expected we'd find unprotected ships waiting for us in Tortola. He was wrong of course, but he kept rambling. Rum got him singing. The crew was used to this and they often joined in with him. One night however, he sang an original set of verses none of us knew. I looked straight at him: he was singing at me, *to* me, like he was teasing me, staring into my eyes—"

"Do you remember his words?"

"I wrote them on sailcloth."

"Tell us," said Emma.

Ben read from the folded canvas: "'*Cold buried clear though seen for miles. Deep top-down thirty, think on it and smile.*'" Ben paused, then added, "'*Cold*' might mean *gold*. '*Clear for miles*'—a lighthouse?"

Gant snarled, "Tell us something we do not know."

"But dig '*thirty*' feet deep? Emma ignored Gant, and remarked, "That is a great way down."

"Not down," Gant interjected, "He meant to *climb* a tower—*up* thirty feet. At the very end, aboard *Raptor,* he acted like he had lost his mind. Jordan often said the opposite of what he intended. I say we start our search in the tower." Gant looked out the aft port while Emma and Briggs reread the notes. Gant broke their concentration, adding, "But don't be surprised if Jordan was lying. About everything."

Gant clutched *Rattlesnake's* wheel tight. Approaching Cuttyhunk to port and Vineyard Sound ahead, he reflected on prison—reeling from cruel turnkey taunts, the slop thrown at the wretched, tangled bodies strewn on the dirt floor. The worst debasement he had suffered, however, was the guards' air of superiority. He felt the same now when Briggs tentatively approached Gant at the helm.

"I say we take the Muskeget Channel. It's the straightest route to Malabar."

"I say we don't!" snapped Gant. "Muskeget's a death trap." Rocks barely concealed at high water on the west side, its shoals to the east were treacherous even at slack current on a clear day. Gant motioned to the distant horizon, growing as red as fire. "And we got heavy weather comin'. We'll take the Sound."

Briggs looked at the sky and cursed the bursting orange and yellow clouds. An approaching gale would exacerbate an already tense day fraught with menace. *Rattlesnake* left Rhode Island waters and headed toward the treacherous shoal-filled waters off Martha's Vineyard and Nantucket Island. Briggs looked at Emma in her solemn, grey dress with its voluminous petticoat ruffling under the hem. She roamed the deck as naturally as a seaman before the mast—steady and assured, in laced leather shoes, low in the heel.

"Your heavy dress, Emma, will drag you down if you slip overboard," offered Ben, "Riding clothes would have been better—"

"I do not intend to go swimming, Ben, thank you."

Briggs realized Emma had traveled past the fight, the knives, and the blood. She did not cling to the recent past. Nor did she make any attempt to explain why she had taken the gunner to her bed. Ben struggled to recall what he might have said to spurn her; he had thought that she was growing attached.

"Damn you, Briggs!" cried Gant, then directed his order to the two young crewmen doing the work of ten. "Trim and come up! Or we'll fall outta the channel!"

Briggs evicted the painful image of Emma and Gant coupling. He tried to concentrate on sailing the ship. As he passed Gant, Q spat a deep chest-load of heavy phlegm, downwind, its effect deliberate and loud. Briggs and the girl evidently had a private understanding, Gant grumbled to himself. Anyone could see it—the way they moved in unison as *Rattlesnake* rode gentle swells, never bumping into each other when the ship took a bow wave from the east, never taking up more room than for one if they climbed a companionway ladder together. It unnerved him how well their bodies seemed to mesh: They talked without speaking, argued with a raised eyebrow, shared plans with a sigh. *They were against him.*

"Jenkins!" barked Gant, turning the wheel of his ship over to the young crewman. The former gunner strode to the starboard rail to confront Briggs alone, the smooth countenance of his partner boiling his soul. "You wanted the *'Snake,* Briggs, but she's mine now. You wanted that girl, but she'll crawl into my bed any night I call her. You wanted your own ships—you greedy swine—a fleet of 'em—but unless we find Jordan's gold, you'll not own an oar. I'm only lettin' you live because *she* says she needs you. But listen to my words—after she gets what she wants she'll throw you over for a rich man. And I'll be laughing on your grave!"

Briggs used his remaining restraint to say nothing. He resolved to meet Gant as an equal. He did not back down, nor play Gant's game of endless recrimination. Better Gant condemn him as a betrayer than a coward, which was, Ben told himself, closer to the truth. Ben could never explain Tortola, never apologize to Gant, nor change the gunner's jaded worldview. Gant had turned away from the only two people who cared if he lived or died. Perhaps it was best, vindication of a sort, to let Gant's misinterpreted version of the truth fester, and over time consume him entirely. And after Gant inevitably sailed away, Briggs thought he and Emma might build a life together. *So let it be for today.* Within an hour, *Rattlesnake* had left the eastern approach to the Vineyard's Holmes Hole astern. On deck, Emma and Gant passed each other silently and he wrenched the wheel from Jenkins. Enjoying the helm's feel, Gant gripped *Rattlesnake's* spoked wheel tighter and steered northeast across the sound.

"Don't be so glum, Quartus," said Emma from her perch near the taffrail. "We have a good notion where to search."

Gant did not respond; he sensed, since their night together he was being played; the lightness to his step after his passion with the girl had long since dissipated. When a gambler is losing at cards, suspecting his opponent is cheating does not improve his hand. His strength was beginning to return despite Briggs' knife wound that Emma had skillfully stitched. And for that he was thankful, though he never said that to her.

Emma Hammond grew up among sailors and ships, cordage and lofts, chandleries, suppliers, and shipyards, but she had never herself sailed offshore. Like her father, she commanded seamen from her window. But this day was different. She was unsure if their pact was as sturdy as a ship's keel or as fragile as a threadbare sail. And what if the two men killed each other before they delivered her safely home with the funds she needed to rescue Hammond and Company's honor? She would be at the mercy of Geoffrey Morris, one known for having none. As a fresh breeze sought to steal her bonnet tied to her head, she looked at Briggs and Gant and an unsettling thought occurred to her: she had entrusted her future to men accustomed to reveling in violence. *I've committed my life to two privateersmen,* she thought. *Bloody hell.*

Before they had embarked from Newport to plunder Captain Jordan's heist, Emma had made a precautionary arrangement, ruminating as she had about how to conceal Jordan's gold from prying eyes. She had climbed aboard her ship by dead of night. In a tool cabinet near the galley was a worn seaman's chest with sturdy rope handles. She had selected loose carpentry tools and utensils from the galley, placing them inside. After eying the available remaining space, she had shoved the chest back into an unobtrusive corner. Perhaps it might prove helpful. Now, Emma looked up at *Rattlesnake's* new captain at the wheel. She smiled faintly at Gant, as Briggs stood far forward with a spyglass in his hands, scouting for British patrols.

"You and I have similar goals, Quartus. We both want our freedom," she said.

"You compare your high livin' ways—to *prison*?" asked Gant, ire dripping.

"I'm referring to a freedom of *spirit*. Do not pretend you don't know what I meant." She stared at the coast moving slowly by in the distance, and added casually, "You're not as cold as you want people to think."

"You should not suppose more than I say."

Emma decided to let it rest. Overnight something had changed between them. A spark had risen to a flame and then dissipated in an instant—a burst of rain had hit a robust forest fire, dousing the flame, leaving steaming ash. Was she afraid of his tightening, lustful grip that threatened to possess her? Should she abandon a man whose face, so controlled as he awoke, revealed duplicity as insidious as her own? She had shuddered as she dressed—ecstasy and fear comingling. She awoke determined neither to cast him off nor allow him to consume her. Wasn't there time in a relationship for a man and woman to learn how to love one another? Why did love have to be so forcefully determined on a person without time for building anticipated desire? And what about trust? She held out a faint hope that after this voyage, she and Q might rekindle a smoldering ember. Only after she had achieved her goal, however, would she allow a man to completely capture her heart. But she feared that, at any time, any two of the collaborators might just as readily turn, savaging the other; they all had good reasons.

At Monomoy Island, cold Atlantic waves crashed on east-facing Malabar beach, while gentle, sandy flats stretched west in the new morning air. Malabar deceived in the morning; gentle now, though the flats cracked angrily each afternoon when the sun hit its peak and the south-westerlies sprang from the Sound churning the outgoing tide exposing the shallow anchorage to crushing onshore waves. Rowing ashore with Emma and Briggs, Gant was first to reach the lighthouse door. Briggs followed close behind with an axe and a spade. Emma followed, struggling at first in the sand before she chucked her shoes and stockings, wishing she had worn her riding breeches after all instead of a heavy, woolen work dress. Gant pressed against the lighthouse door. Hinges creaked. Inside, he did not trust the appearance of the tower's wooden stairs, likely built by winter carpenters from Chatham, manned only by seasonal coast watchers. The season of constant gales had not quite yet arrived, so the tower sat empty of coast-watchers today. Fortunate for us, Gant thought, as it appeared a storm was building from the west. He looked outside for any signs of fishermen or worse. Once he was satisfied they were alone he entered the lighthouse. Looking up, he ascended several steps, then paused. He climbed no further.

"What's wrong?" Briggs asked.

"Would *you* carry a heavy chest up those stairs?"

"So *where*?" Briggs understood yet goaded Gant anyway, "You said you *knew*."

Gant wanted to end it now. His knife was ready. Neither Emma nor the two lads left on the ship could stop him.

"'*Climb for his fortune*,' Jordan sang... but '*bend for none*'," sneered Gant.

"I agree with Quartus." Emma saw the morning ending in violence if she relinquished command. She stepped between the two men. "I see, you are right Captain Gant, these stairs are too narrow to carry up a heavy strongbox."

"For what reason would he want us to '*climb*'?" Briggs' voice echoed within the stone hollow. "If he hid strongbox in here..."

Emma lay her hand on Briggs and directed him to the left. Reaching Gant on the steps, she gently pushed him to her right. Gant, however, did not budge.

"May I pass?" Emma asked, not smiling.

Gant moved his bulk aside. She placed her bare foot on the first step of the circular stairs that led to the top and stamped hard twice. The stairs although small, were sturdy enough. She climbed. "Read us from your notes, Ben." requested Emma, climbing further.

Briggs read slowly,

"*They rose at night and found the block,*
Felt their way, their light unlock'd..."

"'*At night*.' The moon!" exclaimed Emma. She looked up at the open space above her head where the whale-oil lamplight would shine bright during foul weather. She looked down, to where her companions stood. "When do we think Jordan came here?"

Gant looked to Briggs who answered, "Eighteen months ago, Emma. After *Rattlesnake's* raids on England. April."

"Do you have a date?" she asked.

"No. Though to avoid the spring gales, I'd guess not before the second week," Briggs answered.

"You kept the ship's log, Ben. Do you remember: was there a full moon that second week?" asked Emma, looking up the stairs.

"I do not recall, though full then was likely mid-month..." Briggs counted the moon-months backwards seventeen times and guessed. Gant, quick to understand Emma's questioning, strode up the stairs several steps, stopping clear of Emma a few stairs above him. Briggs continued, "Rising from east-southeast."

"Which would cast its '*light unlocked*...'" Gant reasoned, and angled one arm to the eastern sky the other in a straight line back down. Emma angled the same from higher up. They reached a conclusion at the same time: " '...*found the block.*'!" Emma's voice rose above his.

"What? What?" Briggs asked, bewildered at the other two with their arms extended and rising excitement.

Emma flew down the stairs following Gant. Scrambling past Briggs, Emma and Gant fell to their knees at a spot on the floor behind the stairs, next to the circular tower walls. Gant bent over and wiped away sand separating the structure's stone foundation. He found joints where mortar had bound heavy granite floor-blocks to withstand tremors of wind and rain. He knelt to wipe the seams of one block, then another. To the left, a third, then realizing he might be closer than imagined, he wiped the entire floor around him. He cleared the seams revealing mortar paste whiter than the weathered seams near it. On two sides, the blocks were chipped, suggesting force had been applied to remove them one at a time.

"We found it!" Emma cried.

Smug though a bit surprised, Gant smiled and extended his elbow, excluding Briggs from the celebration. "Axe!" he cried. Briggs handed it to him.

Keeping his partners in his peripheral sight, Gant chipped out the seams between blocks, first at the edges until one stone came loose. His axe fell again and again and with his hands he pulled at the loosened edges of stone. After ten or more blows, another block rocked free. Briggs squatted and the two men removed first one and then the other block from the floor. More angry blows and Gant loosened three other blocks nested by the first two. Thereby they created a hole just large enough for a man to enter into what appeared to be a crawl space under the lighthouse floor. Gant thrust his broad torso into the opening. And stopped. Deathly dark within the space, he felt the sandy ground beneath him. The tight space was high enough to crawl into, but not stand. Gant paled at the recollection of Mill Prison's 'lower deck'.

He stammered, "I will not go in there!"

"What is it?" Briggs exclaimed, realizing that he could end his war with Gant with a heavy axe blow to the head. Gant, half entombed, knew the same as he withdrew from the tunnel. Emma heard a low-throated gag of raw jealousy escape Ben's mouth.

She glared at Briggs. "Help him up, Ben. Now! You go."

Gant stood. Briggs shimmied down in his place. Emma peered into the dark hole after him.

"Move, Emma, you're blocking my light!"

She obliged. "See anything?"

"I see a..."

"What?"

"A seaman's chest."

"Only one?" Gant asked, thinking—hoping—Jordan had skimmed an entire boatload of bounty from the Hammonds.

"Come down and look yourself if you don't believe me!" came Briggs' muffled reply.

Grunting, Briggs hauled a heavy wooden strongbox closer to the opening. Simple rope handles hung from its two ends, rusty hinges, and chipped corners. Struggling, the two men lugged the strongbox out.

Jordan had locked it, of course, but one blow from the axe and the three peered inside at a glittering mass.

Privateer

Chapter Twenty-Six

Nobody in the nation's capital paid particular attention to the carriages that arrived late at night at the hotel's service entrance. Men in top hats and long, grey coats clustered together nervously entering the hotel, each followed by a liveried slave who held doors and accepted discarded hats and coats. The group climbed a back stairwell to an inconspicuous room in a wing of its own with no adjacent rooms. No voices might be overheard. The six new arrivals took seats on one side of a long table, opposite three others who waited in silence. From the head of the table, Geoffrey Morris bowed to each man. To his left, Matthew Westerly took his arm, and a third man, unknown to the visitors, sat to his right, a pistol hidden under his coat. Known to one another, the newly arrived shared neither names nor greetings. To each of the visitors, Westerly passed an envelope. Morris lit a cigar and stifled a smile. *Not one of these pompous Southerners shall have a role going forward.* In fact, he knew, if they did not march to his tune, he would throw the lot of them in prison, perhaps in Boston Harbor's notorious Fort Independence, or in an isolated work-camp along Georgia's mosquito-infested coast. Keys would become lost, trials delayed, then rendered unnecessary. British prisons were a good model for these turbulent times, Morris reminded himself. *Tonight, however, requires respect, affected courtesies, and reassurances. Retribution will come in time.*

"Please understand your importance," Matthew Westerly began. "Your state militia must be in place to defend your own shores, where the enemy believes we are weak. They dare not come up the Potomac again. Five hundred men could not dent our Capitol's defenses.

Although a few got through and lobbed firebombs at the Mansion, they shall need ten thousand to capture our entire seat of government. And hardened troops under Wellesley are cleaning up in Belgium, not transiting the Atlantic." As was the custom, the rotund banker presented the syndicate's narrative.

"Where then do you propose we send our men to reinforce the Federal troops under—what's his name again?" A senator from Georgia spoke, his confederates nodding.

"Jackson, Senator," Westerly acknowledged him, "in command of the Tennessee militia."

Andrew-bloody-Jackson, Geoffrey Morris thought, buffered within his cigar cloud. *My people tell me his poor health barely allows him to mount a horse, never mind fight a war against professional troops. Nevertheless, he has spirit. We must keep him far from our invited invaders.*

"And will he take kindly to our assistance?" asked another senator, a bumptious farmer whose South Carolina property he inherited from his father. Conveniently his land had a well-traveled gravel road directly to Charleston. This allowed his exported raw cotton to enjoy the most expeditious route to the mills in the North, and soon again, to the British Islands.

"Has he agreed to cooperate and share leadership with our state militia's generals?" enquired another agitated member without waiting for the answer to his neighbor's question. Each man, uncomfortable with a gathering that exposed his own complicity to the others, spoke in a hurry over his neighbor.

"He will and he has," Westerly responded decisively.

Despite the packets now entrusted to deep coat pockets, the room had not yet fallen in abject capitulation.

"You ask a great deal of us who are entrusted with a sacred honor," drawled a third conspirator, the shortest of the group but with steely eyes and determined full lips. "Calling your confederates 'friends' does not assuage my doubts. How can you, sir, stand before us with the absolute surety that you can deliver everything you've promised? To leave the capital undefended is a great risk—if you are wrong, sir—or have been misled by the British."

One man with knotted, arthritic hands—a seasoned legislator from Charleston who had fought with Francis Marion in the swamps and espoused an ingrained hatred for all things British—sat more stiffly than the rest. He carried a scar from a British ball that once embedded deep into his shattered left shoulder. The Charleston senator stared at Morris, and despite having just received his reward for a simple forthcoming 'aye' vote, remained uncomfortable sleeping with the enemy. Morris leaned back and stretched insolently. He stood and repositioned himself with his entire angular frame leaning in toward the man's face, breathing down on him.

"Madison," Morris let the name hover like a foul epitaph. "is the mud... and we are the tide that shall sweep over him."

"So that I understand, sir..." The Georgia senator turned to Morris again, wanting additional assurances. "...you have the highest confidence that their armies will attack us from the South, from the rear, and *not* with a frontal invasion of the Capitol?

"I do," Morris answered after a careful pause—long enough to ensure the entire table's attention, but short enough to prevent doubt to infiltrate.

Westerly nodded and smiled, as he added to the lies, "Our *communique* to their fleet and their generals, made clear by map *and* written instruction, is that we wish their attack to concentrate on the South, where they think they will encounter only local resistance from farmers and trappers."

The senators murmured amid a bit of chuckling.

"Old Hickory will resist, I dare say," one voice said as many heads bobbed.

"Upon victory in the south, they believe they have free passage up the river, across to the Shenandoah?" the senator from South Carolina pressed.

"They were told the same, gentlemen." Westerly took the lead once more. "They believe in our plan. Their great man Wellesley himself may lead the campaign. And after we crush them on the bayou, our government will force them to forfeit every West Indies port, every wilderness fort, every livery, every outhouse west of Wales." Westerly spoke with finesse and the kind of whiskey boastfulness that churned an evening's excitement among such men.

"And Canada?"

"Indeed. Foremost, Canada. They'll be forced to vacate that province and with that any influence on the murderous savages in the Midwest that they've been secretly arming."

Morris and Westerly promised that after tonight, the top hats would become wealthy beyond ambition, the contents of the envelopes affording them the ability to buy the votes needed to remain in power for life. In return, the newly-empowered senators agreed to pass a hastily-attached rider to a bill to be voted on in Washington, DC as soon as they returned to the chambers. A few men questioned the soundness of so much temporary power bestowed on one man, though Morris had so far delivered what he had promised: extraordinary profits from the increase of free labor, returns that had never seen such heights. The new administration would enrich the country's agrarian economy for its privileged landowners of voting age. Mr. Madison's war, without doubt, had brought a calamity down upon the nation; they had no choice, no choice at all but to deal with it straight-on. All that remained was passage of a lawful adjustment to the manner of governance. Such a model had been best displayed in the Italian wars of the early Renaissance, when closely held absolute power within each kingdom was ably managed by a self-chosen, enlightened few. An American economy powered by free labor, its trade protected by swift naval escorts, would become the model for a truly new world.

"And where do our generals meet up with General Jackson?"

"Here, Gentlemen," Morris rolled out a map across the table before them. "where the frogs and alligators roam and the marshes will suck our enemy as they scamper for dry land."

Morris congratulated himself with his grand deception: he could not have sent American forces to a more secluded outpost. It was a city surrounded by impenetrable swamps and lakes. There an American army could not easily abandon it in order to confront the enemy's actual invasion one thousand miles to the north. Westerly did not feel settled but maintained a smile. He looked over to Morris who sat enjoying his escape into a cloud of cigar smoke, his eyes nearly invisible to the table. Morris listened as the entitled men discussed transport and movement schedules and other soon to be irrelevant logistics. He exhaled a full breath of Virginia's best. Months before, Morris had tried to convince the President of the folly of listening to the rabble rousers, the impressed sailors' families, and the feeble commanders of his miniscule navy. Geoffrey Morris eventually learned of President Madison's lies, but the president advised the banker and his circle to calm themselves and trust his judgment. Instead, two months after, Madison had declared war on the world's foremost empire.

When their great man disembarks on our undefended Virginia shores, I will make sure Mr. Madison's rebuilt mansion burns completely to the ground this time.

Briggs and Gant struggled to drag the heavy chest down the beach to the waiting longboat. The two young crewmen, waved ashore in another boat, helped lift the chest into the longboat. Then, they hoisted it to the deck with sturdy block and tackle lowered from the mainsail yard. Uneasy, Gant's hand never drifted more than a few inches from his long knife. It had not escaped him that Briggs was similarly armed. Never once did either turn his back on the other. Each man conceded, however, he would not have found Jordan's fortune without their triumvirate: Ben and Emma would have sailed forever had Gant not identified Monomoy, one island among thousands along New England's coast. Gant faced eight miles of sand to dig had not Emma led them to the tower. Despite the tenuous fellowship, Gant did not trust any part of the arrangement. He thought about Jordan and the vengeance of the dead. He could never trust Briggs again. And the girl's willful, enticing smiles? Nothing but perfidy and lies!

The three wary collaborators watched Crowell and Jenkins carry the chest below deck through the narrow companionway steps to the captain's aft cabin. In a weak, guilty moment, after the lads were told to tend the sails and ready the day anchor for a speedy departure, the three conspirators, without a word, took turns diving hands and arms deep into the coin, gold and silver raw nuggets, bright bracelets and arm bands, jeweled headdresses of gold, and currencies in European coin: Spanish gold, English pound sterling, even U.S. gold dollars and paper currency in neat stacks six inches thick. *A fortune large enough to buy the world,* thought Gant. But Jordan's fortune was earmarked, owed to Morris and his syndicate, a past-due payment to Westerly.

Emma worried, nonetheless, whether there were enough riches in the chest to buy safety from the crew late of *Rattlesnake* who infested Newport—bitter men whom a dead lunatic had promised a share. These men surely waited for *Rattlesnake's* return. Thus, the successful voyage placed the five aboard *Rattlesnake* at risk. Were they tempted to celebrate ashore, an armed mob would descend to their bedsides.

"A sail! A ship approaches fast from the South!"

"*Rattlesnake's* been followed, Q," Briggs cursed as they rushed to the deck.

Sailing ardently from the Sound, her square sails set including studding sails, flying jibs and topgallants reaching for the clouds, there flew a dark, angry sloop of war. She flew neither pennant nor ensign.

"She'll be a privateer, sir!" Andy cried, his hand cupped over his eyes for shade.

Gant held his father's spyglass to his eye. *Damn, we missed spottin' her in the haze.*

"Three miles away, I reckon, sir," said Thad.

"*Raptor!*" bellowed Captain Gant, as he lowered his glass

"Upon my word—Morris' ship?" Emma's tone hushed, terror rising in her bosom.

"Aye," said Gant, assessing the anchorage. "We cannot escape."

It did not take long for Emma to realize her planned sleight-of-hand was doomed. Jordan's money was her father's money. *Her* money. She would compensate the crew appropriately. Now however, she needed help. But from whom? *Briggs*, Emma mouthed his name. Distant, Gant gazed stupefied at *Raptor*, considering their few options; the two younger sailors fell back to the larboard rail considering the gap closing across the water.

"Briggs," she mouthed the words, "Go below. Empty chest. No one else needs to know about this."

Emma tilted her head; Gant's gaze remained outboard.

"I'll get weapons." Briggs spoke just loud enough for all to hear as he disappeared below.

"Quartus." Emma's urgency was apparent. "Before Ben returns, we must speak plain. If this ship carries Morris' men—"

"It does."

"Then we must have a story to tell about why we are here."

"Aye, I shall enjoy hearing it myself. Perhaps we were watching sharks rip into seals?"

"Settle, Quartus. Our lives may hang in the balance."

"They want what we found. They know what we're doin' here."

"But they do not know what we *know*, only what we found."

"They'll strip the ship. We cannot hide the strongbox. We got no time to take it back ashore."

"Then we bargain. Knowledge is a powerful weapon. They know we have Jordan's chest. But I know *why* Morris needs it," she spoke urgently but of course Gant knew nothing about Emma's dive into political intrigue. "*They're* stealing Jordan's money for the same reason *we're* stealing his money..."

He looked at her, considering not for the first time that she was playing him for a fool.

"Gold buys power and men. We got no powerful weapon against that."

Emma knew that Gant had no notion of how much money she owed, nor the pressures from Morris and Westerly, nor about the political plans their syndicate had conspired with her father's cooperation. Gant, unaware of how Jordan's loot would fund the syndicate's traitorous purposes, considered it simply stolen loot. At this crisis point, Emma had no time to present the stakes in a different light, however. She tried something else.

"Quartus, when I saw your body, your hurt and scarred back and shoulders, your broken bones, I cried myself into your arms and hoped I could prevent you from being hurt ever again. I let you enter my life. Quartus, you're part of me in a way no man has been before. I know you were wronged. We all suffer in this life, but you *thrive* on the memory of your suffering." He looked away. "Do I *disgust* you, Quartus?" Emma asked as she reached for his hand.

"You do not," Gant replied softly.

"When you held me... it was... beyond—"

"We may see the *beyond* before you expect. They have us now, Emma. They'll take everything. Including our lives..." His rare attempt at a joke was affirmation of a sort, she thought as she wiped her eyes. He was not a dead soul beyond redemption. Gant shouted, "Briggs! Where is he, damn it? If they fire on us, we'll die quick. If we surrender,

I fear worse." He turned to her blanched face. He did not hold back his meaning. "You do not know these people, Miss, not like I do."

"Mr. Morris and his crowd? You might be surprised." Emma gathered her courage for the unpleasantness of what would come next. "Besides, some of my father's men sail on *Raptor*. They're our boys, too. They're not all cutthroats."

After ten minutes below, Briggs returned with a few antique muskets and swords, pathetically inadequate, while the armed ship loomed with dozens of men on deck. Gant observed *Rattlesnake's* lethal rows of cannon devoid of ammunition and the many men needed to fire them. He sighed.

"Give me a pistol, Briggs."

"Why not two or three, tucked into your belt?" Emma offered helpfully. Briggs locked eyes with Emma. He nodded.

"I'll only need a single shot," replied Quartus Gant.

Raptor dropped anchor in the small lagoon.

Good, she thought. *These men will take what they want and leave us. Unless...* suddenly terrified understanding his last declaration, she turned to Quartus.

Raptor anchored close to *Rattlesnake*; her escape to sea was blocked. Intent on violence, *Raptor's* longboat had already launched, crowded with six seamen, each carrying a musket or naked sword. Clustered together aboard *Rattlesnake* the five could neither outrun the square rigger nor fight her. Gant considered diving over the side and swimming ashore. Emma tightened the clasp to her dress and held it firmly to her chin. Involuntarily, she reached for Briggs' arm and briefly considered picking up a heavy cutlass to thwart her first attacker.

The first man up the ladder Gant recognized as the master's mate, Gordon Babcock whom Gant knew from his short stint aboard *Raptor*. Up and over the rail Babcock climbed; his look toward Gant not unfriendly but deadly intent to impress his own employer. He opened the gate from the inside and a second man climbed aboard. This man resembled a corpse recently unearthed. He carried a withered stump that dangled obscenely, untethered from his shoulder and without ability to direct it for any useful purpose. His other arm, though functional, was draped in a bandage of a sort that was now dark and bloodied. His trousers were stained, soiled from blood and piss. His shirt glistened with the stale sweat of clothes inhabited too many days. Where in his mouth once shined a disingenuous smile, gaps were evident in tarnished teeth broken during his most recent battle. His entire person mirrored an archive of injuries and self-neglect.

"Good morning, my dear friends," declared Cornelius Jordan.

Privateer

Chapter Twenty-Seven

Cornelius Jordan wasted no time. Briskly he crossed the deck to Gant.

"I am so glad to see you." Jordan held a sword in his one arm and without warning crushed the hilt into Gant's face which split open, blood gushing as he crumpled to the deck.

"Quartus!" Emma shrieked and fell to Gant whose head bled fiercely onto the planks.

"G'day, Mr. Briggs. Got no quarrel with you."

"You might think I'm unhappy, Miss, that you dismissed me from your service. But I secured another command. She's a smart ship, eh? Mr. Morris sends his kind regards. How does your father make out, by the way? Mr. Morris told me he would keep an eye on him when he moves into Great Hill." Emma's face betrayed no reaction. Jordan yanked his head toward Babcock followed by a quick command, "Go below and get it!"

Gant regained his feet, a hand to his bloody face. Shuddering, Emma stood nearby. If they died together today, she was determined to spill her blood too while Gant still breathed.

Grinning, Babcock reappeared from below. Jordan gestured for him use the winch to lower it to their waiting longboat tied alongside.

"So, you found my money. And you got it on board *your* ship. I was on my way to gather my things after my last voyage, but I was forced to take a longer route home." He spat at Gant.

"Then go!" Emma stood proud. "Take your damned chest and leave us."

"Oh, I shall." The sight of the captain repulsed Emma. She failed to recognize any part of the smooth charmer who had once visited her dreams. Jordan motioned to his crew. "Hoist my chest aboard *Raptor*. Make ready a-weigh. Tell Lowery and Bannister to come over and bring a whip. They shall accompany *Rattlesnake* to New York."

"*Rattlesnake's* not going to New York," said Emma defiantly.

"Oh, Miss Hammond, it is."

"You shall not take my ship!" Emma bellowed hoarsely.

"Miss Hammond, your ship is now *my ship*, again. The three of you are guilty of theft. I have been authorized to pass judgment and deliver punishment."

"Emma has committed no crime, let her be. And you said you have no argument with me," Briggs protested weakly, looking at the musket barrel aimed at his head.

"Except she has stained my honor! And now she steals my honest fortune, while giving aid to an officer guilty of mutiny—a scoundrel who left me for dead as I fought for our nation's liberty! No, she will suffer as I have suffered. You shall *all* suffer!" Jordan screamed, spittle scattering downwind. Jordan turned to the bleeding Gant and shrieked into his split face. "You thought me dead, eh? But my wounds did not fester—the Indiaman had a skilled surgeon aboard, you see! And they welcomed the hefty ransom Mr. Morris offered for my release."

Gant waited for the final blow. He balled his fist, his arms ready and his leg muscles taut. He knew he could not inflict serious damage before a pistol's ball found the back of his head or a sword stabbed him deep. But his last lunge would be worth it before he embraced final darkness. He might even hear the girl's weeping as his life ebbed—a woman who might have loved him if the spark in her eyes had not died. How it all turned so cold so suddenly with her, he could not understand. As Jordan rambled on and on, Gant realized he might live even a few moments longer.

"...*Rattlesnake* shall sail down the Sound. Once in deep water, Mr. Lowry and Mr. Bannister will secure your wrists, arms, and legs, and attach weights. And in thirty fathoms, you shall be interred. Miss Hammond, I can offer you a fatal dose of liquid opium or a sharp blade to your bosom, although you must administer the blade yourself. I do not find pleasure in killing a woman—"

"They'll hang you, Cornelius," warned Emma angrily. She recognized the men standing by Jordan, their greasy smirks showing they readily volunteered to act as her executioner.

"Not today." Jordan's attention turned. "I don't admire the look of the sky—my ships must make their way to New York and our bankers. I have a schedule to keep for my new owner who is in a frightful impatient mood for some reason. I cannot waylay watching you three spit up sea water, so I will leave you to your fate. I also fear a squall may be on the nose, so we must make way with some urgency." Jordan gestured and his men came from behind Gant and Briggs to bind *Rattlesnake's* officers. "In regard to the esteem we once shared, Miss, you shall remain free of similar constraints. Since you have refused my kindness, however, I shall ask them to give you a sharp blow to your head before they send you over the side. Unfortunately, I cannot account for your honor *before* this tragic event, eh, lads?"

Emma heard coarse laughter from Lowry and Bannister, hitching their pants, giddy with anticipation.

"Mr. Gant and Mr. Briggs—you, however, shall experience a slow drowning. We shall attach just enough weight to keep your feet down and your head inches below the surface, where your uplifted nose might reach a pinch of air. Like a bobbing buoy, you will breathe air one moment, sea water the next. You will thrash, swear, and scream for deliverance. You will inhale salt foam of whitecaps and the green ocean. As your lungs fill with water, remember it is Cornelius Jordan who has killed you."

Terrified, Briggs called out, "Captain, listen!"

Jordan yelled over to his ship, "Mr. Raca! Boy, take a glass and keep it focused on the *'Snake*. Watch close and tell me if they drown with dignity or beg for mercy. We know you like to watch that sort of thing, eh?" To Briggs, Jordan added, grinning, "I know of your great fear of the ocean. Strange for a privateersman, but so be it. Farewell, mate."

Emma felt faint; her face drained of all color. Briggs, for the first time, saw weakness where before she had held her own. He took her hand and she gripped his. The three conspirators saw their end coming at them like a rogue wave. As the inebriate Jordan was helped awkwardly back aboard the Morris flagship, a drunken crew, Gant knew, would make mistakes. Jordan's two guards on board

Rattlesnake—Lowry and Bannister—held bottles of congratulations, gratefully slurped, then slopped, and drank more as Cornelius Jordan and the *Raptors* returned to their ship. She weighed anchor and loosened her topgallant sails to catch the afternoon's fast-building gusts from the southwest. Jordan and his ship sailed slowly away from Malabar Point in close convoy with *Rattlesnake*. Gant had carefully noted the many bottles passed among Jordan's armed crew. Before long, half of them would be drunk on *Raptor*. Jordan had obviously been drinking already and was even more unstable than when he last stood on *Raptor's* tilted deck. Gant looked to the sky: Increasingly dark now over the distant islands of Nantucket and Martha's Vineyard, a tempest for sure was already upon them, foretold by the sunrise red sky a few hours earlier. Gant recalled young Will Doyle's prison trick. As Jordan's drinking men bound the former gunner, he extended his hands full, his arms muscled hard to their strongest width as the ropes were wrapped and tied. He fought the pressure with all his strength while his face showed only the resignation of despair. Once his captors had finished, Gant relaxed his grip. Pleased with the slackened rope, he waited and sent a silent prayer to the soul of William Doyle.

Emma sat by the rail, balled in her dress, knees to her chin. Bannister, a farm boy from a rural village west of Worcester, bent down.

"Ah, a pretty face, and a nice bouncy chest you got here, eh?" His rum-soaked breath and filthy fingers rubbed over her face.

"Leave me alone, you brute!"

"Ah, but I can be a gentle sort, when my pants are at my knees and…" Bannister whispered into Emma's ears and she shook her head violently. "It'll be nice—for me! And then my mate, Lowry here, will take a few turns. Though he's not so gentle like, he'll come for you like an angry bull. He likes it rough!"

"What are you, an animal or a man?"

"I am what God made me, Miss. Rambunctious, they say!"

"No god made you to inflict pain on a woman. What gives you the right!"

Bannister grabbed his crotch and she gasped. "This'n is all the right I need. Be back for you shortly. Hope you're as ready as us boys!"

Bannister left Emma recoiling in anger. She looked first to Briggs who seemed lost in his own misery, tied hands behind his slumping back. Then she caught Gant's attention. Like the night that had passed in a shroud of delight followed by a strange distance, his eyes told her everything she needed to know. She nodded, willing to risk all.

Briggs had also noted their captors' hearty drinking and wished for the mercy of a final taste. He watched as Lowry and Bannister cruelly whipped *Rattlesnake's* two young crewmen as they hauled the anchor on the capstan turns and hoisted the jib and spanker gaff with unspeakable difficulty. Standing at the mast end of the spanker boom, they hoisted together and got a few inches, then a few feet and lashed the halyard while they grabbed for more slack. They jumped again as the whip came down on their backs and on their bare feet, dragging blood along the deck. Briggs looked at Gant who sat quietly. Briggs thought it odd; Gant had not uttered his usual oaths and promises of retribution, but instead was deadly focused.

Rattlesnake's two crewmen were kept busy—Andy Crowell at the helm with *Raptor's* Lowry behind him, a crack of his whip landing every minute. Thad Jenkins worked the sheets, while Bannister drank at the nearby rail. *Our two lads cannot help us*, Briggs ruminated. And poor Emma awaits the worst—untied, slouched by the taffrail away from everyone. Soon, Briggs feared, Lowry and Bannister would drag her below.

Again, he looked to Gant.

Gone!

Briggs scanned the deck. He spotted Gant running with great leaps towards Bannister at the wheel. At the same instant, Emma, not constrained by any ropes, dashed forward and pounced on Lowery's back. Never in his life did Ben expect such a dexterous motion from the young woman. In all his dealings with her over many months, she moved with grace, yes, but in this one, amazing sprint she exhibited the stealthy physicality of mountain lion. Lowry tried to shake her off and spun himself while she dug her fingernails deep into his eyes. Swirling on the deck until she fell off, she faced him. Her small fist, Briggs could see, carried the force of an enraged woman. It was obvious that Emma had witnessed how seamen fought along the piers. Her back arched, she swung at Lowery with the smooth motion of a synchronized shoulder and arm. She landed her tight knuckles squarely on Lowry's nose. Eyes bleeding, he staggered backwards then raised his whip, lashing blindly at her face. Leaping back, her fighting eyes blazed: in a battle to the death, Ben thought he now witnessed one of the great moments of his life. His heart began to beat with an entirely new rhythm. Emma side-stepped Lowery, tripping him to the deck, as Gant grabbed Bannister by the throat. With his arm, he choked then snapped his opponent's neck. Briggs heard the bones break followed by an angry grunt as Gant picked the man's deadweight off the deck and heaved him over the side. As Lowry raised his whip to strike Emma, Gant grabbed him from behind. He spun him around by his whip hand, looping it 'round Lowry's neck, and drew him in, felling him with a single blow. Senseless, Lowry dropped. Gant dragged him to the rail and rolled him over the starboard bulwark. Briggs watched as Gant strode straight to him with fury in his eyes, Bannister's knife in his hand. *This is it,* thought Ben, looking for a fitting final remark to throw out before the gunner slit his throat. Ben watched Gant stoop down and slice through Ben's bindings. *For what purpose,* Briggs first thought, *to kill me standing up, a less defenseless victim? Because Emma is watching?*

"I'll take the helm. You and the boys trim the leeward braces," ordered Gant.

Briggs caught his breath realizing he had been spared. *Rattlesnake* was theirs!

"Emma, you were marvelous, I had no idea you—" Briggs stuttered as he turned to her.

"Enough coddling!" Gant lashed out.

"Q," Ben heard himself saying, "you saved us—"

"Not yet I haven't! Go! Jordan will come after us with twenty cannon and fifty knives!" roared Gant. Moments ago, he killed two feral able-bodies and was in no mood for anything other than escape. But he weakened as two sets of eyes looked to him with a strange sense of affection. Though she had done his bidding with only a shared look and a nod of his head, he decided to ignore her. At the wheel, Gant steered the ship back to her previous bearing hoping the eyes astern one half-mile had not noticed their sails had momentarily luffed. "I can't beat Jordan by myself, Briggs!"

"Aye," Briggs answered as Gant peered astern.

Raptor followed an earlier course towards the mainland, then was to sail southwest along the coast, past Newport, Long Island, and on to

New York City. The ships were only a quarter mile apart; by no means did *Rattlesnake* enjoy a safe lead over the larger, speedier ship.

"You were right before... We'll take Muskeget. They're headed inshore," said Gant as he sheathed his knife.

"I thought Muskeget was too dangerous," Briggs reminded.

"We'll find out. I heard our frigate *President* made it through last month. *Raptor's* in trouble if she cuts the channel too close. She draws near twenty-five, and without cargo or crew, the *'Snake* barely draws fifteen."

Gant turned the ship south to a course splitting the two large islands. Jordan would surely follow, once he realized *Rattlesnake* was not tracking on his prescribed course nor heaving-to for the capital punishments. Forced to navigate through the narrow Muskeget Gut, a maelstrom of rocks and sand especially when currents and tide collided, *Raptor* would not be able to easily come aside and board with an armed crew. But if *Raptor's* cannon came to bear...

"Will he follow?" asked Briggs.

"Look at the sky. If he does, he's a worse fool than we thought. A gale's on us, about to hit," replied Gant, sure of Jordan's maniacal methods, not as confident, though, about *Rattlesnake's* short-handed sailing capabilities.

"He'll try," Briggs added without emotion.

"Aye. Listen, Briggs..." The two privateersmen, both being skilled navigators and wily fighters, shared a plan aimed to lead Jordan where *they* wanted.

Once the deck had been cleared of Jordan's vermin, Emma collapsed, waving away Briggs' offer of comfort: blankets, water, and biscuit. She reflected her sins might be worse than the ferals Quartus had heaved over the side. The day before, she had been willing to trade innocent lives with her pen in order to reclaim her luxurious life and her family's profitable future. She had embraced trade in the triangular route, she had sinned, grievously, by intent. Today's deaths were because of her; today had been God's retribution.

Today, however, was not over.

Rattlesnake's abrupt course change to the south caught Jordan by surprise. Aboard *Raptor,* he had vanquished the better part of a bottle from Barbados while lazily admiring the storm overtake the sun. Its cooling shadow threatened to send him below to his great cabin for sleep until New York. He had worried if forced to watch the flogging he might have relented, countermanding the death sentences. At least for Briggs—an otherwise decent officer, except for the sides he chose and the company he kept. And for the girl, whom he had once coveted initially for opportunistic reasons until he saw for himself her fair skin and bright face—an innocent blossom he had once hoped to deflower. He admonished himself, as he drained his drink. She deserved to die, no longer to interrupt his sleep. His written instructions from Geoffrey Morris had been explicit:

As a condition of your employment, Rattlesnake's captured crew must mysteriously disappear at sea. Your ship's log will show you came upon a drifting brig. You claimed it as salvaged property—another unexplained story of a ship lost to the whims of the ocean.

"Capt'n Jordan, *Rattlesnake's* off course!" shouted a young thug from the deck.

"Eh, Mr. Raca?" replied Jordan, regarding the youth nearing fifteen years who was unliked and unwashed. Yet Cornelius Jordan kept the boy to clean blood and gore from a battle's aftermath. That the boy had an almost total unawareness of any morality or sailor's decorum made him useful to a captain who clearly understood the laws of man and God and chose to ignore them.

"'*Snake*. Goin' south—not west. Leavin' Cape Pogue to starboard!"

"Muskeget?"

"Aye!"

Jordan realized his mistake: He had left two drunken farm-boys to kill shrewd privateersmen. He stumbled to the deck. Sure enough, *Rattlesnake* had raised her foresails, now nearly full, and headed due south sailing flat and fast.

"Harden all braces, trim every sail! Helm—come up twenty points!" He turned to the sailing master and gave him the new course, "Follow them! Babcock, open our larboard gun ports. Arm the guns with heavy iron!"

"Aye, sir. Will we board her when we catch up?"

"*Sink* her! Clear for action! Take my strongbox down into my cabin!"

As he spoke, he looked curiously at the chest representing several years' theft. Two crewmen grabbed its rope handles and lifted it with an easy motion. Odd. When Jordan had buried his plunder beneath the lighthouse floor, two hearty brutes and himself strained at the strongbox's dead-weight. Now, however, two of *Raptor's* slender lads carried the chest across the deck without so much as bent knee or sagging shoulder. They approached the main hatch and prepared to carry it down the steep, narrow companion ladder. Jordan followed, a sick fear rising in him.

"Watch it, mate!" one boy admonished the other who tripped and fell with the chest thudding down the stairs onto the lower deck where it cracked open on impact.

Jordan looked down at shiny trinkets and whatnots of silver spewed among a scattered rusty pile of loose carpenter's tools, old galley spoons, and dented tin ladles.

"Hell and damnation!" screamed Jordan.

"Captain—we've readied our larboard cannon. *Rattlesnake's* almost in range. We can sink her—"

"No! Belay that! We will come alongside and board! Damn them!"

At the wheel, Gant noticed *Raptor* trimming sails to match their new course. Briggs stood behind him, yelling instruction to Crowell and Jenkins, climbing and loosening sails despite their painful whipping wounds.

"Can we make it, Q?" asked Briggs. He looked back as the larger ship gained. "Tide's going out."

"Current's against us," Gant agreed. "Gonna be tight."

"He'll be on top of us, if not in the channel, Q, then as soon as we cross over the rips, if we both get through the rocks..." *He'll sink us for sure.*

Gant considered Briggs' logic. He recalled they had once been an inspired team.

"Got your current tables aboard—?"

"Aye."

Briggs rushed below. He grabbed the notebook with its careful script of the ebb and flood calculations in this part of the south coast.

He scoured the stained pages, musty after years stowed in canvas duffel bags, splashed with seawater and sweat. *Muskeget: October 10.* Briggs found the time for the expected current change, there: *6:00 p.m. Running hard from Pollock Rip: 3.5 knots northeast, for another two hours.*

"Foul, Q. Until eight o'clock!"

"Breeze is holdin'!" Gant yelled back. "Hope the squall line don't hit us on the nose."

Looking skyward, clouds darkened at each pulse.

"There used to be a narrow channel that cut through to the beach at Wasque... but... it was a long time ago." Gant barely hid his anxiety.

"A channel?"

"Aye, through the shoals. To the west. We once ran a boat in for a midnight delivery."

"Can *Rattlesnake* make it through?"

"Don't know. I'm fair certain *Raptor* cannot."

"They're closing, Q! Briggs, I see smoke!" shouted Emma. *Raptor* gained on them. The two *privateersmen* were focused instead on plotting an adjusted course through rocks and sand, abandoning the safety of the charted channel, so ignored Emma's question. "Why can't we shoot back with one of our cannon?" She persisted.

Gant replied, his tone a grizzled seaman to a lubber, "Cause our guns are pointed the wrong damn direction and it takes six hearty lads to fire one! You see six hearty lads sittin' around, my dear? Or enough sea room to turn the ship abeam, eh?"

Hurt, Emma retreated with a tenuous hold on her emotions, just as a cannonball from one of *Raptor's* six-pound bow chasers crashed into the water not far astern. Staggering, she grabbed the taffrail to stay on her feet. *The next one will be closer,* Gant anticipated. Jordan would mostly certainly aim the sights, firing with skill and a determined ill-purpose—a deadly combination. Gant eased the helm and ordered the two boys to loosen sheets. The passing water was white with violent currents running hard against the bottom lining the eastern edge of the shoal. Less than three feet below, sharp rocks clawed at the water's surface able to rip open the bottom of any ship scudding sideways. To the west, an equally deadly but less defined barrier: sand and rocks above, sandy bottom beyond. The depths near Muskeget ranged from a shallow thirty feet to rocks visible only in daylight on calm days at low tide, and only by ships whose men with strong spyglasses watched in the right places.

Today was not one of those days.

Briggs held Gant's brass spyglass, determined to find relatively calm water—evidence of Gant's escape channel.

"D'ya see Wasque Point? Should be visible by now," Gant cried, "Emma—you too, look sharp now, I need a bearing!"

"I can't see anything," she replied, holding tight to the starboard gunnel. "And we're losing our light."

Emma peered to the west as the afternoon sun disappeared fast into the on-coming storm. The wind increased, slatting lines and sails against the rig. *Rattlesnake's* frantic voyagers looked up when a crack of lightning exploded the heavens.

"This squall-line's gonna be a beast—on top now!" Gant yelled over the crashing waves smacking rocks on both sides of the ship.

Andy Crowell rushed aft from the foremast shrouds. He stood next to Emma and she took purchase of his arm for reassurance. He looked at her steady and spoke with a gentle smile.

"He'll make it through them rocks, Miss. I seen Mr. Gant do it before. Don't you worry, now!"

"Thank you, Andrew. Peel your eyes, we both must look to find the cliffs." Emma smiled—a boy not much older than her Thom here comforting her.

"Aye, Miss." He did not flinch at the huge bolt of lightning ahead nor the thunder that followed immediately.

"There—in the flash—I see it!" Emma cried out, pointing to bluffs one mile distant.

However, to larboard Gant saw only dangerous whitewater. He craned his neck to the right; there he saw white water, too—as expected. But with the help of Emma's shore bearing, he steered ten degrees further north. Where he pointed the ship's bow suddenly appeared less boiled. *Rattlesnake* sailed into Gant's narrow channel with no room to retreat. Gant did not say to the others what he knew: Thus committed to this unmarked gap, they could not change course. They could not sail higher or lower, nor jibe, nor come through the wind in a desperate attempt at escape. If their bow, keel, or rudder hit rocks, the ship would shudder and stop; ripped apart in the fast-moving current, it would turn on its side, and dump its doomed passengers into the false channel. Briggs knew how Jordan reacted to fleeing prey. To defeat Jordan, one had to think like *The Curse of the Coast.*

He'll follow us as fast as he can, Briggs told himself. *He'll search for an advantage to weather, fire his broadside, and sink us. He has abandoned all thoughts of selling* Rattlesnake *at auction...* Jordan's was a blood sport.

"Raise more sail! All of'em!" cried Briggs suddenly.

"No! We'll be overpowered," Gant argued reasonably.

"Listen, Q, think like Jordan! Over-canvased, the ship will heel! We'll *slow down—*"

"Aye, *we'll* slow..." Gant slowly came to understand Briggs' logic.

"Jordan will think we've cleared the shallows, about to gain speed in the open water. He'll think he has a fleeting advantage, if he acts fast."

"Right. He'll try to sail *above us* so he can bring his larboard guns to bear. When he does, he'll fire a broadside. He'll know he won't have that same chance once we're over the rip." Gant looked aft and considered Briggs' idea. He glanced to windward.

"Q, with the squall about to hit, he's going to try to sink us *now.*"

Gant agreed. *Think like Jordan.* They looked at each other. *But he'll find no channel north of* Rattlesnake. *If he tries to sail above us—there's only rocks. Below us—more rocks.*

"Hoist every stitch of damn canvas we can raise," ordered Gant, manhandling the wheel, straining for all his life to keep the ship on course.

And as the boys unfurled the fore and main courses that cracked as they caught the building wind, the desperate crew felt the ship heel hard to leeward, thrashing in the rising gusts.

Rattlesnake slowed.

"*Rattlesnake's* hoisted more sail, Captain—fools!" reported Jordan's first mate, wishing now he had resisted finishing the bottle each man was allowed as they geared up for their victorious voyage to

New York and a week of drunken carousing in the many dockside brothels along the East River. "She got too much canvas up! She's over on her side. We're catchin'em!"

Aye, we are, thought Captain Cornelius Jordan. *I can cripple her in one broadside aimed at her masts and deck here and now, and board her before the gale hits.* He wished to blow her away. But he had to board her in order to recover his twice-stolen strongbox. To accomplish this, he knew, *Raptor* must sail above *Rattlesnake's* course, then steer down and come aside her with men hanging on the shrouds and gunnels armed with pikes, pistols, and cutlasses.

"Helm, steer up ten degrees, west-sou'west."

"Captain, we got enough water in there?"

Jordan did not know. He had never sailed through Muskeget Channel. On most voyages east, he had sailed safely around Nantucket's rips and shoals. Or he took Vineyard Sound, crossed Nantucket Sound, and passed through Pollock Rip Channel. Yet today *Rattlesnake* was forcing him to split the islands. *If Gant can do it...*

"*Rattlenake's* got room, so we got room! Steer up, damn you!"

Raptor did not hoist as many sails as the smaller *Rattlesnake*. And by keeping her hull trim and flat, Jordan's ship enjoyed greater speed in the increasingly heavy gusts. The flatter angle also gave *Raptor* an advantage every captain at sea fought for: to gain the weather side, upwind, placing his ship—and his cannon—above his enemy. To accomplish this maneuver, however, *Raptor* must also battle her more pressing foe: the rising gale. The narrow Muskeget Channel presented an ominous risk of ocean water outflowing hard with current and tide.

This boarding will take but a minute, Jordan congratulated himself. *Then we best find open water away from these damned shoals.* He intended to watch the three die by his own hand. Gant first. No more mistakes. "Grappling hooks ready and small arms for every man! We shall come aside in two hundred yards and board!"

"Forty feet, Captain!" Came a cry from the rail. *Plenty of water,* thought Jordan.

Cornelius Jordan relaxed in his imminent glory.

Suddenly, a scream from the rail, "Thirty!"

Hmmm. Rising, a bit fast...

"Twenty!" Eyes wide with terror, the man with the lead line looked aft to Jordan—*Raptor's* draft, with an empty hold, was twenty-five feet. "Channel's disappearing, sir!"

"Rocks awash! Clear ahead!" Came the cry from the foretop.

Over, over! Gant prayed to any gods still protecting his own pitiful life. The ship fell off a few degrees, her keel rose, and though her progress through the water had slowed, the hull near on her side had less draft; they might yet pass over the rocks. Gant could not spare a man for lead lines to measure depth, so he could only guess—and whisper snippets of long forgotten prayers. Emma looked back at *Raptor*. Morris' privateer sailed high enough above them for a lethal broadside of cannon to rain hot metal at any moment. She assumed Jordan would sink *Rattlesnake* with all the powder and shot he had aboard; he'd keep firing until not a living person, cat, or rat breathed. She did not know Jordan planned worse.

"Quartus, they have men at every cannon!"

Gant scanned the water rushing by. He looked forward and where the blackness of the incoming storm met the quiet of ocean beyond a line of rocks and unsettled waves, he could make out the sudden end to the rough water. *Not far now, the brig could make it!* *'Snake*'s keel had not hit bottom. Gant looked behind to *Raptor*, fast overtaking them. If she fired, he would not live long enough to recall the most grievous of his many sins. The enemy privateer was gaining, but then she steered down as if to board instead. She was cleared for action but did not fire. This made no sense. He saw Jordan by the rail, broadsword swinging madly in the rain delivered by a lightning flash.

"They've hit!" cried Briggs, the glass hard to his eye.

Gant and Emma stared back at their pursuer: *Raptor's* forward hull ran-up hard against rocks. The heavy ship, sailing steady in an increasingly rising wind, stopped abruptly. Her bow dipped low in the water as her stern rose high in the air and seemed to follow the motion of her mainmast bending unnaturally forward. *Raptor* suddenly fell with a crash echoing the real thunder's tumult closing in from the west.

Men screamed over the roar of breaking water. Men were hurt. Dying. Shrieking in shock and anger. Rain increased. Suddenly a gust hit both ships from the gale's leading squall line. *Raptor* turned clockwise, her large, wide stern pushed by her forward momentum higher onto the rocks. The bow turned with initial explosive thrust from the gale. Opposing forces, wind and current, sent the ship to its death in mere seconds, not the minutes even a catastrophic grounding might take, or the hours of a more benign grounding when longboats might be lowered and crew saved. *Raptor* toppled onto her side. Men on deck were tossed into the sea. Sailors aloft dropped, clinging to any tarred rope or stout yardarm they could grasp for a moment's hope of deliverance. She bore too many men, too much confusion. The longboats for rescue were themselves swamped as the ship turned in a continuous roll. Now dismasted, *Raptor* was upside down on its main deck with its stringy, foul bottom rising high into the storm, as if defiling the honest world with one last profane insult. *Rattlesnake,* however, was not yet in the clear. The helm's shaking motion confirmed the relentless force against her. By the press of sail and loss of speed needed for the deception, Gant had forfeited precious forward traction against a running current, forcing the ship backwards.

"Ain't got steerage!" cried Gant, turning from the disaster behind to his own ahead. If *Rattlesnake* slowed any further, or came to a halt, the opposing current would toss them into the same rocks that consumed *Raptor*, the building gale finishing the job. "Jibe the spanker and stay'sls! Cut the braces for topgallants and course's—we must escape the current!"

There was no discussion. Briggs flung the spanker boom over with its heavy sheet, while the two lads cut the windward braces. The course change brought the angle of the large square sails onto the other tack. Trimming to a proper angle, however, with only two crewmen aloft and one on deck was impossible. Sails fell away losing their wind; as a result, the power Gant desperately needed had been forfeited although the hull settled into a steadier course. *Rattlesnake,* however, slipped sideways a bit; her hull riding flat. But Gant deftly angled the ship to the approaching wind driving her high enough to avoid the rocks while maintaining a modicum of essential forward progress. *I must hold this course another minute and let nothing break my concentration—*

"Q, are we in deadly peril?" asked Emma, her fears on the surface.

To hell with false assurances, Gant thought. "We're fighting Muskeget for our damned lives. If the ship hits those rocks, we're dead!"

"What can I do to help?"

"Shoulda' lowered the longboat, in case. Too late—got no hands to man the davits."

"I can row, Quartus… I—"

"Leave it, girl! I need to steer! Sit quiet, will you now?"

Emma looked back at Jordan's ship splitting into long planks enveloped by sails wrapped over the wreckage. *Raptor's* small longboats, having never been lowered, were rent into splinters, or capsized under the mass of her sinking hull.

"Briggs—trim the jib hard! And hoist our fore stays'l—we need to climb!"

"Aye!" yelled Briggs from amidships. "After, we'll set your uppers stays'ls,"

The betrayer can sail. Gant nodded. *Give him that much.*

"Did you not hear me, Q? I can lower the boat—" Emma screamed.

"Fightin' for our lives, woman!" cried Gant. "Be still!"

"This is *my* ship!" Emma shouted back at her captain.

Gant ignored her and struggled with his entire strength to control the wheel, to maintain the bow pointed west when the ocean pushed east. Survival depended on the hull clearing the bottom. Had Emma felt Gant's helm, it would have told her how hard the current was crushing the ship back toward the rocks they had escaped only moments before. But she did not understand the motions of the sea. Emma stared at *Raptor*, now turned on its side after a complete roll, no masts or sails left. Ribs showed where minutes before cannon had aimed at her head. She saw two bodies sucked out an open gun port as the ship rolled, the two men, lifeless. Emma dropped back to the taffrail, angry, useless, and feeling responsible for this disaster. Staring at the shipwreck astern, she noted a clump of rope draped over the edge of *Raptor's* upended stern like a wayward window sash in a ransacked home. Halfway up *Raptor's* sides, caught in the ropes by his only arm, Captain Cornelius Jordan struggled desperately for a hold. Emma envisioned another time: An overview of the harbor, a warm summer evening, and a proud, virile captain dismounting a noble steed, and bowing, holding out his hand to welcome her with sophistication, kind eyes, and a smile. She remembered his talk of a tropical place where splendid birds flew over waters of cobalt blue so unlike the greys and greens of New England. Now, here today she only saw a wrecked ship with a broken spine and drowning men. Splintered planks, sails, and rigging floated astride corpses towards Wasque and the distant Cape. Men struggling in the rushing water suffocated beneath the foam and whitecaps; bloated bodies making shore if they did not sink first. Emma turned away. She noticed Briggs struggling alongside the two sailors to bring a huge sail aloft into trim while cutting lines to free others that hindered Gant's maneuvering. *Rattlesnake*, it seemed, had responded well but was still clearly in mortal danger of foundering like *Raptor*. She decided she must make a contribution to possibly save lives. As Gant had explained, the poor souls on *Raptor*—some of them her father's men, *her* boys, not all cutthroats like Jordan—had no chance to find the shore once their longboats had been crushed. She stared at *Rattlesnake's* sturdy, seaworthy longboat swaying on its davits, not riding high in the water where it might save people in desperate need.

I initiated this folly! She felt compelled and determined to not follow *Raptor's* demise. *Rattlesnake's* people must be given one last chance to live. While Gant's furious focus remained forward, Emma could not take her eyes off the tragedy behind. Gant concentrated as if it might propel the ship a knot faster, away from the rocks to safety. Emma understood the ship was hard against a foul current. A landswoman, alas naturally she lacked a sense of the water's force. The heavy pressure of the angry weather helm that Gant struggled against at the ponderous wheel, that two or more men would normally handle, meant nothing to her. Gant fought the roaring gale with every ounce of his skill. Icy rain streaked the deck obliterating the view from stern to bow. Torrents sliced the sails and the deck. The violent downpour stung Emma's face and pierced her woolens. Yet, she did not respect Gant's blistering attention to the trim of the sails, nor recognize the desperation in his voice as he called out commands to Briggs and her two young crewmen to hoist or ease. She did note that Briggs and the boys snapped to Q's words, ignoring her.

This was *her* ship, she decided.

Emma ran to the stern rail. Her longboat had not yet been stowed on deck after the partners' expedition to the lighthouse but dangled over the water above the taffrail. At each end hung a set of blocks connected to davits that swung out over the stern to ease the longboat down onto the surface of the water. To lower the heavy boat, however, required two men standing on deck releasing its line synchronously. Lacking that knowledge, she scrambled to reach the davits as best she could with her rain-drenched dress and petticoats, heavier now as the cold downpour pelted sideways. Emma untied two securing lines from belaying pins and with one line in each hand she climbed aboard the longboat, holding the tension tight as she found a seat and braced her straight back. First, she let go a bit of line, and the boat jerked down a measure. She eased and lowered a foot or more again. *Good,* she thought. Then the other line and the boat remained balanced a few feet below deck-height. She lowered the bow another foot. Back and forth, back and forth... lower... she watched the lines until a wave hit the hull.

The gale surged, ferocious at its leading-edge. Gant saw the topsails blown out from the over-trim they had needed for the deception. With no men to send aloft, the topsails were now useless; power to steer and aim the ship was nearly lost. All he could do was hold his present course. *Another twenty yards or so*, he thought... Then, he heard the woman scream. *Where the hell is she?*

Emma having lowered the longboat below the aft port windows, its stern nearly reaching the waves, when the huge ghost roller belted the ship. Emma did not anticipate the hull's reaction: A surge under the hull, unseen and unfelt until too late, toppled her, costing her grip on one line. One loose line sped through the blocks and sent the stern of the longboat crashing into the water while its bow hung several yards above. At the awkward angle the boat had dropped, Emma could neither stand nor sit. Climbing back aboard was impossible. She fell to the floorboards, and then over the gunnels into the rushing Muskeget channel. Her left leg did not follow however; her foot was caught in the longboat's running loose davit halyards wrapping around her shin. Her torso fell half in the cold seawater. She could neither free herself nor tread water. With all her strength, she held onto the side of the down-turned boat as her sodden clothes dragged her under. A drab but precious garment she had imported from England before the war, featuring delicate lace, comfort, fashion, and warmth, had transformed into an anchor forcing her head underwater. Only if she could free her foot and climb back aboard would she survive. No, she realized, should her foot release, she would immediately sink. Without an act of God,

Emma was moments from drowning. With all her strength she screamed, one word, her last and only chance for rescue; she called for the one man she believed she could forever count on.

"Briggs!"

When they heard her scream, Briggs rushed to Gant focused at the wheel. Exhausted, Ben had finished trimming a topsail brace, and had been leaning against a shroud. He and Gant had just exchanged glances: *We're gaining.* He expected to see the girl where she had last been sitting, just aft of Gant's wheel. He glanced fore and aft but did not find her. Leaping to the stern rail, Ben looked over. There he saw her face dip repeatedly under water with each swell. Gasping between each plunge, her snagged foot secured her from immediate drowning, but her garment forced her head under.

"Q! Help! Emma's caught in the longboat, we gotta haul it up!" yelled Briggs.

"If I let go the wheel for one moment, we'll be on the rocks! Leave her be 'til we're through!" *Serves her right*, Gant thought.

Briggs glanced around for the two other sailors. He found one boy high aloft and the other halfway to furl the flagging topgallant. There was no time! Briggs leaned far out over the stern. Alone, he could not raise the boat on its davits and tackle.

"Q! She's drowning!"

"Then she's dead already!" Gant heard his own pitiless words. Save the ship, save the girl, save a man he hated, no difference. Sink *Raptor*, save her crew, abandon her captain; rush down the prison's corridor, avoid the light—save the woman sacrificing herself in the dark. Nothing mattered. A blue face forever haunting his dreams. A friend lost forever, betrayed by weakness and foolish ambition. And for one night he thought he had found a light, only to feel the knife's blade of a morning sun. Instead, his life ahead would forever feed on a festering corruption of hate. It filled him. *Yes, I shall abandon the girl to her folly, but I will survive. She matters not.*

"I'm going over, Q!" Briggs cried above the gale. "Lash the wheel and pull me up when I yell! Do as I say, for the love of God!" Briggs screamed with the force of all his past battles compressed into a single, frantic plea.

Gant made no immediate effort to respond. He felt little compassion for the self-serving young woman. But for a fellow privateersman who had once, nay more than once, saved his life... *Do I owe that man a hand? Or forever be done with him?* He glanced over his shoulder as Briggs tightened a loose line and climbed tentatively over the stern rail. *Look at Briggs! The coward's terrified of the ocean...* Gant shook his head, eased his grip on the wheel, and held its spokes with his knees as he reached grudgingly for a loose line. With a practiced hand, he cut a piece with one hand as his other grappled with the wheel that wanted to come up hard with each gust from the storm's crescendo. Moments before, he had estimated only twenty more yards to reach safety. Now, on account of a woman's whim, his ship became secured only by a piece of thin manila rope and a double half-hitch. *Never again shall I risk a ship for a body gone overboard.*

"Now! Pull!" cried Briggs.

Reluctantly, Gant let go the wheel; the hitch held. He ran to the stern and yanked the second rope. The unconscious girl in Briggs' arms slid repeatedly in his grasp as he struggled to keep her from falling back into the ocean. Gant pulled one line, Briggs the other. Ben attempted to climb despite sodden deadweight drawing them toward the rushing water below. Briggs had only enough strength to grab her by the waistbelt on her dress. It held firm for a moment and then snapped free just as his arm reached under her armpit and shoulder. He pressed his head against the line to keep her body balanced with his own weight. He found a foothold and climbed.

"I must take the wheel!"

Gant's knot was slipping, loosening the wheel. *Rattlesnake* was moments from disaster.

"No Q, another few feet!" Briggs screamed when the rope he held fell slack.

Briggs smashed the port cabin window with his elbow. He grabbed a window frame for support, but his foot fell away. As Briggs and Emma slipped into the void, the line drew taut again. Gant looked over.

"Got ya!" Gant heaved.

Andy Crowell, seeing the wheel untended, had slid down the starboard main shroud and rushed to join Gant at the rail. The two hauled the exhausted Briggs and waterlogged Emma over the rail and lowered them to the deck. Briggs gasped heavily. Emma lay immobile.

"Gant looked at her curiously. "She alive?"

As Briggs glanced up at Gant, the ship lurched, and he saw the wheel spin suddenly loose.

"The helm!" he shouted.

Briggs leapt up and flung his body at the spokes turning out of control; Gant's knot had failed. In that moment, the wheel spinning free, Emma gurgled and coughed. Gant knelt and bent closer to her face. She coughed again. Gant rolled her body toward him, so she lay on her side, and she jerked awake. Gagging and vomiting, she cried as she looked at Gant through hazy, grateful eyes.

"Quartus, you came..."

Gant watched Briggs fighting the wheel. The two men looked harshly at each other until Gant's face broke out in a smile.

"Lie quiet and rest." Gant leaned down to Emma and touched her shoulder tenderly. "I told you to sit quiet."

Striding back to the helm, Gant grabbed the wheel from Briggs. The wind shifted easterly as the worst of the storm-front blew through. He steered *Rattlesnake* onward, past the rocks and the last of *Raptor*. The going remained rough, but they had made it through the cut where the current ran hardest. Briggs stared back at the wreckage. Faintly in the distant water, he could see a man in the surf looking in their direction as *Rattlesnake*, free from the roaring current, sailed clean away. The distant survivor had nowhere to go although he had freed his arm of the tangle of lines and debris. He did not cry out or grimace, he merely stared after *Rattlesnake*. As the coming darkness obscured the horizon, Briggs saw the silhouette of the man's one arm raised in defiance before the sea swallowed him. With Gant at the wheel, Briggs tried to help Emma to her feet, but she pushed him away.

She nodded to Crowell and whispered, "Andy, my heartfelt thanks."

Privateer

Chapter Twenty-Eight

Cold night descended as *Rattlesnake* limped into Newport Harbor. Emma, wet and miserable, mumbled her thanks to Gant who doffed his cap. She noticed his gesture extended to Briggs, accompanied by a smug raised eyebrow as if Gant had won an unexpected advantage. *Odd*, she thought. Once lines were secured to the pier, she thanked Crowell and Jenkins, handed them a few coins along with advice for their injuries. Ignoring Ben, Emma led the small departing crew off the ship, she to a summoned carriage home to Great Hill, Briggs to his boarding house. Gant remained on his new ship, the only home he had known in years. He took out his pipe and replayed the day's events, marveling that he had miraculously won Emma's favor while once again avoiding death.

"Father, I have so much to tell you. Can you hear me?"

After a night of disturbed sleep visited by the cries of drowning men and the leers of Jordan's hateful creatures, Emma rested her head on Colonel Hammond's chest and listened to his faint breathing. Her father remained warm. Still with her, but where *was* he—in between one life and the next? His silent sleep seemed a cruel punishment for such an active man. Yes, he had sinned; the returned schooner from Africa betrayed him. She hoped this cruel repose might wash his soul, leading to renewed health. Or perhaps this sleep was a gift before his ultimate judgement, a small reward for the love he had always shown his family. *And for what?* she wondered. *Thomas is dead. Mother's run off. The one man I trusted failed to come to my aid. The other wants my embrace only in the dark.* She scolded herself, *Neither cold indifference nor unbridled passion is sustainable. At least I escaped Cornelius Jordan. And though I've captured my stolen fortune, I fear I may never be free of that despicable Morris. Why did I write that foolish note with its lying promises? He will come to redeem them, I know it.*

Quartus Gant sat in the shadows within the *Scarecrow Tavern* and emptied another tankard of ale. He, Briggs, and Emma had agreed to keep their recent voyage a secret. Gant was sorely disappointed Jordan's plunder had followed *Raptor* to the bottom. Nevertheless, that turn of fate had at least killed Jordan. Nor would Briggs ever enjoy the gold. Gant remained comforted to a degree: there would be other strongboxes to steal. Still, he had enjoyed the unexpected pleasure of watching Briggs lose face with the woman Gant coveted. Draining the ale, he reflected on why Jordan had changed *Raptor's* course at the last minute. They should all be dead, *Rattlesnake* sunk. What had changed Jordan's frazzled mind? This bothered him greatly. Sufficiently numbed to face Emma, the gunner made his way to meet with her in her father's harbor-side office. Per their agreement, for his contribution to the failed search, she deeded him *Rattlesnake*. Seated across from her large desk, he stared at the strange writings she passed to him. He wondered aloud another question that had kept him awake since their return.

"What took Briggs so long to find weapons during those final moments before Jordan and his men boarded the brig?" His query to Emma was not a straight-up accusation nor did he expect a truthful answer. When she did not reply, he reframed it. "You instructed Briggs to go below to find weapons that day. He stayed a lifetime."

"I hadn't noticed, Q. I was too terrified of *Raptor* blocking our escape."

"Aye. And one more thing," Gant said as he made his mark on *Rattlesnake's* deed. He put the quill down, watching her eyes. "*Raptor* was intent on sinking us, her broadside within range. But then she suddenly sailed down on us, as if to board instead. Why would Jordan do that?"

"Are you sure *Raptor* was close enough to fire on us, Q?" Emma countered, nonchalant.

"Aye, sure. Her course was high, parallel our own."

"Perhaps Cornelius sailed nigh so his cannon would not miss?"

"He was comin' t'board us. By doing so, he ran his ship onto the rocks. Why'd he risk that, Emma?"

"I have no idea," she parried. Stone-faced, he observed her every twitch and gesture. Her expression had shifted from frank to evasive. It did not sit right. Emma continued, "I assume they'd have sunk us if they'd been able to." She paused a moment to grace him with an open smile, aiming to redirect his attention. "Your escape was masterful, *Captain Gant.*"

"I thought so too, at first—but Jordan chose *not* to sink us. Why?"

Emma offered nothing useful. Instead, her tone changed. "Quartus, although you didn't come home with your share of Jordan's stolen fortune, your service to me and my father has rewarded you with a fast ship." Adeptly, she sidestepped a patent lie.

"Aye," Gant admitted flatly.

"Now, if you please, I have business to attend—"

Gant looked straight into her eyes. He wanted more riches than a ship. Quartus Gant made Emma an offer.

She paused before answering. She would need to think about it. "Let us talk more about this later." She rose formally, extending her hand toward the door. "Please visit Great Hill for dinner before you set sail, Captain?"

"Will *he*—? "

"I shall ask Mr. Briggs to conduct company business... out of town."

"You'll make five separate deposits, Ben," Emma announced. The Hammond and Company office was as busy with business paperwork as the yard outside, bustling with men provisioning ships. "Ensure the receipts from each Boston bank are not tied to one another. You may need to pay for each banker's silence."

"Agreed. We can't touch it until *he* leaves," Ben replied. *Until the damned gunner is far out at sea.*

"I've meant to ask…" Emma looked up from her desk. Although they were alone, she lowered her voice. "How much?"

"I transferred all the coins and currency. I left a top layer of silver ornaments to hide your galley utensils."

"Well done, Ben." Emma studied her partner with increasing admiration. His business acumen proved shrewd, and he did not question her methods or motivations. Though his jealousy simmered, he did not direct any discontent at her. His antipathy to Quartus was obvious since that fateful morning in her destroyed kitchen. *Was it only days ago? That I stand between them is regrettable, albeit unintentional.* She convinced herself.

Ben Briggs also had a question, one that disturbed him so much he kept a loaded pistol and a boarding knife by his bedside. "What does Q say, since we've returned?"

"He suspects."

"He doesn't need another reason to slit my throat, Emma." Briggs grimaced. "How did he come into enough money to buy *Rattlesnake?*"

"I asked Mr. Westerly to extend him credit. I endorsed it." Lie upon lie, she continued, "The least I can do for a man who saved my life, while you, Ben, shall see your name next to ours on the office sign, as agreed."

"Saved y—? Emma, I need to explain someth—" Ben caught himself. *Who'd verify my account if she won't accept it? Not Gant. The crewmen? Aloft when I first climbed down after her. She'll think me a liar.* Briggs collected himself. "You sold him what he wanted."

Emma noticed Ben's change of course. She placed it tactfully away. "And on his new ship, Quartus will sail off. You *both* get what you asked for, Ben."

"Better for all of us," remarked Briggs.

Perhaps you will be, she thought, *but my dreams are cursed with the image of that hateful Providence man, however, bent on trying to drain a fortune from Father's empty vault.*

Ben Briggs returned to Boston to conduct *Hammond and Briggs Company's* mission. In Newport, a northerly wind turned uncomfortably brisk, and Emma welcomed Captain Quartus Gant for a quiet evening alone. His ship scheduled to embark, yet they had settled nothing. Before Great Hill's bellowing hearth, they sat comfortably and spoke of a possible future together or apart, or variously together and apart. It was a difficult discussion.

"I've noted the Hammond Company's fortunes seem to have suddenly improved since we returned from our adventure." Gant let his remark hang in the air. In recent days since their short cruise, he had replayed the events at Muskeget and Malabar beach over and over but could not decipher the conflicting happenstances. To Emma's vacant look he added, "You bought new topsails for the schooner."

Feeling guilty, Emma was tempted to admit her deception. To reconcile her duplicity to the man she held in her arms, the man she believed had saved her life, she held back and would do so forever. Yet to the other man rescuing her family estate through hard work, she had bestowed her confidence. Nonetheless, neither man solely held sway over her heart. Surrendering to Quartus' most recent proposition would mean a lonely life waiting for a ship; Briggs, on the other hand, affectionate in his quiet way, growing in her heart for his patience and consideration, stood near. Ben was obviously besotted with her, but reticent to show it. And neither man flowed with the heart-stopping passion of that soul now departed, taking with him to the bottom of the sea her adolescent dreams of far-away islands with warm coves and crescent laps of sand and shell.

"Ben has made amazing progress, Quartus. Our trade is increasing ten-fold. Mr. Westerly has therefore agreed to refashion our debt." Emma left his side on the sofa and stood.

"*Refashion*," echoed Gant flatly. Emma detected a hint of mockery.

"Many things have changed since you went away, Quartus." She stoked the fire, avoiding his gaze. "I want to live my life with no constraints."

"With *me* you can have such a life."

"When you're always at sea? What kind of life—"

"I'll make honest trade."

"So you say." She took his large hand in hers and gazed at him. "But when Newport disappears in your wake, you'll be in command of ruthless cutthroats."

"I need strong men. We face dangers—"

"Captain Gant, my word—*you're* the danger! You spread violence because you enjoy it!"

"But I come back, don't I? Alive and rich."

"You sound like Jordan." She turned away as Gant watched the flames spit and dance in the hearth.

"I won't disguise who I am." Gant could not find the right words to reconcile the chasm between the lovers. "You have my offer, Emma. It's up to you."

"The privateering life is over—"

"It ain't for me."

Emma looked at her hands as she turned back. "Then go. Live like an angry scavenger," she added, absent forethought as sometimes an honest thought escapes without warning. "You should have renamed your new ship *Predator*. It's a better fit to replace *Rattlesnake* on the stern than *Wasp*." Emma retreated from the fire into Gant's embrace, afraid to let him go, yet afraid to fall into his arms forever.

Gant smirked. "Have you never felt the sting of a wasp?" Emma made no reply as she held him tight. "Life at sea suits me," he added. "Nights ashore with you… fills me."

"That may be an impossible balance, Quartus. You want the freedom to extract your revenge on the world. You come alive only when you're angry."

"I'll run an offshore trade. Canton… England," Gant added, as if he had not heard her. "I'll always come back for you."

"So you say." Despite her harsh, accurate profile, she regarded him with heartfelt affection and a wry smile on her lips. But instead of returning a tender, knowing look as between two closely-bonded people, Gant stared into the embers snapping in the hearth. He felt the last remnants of his heart turn to ash, consumed in the flames.

Emma shivered despite the warmth. She knew he would continue to sail, fight, and steal. He would unleash his unhappiness on all men and any woman unfortunate enough to cross his path. Emma recognized she had been a fool, casting her line like a fisherman on the rocks, hoping for one last landing before losing the tide.

"I challenge you, Quartus. Sign honest lads for your ship, boys off the farms. Boys new to ships... and teach them the ways of the sea. Show them how to live well, come back to their families with accomplishment in their hearts and coins in their pockets." Gant said nothing, only staring at the flames, trying but failing to reconcile her words with his desires. "I see into your heart, Quartus," Emma continued as she raised her head and looked him in the eye, seeking to reach that place he had locked. "Your eyes give away your true feelings. More so than the words you whisper when we touch. I shall soon watch your crew as they board your new ship. These men—whether you've selected honest lads or cutthroats—will be your answer. If you find me by the gangway on the last of the ebb, I shall sail away with you. If I am not there, however, my answer is goodbye forever. You can have my heart, Quartus, but *you* also have a choice to make."

"Your fantasies, Emma..." Gant took his time; he knew he would never return to this time or place. He understood what she wanted. *So be it*, he decided. He had suffered loneliness and cold before; he could live with it. "Your fantasies block your vision. Jordan was no gallant privateersman. Briggs, no genius shipbuilder. Nor am I a godless, cursed cutthroat."

Quartus Gant might have captured her heart, but she recalled her father's words about the Gant family from Newport's Northside: "*He'll marry a girl to warm his bed on the nights he returns from sea, Emma. He'll raise little fighters...*"

Shifting her weight, Emma Hammond leaned in to kiss him. "Take care of my ship, Captain Gant. She has fine lines." She dabbed her eyes.

The day before Gant was to cast off, Emma left Great Hill early and came aboard *Rattlesnake*—now renamed *Wasp*—to gather her father's sextant. Gant had gone to town to purchase last-minute provisions. On board, former *Rattlesnake* crewmen mixed with Gant's new deck hands stowed barrels of cod from the saltworks. To Andy Crowell late of their expedition to Malabar Point, she smiled cheerfully—they had a special bond, having escaped certain death. A generous deposit made to his mother ashore bound Andy to Hammond and Company and kept their secret.

"Mr. Crowell, I am pleased to see you up and about after our ordeal. How do you fare?"

"I don't mind sayin' they hurt us good with their whip, Miss. Nasty lashes make it hard to wear shoes. Your surgeon gave us herbs and an ointment, though, thank you!"

"Of course, you're one of our boys."

"Aye, Miss, but those *Raptor* ruffians got it worse—eh?—when Captain Gant broke their boney necks and threw'em o're the rail!" Emma shuddered at the memory of bones snapped by hands that had so recently caressed her. "But, Miss, I should be asking you how *you* are after your near drownin'?" She smiled her gracious thanks and turned swiftly to leave Crowell for her more pressing matters, when the lad bridged the distance, hollering, "You sure were lucky Mr. Briggs climbed over to haul you back aboard, Miss!"

Emma whirled around. "What're you saying—? Mr. *Briggs*?"

"Aye, Miss. Of course, you couldn't see what happened. When you cried out from over the stern, me and Thad were about to furl the main t'gallant, but then we saw Mr. Briggs rush to the stern and jump over the rail—we was surprised, Miss, since he don't swim."

"And where was Captain Gant all the while?"

"Oh, he never left the helm—fightin' the current, I reckon, Miss, until Mr. Briggs had you most of the way up. We all pulled you the last few feet up'n'over, too sodden heavy for Mr. Briggs to haul you all the way up, with all due respect Ma'am, you'd have drowned if Mr. Briggs hadn't got you and laid you safe on deck. Then Mr. Gant come over to look if you's dead, and the wheel spun loose, and Mr. Briggs grabbed it before the ship wrecked on the rocks!"

Emma sat on her father's bed, tenderly holding his hand.

"Father, if you can understand me..." She spoke softly, "The war's almost over. I'm not sure why we fought it. I am safe, but Father, since we lost our dear Thomas at sea... bravely in battle... I placed a marker with his name in the spot you admire on the bluff overlooking Saltmarsh Cove. Thom asked after you every day... Mother has not yet returned but has explained her lengthy absence. I, too, despise your triangular trade, but unlike her, I forgive you. I know why you did it, but Hammond ships shall never sail the middle passage again, Father, never." Emma took a few deep breaths and continued. "I have two suitors, Father. Two good men, well, one of them is good. I admit my heart is torn."

Colonel Hammond groaned. His hand twitched.

Excited, Emma leaned in. "Father?" She waited. Watched. A finger on his left hand curled then straightened. *He understands me*, she thought and wedged her long, slender fingers into his gnarled fist. With renewed enthusiasm, she continued, "Oh Father, I understand you desired peace. But your contributions were abused by your so-called friends. They used our money to fund a detestable plot against our own government. Geoffrey Morris threatens me still and although I am not alone these days, he terrifies me with his threats and evil eyes. I intend to retain a banking relationship with Mr. Westerly, however, until I tap into other available resources. I am also considering leaving Great Hill. I need to live where people don't know about *Windslayer*. Perhaps in Massachusetts or Connecticut nearer Cousin Cecilia. Father, I wish I could do more for you. I love you so. I will hold you in my heart, for always and a day."

Emma suddenly felt her father squeeze her hand gently. Her heart swelled with joy for the briefest of moments before Colonel Samuel Hammond's fingers turned cold.

Ben Briggs rode his mare along the ocean past Eastern Point where acres of rocks stretched into the bay. With the United States and Britain expecting peace any day, the offing to Newport Harbor was clearing of black ships with yellow streaks; American vessels soon would enjoy trade with the entire world once again, including, thankfully, Britain. Thanks to fate and Emma Hammond, a golden future lay before Ben. During the days after Colonel Hammond's death and burial, Briggs had the good fortune to spend time alone with Emma. Amidst all the struggles, however, and with deep regret, he had lost his friend. *Tortola will always stand between Q and me*, he knew. He reconciled that some wounds are simply too painful to set aside. The young woman, however, remained available once he found the right words and rose to the challenge. He remembered her blank expression ages ago when he had failed to convey how he felt about his passion to design the fastest, most beautiful sailing ships the world had ever seen. He could speak of ships, but about the heart he stumbled like a lubber aloft.

He nudged his horse down the path towards the cove. Ben could do nothing these last days but think about Emma Hammond. Of recent encounters with her, however, she had acted tentative, a hint of hostility not far beneath the surface. She reminded him she needed him for his business acumen and, of course, they both needed to protect their dangerous, shared secret. What were her eyes saying that her words did not—Could she be his?

But due to Gant's successful advances reinforced by Emma's misunderstanding of what happened that night off Muskeget, Ben knew his own path to her heart might be forever blocked. Ben had always assumed that he would someday marry—after making his fortune. But on the day they had escaped *Raptor,* when Emma dashed across *Rattlesnake's* deck and tackled Jordan's murderous sailor, Ben Briggs wholly lost his heart to her. She rose above hate and fear, her actions a marvelous revelation. Two years prior, he had viewed her and Thom as perhaps a means of career advancement; now Emma Hammond had become his future's sole and defining purpose. There were thousands of ships he might build, but there was only one Emma Hammond. Ben felt eager to show her a new ship sketch: a daring brig design to replace *Rattlesnake* in the Hammond and Briggs fleet. A graceful ship with extra-tall masts, built to sail faster than any packet on any ocean. Painted brilliant white, with spars and halyards hoisting hundreds of acres of gleaming sails, every man and woman along the coast would admire it. His first-built ship would be christened with the name Emma's father gave her twenty-one years earlier: *Mary Celeste*.

Ben dismounted and tied the horse to a nearby tree, scanning the bay. It was evident why Emma had chosen this bluff for the colonel's grave and Thomas' marker: *The people we've lost cannot enjoy the view, but those who miss them, can.* Here high on the bluff, gentle summer breezes drifted from the southwest, rustling pine trees and bushes with their orange and red plum-berries. After a few minutes building his confidence, he turned to ride up the path to Great Hill. With the drawings of his new brig, he would call at the front entrance as an eligible suitor and her new business partner, no longer arriving by the pantry door as an employee. He planned to boldly announce his intentions in her grand salon with its tall ceilings and polished furniture. Dressed in a gentleman's knee-length evening coat, he had also purchased a tall beaver-skin hat and trousers clean of a seaman's ever-present salt-spots. Twice shaved, he shone like a healthy, successful sea-officer-turned-man-of-trade.

When a horse suddenly appeared, galloping from down the path behind him, Briggs glanced up. High on her steed, Emma Hammond smiled at Ben, her face brighter than he had ever seen. *Was she happy to see me or only because I'm paying respects?* She dismounted and approached him gracefully.

"Ben, it is so wonderful to find you here!" She stood so close he could smell rose water on her skin. "I went to look for you in the office after I made my final visit to *Rattlesnake*. I have been terribly inattentive to you these last few days."

She embraced him—a surprise. He awkwardly reached around her waist and held her in return, perplexed at her overt expression of affection. This was the first time he had touched her since dragging her unconscious body from Muskeget Channel. He gently released her. She kept her arms around him long enough to send a subtle signal, but not too long in case she was wrong. Her face tilted upwards, her full smile rich with bright teeth and skin shining from her morning ride.

"What's this in your hand, Ben. Another one of your little ship drawings?"

His ruinous plan slapped him in the face like a gust of cold North Atlantic wind.

"It's nothing, Emma. Perhaps... for another time." He quickly placed the roll back into his saddle bag. He was thankful she did not press him.

"Have you come here since we buried my father?" asked Emma.

She walked towards the edge of the cliff where trees parted, and grave markers stood overlooking sea grass with wild rose and blueberry bushes that grew by the sloping sand.

"Honestly, no. I was on my way to the manor... to see you."

"To offer your condolences *again*? Thank you. I so very much appreciate all your help, Ben. You're a great comfort to me. Do we have business today?"

"I was not coming about business."

"Ben..." Emma's heart beat faster. She turned away, staring at the grave markers, then toward the cove. "Everything I'm facing, I did for my family. But my family is gone... What was it all for? I mean, Morris, our debts, my nightmares of Jordan's perversities—"

Ben took her hand.

"You do have family, Emma," said Ben. She stood close but did not speak. "You once thought I befriended Thomas only to gain your father's trust. I admit it briefly crossed my mind. However, I came to admire your brother. He was an intelligent lad, braver than men twice his age. He taught me to respect the mission and protect the men we fight alongside. I think of Thom every day, Emma. To my last breath I shall regret his death." Emma's eyes welled. "My life's ambition has been to build a fortune, design ships and sail the trades. But when Thom fell, he only wanted to know who won. I'm tired of being judged on winning or losing, Emma. I want to build a life near the shore without the fighting and the blood. I want to raise a strong family of youngsters like Thom. To do this, I need a woman smart and brave... a dashing, beautiful woman to help me become a better man. That woman, Emma, is you." Ben held Emma's hands in his and looked into her eyes with all the intensity he felt. "Since the moment I saw you at your father's reception nearly two years ago, I thought if I were ever to marry, it would be to a woman like you, living life on her own terms. Emma, I cannot imagine my life without you. I came to the bluff today to ask for your father's permission. I thought I might hear a rustle of wind or a gull's cry and receive my answer. But I don't need a sign. I know my heart. I love you more than life. So, I ask you, in this special place, will you accept my offer?"

For once, Emma's response did not include a quick retort. She leaned up on the toes of her riding boots, grasped Briggs around his waist and kissed his sunburned lips.

"I only ask that our engagement be a short one, Ben," she said with a slight giggle, feeling a new and unexpected pleasure deep within her. Ben smiled in return. They stood quietly, heads tipped, leaning into one another, eyes to the cove and deliriously happy as the sun splashed the town of Newport. Emma continued, "Otherwise, I had planned a sea voyage to India to meet up with my mother. We could always marry once I've returned in a year or two, if we were not otherwise committed…"

Ben agreed their wedding would take place in a fortnight.

Emma received an unwelcomed message delivered to Great Hill by a young boy: she should expect a visit from the Providence investor within the hour. She panicked and rushed to change out of her riding habit.

"Rebecca!" she called for her maid. "Quickly, have Pete take you to the office in my chaise, and request Mr. Briggs attend to me as fast as he can ride!"

"Don't you mean Mr. Gant, Miss?

"No! Mr. *Briggs*! Go now, quickly!" *Ben will come, I am sure.*

Morris had threatened to take all she had left in her life—her home, her family's reputation, their ships. She felt a suffocating fog rolling ashore as he crept closer. The voyage to Malabar Point and their escape provided a bright future only if she could carve out enough time to find a safe haven and start over. Before that promising future, she must stare down Mr. Geoffrey Morris one last time.

After her return from Monomoy lighthouse with Captain Jordan's plundered treasure, Emma had hired a local man to guard Great Hill's front entrance: Mac Flynn, a drifter her father had once employed in the storehouse. She was therefore horrified when Morris presented himself *inside* Great Hill's foyer, opening her grand parlor door, unescorted.

"Mr. Morris, I won't pretend I'm happy to see you."

"That's rather a shame, Miss Hammond, since I can solve your pressing issues."

"So Mr. Westerly reminds me."

She would not let Morris have his way again. In her black, loose-fitting dress, billowing in front to obscure her shape, she had sequestered a small knife with a straight blade, its tip honed, able to pierce leather. A loaded pistol lay hidden under her chair cushion. Aside from the upstairs maid and Mr. Flynn—probably still asleep in the stables—she was alone at Great Hill.

"You heard we lost *Raptor,* Miss?"

"Is there no hope?"

"Only wreckage strewn on the beaches, Falmouth, Wasque, even Holmes Hole." His eyes narrowed. "…as well as many bodies."

"Were there no survivors, Mr. Morris?"

"Only one. A strange lad, Gregor Raca his name. He washed up half-dead on Wasque. A violent boy, not quite right in the head. I don't trust him and I'm not sure I believe him, but he said *Raptor* spoke a brig in the Sound."

"And your Mr. Raca, despite his mental deficiencies, has sent you in *my* direction?"

"He has. He nearly killed two of my men who were kind enough to escort him back to Newport. Nevertheless, I have considered his account with close attention." Expressionless, Emma folded her hands in her lap, having learned from Quartus Gant the power of silence. Studying her closely, the banker continued, "I wonder why my ship was sailing through a dangerous channel—in a gale no less."

"*Rattlesnake* too encountered rough weather. She returned safely."

"This boy, Raca, reported *Raptor* was close behind an armed brig."

"And how does this concern me?"

"Raca's memory left him unclear of the brig's name. But he said Captain Jordan transferred a sea-chest from this brig onto *Raptor*. We presume that box went down with my ship. Miss Hammond, I need to know if his account is accurate."

"I don't know anything about a chest, nor *Raptor's* misfortune. Where did she sink?"

"Muskeget Channel."

"Well, Muskeget is deep and the current there runs hard. If *Raptor* sank in Muskeget, any chest stored on board will surely lie on the bottom until the Lord comes to judge us."

"Unusual, for a rich girl who has never gone to sea to know about such an obscure passage," noted Morris through narrowing eyes. "It must have been terrible," he continued, "Men and boys dying in the rip currents, clinging to rocks and debris, calling out for their mothers and God's forgiveness, drowning in the cold water. With no ships nearby to save them!"

"Are you here for a purpose, other than to complain of your misfortune?" Emma fought to push away the memory of drowning sailors.

"Yes—I'm here to collect a debt. You owe us a great deal of money!" At this, his long finger extended from his cuff like the tongue of a serpent. *This devious witch knows something.* "With interest," Morris continued, "compounded to the many thousands of dollars. The war is nearly over, and it is absolutely critical for the salvation of this great nation that certain actions take place *prior* to that treaty! To effect those arrangements, we need the commitments your father made in good faith to his friends and partners—"

Her eyes flashed. "My father is dead."

Morris stepped back. "My condolences. I shall gladly deal with *you* then." Having shed his hat by the door, he now doffed his gloves and coat. Approaching Emma with a determined stride, his hatred comingled with lust. "Your balances of liquid assets, Miss Hammond, have mysteriously grown suddenly," said Morris as Emma looked to the door hoping for help to arrive. "I've learned you have opened cloaked accounts in banks across New England. I could seize your funds as I sit on the boards of many institutions, but time is pressing. Are you surprised I know this? Oh, our friend Westerly may preen about financing the Hammond trade, but it is *my* money that's invested in your ships. And when your ships return with profit, I see every penny, every gold dollar. Your father cannot buy a cask of wine without its invoice coming to my notice! You can imagine my surprise when I learned of your secret accounts—flush with deposits coinciding with

Rattlesnake's mooring, while *Raptor* did not!" Morris grabbed Emma's arms and yanked her out of her chair, hissing, "You found Jordan's fortune. You owe it to me!"

"Help!" Resigned to the fact this conversation could only end badly, Emma continued to shout, "Mr. Flynn!" Her hand searched for her knife within her dress pocket. "Flynn!"

Morris directed his pent-up fury at Emma. He balled his right hand with its diamond ring protruding obscenely.

"We had an understanding, Miss Hammond. Your visits were to continue until—"

"I recall your demand!"

"I *will* have my debts repaid today—"

"I need time—!"

"There is no time! Give me what ready money you have—now! Or I shall take payment in another manner." She felt the knife. "I tire of your excuses."

Emma gripped her knife. Praying the truth would shock him and buy her time, she screamed, "You're a traitor!"

"How dare you make such a vile accusation!"

The sordid truth was not her ally. Emma realized no one was coming to her aid. She was armed with only a short blade without room to maneuver.

"The British army will not land in Virginia," she blurted. If her plan was to startle and further enrage a man already bent on violence, she succeeded. She could not stop herself; *this must end tonight!*

"What…" Dumbfounded, Morris paused. "are you talking about?" His eyes slits.

"You arranged for the British to land troops in Virginia. You made sure they would not meet armed resistance. You knew our armies would be sent elsewhere. You and your friends conspired so the British could easily capture our capital and remain to occupy it this time. However, I altered your plans."

"You?" he asked, aghast.

"The British will not sail their fleet up the Chesapeake. Nor will they land ten thousand troops on the Potomac."

"How do you come to learn this from your sanctuary here?"

"The British are moving their invasion elsewhere." Her voice shook.

"Where will they—? Tell me!"

"Your British friends received new instructions they believe came from you."

"What friends?"

"Captain James Breton of His Majesty's Royal Navy. He requested clarifying information about the details of our defenses. He has come to know my captains and my captains have confided in me, as they did with my father. I learned a great deal about you and your so-called 'syndicate'."

Hearing the British captain's name from her lips came equally unexpected. "You don't say... Breton, eh?" Morris' eyes, as stony as any adversary he had ever fought, yet he foundered in uncharted waters: at war against an intelligent woman.

In Colonel Hammond's office, Ben Briggs and Matthew Westerly finalized temporary credit terms.

"No other shipping concern will receive such generous financing, Ben." Westerly smiled.

Briggs was tempted to refuse the offer with its usurious interest the two men understood was only available through smuggling or the triangular trade. *With Captain Quartus Gant sailing away forever, however, I'll be free of the gunner's accusing stares, and Emma as well, of his leering.*

"Hammond and Briggs will no longer require loans from Providence or anyplace else." Ben sighed. "Not even Morris."

"His loss of *Raptor* stings, though he has other matters on his mind."

"You spoke with him recently?"

"Yes, we shared a chaise from Providence. En route, Geoffrey requested I drop him and his man to Great Hill where he is at present meeting with Miss Hammond. I shall rejoin them when we have finished."

Briggs stood immediately, reaching for his coat and hat. Surely Emma had not arranged a covert meeting— In that moment, stampeding feet up the wooden stairs thundered outside.

"Mr. Briggs, sir," Frantic, Rebecca Malone, Great Hill's kitchen maid burst into the office shrieking, "Come quick! Missus is in distress! And our Flynn lies by the front—he ain't movin'!"

"Morris—?" asked Ben, following her out the door.

"The severe-lookin' man from Providence who Miss Hammond..." the maid glanced back at Westerly who followed them, "vowed she'd never again invite to the manor."

"We'll take my chaise," Westerly offered.

"You said something about his *man*?" Ben blurted out as they climbed into the chaise, a light buggy drawn by a single mare.

Westerly's chubby fingers flicked the reins and the horses sped off.

"Yes. When Captain Jordan commanded *Raptor,* he kept a man near him for, let us say, *company*. Mr. Morris now employs this same man, McSweeny is his name."

"Faster!"

"What are you afraid of, Mr. Briggs? I understand Miss Hammond handles her affairs quite capably."

"I don't trust Morris alone with her."

"Why does Mr. Morris not sit well with you, Mr. Briggs? Thanks to you and your estimable services delivering our concluding correspondence, Geoffrey Morris is in your debt. He is an influential gentleman. I believe he will become even more influential in the very near future."

Before he could stop himself, Ben blurted, "We'll see about that."

The young man's insubordinate tone, more than his words, struck Westerly like hitting one's head on a low hanging door frame. Matthew Westerly had trusted Briggs to deliver Morris' final instructions to the British. *Sealed, secret instructions.* He had assumed the promise of a ship command would bind the young man to their nefarious purpose. Had Briggs turned? Who else knew of the syndicate's plans? *Hammond, of course!* Westerly scolded himself. The colonel had likely been plotting behind the syndicate's back, making his own arrangements with the British. Was this how Hammond privateers met with such astounding success? Had the colonel used the syndicate's back-door communications with the enemy as a pretext for his own secret negotiations? *What fools Morris and I have been! Hammond had, from the syndicate's early days, intended only to safeguard his own interests while feigning support for our coup!* Ncw, Westerly sorely regretted Morris' desperate gambit, traveling to Great Hill to wring from the girl enough funds to pay the final three senators and arrange for key departments of government to stand down... their doors open for his glorious approach arm-in-arm with the men in red.

But if Morris had guessed wrong, if the Hammond girl had not uncovered Jordan's stolen loot, then Geoffrey Morris' final foray today would certainly fail. And worse, Morris might unleash his frustration against the colonel's captivating daughter. Fearing the worst, Westerly sensed the chafe of a noose, as he loosened his collar and wiped his brow. The banker's sticky hands on the leather reins urgec his horse up the stony path to Great Hill.

Emma enjoyed only a very brief respite after her shocking confession threw Morris off balance.

"And on receiving this false information, what did Captain Breton tell your man?" asked Morris.

"They welcomed the intelligence."

"I can counter your scurrilous libel with an immediate message."

"You may try. Your original correspondence, however, is in safekeeping with my solicitor instructed to open it if I am in any way incapacitated. He shall then deliver it directly to the governor."

"You miserable whore!" Morris barked.

"Would you care to renegotiate my father's commitment?"

"My privileged correspondence between representatives of the United States Government—"

"You represent nothing but yourself!" Emma remained calm.

"And my counterparts in His Majesty's Government."

"You told our enemy you would deliver a '*disbursed Congress*', a '*disarmed*' Federal Army and a '*scuttled*' fleet of frigates under forts with '*spiked*' cannon? And you organized certain representatives of Southern States to support you?"

"Yes, damn you, and more! Ours is presently a pathetic excuse for a government! No one gives a rat's fart about whether people live free or in shackles! Our President doesn't answer my slaves' cries for freedom, does he? And yet I watch my profits go to rot in this idiotic war while the British economy rolls over Europe. They're making their trading partners rich beyond imagination."

"I wager *you* imagine those riches?"

"Damn it, but I do! And I make things *happen!*"

"With proceeds from smuggled goods for which people must pay exorbitant prices—"

"You call *me* a traitor, when your father expanded his interests to slave trading! I am working to fix the failings of a colonial system that was mishandled thirty years ago, Miss Hammond." She opened her mouth to object; he plowed on, "It plays like this for people like you who can afford a Great Hill. Money begets power. With that power, we write laws to our manner of thinking. And, *these* laws, *this* Constitution, this *flaccid* presidency and *meddling* Congress are NOT what the great men of trade in this country deem appropriate! Laws, therefore, shall be recast! By doing so we ensure that the freedoms for the common people never again infringe upon the profits of its most able citizens. Your father at one time was one of us. He knew it was wise to regain Britain's trust. But he evidently lost heart. 'Twas his weak backbone killed him!"

"My father never lost heart," Emma threw back. "You, however, care only about power."

"I care about many great things. I do not hide from that. And it's through those efforts that I made you an offer—a coveted place by my side—"

"Your drunken talk of marriage? A lie and you know it! You meant to set me up at *The Arms*'—a kept woman in a suite of plush rooms!"

"And I shall have what I paid for!"

Looming over her, hand raised to strike; Emma despaired for a savior. *Jordan—a dead lunatic. Morose Gant unmoored. And Briggs—head-down, dreaming of ships or reveling in the new signage on her company door.*

Disbelieving the violence and pain, Emma felt Morris' open hand slap her face with the full force of his entire body. His ring—deliberately aimed—sliced her delicate cheek. His blow threw her over the back of a chair onto the rug. Her head rang, her senses faltered. Without time to defend herself, she reached for the pistol beneath disheveled seat cushions, but Morris sprang on her, his full weight straddling her waist. He grabbed at her bodice and ripped her dress open in a violent rage, its soft imported silk torn apart. She twisted, turned, and pulled one arm free. Again, she attempted to reach around but could not find her knife that she hoped was still wrapped in her the folds of her voluminous dress.

The moment the little wench had admitted her treachery, Morris knew all was lost. He had promised the holdouts in Washington he would personally deliver funds with an additional five thousand dollars to each man, greasing the skids while easing his governance of a new Atlantic States into the future. But without grease on the ways—and without the British Army on the way—a rally cry by itself would not move timid men to bold action—only largess, hard currency, and gold.

Emma recalled the damage she had inflicted upon the face of Jordan's sailor. A man does not expect a woman to fight with uninhibited ferocity. Emma enjoyed an equestrienne's strength and healthy teeth. Her nails ripped at Morris' exposed cheeks, his surprise equal only to his fury. Her teeth continued the assault, biting deep into his neck, filling her mouth with his vile blood, her nose nearly overcome with the stench of his cloying French cologne. Morris screamed profanities as she latched onto him like a mussel to a rock: she clawed at his eyes as his oaths promised retribution ending her miserable life. But despite her fevered tearing and scratching she could not overcome his bulk. His hands reached under her dress, ripping, tearing. His lips, white with spittle, roared against her bloody face as he opened his trousers. Unable to recoil from his powerful thrusts, she bit his ear lobe clean through. Gritting tight, she shook her head like an angry cur. Morris screamed, backed off, and, forever disfigured, felt for his desecrated ear lobe. Emma's arms and hands suddenly free, she found her knife nested in her dress folds. In one swift, deliberate motion she plunged steel to the hilt into Morris' paunch. Committed now, she would fight him as long as she had a pulse. She thrust her knife, twisting it with both hands. Morris tried to pull himself away but, as he retreated, Emma sat up and drew the knife upwards in a tearing motion. As his body convulsed, she shoved her blade ever deeper. His panicked attempts to squirm only drew the knife into his defenseless vitals. His blood spewing, she jerked the knife back out all the way and found a new, uninjured place in his side. With all her remaining strength, she delivered a final thrust with her blade, grunting while forcing the knife through his stiff vest and tailored shirt. Staring into her eyes in

disbelief, Geoffrey Morris of Providence and New York fell away, howling in unimaginable agony.

Briggs and Westerly heard screams as they jumped off Westerly's chaise at Great Hill's main entrance. Briggs saw a stranger guarding the front door and forced his way past.

Westerly shouted, "McSweeny, stand down!" Westerly jerked his head toward the woods. Morris' man ran off.

Briggs noted Flynn's body on the ground beside the door. He flew past the deceased in a fever to find Emma. Westerly drew his pistol as he quickly followed Briggs inside. In the parlor, they found a bloodied Emma Hammond breathing heavily, her dress torn, her hair in tangles. Convulsing a few feet away lay Morris, his hands desperately failing to stop the blood, now seeping across the carpet. Rushing to Emma, Briggs gently cupped her head in his hands. Unable to speak at first, she looked at him gratefully—unlike the dark day of *Rattlesnake's* escape from Muskeget Channel. Ben smoothed back her hair, matted with blood.

"You came for me, Ben," she whispered. "Thank you, my love."

With the assistance of the upstairs maid, Ben gently helped Emma to her sitting parlor adjacent to her bath and bedroom suite where she pronounced herself safe.

"I need only Rebecca's nursing after I bathe, then a night's rest."

Emma Hammond had promises to fulfill; *Wasp* was setting sail.

With Westerly's first glance around the Great Hill salon, it betrayed a sordid narrative. He stared at the pitiful figure bleeding on the rug. He *tsked, tsked* to himself: *How badly everything has gone!* Westerly stood over Morris. He made no attempt to investigate the seriousness of the wounds nor to soothe with an offer to help. On their ride from the port, he had gotten from Briggs enough of an admission to anticipate the end of Morris' dangerous game had arrived; an overly ambitious foray that had embroiled both bankers and the unfortunate Colonel Hammond and his family. Briggs had admitted to Westerly that the British forces the syndicate had so carefully steered to the lightly defended capital had been re-aimed by Emma Hammond's letter that replaced Morris' original. That her intuition might be her own (had she eavesdropped on nights when syndicate voices climbed through the night?) or a secret instruction from her father prior to his death, was unknown and forever destined for the crypt of lost causes. Where would the British army come ashore? New York, capturing the Hudson's trade route to Canada, the Lakes, and the West? Boston, severing British-friendly New England from the Mid Atlantic States? God forbid, not to the South! Not New Orleans! Their secret syndicate—if their treasonous plan and identities were discovered, if Morris once arrested betrayed his confederates (as Westerly deemed likely)—would be hunted down as the traitors they were. It must either end here or Matthew Westerly would likely meet the hangman.

"Your wounds appear painful, sir." Kneeling, Westerly spoke calmly to his bleeding comrade, "Not so serious that a skilled surgeon can't repair you to good health though." Listening hopefully, Morris lifted his head weakly towards Westerly. "But we cannot have that, my friend." Westerly placed a plump seat cushion between his own fine coat and his target before his pistol fired.

Returning to the parlor from Emma's boudoir, Ben heard a pistol shot.

The two men exchanged a knowing glance as Westerly made a speedy exit, his gun still smoking. Ben arranged for the undertaker to remove the corpse, neglecting to explain the unfortunate hole in Morris' head. Ben told Emma that Westerly had helped Morris out of his misery: a horseman shooting his lame beast. She only nodded. Rebecca cleaned the blood, the glass, and broken furniture of what would soon again become Newport's finest salon.

Later, on his route to the Hammond and Briggs office, Ben found himself on Hammond Pier. *Rattlesnake*, now renamed *Wasp*, was to cast-off on the ebb. He felt an urge to speak to Gant presently or stifle his words forever. He spied the new captain busy on deck impatiently directing men stowing crates and barrels. Gant looked at Briggs standing alone, turned away, then reconsidered, and stomped down the gangway. Captain Gant carried both a pistol and a boarding knife in his belt and made sure Briggs could see them. As Gant approached, it occurred to Briggs the gunner might yet extract his avowed vengeance, sailing away before the crime could be reported. He reached for his knife until he remembered Emma had asked that since he was a partner now, an honest man of trade, he should no longer carry a privateer's weapon.

"The girl's not on board." Gant spat on the ground.

"I know," Briggs replied flatly. "I only came to give you this." Briggs held out Gant's brass spyglass last shared in the Muskeget channel. "Won't be needing it."

Gant looked at his father's telescope, the last reminder of his Northside childhood, of life before the war, a time of poverty and a leather strap.

"Keep it." The two stood awkwardly for a few moments. Gant turned away, then back. "I don't believe you're innocent, Briggs, no matter what she says. If we meet again, I'll doff my cap. But don't expect anything more."

Ben considered offering his hand to the man once a brother-in-arms. "We were a force, Q. Privateersmen."

"Aye."

Gant retreated up the gangway to *Wasp,* knowing Briggs could not begin to fathom the intense pain he had suffered in Mill Prison. The Hammond girl did not understand it either, though he would forever be grateful to her for his release. He wanted her, needed her, but knew he would never again hold her in his arms. She lived behind Great Hill's stone walls, while he hungered for the freedom of the world's oceans. The girl would be happier without him, he knew. All the way up the gangplanks, Gant shouted commands to undock so to catch a fresh-building offshore breeze.

He stared hard back at the pier, beyond Ben Briggs, to the stairs leading from the Hammond office. Emma had not come. If she was watching from the window, he did not want to catch her eye or her final indictment against him and his ways.

Reaching *Wasp's* deck from the gangway, Gant met with eyes as green as Emma's gazing back at him—a young woman hefting with a large wicker basket.

"Claire Shortell," she introduced herself. Her long wavy hair shone bright copper. "I got here fresh loaves of bread a Captain Quartus Gant ordered from the bakery."

"A 'wash-ashore' new to America, are you?" he gruffly chided the lively Irish lass. He admired her lovely smile that seemed to stretch from his ocean to the up-island hills. He inhaled the fragrant bread and palmed her a generous handful of coin. "I'm Captain Gant."

"I know." She curtsied, keeping her eye on his.

Over her shoulder, she thanked him kindly for his overpayment. Gant took in her swaying gait as she walked away and down the gangway. To his pleasure, she turned back. Holding his gaze, Claire hollered from the gangway, "You must learn to smile, Captain!"

Gant's eyes followed her skipping along the pier until she disappeared into the crowd.

After her bath, Emma regained her bearings with surprising speed. Except for a badly bruised face and a bandaged cheek that her maid, Rebecca proclaimed did not require a needle and thread, Emma felt more energized than she had a right to. Earlier she thought she might leave Briggs in charge and sail away with Gant as her lover had offered, living a life of endless horizons and tender nights beside a coal stove. But she remembered the conditions she had required of him; she knew Gant would meet none. The Quartus Gant she knew would never change, and she had. Mourning her father's death must be set aside for a time. Today, her former ship was setting sail for a cruise to unknown destinations. Torn about Captain Gant's offer, she had prepared a sea-chest. She had left it at Great Hill, however, along with the foolish fantasies of an emotional girl. Surrendering a life of passions unhindered by the responsibilities of a new family and a growing enterprise, she felt sure of her decision despite feeling that a part of her heart had been cut away. Her feelings for Ben, though having grown over many months, now bloomed when she learned that it was he who saved her life off Muskeget. If not for the foolish distractions of two sea captains, she might have fallen into his arms sooner. Her choice to accept Ben's marriage proposal, however, did not make her decision any easier as she stood by her father's desk chair gazing out at *Wasp*. She smiled, watching Claire swan away from the wharf, her mass of red hair swiveling back at the captain. Emma felt ill. Though Ceci was recently married, the judgmental cousin could offer no insights of what to expect. Emma found Ceci's words pitiably naive, while her own thoughts roamed toward guarded optimism for the future despite the finality of recent chapters near their end. *Strange* thought Emma, *to feel this way with new life abounding.* The war's successful finale had just been announced; Emma felt a certain pride with the role she had played in it. The treaty would be signed two weeks before President Jackson mauled the invading British troops in a battle near New Orleans. She admitted to herself she had acted not out of patriotism nor for an ideal she barely understood. *Freedom?* Available only for white men with property. *Rights?* Although a woman of wealth and influence, Emma could buy a governor's favor, yet could not vote for one. She had turned on Morris and his conspirators primarily to protect her father and the family's reputation as much as to spite Morris. As she had watched him bleed out on her fine carpet, she had felt relieved, his death a blessing to her and her countrymen. Emma no longer felt tempted by the illegal slave trade which continued to flourish, limited to the most disreputable ship-owners. Respected trading firms that had made earlier fortunes selling humans in return for sugarcane had quickly reinvested those triangular profits in respectable industries of the new century. Churchgoing men of the leading trading families in Boston, Salem, Newburyport, Newport, and Mystic would forever deny their ships had sailed the wretched middle passage. And no one ever asked.

Emma sat quietly in her father's office. She watched crewmen with duffels—clearly rough and tumble sorts—saunter up the gangplank leading to *Wasp*. Two young men full of energy and promise bumped into each other on the narrow gangplank. One lad fell onto the wharf, his bag spilling on rough cobblestone. Foul, threatening words erupted from men with drink in their bellies and hurt in their hearts. The one standing upright jumped down off the gangway, sprang to the other sailor who had regained his feet and wailed at him with fast, furious blows sending the downed man's head a-jerking. Blood splattered both sailors as one drew his knife and slashed the other man across his cheek. Men from the ship's deck cheered one, then the other. Gant had hired men like himself, she realized.

Captain Gant stood imperiously at the ship's rail overlooking the action. Arms folded at first, he watched the scrum, a pipe protruding from his mouth. *Is he shocked?* Emma watched from her office window. *No, he is entertained.* Gant had gathered violent men. Violent men fight.

Finally storming down the boarding plank, Gant intervened. And with the back of his heavy hand he sent one man flying, his boot slamming into the other fighter's stomach.

"*Wasp* is a fighting ship," he shouted to the rest of the crew. "Victors, come aboard! The rest of you lubbers can go to the devil!" Gant put his arm around the winner, slapping the back of the young man's. The vanquished sailor gathered his belongings and stood alone with a dumb expression—lesson learned. A vulgar rule for future engagements had been established for *Wasp's* twenty young crewmen.

"Ben, please hold me."

As they embraced, Emma stole a final peek out the window, stifling unwanted tears. The sailing brig *Wasp* had cast free the heavy dock lines and her days as *Rattlesnake*. The privateer watched her ship clear the rocky point, heading southwest, the future possibility of a warm breeze, unknown and distant.

THE END

Glossary of 19th-century Nautical Terms

Abeam: centerline on a ship

Abaft: in or behind the stern of a ship

Brace: a line that moves the yardarms to better catch the wind

Cable: an anchor line

Clew: a sail's lower corner(s)

Companionway or companion ladder: an opening through the main hatches where sailors can climb down to the deck below; in the companionway opening there is a steep wooden ladder

Capstan: a mechanical device that makes it easier to raise a heavy anchor

Come About or 'about' or 'tack': to change direction by losing wind from sails; a ship's bow comes across the direction of the wind

Course: another name for a large 'square' sail; also, the direction a ship is sailing

Ease: to loosen a line attached to a sail; this makes a sail lose its wind and power; a ship will slow down when sails and lines are eased

Founder: when a ship sinks due to extraordinarily heavy seas or storm, often without witnesses

Frigate: a medium size warship with between twenty-eight and fifty cannon; fast, often used to carry fleet messages or patrol an enemy's coast

Gaff: top wooden support for the spanker; heavy to hoist

Halyard: a line that raises or lowers a sail

Hove to: Stop sailing with sails backwinded

Jibe or jybe; also, to 'wear': to change direction quickly away from the direction of the wind; the wind remains in the sails; requires more sea room to execute than a tack; safer than tacking and so preferred by captains whose ships are far out at sea

Leechline: lines used to furl (tie-up) or let down a sail

Lines: ropes that are attached to a sail and have a particular function— e.g., a jib sheet is a line (a rope to trim a jib sail) or a spanker halyard is a line (a rope to raise a spanker sail)

Log: a spool of line with a weight attached to measure a ship's speed. ALSO

Logbook: a written record of a ship's navigational data plus all shipboard activities like coming upon another ship, if, for example a ship "speaks another", or you might hear that two ships "spoke". Note, not "spoke to": speaks another only means they both hove to (stopped sailing with sails backwinded) and communicated, often through a speaking trumpet across the water or sometimes they visited each other by ship's boats

Lubbers Hole: an opening in the platform high on the mast through which a sailor can climb avoiding the near upside-down climb over the outside of the platform which is quicker; stands for "land lubber" or a non-sailor (e.g., only non-sailors would chicken out and use a "lubber's hole")

Mess: a group of sailors who eat together; often a friendship group develop

Moonraker: the top-most sail on a clipper ship

Mooring ball and slip knot: in the event a ship must depart quickly—perhaps escaping an enemy ship or a smuggler trying to sneak away with stolen goods—she can leave her anchor in the water tied with a slip knot to a floating mooring ball

Orlop: the lower deck on a multi deck ship such as a frigate or ship of the line (a man-of-war)

Packet: a swift sailing ship most often used to transport paying passengers with a schedule

Peak: top of the mast; also called a 'truck'

Pilot: a seasoned seaman hired to guide a ship into a harbor, avoiding rocks, sandbars, shoals

Port: a window in a ship; also: a harbor in a town; also: a type of wine with added hard liquor (brandy) made in Portugal; also, after the time of our story—larboard was changed to port, meaning left-looking forward-toward-the-bow. Imagine the confusion in a storm, yelling larboard and starboard! With the change from larboard to port, commands were no longer confused between starboard and larboard.

POSH (acronym) "Port Out, Starboard Home": meaning the preferred, cooler side of the ship for passenger cabins on a voyage to the far east; it came to mean anything upscale or luxurious

Larboard: left-hand side of a ship looking forward (to the bow) (renamed 'port')

Line: see Rope

Longboat, gig, pram, pinnace, jolly boat, etc.: different types of rowboats on a ship

Luffing: flapping of the whole sail, the opposite of a "trim" sail

Privateer: a converted merchant ship—light and fast—approved via a 'letter of marque' issued by a government to attack, burn, and sink enemy merchant ships; also, the name attached to those sailors on board a privateer—also referred to as "privateersmen"

Mid (abbrev. "midshipman"): a young officer, as young as 10 and as old as 30; often sons of high-born families looking for a naval career; also called "young gentlemen" in the British Navy

Rake or mast-rake: the vertical angle of a ship's mast (e.g. tilt) that can determine sailing speed

Ratlines: a rope ladder on a ship—how sailors climb up the mast; attached to shrouds or stays—heavy lines that keep the mast in place; sailors were taught to climb ratlines with their feet alone, as their hands were often on a much stouter shroud

Reduce sail: to reduce speed and, thereby, increase safety in high winds or storms by hauling up a sail and tying it to its yardarm

Reef (or, v. "to reef"): to "reduce sail" by hauling up a sail and tying it to its yardarm; this reduces speed and increases safety in high winds or storms

Rip: an underwater cliff; the water driven by currents hits a wall of a rip and rushes to the surface creating waves and violent seas; any ship caught in a rip can be turned sideways and pushed on its side which, of course, will cause it to fill with water and sink

Rope (versus "line"): all lines are made of rope; a rope becomes a line when attached to a sail or spar (e.g. yardarm); note that all lines have a specific name and are found in the exact same location on all sailing ships during the *Age of Sail*; this allowed sailors from different ships, countries, and languages to be able to sail together on a new or unfamiliar ship without re-training

Saloon: No, not a bar in West Texas, rather, saloon is another name for the main cabin, where multiple passengers might congregate, eat, and socialize

Sea Room (or just "room"): enough navigable water between a ship or ships and an obstruction, like land or reefs

Sextant: a navigational instrument used to measure the angle of heavenly objects in order to determine a ship's location at sea; most often used by the captain, first mate, or a sailing master on a merchant ship, and by all naval officers on a navy vessel

Shanghai: 19th-century slang, to kidnap a sailor and add the unfortunate to a crew for a long voyage

Sheet: a line attached to a sail's lower corner(s) (or clew) that controls a sail's trim, while a "halyard" is a line that raises or lowers a sail, and a "brace" is a line that moves the yardarms to better catch the wind

Slip knot: see Mooring ball

Spar: the yardarm attached atop a mast, supporting the sails

Speak another, speak, spoke: one ships speaks to another and two ships speak;. note: not "spoke *to*"; speaks another means that two ships hove to (stopped sailing with sails backwinded) and communicated with each other; often, sailors used a speaking trumpet in order to be heard across the water between the ships; or sometimes seamen visited each other by ship's boats

Stays and Shrouds: heavy lines or cables used to support the masts and the incredible strain of sails full of wind

Stem: the angled, vertical beams that form the shape of the ship's bow

Steerage: the cheapest, humblest compartments for passengers (e.g. miners, immigrants)

Strike: to take something down, e.g., a sail, a flag in surrender

Studding Sail or stun's'l: a rectangular, extra sail placed outside the main sails for extra speed, most often in light or moderate air

Trim (v., n., adj.): to pull the sails in; the angle of a sail; how efficiently the sails are balanced relative to a ship's load; also, see Sheet

Wear ship: see Jibe

Yardarm: the spar atop a mast, supporting sails

19th-century *Age of Sail*: resulted in a huge industry of smugglers, thieves, and privateers aiming to avoid them

About the Author

Photo Credit: Cathy Dahill

Best Historical Fiction Award-winning author, sailor, and former software executive, Steve Dahill lives in Marion and Boston, Massachusetts overlooking Boston Harbor and the *USS. Constitution*. He is a direct descendant of a privateer captain whose ship foundered off France bringing supplies to George Washington's army in 1776. The privateer's brother was Revolutionary War hero Captain John Barry cited as the "Father of the United States Navy". Steve is also a direct descendant of revered rebels hanged by the British during the Irish uprising of 1798.

Dahill's *Age of Sail* historical fiction trilogy explores the violent adventures of 19th-century American smugglers, privateers, slave traders, and clipper ship captains. Fans of the sea adventures by Patrick O'Brian or C.S. Forrester enjoy Dahill's novels about strong protagonists, including sailing wives and daughters, as New England families fight each other for dominance in the exploding 19th-century American seafaring economy. Dahill spent many years as an executive in the software industry. He sails *Riva*, a racing sailboat, along the Southern New England coast, often crewed by his wife and three children. *Secrets of the Mary Celeste*, his acclaimed debut novel, is the winner of the *Best Historical Fiction Novel 2024 Imajinn Award* presented by *Imaginarium Film & Book Awards*, followed by *Clipper Wars*, and *Privateer*.

Acknowledgements

Privateer completes my *Age of Sail* trilogy which highlights the years of the first half of the 19th century when most arrivals to America came by sailing ship, when most commerce along the coasts and between the United States and the world commenced from the wharves of Boston, Newburyport, Salem, and New York. I would like to recognize all the families, adventurers, and outcasts who arrived on these shores with hope in their hearts, near to nothing in their pockets but an ardent will to adapt, learn, and prosper in this new land, bound by the sea on which vessels of sails and ropes sailed over the horizon and made the American experience possible.

In addition, I want to thank my family, and most notably my father, Arthur Dahill, who taught me how to sail and who helped ingrain a love of sailing and sailing ships. Arthur was never so happy as when he was "messing around with boats" whether at the local sailing club on Cape Cod or in our family's back yard, taking his turn at painting and varnishing one of the beetle-cat sailboats that the entire family sailed. Also, I would like to acknowledge my long-time friend, Jerry Pallotta, the celebrated author who encouraged me to turn my sea-tales into books. None of this would have been possible without the expertise, guidance, and patience of Ghia Truesdale, my editor who took rough and tumble manuscripts and taught me how to sculpt them into polished stories, and the ongoing support from my publisher, Jumpmaster Press; Gene and Kyle have made my life-long passion for writing a reality.

Author Q&A - Steve Dahill

Award-winning *Age of Sail* trilogy Book #1, *Secrets of Mary Celeste*

Q. What inspired you to write *Secrets of Mary Celeste*?

A. My historical fiction novel is inspired by a real maritime event that remains a Top-10 unsolved mystery.

Q. Who's Mary Celeste?

A. There was a 19th-century ship named *Mary Celeste*, and that's what the book is about. In my telling of this true story, I created a character called Mary Celeste, for whom the ship is named. So Mary Celeste is both a ship and a person.

Q. What's the mystery of the *Mary Celeste*?

A. About 150 years ago a brigantine sailing ship, the *Mary Celeste*, was discovered adrift in the mid-Atlantic Ocean. No one was on board. So I used that base fact and created a story around it. To this day, there are many theories as to what happened to crew and passengers. Even Arthur Conan Doyle tried to solve it in his 1884 short story, *J.Habakuk Jephson's Statement*.

Q. Why did you choose to write this particular mystery?

A. The disappearance of the crew of the *Mary Celeste* has been a hotly contested subject for many decades. Growing up, my aunts and grandparents debated it, as my grandfather had lived in the next town over from Marion where *Mary Celeste's* owners once lived. Sort of a local story gone big time. Descendants of the lost family are still alive, so the story has lived on. With my personal connection to the story, living as I do during sailing season in Marion on the Massachusetts coast, I felt I could do a good job bringing it to life.

Q. But your book is a novel, not a historical depiction of what happened.

A. Correct. As Hollywood says it, "Inspired by real events" or "Based on a true story." I took the actual event—a ghost ship found abandoned—then I did a lot of research, and created an entire backstory. Then, I wrapped it around unique characters, plumbing the depths of what might have happened to the people on the *Mary Celeste* as well as those who went to search for them.

Q. So, what did happen?

A. Read it! You may come to your own, perhaps different conclusion than I did, which I welcome. As you witness my characters ardently seeking to solve the mystery, you'll see, more importantly, that my story stands on its own as an original work of fiction. The characters in my story ask the same questions scores of people, sailors, part-time sleuths and mystery buffs have also asked since it took place. Given that the ship no longer exists, and the people went missing at sea, no one will ever really know.

Q. You're a sailor?

A. I sail a small racing sailboat called *Riva*, a 35-foot racing sailboat that my family and I also use to cruise along the New England Coast. For many years we've raced in handicap fleets in Buzzards Bay, Edgartown, and Boston.

Q. Why does *Secrets of Mary Celeste* resonate with today's reader?

A. *Secrets of Mary Celeste* is about fundamental human emotions and what drives people to do great, heroic things. In it, a young man of 17, Alexander Briggs, fends off a captain and despicable first mate who mistakenly think Alex is keeping a secret from them. They hold all the cards while Alex is captive on their small ship. Yet he prevails. My book is about families—brothers who don't care for each other, a father, Captain Quartus Gant, who blames his innocent daughter Pricilla for his failings in life, a former slave who gives up a comfortable life to do his duty to the man who set him free. And female readers may see themselves in the strong female protagonist. I explore relatable human conditions that many people face. My characters have it tough. Sometimes reading about another's misfortunes makes our own foibles feel more palatable.

Q. In *Secrets of Mary Celeste* where does the real event leave off and your fictional story begin?

A. Great question! That is one that I wrestled with as I wrote the book. The event takes place in a real town on the Massachusetts coast. In real life, it was renamed Marion long after the time of our story, so

GPS won't find the town of Rochester on the coast (they split up the town many years ago)

Countless times over many years, I've sailed from Sippican Harbor, and it still looks the same as it did in the renderings and daguerreotypes of the 1800s, with the exception of a few sandbars that the weather has relocated. So, the descriptions in my novel are real, augmented by my imaginings of what the landmarks looked like in 1832 based on things from that time that are with us today. As an aside, I grew up in a sea captain's home built around this time, so my descriptions of houses of that time, too, are genuine. The characters, however, are all my own, including Alexander Briggs whose last name I kept because I liked how it sounded, and it wasn't too long to type a few hundred times! My accounting of the rescue is pure fiction—to my knowledge, no rescue was ever attempted. The conflict between the various captains lusting after the ship's valuables is also my own invention as is the plot point wherein the antagonist has his own reasons to search for the missing family.

Q. When did you start writing this book and how long did it take to write it?

A. About six years ago, I was thinking how nice it would be to watch a movie on the subject of the *Mary Celeste*. And so I wrote the screenplay of the ship and its missing crew. I hid that away until I finished writing the novel, and had it published.

Q. Did you struggle with the writing of *The Secrets of Mary Celeste?*

A. The writing part came fairly easily, and I enjoyed the research and fact checking. Editing unfolded over a couple years.

Q. Your bio says you are part of a famous seafaring family yourself.

A. Aye. And descendant of notorious rebels to boot!

Q. Tell us?

A. On my father's side, my Dahill lineage goes back to at least 1798, the 'Year of the French' when Irish rebels organized to fight the British. My forefather and his son were both hanged by the British and are revered to this day by Irish Nationalists. On my mother's side, I am a direct descendant of the brother of Captain John Barry, a famous Revolutionary War naval hero who is called the "Father of the US Navy". You can find his plaque on the Boston Common and a statue in his honor in Philadelphia. Captain Barry's brother, my direct ancestor, was also a sea captain as well as a privateer. He died at sea during the Revolution bringing needed supplies back to George Washington's troops from Bordeaux, France; his foundering ship was never seen again.

Q. Back to the ship *Mary Celeste*. If the ship had been found, why would it have been difficult to determine what happened? Even in 1872 there surely existed sophisticated scientific means sufficient to determine the cause of such an event.

A. A British prize court did conduct an exhaustive three-month inquiry into the claim brought by the shipowner who discovered the drifting *Mary Celeste*. After interviewing all involved, it was concluded that there was no "evidence" of foul play. But that did not satisfy the underwriters who awarded only 6% of the salvage value, thus signaling disbelief of the testimony of the *Dei Gratia* captain and crew.

Q. Why does this mystery still resonate today?

A. People today may not fully appreciate how much a sailing society America was in the early 19th century. Our commerce was predominately carried out on ships just like the *Mary Celeste*. Along the shores and across the oceans, such vessels carried commodities and manufactured goods—molasses and slaves, troops and lumber. There were few roads, the railways sparse. So ships were as common as trucks today, sailors as prevalent as businesspeople at a convention. And so, the general understanding of ships and sailing was widespread. The language of the sea infused common language even when taken across the continent, and used in the plains or the mountains. Most of America's residents today, save for Native Americans, came to these shores by sailing ship, or their families did. My point is, back then there was high-level expert understandings of ships and the sea. Every city had many sailing masters, captains and crews. Hundreds of thousands of people had endured long ocean crossings to get here. So, back then, amateur sleuths, writers, and novelists knew what to look for when they were trying to decipher what happened aboard the *Mary Celeste*.

Q. You're not going to tell us what you think happened, are you?

A. Shakespeare once complained about those who wanted the answers to his mysteries before he released the play. That was good advice then, think I'll stay with it.

Q. Just tell me this, then: were aliens involved?

A. Involved, and they seared the story in stone with lasers… at the bottom of the Atlantic. And I alone found the location.

Q. Very funny! So, what makes sea stories so much fun to read? You're a fan of Patrick O'Brian and CS Forrester. Tell us what inspires you.

A. O'Brian and Forrester wrote sea adventures as if it was the Wild West, and *truly* at that time, seafaring *was* the Wild West. I am a fan of both authors and wish they were still writing new books. Sea adventures are exciting because the ocean, to most of us, is an unknown world full of strange and beautiful seascapes, dangerous wild creatures, and a lawless society where danger lurks beyond every horizon. In the Wild West you can find a nearby town or Army fort. In outer space, there's always a starship or a Deep Space colony with gravity. But far out to sea—readers find themselves in a mysterious world. At sea, every character's resolve and abilities are pushed to an extreme that few land-based tales can match. A trek across a desert, swamp, or jungle might compare. Those who sail, who travel across what often seems like endless treacherous water, capture our imagination like few other stories can. Notably the scrappers and murderers on board an ocean-crossing vessel escalate that tension. Will Mr. Fletcher find an island for his mutineers? Will Jack Aubrey finally get the promotion he deserves? Will the taciturn Hornblower find peace amidst a world of turmoil? These stories of fictional men and women inspire me, as do their real-life inspirations.

Q. What historical characters have influenced your writing? Is there a real-life Alexander Briggs and Pricilla Gant who inspired you? Or a Captain Quartus Gant or Mr. Raca who strike terror?

A. Any writer of nautical fiction, at least those in the Anglo-Saxon tradition, pays homage to Horatio Nelson and the naval heroes of his time, including Captain Cochran. O'Brian clearly modeled some of his characters from those historical figures of the Napoleonic Wars, as did Forrester. For my part, I learned of a Massachusetts privateer, Captain William Nichols, who ravaged the British homeland—*this*, I thought, was outrageous! But my own stories in my *Age of Sail* trilogy aren't naval stories, but the purported *peaceful trades* that were anything but. That interested me more: privateering, smuggling, and the abhorrent history of slave trading. Life at sea was brutal in the 1850's aboard clipper ships.

Q. You touch on the slave trade in *Secrets of Mary Celeste*.

A. I skirt it. In coming books in my trilogy, I delve into the slave trade in more detail. In those days, it was very common to have crews comprised of men and boys from all nations, colors, and languages. The presence of slaves and former slaves was common—alongside conscripts and convicts. In some industries such as whaling, crews with sailors of color were common.

Q. Your main antagonist in *Mary Celeste* is a smuggler, Captain Quartus Gant. A former privateer. And a slave trader. Was this common or unusual during that period in history?

A. For all three trades—smuggling, privateering, and slaving—fast ships were pivotal. Each had the same requirements: speed, stability, easy-to-sail with a short-handed crew when necessary. And a ship's draught had to be shallow enough to enter small harbors and coves. Therefore, the owners and captains of these ships—mostly schooners and brigs with only two masts and larger square riggers with three— easily went back and forth between the trades. Some ships and their owners started out in peaceful trade, found smuggling more profitable, and when wars erupted in 1775 and 1812, privateering became top dog. All on the same ship, an armed coastal ship packed with crews of armed and angry sailors. It was not a jump to send that same ship to Africa for a middle passage of slaves for the West Indies' and Southern States' plantations. Many ships did both or all three trades.

Q. What kind of research went into this book?
A. First and foremost, I've *lived* sailing. I've been sailing since I could swim, which I could do before I could walk. My first *real* sail was on a wooden sloop across Provincetown Harbor to Race Point where I was stuffed under the bow in a lifejacket. I've owned sailboats since I was nine or ten and for over the past twenty years I have raced and cruised extensively all along the New England coast from Maine to New York. I have a cottage on the coast and live overlooking Boston Harbor where I can observe the *USS Constitution* out my window. I've done extensive research on tall ships, including a tour of the *Mayflower* as she was being rebuilt a few years ago in Mystic Seaport. I grew up near, and now live half the year in the same town where the real-life family of the *Mary Celeste* lived, and where the descendants
still live. I've interviewed captains and sailing masters about points of sail on numerous tall ships, including the captains of the *USS Constitution, USCG Eagle* (both women commanders), as well as privateer reproductions, training ships, and even a reproduction of a Viking longboat. My library of sailing reference books, both fiction and non, is extensive and continues to grow with me after nearly six decades. I have researched original logbooks at libraries and museums including the Massachusetts Historical Society and the Boston Maritime Museum as well as the *USS Constitution* and Hereshoff museums. I've interviewed the first mate of a modern clipper ship (*Stad Amsterdam*) about how to sail, jibe, and tack a square-rigged sailing ship. I've interviewed a mate on a square rigger that rounded Cape Horn in a gale. I've sailed myself offshore across the Gulf Stream to Bermuda where we dodged tankers and found flying fish on our deck most mornings. As a youth, I even built two ship models of the clipper ship *Cutty Sark* and the *USS Constitution* which I keep in my office as I'm writing this—for instant visual accuracy. Some of the sailing scenes in the book, including my other two novels in my *Age of Sail* trilogy, are descriptions of tactics I have personally used racing my own boat. So the research is both scholarly, personal experience, and first or secondhand research of like-ships and their sailing masters.

Q. Who is your target reader?

A. Anyone who enjoys adventure stories. Sailors are obvious targets, but the book is not overly nautical and the language is accessible to non-sailors and sailors alike. It's the kind of book I'd want to read at the beach or the pool, in a plane or before falling off to sleep at night. So, all ages, 12 and up, male and female. Having three daughters and three sisters (no sons or brothers!), I've tried to relate to how a young woman would deal with the challenges faced by the captain's daughter, Priscilla Gant, on a gloomy ship with a dangerous crew. I am told that she is an inspiringly strong female protagonist. I believe all readers will enjoy the action, mystery, and suspense, and relate to the family saga, conflicts, and emotions between the characters.

Q. How would you compare yourself to your influencers, O'Brian and Forrester?

A. Unlike O'Brian, I didn't invent a fictional biography. Stephen King cites O'Brian as one of his most admired writers, and I agree. I only hope that readers of his Aubrey/Maturin series of novels might also enjoy mine, though he deals with the British Royal Navy during the Napoleonic Wars—as does Forrester with the Hornblower books— while my subject is American 19th century smugglers, privateers, and clipper ship captains. So, old world compared to new world, O'Brian's writing style is unique and perhaps unparalleled in historical fiction literature. He claimed he never went to sea, but that was not true—he is an expert sailor and historian; and his writing style is both fluid and mesmerizing. Forrester's stories remind me of 18th century writers like Dumas for classic storytelling, exciting action, and memorable characters. If my books were ever listed in their company, I would be deeply honored.

Q. Tell me about the other books in your *Age of Sail* trilogy?

A. Next to be published is *Clipper Wars*, the sequel to *Secrets of Mary Celeste*, with a new antagonist. Set at the height of the California Gold Rush, it is a story about a fictional race between the fastest clipper ships ever built. It begins in Boston and in New York, careens around the treacherous Cape Horn, then survivors struggle onward to San Francisco. Warring characters from *Secrets of Mary Celeste* appear in

Clipper Wars, so it is a sequel with a new plot and new conflicts. My *Age of Sail* trilogy wraps up with the prequel to *Secrets of Mary Celeste*. Titled *Privateer*, it is set during the War of 1812. A wealthy woman inherits her father's fleet of private warships. Then she must deal with his deadly political legacy that nearly bankrupts their trading company. While fighting off creditors, she deploys the skills of three violent privateersmen to help her find a hidden fortune. A number of *Privateer's* characters live on in *Secrets of Mary Celeste*, one of whom anchors all three books. My *Age of Sail* trilogy depicts two seafaring families in three different sea-going businesses over a forty-year period when the American economy was expanding at an explosive rate.

What Readers Are Saying
About Author Steve Dahill

Steve Dahill's novels have been favorably reviewed by *Sail Cruising World* magazine, *WJNET Cape Cod Smooth Jazz Radio*, *The Wanderer*, *Sippican Week*, *Points East* magazine, and other news media.

I can't wait to recommend it to my book group… a fabulous story wonderfully told. I couldn't put it down. I wasn't expecting to like the book as much as I have. It's really well written with vivid details into an era and sea setting I knew little about. Thanks for such an enjoyable adventure.
—Bruce Gellerman, former NPR reporter, Here & Now Host

Steve Dahill exhibits a remarkable prowess in weaving characters into the intricate tapestry of historical and geographical context. His writing possesses a substantial and robust quality, immersing readers in a tangible and vivid experience, a testament to his skillful storytelling.
—Maureen Gillis, Development Director Hull Lifesaving Museum

Dahill gives us a reasonable explanation for the missing ship, surrounded by a family saga with lots of excitement. Enjoyable reading about one of the great maritime legends!
—Jerry Pallotta, best-selling author and sailor
I smelled the salt air as I read Steve Dahill's fast-paced, suspenseful, Secrets of Mary Celeste. Enjoy it by candlelight with a tin cup of grog at your side before it comes to a theatre near you.
—Dan Shaughnessy, *The Boston Globe* sports columnist,
author *Wish It Lasted Forever, Francona, Curse of the Bambino,*
Major League Baseball Hall of Fame Member
Dahill's nautical knowledge brings serious dimensions that enrich the story… he masters the current that sweeps through the story.
—Westy Egmont, Professor at Boston College
Author of *Immigrant Integration in the United States*
While many people have tried to solve the mystery of *Mary Celeste*, Steve Dahill re-imagines the disappearance of her crew and

the recovery of the ship in a tightly plotted narrative that keeps the reader turning pages until the very end. Dahill writes with the ease and confidence of an experienced mariner, setting scenes above and below deck that rock with every passing wave. With clever turns of phrase and vivid command of the language, Dahill fills the story with characters both fair and foul whom we are not likely soon to forget as he sends them on an adventure designed to thrill fans of both historical and nautical fiction.

—Corinne Woodworth, sailor on 40' sailing yacht *Tango*

I really enjoyed it. I couldn't put it down. It was pretty brutal in parts and I hated Gant and Racca—some miserable men back then including Alex's brother. I was glad to see Racca go overboard. I had a little trouble with the nautical terms but the *Glossary* in the back is very helpful.

—anonymous reader

It would be a good movie! You inspired us and we are now watching *Master and Commander*. Looking forward to your next book!

—anonymous reader

My wife got this book from a book club. Since we owned the book, I read it… I couldn't put it down.

—anonymous reader

The subject of old sailing ships is not of great interest to me but your descriptions and the interesting plot kept me going. I really enjoyed it.

—anonymous reader

On my own I would not have chosen it because of the cover, it turned me off, it looked like a romance novel. But I overcame that.

—anonymous reader

I am a lifelong sailor, but I also love character development within an accurate depiction of time and place. Dahill slams this one out of the park! His writing is meaty, his descriptions of geography and the sailing environment of the time are gritty and real. Best of all, he carefully posits the likely solution to the Mary Celeste mystery. It's a delightful work of historical fiction. Buy it! Thanks very much for keeping me entertained and maybe educating me a little.

—anonymous reader

This book held my interest from the beginning. It was an incredible journey on a sketchy ship in search of the *Mary Celeste* with a captain with less then honorable intentions and it was brutal in parts.

—anonymous reader

The depiction of the characters is so real—some I loved and some I hated. I am not a sailor, so the *Glossary* helped me with nautical terms. Well written and I'm looking forward to Dahill's next book. It would be a good movie.

—anonymous reader

Got home tonight around 8 pm, and started much-needed catch-up work. But passed the foyer table where *Secrets of Mary Celeste* innocently lay. Unfortunately, that was it, since it's midnight and 55 pages in, I have accomplished nothing else, being immersed in the world of the 1830s with rough seas and hard men in our seaside Rochester (now Marion).

—anonymous reader

So, Bravo Zulu (BZ) to you, i.e., *Well Done!* as we say in the CG... It's great.

—anonymous reader

The sea and the great sailing ships of the 19th century are no mystery to Steve Dahill. This maiden literary voyage is a treasure chest for those "who go down to the sea in ships." It will especially engage mystery readers and lovers of New England who relish the tales of history, of family intrigue, treachery, and search for answers about the disappearance of treasure and kin. Dahill's nautical knowledge brings serious dimensions that enrich the story, and, like his racing of his own yacht *Riva* on Buzzard's Bay, the author masters the current that sweeps through the story. The characters are strong and interesting; he brings the boats and coastal people to life and spins a good mystery about family fortune and the villainy of those who would claim the success of others for themselves. You can feel the gale come hard aboard ship and Dahill's detail makes the clinging crew a visceral experience.

—Prof. Westy Egmont, Author,
Immigrant Integration in the United States,
Founder, Immigrant Integration Lab at Boston College

As a Professor of Global Practice in the School of Social Work, Westy taught social policy and multiple courses focusing on immigrants. He has also lectured in San Miguel the Azores, overlooking the harbor, long after the great era of sail.

[Until now, I'd never read]...a book that so perfectly captures the essence of a sea voyage that I felt myself to be completely transported to the energy and excitement of an ocean adventure. For those who love boating or water, I recommend this book highly, to be swept away in your seafaring fantasies.
—Nicole Watkins, Producer, TV Writer
Berkshire Hathaway Home Services Verani Realty
#nicolewatkinsnh

[Steve Dahill's *Secrets of Mary Celeste* is] a captivating novel sure to please anyone who appreciates a challenging seagoing experience
—CWO Ken Lawrence, U.S. Coast Guard (retired)
Producer, WJNET Cape Cod Smooth Jazz Radio

Other exciting titles from

JUMPMASTER PRESS™

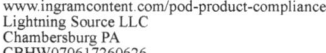